DOGCHILD

Also by Kevin Brooks

Born Scared

DOGCHILD

KEVIN BROOKS

First published in Great Britain 2018
by Egmont UK Limited
The Yellow Building, 1 Nicholas Road, London W11 4AN

Text and illustrations copyright © 2018 Kevin Brooks

The moral rights of the author and illustrator have been asserted

ISBN 978 1 4052 7620 7

58761/1

A CIP catalogue record for this title is available
from the British Library

Typeset by Avon DataSet Ltd, Bidford on Avon, Warwickshire

Printed and bound in Great Britain by the CPI Group

Stay safe online. Any website addresses listed in this book are correct at the time
of going to print. However, Egmont is not responsible for content hosted by third
parties. Please be aware that online content can be subject to change and websites
can contain content that is unsuitable for children. We advise that all children are
supervised when using the internet.

Egmont takes its responsibility to the planet and its inhabitants very seriously.
All the papers we use are from well-managed forests run by responsible suppliers.

Out of civil states, there is always war of every one against every one.

Thomas Hobbes, *Leviathan*

For the animal shall not be measured by man.

Henry Beston, *The Outermost House*

I dont know how to do this.

Ime sitting here on the floor with my writing book open in my lap, the whiteness of the empty page flickering orange in the flamelight of the fire, and I still dont know how Ime going to carry out Gun Surs order. How can I write an account of this world when I know so little about it? What do I know of our times, our lives, the war? What do I know of anything?

Its cold, I know that. The nights are always cold.

And when the sun rises in the morning, and the cold of night melts away in the blazing white light, and the rocks and sand and the dustblown air begin to shimmer and burn in the searing heat---
It will be hot.

I know that too.

The days are always hot.

And above all I know that tomorrow the Dau will still be there – just half a mile away across the empty black glassrock of Nomansland – still watching and waiting, biding their time, just waiting for the day when the time is right to storm our wall and swarm into town and slaughter every last one of us---

But what else do I know?

What else is there to know?

Its late now, getting colder by the second.

I need to sleep.

Tomorrow---

When the sun rises in the morning and the cold of night melts away---

Tomorrow Ile go and see Starry.

Starry isnt just my uncle and mentor – the man who rehumanised me and taught me all I know – hese the only human whose ever meant anything to me.

Most men of his age – hese 26 – are Fighters, but Starry was retired as a Fighter when he lost his left leg after the attack by the Wild Ones nearly 10 years ago, so hese only a fighter now in the same sense that all of us are. We all have to be ready and able to fight, from the youngest child to the oldest of the Olders, and none of us are ever without a weapon of some kind. Starry has an ancient Colt Dragoon revolver that he carries in a holster on his right hip. It was probably a perfectly good weapon once, but its been fixed and refixed so many times over the years that these days its mostly held together with wire and mismatched nuts and bolts.

I dont have a firearm. I have a 3-foot leather sling that I carry on my belt, and a bonehandled knife with a 9-inch blade that I keep in a sheath on my thigh.

It wasnt hard to find Starry that morning. Hese a man of habit, and at sunrise every day he takes his fishing pole down to the beach and sits on the same ruined remnant of the old sea wall, fishing until noon for whatever he can catch, which usually isnt much.

It was still early when I got there, the sun only just clearing the horizon, but the air was already thick with heat, and the smell of the sea – a putrid mixture of salt and oil and rotting flesh – was growing stronger as the temperature rose.

Caught anything yet? I asked Starry, clambering up onto the wall and sitting down next to him.

He shook his head. Its getting harder every day, Jeet. Everything out there is dying.

I gazed out at the sea. The ruins of the old sea wall arent that close to the waters edge – between 25 and 40 yards away, depending on the tide – but its not safe to be any closer. As well as the stinking black mud on the shoreline that can suck you down into its depths in seconds, there are all kinds of dangers in the shallows. The great black jawfish usually only hunt in the open seas, but if theyre hungry enough theyre sometimes forced to venture closer to the shore, and theyve been known to leap from the sea after prey. But the far greater risk comes from the giant eels that lie in wait for hour upon hour just below the surface of the oily black mud, waiting with mindless patience for the slightest sound or vibration to indicate a possible meal – usually a towndog or some other scavenger searching the beach for scraps. The eels are naturally nocturnal hunters, and they usually let their prey come as close as possible before launching their attack, but – as with the jawfish – their behaviour is dictated by their levels of hunger, and over the years theyve become more and more brazen, often hunting during the day, and not always prepared to just lie in wait. Theyre becoming active predators, lunging out of the mud and slithering across the beach with astonishing speed after their prey, and theyle go after anything that moves. A fullgrown giant eel is a massively powerful creature – up to 25 feet long and 3 feet thick – and theyre perfectly capable of hunting down and killing a man. Theyre also capable of travelling far enough on land to reach the edges of town. Only a few nights ago, a 3-year-old boy was taken by an eel just a few yards from his home on the Beach Road.

Which is why Starry always fishes from the same 12-foot section of ruined wall. As well as being a relatively safe distance from the shoreline, its also the highest remnant of all the ruins, putting him 20 feet above the beach. And the one thing a giant eel cant do is climb.

As I carried on gazing out at the sea, I remembered the time a few years ago when I thought Ide seen a ship, far out in the distance, moving slowly across the horizon. I didnt know what a ship was back then, but when Ide told Starry what Ide seen – describing it as a long dark thing, as big as a wailfish, but straight like a plank and with little square bits and poles sticking up – hede said it sounded like a tanking ship, and hede then explained to me what a tanking ship was and told me that I must have been dreaming or seeing things, as all the big tanking ships had disappeared a long time ago. I was sure Ide seen what Ide seen though – how could I have dreamed of something Ide never seen before and no longer existed? – but Ide kept my thoughts to myself.

There was nothing to be seen out in the ocean today. It was as still as it always is, and the dark yellow haze that hung over the surface in vast crawling clouds made it almost impossible to see anything. Even the float on Starrys long fishing line was invisible. All I could see was the silvery twinkle of sunlight on the line as it

4

disappeared into the yellowy-brown mist.

So, young Jeet, Starry said after a while, what can I do for you?

After Ide told him what Gun Sur had asked me to do, Starry didnt say anything for a while, he just sat there peering out to sea through his permanently sun-narrowed eyes, a slight frown furrowing his brow.

Eventually, after leaning to one side and spitting a small fly from the tip of his tongue, he turned to me and said, Tell me again what Gun Sur said about the battle.

He told me that weare nearing the end now, I said, and that when the final battle is over, there will only be us or the Dau left standing. He said its the victors who write the history of war, and that will be us, so our history needs to be written.

Those were his exact words?

Yeh, and after that he went on to tell me that as well as chronicling the battle itself he wanted me to make a written account of the times and lives of our people in the days and weeks leading up to it.

Starry nodded thoughtfully.

What do you think it means? I asked him.

It means Gun Surs finally accepted the truth.

What truth?

The truth that everyones known for a long time – weare running out of water. Theres been no rain for nearly a year now and the spring is almost dry. If the weather doesnt change in the next month or so, and theres no sign that it will, we wont have anything left to drink.

Starry stopped speaking for a moment, concentrating on his

fishing line, as if hede detected a possible bite. But after a few seconds he shook his head and continued talking.

We cant survive without water, he said, and we cant go out looking for it because the only sources that havent dried up are either way out in the Deathlands or to the north of the Dau. But if we stay here and just keep waiting and hoping for rain, wele eventually become too weak to defend ourselves. So Gun Sur has decided that our only option is to attack the Dau now, before its too late, and finish them off once and for all.

But how can we possibly beat them? I said. They outnumber us by nearly 5 to 1. Theyve got more Fighters than us, more weapons and ammunition, better equipment---if we try crossing Nomansland, even at night, we wont stand a chance. Wele be picked off one by one, shot down like---whats the word?

Sitting ducks, Starry said with a grizzled smile.

Wede be lucky if even a handful of us reached their camp alive.

Starry said nothing, just nodded.

Gun Sur must have a plan, I said.

Starry nodded again, and this time he looked at me. Whatever you think of him, and theres many who think hese had his day, the Marshals no fool. Hele have a plan. Hese probably been working on it for months, maybe even years. Its just a matter of what it is and whether it stands any chance of working or not.

As Starry gazed out to sea again, I wasnt sure if he was thinking about Gun Sur or just focusing on his fishing, but whichever it was, I knew it was best to wait. So thats what I did. And after a minute or 2, he took a deep breath, let out a long sigh, then turned to me and put his hand on my shoulder.

Ime proud of you, Jeet, he said, looking me in the eye.

For what?

Gun Sur could have chosen anyone to write an account, but he didnt. He chose you.

Only because I can write.

There are others who can write. Not that many perhaps, but he still picked you. And do you know why?

Because Ime younger than the others, so Ime more likely to live long enough to finish the account.

No. He chose you because youre outside of things. Youre not the same as the rest of us, and that gives you a more objective view of our world.

Because Ime a dogchild.

Youre special, Jeet. Dont ever forget that.

He patted my shoulder and turned back to his fishing line.

How are you going to manage for writing materials? he said, reeling out a few inches of line. Ive still got those old pencil stubs somewhere, and Ive got a few scraps of paper I can let you have, but its nowhere near enough to write—

Gun Sur gave me a writing book, I told him.

He turned to me, his eyes wide with astonishment. A writing book?

I know, I said. I couldnt believe it either. Its a complete book, about 100 pages---all of them unused. And he gave me 2 pencils as well. Not stubs---fullsized pencils.

Starry shook his head, dumbfounded. Where the hell did he get a writing book and pencils from?

I didnt ask. He just told me not to waste them.

Starry carried on staring at me for a few moments, the disbelief evident in his eyes, then he shook his head again and turned his attention back to the sea. I stayed quiet for a while, just gazing out at the endless haze of ocean and sky, listening in wonder to its vast and empty silence---

Then I turned to Starry and began telling him of my worries.

I told him the truth – that I had no idea how to carry out Gun Surs order. I didnt know what to write or how to write it. I didnt know if I should simply recount the facts, such as I knew them, or if I should include anything about myself – my story, my thoughts, my feelings – and I had no idea how I could write anything at all about the multitude of things I didnt know anything about---I dont even know where to start, I told him.

Did Gun Sur tell you what form the account should take?

He just told me to write it.

Then if I were you, Ide simply tell the story of everything I know, Starry said. Ide describe myself and my world – the place, the people, the way it all is – and I wouldnt give any thought at all to the things I dont know or dont understand. Once Ide done that – and believe me, Jeet, you know a lot more than you think you do – Ide be in a much better position to reevaluate those matters that I thought I knew nothing about.

He smiled quietly to himself then. It was a smile I know well – a smile of contentment that he sometimes allows himself when hese pleased with a turn of phrase hese just used. I always like seeing him smile. Starry has a heart of great sadness, and he deserves every moment of happiness he can find.

And then, he continued, once Ide worked out what I really needed to know, thats when Ide start asking my questions.

Who would you ask? I said.

Well, you know you can always ask me anything you like, Jeet, and Ile help you out as much as I can, but if you really want to do this properly, you need to talk to the Olders. Of course, youle have to bear in mind that some of what they tell you will be muddled and mythologised, or even completely untrue, but theyre the only ones who know anything of our ancient history.

And if you were me, I asked him, and youd gathered as much information as you could, how would you go about putting it all together?

However it comes out, he said. As long as it tells the story, thats all that matters.

But thats the problem, I said, I dont know how to tell the story. I dont know how to put things into words.

Close your eyes, he said.

What?

Close your eyes.

I closed my eyes.

Now tell me everything you can hear and feel and smell and taste. Dont think about it, just feel it and say it.

I did as he asked, describing the feel of the heat on my skin, the smell of the sea and the air and the beach, the faint murmuring whistle of the sea breeze, and the taste it brought to my throat of salt and dust and ooze and decay.

Now open your eyes, Starry said, and tell me what you see.

The beach, I told him, the sea, the cliffs, the sky, the sun---

What colour is the sea?

I hesitated, studying it.

Dont think about it, he reminded me. Just tell me what you see. What colour is it?

Dark. A kind of greenish black.

And the beach?

Brown, sandy, with patches of oily black---and at the base of the wall its kind of gravelly grey and white.

And what does it feel like?

What?

Everything. What does it feel like to you?

Like its all I know---like its dying.

Thats it, Starry said, smiling at me.

What do you mean?

Thats all you have to do. Just take all the feelings from your heart and mind and put them into words. You can do it. You just have. Its as simple as that.

I nodded slowly, not fully convinced it was quite as simple as he was suggesting, but at least the idea of writing an account didnt seem quite so impossible anymore. There was something else I needed from Starry though, something I knew he wouldnt want to give me. But I needed it. I didnt know why I needed it, but I did. It would hurt Starry to do it, I knew that. And I hated myself for having to ask him, but I had to.

What is it? he said, seeing the concern on my face.

I turned to him. Theres something I need to ask you now--- before I do anything else.

And whats that?

I want you to tell me my story.

Your story?

The attack by the Wild Ones and the dogs---

I could see the pain and sadness in his eyes.

Ime sorry, I said, I know its not fair of me to ask, and I know you must be wondering why I need you to tell me when I know it all myself, or at least most of it. And it doesnt make any sense to me either. But for some reason I just need—

Its all right, he said quietly, I understand.

Do you?

He nodded. You need to know who you are and where you came from and how you got here before you can begin telling anyone else what and where here is.

But I already know where I came from and how I got here. I know my story.

You know the inside of it, the story from your world. You need to know it from the outside world.

I didnt know what to say to that. I wasnt sure I understood what he meant. But at the same time, I somehow knew he was right.

He squinted up at the sun, then lowered his head and stared down at the sand for a while, just gazing blindly at the dry red dust---

And then he began telling me my story.

It became known as the Long Walk, Starry told me. It began so long ago theres no one left who remembers for sure where it began, but most of the Olders believe that it started as a tactical retreat from a battle with the Dau and that it was originally intended as a temporary measure, a means for our people to regroup and reassess their options, but for some reason our people couldnt find a safe place to stop, and they just had to keep going, keep retreating, in the hope that eventually theyd find somewhere suitable to hole up and rest for a while until they were strong enough to take the fight to the Dau again---but it just never happened. They never found the right place – or if they did, the Dau must have forced them out again – and in the end, the retreat just kept on going. It became all there was – a decades-long exodus across the Deathlands in search of a place of sanctuary.

Starry paused for a moment to gather his thoughts, then continued.

Again, no one really knows the truth, but the best estimates are that at the beginning of the Long Walk the Dau numbered somewhere between 2 and 3 thousand, and our people were perhaps a thousand strong. There were still bands of Wild Ones roaming the Deathlands then, but their overall population probably didnt add up to more than a few hundred. And as far as anyone knows, in terms of the human race, that was it. Its impossible to know for sure that others didnt exist elsewhere on the planet, but then – as now – theres no evidence to support the possibility. The 4 thousand or so humans alive at the beginning of the Long Walk were more than likely the only ones left.

He stopped briefly again, this time absentmindedly scratching his head.

I dont know how many wagons and horses our people had when the Walk began, he went on, but by the time I was born there couldnt have been more than a handful of horses left, and perhaps 25 to 30 wagons, so even then we were pulling most of the wagons ourselves---

He smiled sadly to himself.

I was always frightened of the horses when I was a child---I thought they were monsters – dirty and foul-smelling beasts, evil-eyed, skeletal, covered in dripping sores and clouds of flies. But they werent monsters, of course, they were just pitiful, like the rest of us – starved and sick and permanently exhausted---we were all simply struggling to survive. The Deathlands had taken their toll. The land was just so dead and empty, just thousands of miles of nothingness – vast plains of either hard black glassrock or ashes and dust where nothing could grow and virtually nothing could live---no plants, no grass, no trees, just dead forests of blackened stumps. The white heat of the sun burned down all day, and the nights were so cold the ice ate into your bones---it was a miracle that any of us lived through it. But somehow we did. We just kept going, stumbling on in the hope that wede come to another waterhole before we ran out of water---and then, if we were lucky, we could slake our thirst and maybe rest for a little while if the Dau werent too close behind---

He stopped speaking then, peering intently down at the shoreline.

What is it? I said, following his gaze.

I thought I saw something in the mud.

An eel?

I dont know. I just thought I saw something moving.

We both sat there in silence for the next few minutes, staring hard, scanning the black mud for any sign of movement, but there was nothing, not even an air bubble. But as Starry began talking again, we both kept watching, just in case.

Anyway, he said, where was I?

Waterholes, I reminded him.

He nodded. They were few and far between, and most of them were little more than lifeless mudpools with just enough water to keep us alive. There were a few places with good water and some scatterings of life – patches of greenery, leaves growing on blackened shrubs, small animals and birds – but for the most part it was rare to see any other living things at all in the Deathlands--- apart from the dogs, of course. The packs of Deathland dogs were always there, always following us. During the day they kept their distance, never coming within rifle range, but at night they were bolder. We had to post guards. Theyd take anything – food, bones, bits of hide and leather, even scraps of wood. And if the brutes could take a sick horse or an unguarded child---

Starry hesitated, as if hede suddenly remembered who – and what – he was talking to.

Sorry, Jeet, he said. I didnt mean––

We all have to eat, I said, my voice colder than I meant it to be.

I know. I was just saying––

I know. Its okay. Carry on.

After a moments silence, he continued.

There were no horses left by the time we reached the Black Mountains. The last one had died a long time ago. The majority of our people had died in the Deathlands too. Of the thousand or so whode begun the retreat, there were less than 200 left when we came to the mountains, and many of those had been born during the Walk. Me, your mother, your father, you---we were all children of the Walk. And we were the lucky ones. Most of those born in the Deathlands didnt survive. And the Dau didnt fare any better either---they suffered their losses just as much as us. At the time of the ambush they were down to less than a thousand, and all their horses had long since died too.

He went quiet again, gazing emptily at the shoreline for a minute or 2, then – without looking up – he carried on with the story.

The canyon was the only way through the mountains. There were trails that led up and over them, but they were too steep and treacherous for the wagons, and if wede chosen to go all the way round the mountains it would have taken us a lot longer, and the Dau were only a few days behind us. If wede gone round, and the Dau had gone through the canyon, they would at the very least have made up a lot of time on us, and they may even have overtaken us, and then all they would have had to do was lie in wait on the other side and wipe us out when we got there. So the canyon was our only choice. We knew it was dangerous, an ideal place for an ambush, and our scouts had told us theyd seen evidence of the Wild Ones in the mountains, but there were very few of them left by then, and their bands never numbered more than a dozen anyway. So as long as we stayed together, it would be suicidal for them to attack us. But unfortunately we underestimated them. We knew they were ferocious and savage, but the fault we made was in mistaking their savagery for stupidity, and it was a mistake that ultimately proved fatal.

Starry shook his head, and just for a second I sensed a deep-held anger in him, but it flickered and died almost immediately, and when he began speaking again – still staring blindly at the shore – he just sounded sad and resigned.

The canyon was about 3 miles long and for the most part around 40 to 50 yards wide, but there were places where it was considerably narrower. The great black mountains towered so high above us that the canyon walls blocked out most of the light, and although it was the middle of the day, it was dark enough at times to feel like the middle of the night.

He closed his eyes, and I could tell he was replaying the scene in his mind. I waited for him to go on, but his silence continued – he was just sitting there, perfectly still, his eyes closed, totally lost in his memories.

How old were you then? I asked him quietly.

He stirred at the sound of my voice, and his eyes opened. He blinked several times, then rubbed his eyes.

What? he said.

How old were you?

I was 16---

He momentarily squeezed his eyes shut, then opened them again and shook his head, as if clearing something from his mind.

I was 16, he repeated. Kesra, your father, was 15, and my sister Pooli – your mother – was 13. You were just a couple of months old. We were all with the same wagon. There were 3 of us pulling it – me, Kesra, and a cousin of his called Rahmat – and Pooli was in the back with you and another baby, a little girl called Jele. Jeles mother had died during childbirth and Pooli had taken her on. Wede been having some problems with the front axle of our wagon, and wede had to stop a few times to fix it, so when we reached the point where the ambush happened, we were some way behind the rest of the wagons. It was the narrowest part of the canyon wede come across so far, only just wide enough for a single wagon to squeeze through. At first I was pleased to see it. With all the wagons having to queue up to get through, the delay would allow us to catch up with everyone else, and once wede reached the back of the queue it would give us the chance to rest up for a while. But the closer we got to the pass, the more uneasy I became. I didnt know why, but something didnt feel right. There was something out of place. I couldnt work it out, and I kept looking all around – behind us, above us, in front of us, everywhere – trying to see what was wrong, but everything appeared perfectly normal. Kesra could see I was worried about something, and he started to ask me what it was, but just as he opened his mouth to speak, the wagon in front of us moved off, heading through the pass, and we hitched up our harnesses and began pulling the wagon forward to take its place. I was still looking around as the wagon in front of us edged slowly through the narrow gap, but I was beginning to tell myself not to worry anymore. Even if there was something wrong that I wasnt seeing, wede soon be passing through the gap ourselves, and once we reached the other side and joined up with everyone else, wede be safe.

Starry stopped again, letting out a sigh, then went on.

Wede just started moving towards the pass when I finally realised what it was that had been bothering me. It was still far from obvious, but if you looked really hard you could see there was something unnatural about the look of the canyon walls. The way some of the loose boulders and rocks were positioned---they were too precarious, too finely balanced. If theyd been like that naturally, they would have fallen years ago. As soon as I realised what it meant, I opened my mouth to shout out a warning, but I was too late. A bloodcurdling scream suddenly rang out from somewhere above us – the Wild Ones signal to attack – and a moment later all we could hear was the massive rumbling and thudding of vast boulders and slabs of rock crashing down into the canyon, filling the air with great clouds of dust---

He slowly shook his head again.

It felt like the end of the world, Jeet---like the whole mountain was coming down on us---and it seemed to go on forever. The air was black with dust. I couldnt see anything, couldnt breathe--- everything was roaring and crashing all around me---and I remember hearing the shrieks and whoops of the Wild Ones as they came pouring down the canyon walls, screeching like devils---and then something hammered into my head. I dont know what it was---a piece of flying rubble, a rock from a Wild Ones sling---but it knocked me to the ground, and I think I blacked out for a few seconds---and when I came round again---

He hesitated, struggling with the memory.

I cant really remember anything after that. It was all just a blur of dust and darkness and terrifying screams---

He sighed again.

It wasnt until much later that I found out the Wild Ones had planned their ambush and carried it out with so much care and precision that if it hadnt been for the dogs, it would have worked perfectly. The landslide theyd set up had completely blocked the narrow pass through the canyon, isolating our wagon from the rest, but barely damaging it at all. They knew exactly what they were doing. By cutting us off from the rest of our people, theyd nullified our one big advantage – safety in numbers. They werent outnumbered anymore. We were the ones who were outnumbered. No one knows for sure how many Wild Ones took part in the ambush – I never actually saw any of them – but its generally agreed now that there were only about 7 or 8 of them. But there were only 4 of us, including Pooli, and they also had the element of surprise. We never stood a chance. But as I said, I didnt find out any of that until later. I was so dazed and confused at the time – and frightened to death – that all I remember is stumbling through the dust, not really knowing where I was going, just heading instinctively towards the pass, or at least where I thought it was---

As Starry went quiet, momentarily closing his eyes and letting out another weary breath, I knew what he was going to say next. I could feel it coming---I could feel his eternal guilt and sorrow rising up inside him.

I never even thought of helping anyone else, he said softly. Kesra, Pooli, you, Rahmat---I just abandoned you all. The idea of staying with my family, of fighting with them---it never even entered my mind.

He wiped a tear from his eye.

I left you all to die, he muttered.

You werent thinking straight, I told him, as Ide told him a hundred times before. Youd been knocked out, you were concussed—

I was a coward.

I said nothing. Wede talked about this so many times before that there was nothing left to say. There was no way of changing his mind. And besides – and again, this was something Ide thought about countless times before – it was possible that he was right, that he had been a coward that day.

But even if he was, Ive never held it against him.

We are what we are.

Anyway, he continued, wiping his eyes again and clearing his throat, the dust was so thick that I couldnt see anything at all, so I didnt know that the canyon pass had been completely blocked off by the landslide, and it wasnt until I actually stumbled into the wall of boulders that I realised it was there. And it was then, just as the dust cleared for a moment and I saw the great pile of rocks in front of me, that I was hit by the first arrow. I didnt know what it was at first. I just felt a sort of thumping sting in my leg, and when I looked down I saw the feathered tail of an arrow sticking out of my thigh. It didnt seem to hurt all that much – at least I dont remember much pain – and when I began clambering up the boulders, and another arrow took me in the arm, that didnt seem to bother me much either. I just kept going, climbing blindly upwards. I was vaguely aware of the sounds of fighting coming from the wagon – screams and shouts, crying and wailing – and there were muffled shouts coming from the other side of the landslide too, but none of it seemed to mean anything to me. It all belonged to a different world. My world was just the dusty silence of the fallen boulders, the feel of the rock under my hands and feet as I climbed, and the absolute and only desire in my gut to keep going, to stay alive, to keep going, keep going, keep going---

He went quiet again, staring way out into the distance, and then after some time he blinked ponderously and went on.

The next thing I knew, he said emptily, I was lying in the back of a moving wagon and my leg had been amputated. It was only a few days after the attack, but the arrow wound had become infected so quickly that if my leg hadnt been taken off I would have died. I was still very ill, feverish and hallucinating, so it wasnt until some time later that I found out what had happened. The rest of our people – the ones whode passed through the gap before the ambush – had realised straightaway that wede been attacked, and as soon as the rocks had stopped falling theyd done their best to save us, climbing up and over the blockade as fast as they could, but by then it was too late. The wagon was already disappearing into the distance, moving at some speed, and there was no sign of anyone at all – your mother and father, Rahmat, you and Jele---you were all gone. It was assumed you were all in the wagon – the 2 men unquestionably dead, the rest of you probably still alive.

Starry looked at me.

The Wild Ones would have raised you and Jele as their own and kept your mother for breeding.

And my father and Rahmat were just fresh meat, I added.

Starry nodded. The Wild Ones knew every inch of the mountains, and there was no doubt they would have had an escape route planned, which meant that once theyd left the canyon and disappeared into the mountains thered be no chance at all of finding them. So our people took off after them, running as fast as they could. They must have known it was pointless, that theyd never catch up with the Wild Ones, but they kept going, more in hope than anything else---and then all at once they saw the wagon veering sharply to one side, almost toppling over, and then suddenly it stopped. It was about a quarter of a mile ahead of them at the time, and at first they couldnt work out what was happening, but then they saw the dogs. There were dozens of them, at least 30 or 40, the largest pack of Deathland dogs anyone had ever seen. And they seemed to have appeared from nowhere. One minute there was no sign of them at all, and then all of a sudden they were everywhere, tearing into the Wild Ones and the wagon like a horde of crazed demons. Whether it was the smell of blood that had attracted them and sent them into a frenzy, or they were just mad with hunger---

He glanced at me, as if looking for an answer.

I just shrugged.

Well, anyway, he went on, whatever it was, by the time our people reached the wagon there was virtually nothing left. The dogs had gone. The Wild Ones had gone. Your father and mother, Rahmat, you and Jele---just gone. All that was left was the bloodstained wagon, a few scraps of flesh, and clouds of flies buzzing in the heat.

He wiped sweat from his brow.

Our people found me on their way back. Ide passed out and fallen down into a gap between some boulders, and luckily one of our men heard a faint groan as he was clambering back to the other side. They pulled me out, carried me back over the rockfall with them---

Starry turned and looked at me.

And thats just about it really. Thats as much as I know of the story from the outside, or at least as much as I can manage for now. The rest of it is yours, Jeet. And only you can---

He stopped suddenly, his attention drawn to the beach, and he swore violently under his breath. I didnt have to ask him what hede seen. I could see it myself. A small girl, no more than 3 years old, had appeared on the beach – seemingly from nowhere – and was skipping down towards the shoreline, stopping every now and then to pick up pebbles that caught her eye.

Its Sheren, Starry muttered. Laolys little girl.

She was lost in her own small contentment, totally oblivious to potential dangers, and completely unaware of the vast black head that had risen from the oily ooze at the shoreline – a head dripping with black slime, its small yellow eyes gleaming like glass, its half-open mouth showing rows of brightwhite needlelike teeth.

Even as Starry opened his mouth to yell out a warning, the giant eel launched itself from the pool of black mud and began streaking across the beach towards the little girl.

As I leaped down off the wall and began racing across the beach, the dog in me instinctively took over – heightening my senses – and I could see and hear everything all at once and with perfect clarity. I could see little Sheren, alerted by Starrys warning shout, looking over at him, then seeing me running towards her, her previously happy face fading into an expression of confusion and wariness. And then – as she heard or sensed the eel, and looked round to see it arrowing towards her across the beach – her wariness turned to outright terror. The eel was about 20 feet long and 2 feet thick, and it was moving incredibly fast, not snaking or slithering, just streaking across the sand like a great black spear. I heard a scream then, not from Sheren but from a young woman of about 15 or 16 whode just appeared at the top of the beach. It was Laoly, Sherens mother. I saw Sheren turn at the sound of the scream, and I saw Laoly waving wildly and yelling at her daughter to run to her, but Sheren was too petrified to move.

A gunshot cracked loudly from behind me.

Starrys pistol.

The eel kept going.

I kept running.

I had my knife in my hand now, and I was running so fast my feet were barely touching the ground, but I knew I wasnt going to make it. Despite my speed – and although Ide never been able to keep up with the dogs when they were running at top speed, I could still easily outrun any human – the eel was faster than me. And it was already closer to Sheren than I was.

I was maybe 10 yards away from her now.

The eel was no more then 5.

I heard another gunshot, but this time it didnt sound right – too loose and cracky – and at the same time I heard a yell of pain from Starry. I knew what had happened – his ancient Dragoon had blown up in his hand – but I gave it no conscious thought. The eel was almost upon Sheren now. She was frozen to the spot, petrified, not even making a sound. Just standing there, as if she knew it was already over. Her mothers screams had turned to hopeless sobs.

As the eel closed on Sheren, I fleetingly thought about throwing my knife at it, but it was moving so fast that even at close range I couldnt be sure of hitting it square in the head, which was the only way of stopping it, and if I threw the knife and missed, my only chance of killing the beast was gone. It was probably gone anyway. The giant eel was lunging at Sheren now, its monstrous jaws wide open, and I was still a few yards away.

I took my only chance and leaped as hard as I could, launching myself off the ground and flying at the eel, swinging the 9-inch blade at its head. I very nearly made it, but just as the blade was about to sink in, the eels jaws engulfed Sheren with a crunching

24

snap and it instantly twisted its head away from me. I still caught it a hefty slash with the knife, but the impact was nowhere near its head, and as it doubled back on itself and began streaking back towards the mud – with Sherens poor little head and shoulders hanging limply from its jaws – there was absolutely no indication at all that Ide hurt it.

By the time Ide got to my feet again, the eel had disappeared back into the oily black ooze, and the only sign of its existence was a few glooping air bubbles on the surface. I could hear the frenzied buzzing of flies now, and when I looked down I saw the reason why. Sherens body had been severed by the eels powerful jaws – it had probably happened when the eel had twisted its head away from me – and the lower half of her body was still lying in the sand. 2 little legs and 2 little feet, perfectly unharmed, attached to a bottom and waist that had been severed from the torso with such massive power that it looked as if it had been sheared off with a giant sword.

Blood was oozing from the severed remains, the liquid redness soaking into the sand, and the smell of it was already attracting the beach scavengers – tiny crabs, sandworms, small yellow flatbacked beetles. The scavengers were also being drawn to a thick slab of dark meat lying in the sand just a few yards away – the slice of flesh Ide hacked off the eel.

I went over to it, skewered it with the point of my knife, and lifted it from the ground. It didnt smell good – sour and sharp, with a faint scent of ammonia – but it was meat.

Food.

You cant waste food.

I glanced over at Starry. His useless old revolver was lying in pieces at the foot of the wall, bits of it still smouldering, and he was holding his bloodied hand to his chest. When he saw me looking at him, he raised his good hand and gave me a quick wave — and a quick shake of his head — to let me know he was okay.

I looked across at Laoly. Shede slumped down to the ground and was just sitting there — ashen-faced and empty-eyed — not making a sound, not even crying, just sitting there staring at nothing.

I gazed down again at the fly-covered remains of her daughter. There was nothing to think.

I pulled my knife from the slab of eel meat, wiped the blade on my shirt, and started heading home.

Ime back home now, back in my house, back in my room, back to where I was last night — sitting on the floor in front of the fire with my writing book open in my lap. Ime still not sure if I can do this or not, but Ime going to take Starrys advice and begin with the story of everything I know about myself and my world — the Deathlands, the dogs, the town, the people---the way it all was and the way it all is. And I might as well start at the point where Starry finished   my life with the Deathland dogs.

I remember nothing at all of the day the Wild Ones attacked us, and very little about the following weeks and months. No remains were ever found of my mother and father, and I have no doubt at all that they were killed and eaten by the dogs — or possibly, in my fathers case, killed by the Wild Ones and eaten by the dogs. Ime not quite so sure about Jele though, the orphan baby my mother was suckling. I came across other dogchilds during my time with the dogs, and its possible that one of them was Jele – neither of us would have known, after all – but although theres nothing to say that she wasnt taken by the dogs and raised by them as one of their own, in the same way that I was, I think its probably more likely that she suffered the same fate as my parents. I dont have a rational explanation for believing shese dead, its just that whenever I try to imagine her, whenever I try to bring her to life in my mind, all I ever see is an emptiness.

Theres just nothing there.

And every time her life wont come to me, I ask myself the same question – if the dogs killed Jele, why didnt they kill me too?

I dont know the answer.

It could simply be that my dogmother was quick enough to get to me before I was torn apart by the starving dogs, but Jele wasnt so lucky. Or perhaps there was just something about her that the dogs didnt take to – a wrong scent, a wrong sound, a wrong look.

Who knows?

Dogs have very complex and often seemingly irrational sensitivities.

The only thing I know for sure is that I was taken.

All I can really remember of my early years with the dogs is a fragmented series of vague sensations and 1 or 2 isolated experiences. I remember the thick sweetness of my mothers milk, and the comforting warmth of her fur as she sheltered me during the icecold nights. I remember the rasp of her tongue on my skin, the meaty smell of her breath, the sound of her voice, the soft grip of her teeth on my neck as she carried me for hours at a time, day after day, month after month, until eventually I could walk well enough on all 4s to at least keep up with the pack without getting left behind too often. I remember being hungry too – waiting in the den with the other pups, our empty bellies aching as we listened out for the pack to return from hunting, hopefully with half-digested meat in their bellies which theyd regurgitate for us to eat---or if we were very lucky they might even bring back a whole carcass of something for us to rip apart and eat ourselves – a rabbit, a bird, a human child---

Yes, at times, I ate human flesh.

But I have no remorse, no shame, no guilt.

I was, and still am, an animal.

A carnivore.

I ate, and eat, the meat of other animals.

Humans are animals.

We all have to eat.

I had to stop writing for a while just now. Its not of any importance what I did, but as Ime telling the story of everything I know about myself and my world, I might as well write it down. I put some more wood on the fire. I boiled a pan of water. And then I just sat there for a while – sipping hot water, picking at a few pieces of dried meat, staring into the flames---trying to think, trying to remember things--- trying to go back to the times and places Ive spent so long trying to forget---

Most dogchilds dont live very long. Weare so much weaker and slower than dogs, so much more helpless. Our hairless skin

28

burns in the sun and doesnt keep us warm at night. Our hearing is poor. We can barely smell anything. We dont even have the teeth we need to rip into raw flesh or crack open bones. Weare just not made for living in the wild. So most of us die very young. The ones that survive are the ones – like me – whose mothers are strong enough to provide the extra protection and care we need, and committed enough to continue providing it long after theyd naturally have to.

I was lucky. My mother gave me the help I needed to overcome most of my deficiencies.

Apart from that, the only advantage I had over the dogs I was raised with was my mind. It wasnt that I was smarter than them – far from it – it was simply that I had a different way of thinking, which sometimes gave me an edge. Most of the time my human mind was of no use to me at all – and quite often it was a positive hindrance – but very occasionally it worked to my benefit.

One of the few moments I remember with any real clarity – and I have no idea why this remains so clear in my memory – was a fight I had with another dog over a scrap of meat. It wasnt much more than a gristly piece of bone, but we were both half starved – as all of us usually were – and we hadnt eaten for days, so both of us were desperate for the meat, and sharing it wasnt an option. We both wanted – and needed – all of it. Wede grabbed at it at the same time, each getting a good grip of one end, and a tugging match had begun – both of us snarling through our teeth, digging our feet in and yanking as hard as possible, jerking our heads from side to side. It was no match. I was maybe 3 years old at the time, and in human terms I was incredibly strong and tough for my age, but although my opponent was much younger than me, no more than 6 months old, he was virtually a fullgrown dog, which meant he was at least 4 times the size of me, and easily 4 times as powerful. His body was all rocksolid muscle, his jaws as strong as a vice, and his massive teeth were as hard as steel.

I didnt stand a chance.

And I knew it.

I knew I couldnt win.

But I also knew that I couldnt back down. If Ide just given in and let the other dog have the meat without putting up a fight, it would have been seen – and remembered – as a weakness. And not just by the dog I was fighting. All the other dogs watching us would have known that in future they could take whatever they wanted from me without having to fight for it. So I had to keep going for as long as I could, putting up as much of a fight as I could.

And thats what I did.

Within a short while though I was so exhausted that I wasnt really fighting anymore, I was just holding on to the meat and being dragged across the ground by the young male. He knew he had me, and that all he had to do was keep pulling and sooner or later Ide let go of the meat.

So thats what he did.

He just kept moving backwards, step by step, tugging me along with him, his eyes burning fiercely into mine. But I wasnt looking back at him anymore. I was looking over his shoulders at the dried-up river bed behind him. It wasnt very deep – 7 or 8 feet at most – but from what I could see of it, and what I was hoping, the banks were so steep they were practically vertical, and because the young dog was backing towards the river bed, he couldnt see it coming. The only trouble was, he was so convinced of his coming victory that he was hardly putting any effort into tugging me anymore, almost casually pulling me backwards, at no great speed at all. And if he stumbled back into the river bed at that speed, there was no guarantee hede fall into it. So I took a deep breath and dragged up every last ounce of strength I had, and just for a second I dug my feet in and yanked on the meat as hard as I possibly could. It barely stopped him for more than a moment, but it gave him a bit of a surprise, and – more importantly – it annoyed him. And he reacted exactly how I was hoping – by suddenly putting all his power into the fight and lunging backwards as fast as he could. Instead of fighting back, I tightened my grip on the meat and just let him drag me across the ground, and within seconds I saw the sudden shock in his eyes as he felt his back feet disappear into thin air, followed instantly by the rest of his body, and as he began falling backwards down into the river bed, his shock was so great that he simply let go of the meat.

And that was it.

Ide won.

Ide used my mind to beat him. And Ide not only beaten him and won the meat, but Ide humiliated him in front of the other dogs too. So next time a dog tried to steal a piece of meat from me, they might think twice. They might just hesitate for a moment. And sometimes a moment is all you need.

Moments---

I remember other moments with the dogs, most of them hard – always hungry, always hunting, always hunted. There were other packs in the Deathlands, at least a dozen or so in our part of the country. Occasionally some of the packs would come together, as they did when they attacked the Wild Ones whode

31

stolen the wagon, but most of the time they remained rivals – forever fighting over territory and food, stealing and eating each others pups, sometimes even annihilating one another. And all the packs were in constant battle with humans too – the Wild Ones, the Dau, our people. The dogs were a threat to them, and they were a threat to us. Wede kill and eat them if we got the chance, and theyd do the same to us.

It was, and still is, a world of war.

But I also remember some good times with the dogs. These memories are buried away deep inside me now. They have to be to let me live. One of the very first things Starry taught me was that I had to forget everything about my life with the dogs. You can be a dog, he told me, or you can be a human. But you cant be both. If you try to be both, youle die.

And he was right.

But even now some of those hazy memories of the good times still come drifting back to me every so often – running with the dogs, resting together after a meal, sleeping together in the lazy light of a setting sun, just being together---

Moments of pure belonging.

Theres a hurt inside me as I write these words. Its a feeling I cant forget but at the same time cant remember, and I know it will never go away.

It was a combination of hunger and overconfidence that led to my recapture and the massacre of my pack.

Even though the town and the Dau encampment were relatively rich sources of food, we didnt normally go anywhere near them. It was too risky. The humans could kill us from a distance, and their settlements were too well guarded. The potential rewards of a hunting raid were outweighed by the more likely possibility of serious injury or death. So despite the temptations, we kept our distance.

But there came a time when the hunting was so bad that wede barely eaten anything for weeks, and we knew that if we didnt eat soon wede all starve to death. And that turned the scales. It was a simple choice – if we didnt raid the town or the Dau encampment for food, wede almost certainly die of starvation. The likelihood of at least some of us being killed or injured during the raid was high, but it was a chance we had to take. And it was better to go down fighting than to lie around getting weaker and weaker until eventually we just wasted away.

So the decision was made to attack the humans.

And in the end it turned out to be remarkably easy.

The first thing we had to do was choose which of the 2 settlements to raid – the town or the encampment. They both had their advantages and disadvantages. The town was protected on the northside by a great stone wall that stretched in a vast crescent all the way round from the cliffs on the east to the cliffs on the west, and the south of the town was only accessible by the sea – and dogs are born knowing that the sea is a place of certain death.

The encampment wasnt protected by the sea, and it had no walls or fences either, so it was much easier to get into than

33

the town. But there were far more humans in the Dau camp than there were in the town, which meant the chances of being seen were much greater.

The decision was finally made when, after scouting both areas for a couple of nights, one of the dogs came across an unguarded entrance into the town – an ancient animal burrow on the westside clifftop that tunnelled down under the wall. The entrance to the burrow was hidden beneath a fallen tree in a patch of scrubland on the northside of the wall, and the tunnel came out in an overgrown earthbank in a dense thicket of thornbushes just the other side of the wall. It was obvious from the smell of the burrow – or lack of smell – that it hadnt been used for years.

It was perfect – an unknown and unprotected way in and out of the town.

We knew thered be towndogs in the town that would sense our presence and raise the alarm, but there wasnt anything we could do about that. They werent a physical threat – a fullgrown Deathland dog can be up to twice the size of even the largest towndog – but theyd make a lot of noise, alerting the humans, and while it wouldnt be a problem to kill the ones we came across, we wouldnt be able to silence them all. We werent planning on staying in the town for long though. It was going to be a lightning raid – swooping in as fast as possible, grabbing whatever food we could, and hopefully getting out before the humans had time to realise what was going on.

There was a good chance that it wouldnt happen like that – all sorts of things could have gone wrong – but surprisingly it went almost exactly to plan.

It was a moonless night, pitchblack and freezing cold, and the whole pack had made the long journey across the Deathlands to the town. There were 10 of us at the time. My mother, the pack matriarch, and her mate – a jetblack male – together with 5 adults – 3 males and 2 females – 2 young males, and me. The burrow was fairly narrow, so we had to pass through it in single file, and in places it was a very tight squeeze, especially for the adults, but we all made it through, and – as planned – none of us moved from the shelter of the thornbushes until all 10 of us had exited the tunnel. We waited, listening and sniffing for any sign of trouble, but the night was quiet and all we could smell was the thick perfume of the thornbush flowers, a heavy sweetness that hung in the air all around us.

Everything seemed fine.

My mother gave the signal and the raid began.

We stuck together at first, all 10 of us loping steadily into the town, but almost immediately we came across 2 young towndogs who began barking and yowling as soon as they saw us. They didnt even think about standing their ground, they just stood there for a moment or 2, barking like crazy, then turned and ran. At least thats what they tried to do. Theyd barely started running before the jetblack male and the 2 adult females caught up with them and took them down, and within seconds they were both torn to pieces. But the damage had already been done. Their barking – and their death cries – had alerted all the other towndogs, and the night air was now filled with an alarming cacophony of howling and baying.

We split up then, each of us running off in different directions, searching for whatever food we could find. The longer we stayed there, the more likely it was that wede never get out, so the plan was that each of us would grab whatever we could find as quickly as possible and then make our escape, regardless of what might be happening to the others.

As always, my big disadvantage was that compared to the dogs my sense of smell was close to nonexistent. They could smell the tiniest morsel of food from miles away, whereas I had to rely almost entirely on sight, which in the near total darkness wasnt much help at all.

But I couldnt let that stop me.

So I just kept going.

The whole town was awake now – dogs barking, humans yelling and shouting, torches being lit. And it was in the flamelight of a burning torch that I finally saw what I was hoping for. At the first sight of the torch, I froze for a moment then ducked down out of sight behind a low stone wall. I saw a human coming out of a building, the burning torch in his hand, and as I watched him looking around to see what all the noise was about, I saw the dead birds just off to his right. There were 3 of them, all hanging by their necks from a rope that was strung between 2 wooden poles fixed in the ground. The poles were at least 12 feet tall, so the hanging birds were well out of reach. But as the human carried on looking around, I saw another long wooden pole leaning against the wall of the building. It was thinner and lighter than the poles fixed in the ground, and it had a metal hook attached to one end.

I waited, watching the human.

He glanced across at the birds, making sure they were still there, and then – after calling out over his shoulder, presumably to someone else in the building – he ran off into the darkness.

I considered waiting a while to make sure that no one else came out of the house, but I couldnt afford to waste any more time. So I jumped to my feet, ran over to the wall and grabbed the hooked pole, then ran back to the hanging birds, raised the hooked pole high above my head and unhooked the birds from the rope, dropping them to the ground one by one. Then I just picked up the birds and raced off back towards the tunnel.

There was a lot of commotion going on now – more shouting, more barking, even a few gunshots – but I ignored it all and kept running. At one point I turned a corner and ran straight into a human with a gun. He swore at me first, assuming I was just a clumsy child, but it only took him a moment to realise he was wrong. I dont know how I must have looked to him – a human child of sorts, but naked and filthy and wild, with long matted hair and dirtblack skin, and fingernails and toenails hardened into claws---but whatever he thought I was, he knew I wasnt one of his people. And when he saw the 3 dead birds I was carrying, he knew I was the enemy. He took a step back from me and began raising his rifle. Ive no doubt he would have shot me – human child or not – but I didnt give him the chance. I lunged at him and sank my teeth into his leg, ripping away a chunk of flesh, and even as he screamed in pain and stumbled backwards, dropping the rifle and clutching his savaged leg, I was already running away.

I kept going, hurtling on through the darkness – slowing only slightly to stoop down and scoop up the severed leg of a towndog – and when I reached the tunnel I didnt stop and wait for the others, I just dived inside and crawled through it as fast as I could. And when I came out at the other end, I still just kept going.

That was the plan.

Once youre out, dont wait for the others, just go. Keep running. And dont stop.

And thats what I did.

Its midmorning now, and Ime sitting by the window in my downstairs room, writing in the light of a shimmering white sun. Ive been writing all night, stopping every now and then to just sit and think and watch people going by on the sunbaked dirt street outside---

I know this is all wrong.

This isnt what Ime supposed to be doing. Gun Sur didnt tell me to write my life story, he told me to write an account of the times and lives of our people, so I know that at some point soon Ime going to have to tear out these pages and start all over again---

But not just yet.

Starry was right when he said that I need to know who I am and where I came from before I can begin telling the story of our world. But Ime starting to realise that the need to know who I am and where I came from is the emptiness thats ached inside me for as long as I can remember, and now that Ive begun to fill that emptiness, Ime not sure I can stop.

I will---

I have to.

But not just yet.

The raid on the town was a success. We all managed to steal some food and get back out through the tunnel, and we were all unhurt apart from one of the young males who took a rifleshot in his shoulder. It was only a flesh wound though, the bullet barely grazing his skin, and it didnt cause him any problems.

Although we didnt leave town together, it wasnt long before wede all caught up with each other and were running as a pack, and once we were all back together again we just kept on going at the same steady pace, our jaws – and my hands – weighed down with plunder, making our way back into the Deathlands. When we finally stopped, we must have covered at least 20 miles, maybe even more, and wede seen no sign at all of anyone following us.

We were safe.

And tired.

And hungry.

It was time, at last, to feast on our haul of plundered meat.

We ate all kinds of wonderful things that night. Dried meat, salted meat, cooked meat, bird meat, various bits of towndog – limbs, a head – fish, cornbread, and all sorts of other things Ide never eaten before. We gorged ourselves until we couldnt eat anymore, and then we lay down – our bellies bursting – and slept. And when we woke again, we ate again, and then once more we slept.

For the first time in months, our hunger was sated.

It was a magnificent feeling.

But it didnt last long.

The hunting in the Deathlands didnt improve, and within a week or so we were all desperately hungry again, and the decision was taken to carry out another raid on the town. This time though, the decision wasnt unanimous. My mother was against it. She thought it was too early to go back, that it wouldnt be so easy this time because the humans would have learned from their mistake and increased their security. They werent stupid. Theyd know we might try again. And theyd do everything possible to make sure that next time we wouldnt succeed. But the rest of the pack didnt agree with her. The humans might be smart, but we were smarter. Wede outwitted them once, we could do it again.

My mother did her best to persuade the pack from going, but she couldnt forbid them.

Dog leadership isnt the same as human leadership. It isnt absolute. Pack leaders – male or female – dont just give orders that have to be followed without question. If the majority of the pack dont agree with the leader, theyre entitled to make their own decisions. And thats what happened in this case. The pack went against my mothers advice and decided to raid the town again.

Even though she thought it was the wrong decision, my mother still would have come with us under normal circumstances, but on the day of the raid she gave birth, so she had to stay behind to look after her pups.

I could have stayed behind with her, and part of me wanted nothing more, but if Ide stayed behind I would never have been part of the pack again. I had to go with them.

We didnt look back at her as we set off that night, and I didnt say goodbye to her either. That wasnt how things were done. But I wish now that I had said goodbye, and I wish wede listened to her advice.

These words Ime using – saying goodbye, listening to her advice – theyre only very vague approximations of how things actually were. Its impossible to translate the language of dogs into human words. Theyre not just 2 different languages, theyre entirely different things altogether. A dogs sense of communication is as alien and inexplicable to humans as the thoughts of a bird or the feelings of an insect. Dogs know each other rather than talk to each other. We know our bodies, our eyes, our mouths, our lips, our tails, our postures, our movements, our space, our scents, our breath, our hearts. We know who we are and what we want from our world.

Despite going against my mothers advice, we knew she could be right, and we were all very wary as we approached the town that night. We stopped half a mile away and spent a long time just standing there, looking and listening and smelling the air, searching for any sign that the humans were waiting for us.

We saw nothing.

Everything seemed the same as before.

We moved on, cautiously confident.

When we reached the entrance to the tunnel, we stopped and waited again – watching, listening, sniffing – making sure everything was safe. There was no sign of any increased security. The tunnel hadnt been filled in or blocked up, and – apart from the faint trace of our own scent – it smelled and looked exactly the same as it had before. And when one of the young males was sent ahead down the tunnel to check the exit, he came back and confirmed that it was perfectly safe. It hadnt been secured, and the thicket of thornbushes hadnt been disturbed.

Everything seemed fine.

We entered the tunnel and passed through it as before – in single file, one by one. We all made it through and gathered together in the shelter of the thornbushes. Ime sure that some of us had the feeling then that something wasnt quite right – a hint of an alien scent mixing with the sweetness of thornbush flowers – but there was nothing obviously out of place, and the jetblack male was so confident now that he either forgot, or didnt think it was necessary, to stop and wait again to make absolutely sure it was safe to go ahead. He just gave the signal and the raid began.

Once again, just as before, we set off together, all 9 of us loping out of the thicket---

But that was to be the last thing that happened just as it had before.

Wede only just emerged from the thicket when the jetblack male suddenly stopped, and as the rest of us stopped behind him we could see what the problem was. The way ahead was barred by a high, and impenetrable, wiremesh fence. The male turned to his left in an effort to go round it, but almost immediately he was stopped by another fence, and he knew then – as we all did – that wede walked into a trap.

We all turned at once and began racing back towards the tunnel, but before wede got anywhere near it a heavy iron grid came crashing down in front of the entrance, blocking our way out, and a moment later the darkness erupted in a blaze of light as dozens of torches burst into flame all around us.

We could see what had happened now. The humans had been waiting for us, just as my mother had warned. Theyd erected a large wiremesh cage around the tunnel exit – with a cast-iron grid fixed to the top of the open end – and once we were all inside the cage theyd triggered a mechanism to release the grid and it had slid down and blocked the cage shut.

We were trapped.

No way out.

And the cage was surrounded by dozens of torch-wielding humans, all of them carrying weapons – rifles, pistols, clubs, axes---

We flung ourselves at them, throwing ourselves against

the fences, tearing at the wire with our teeth, doing everything in our power to get to the humans and rip them to pieces--- but our efforts were futile. The fences were too strong – unbreakable, impenetrable.

We never stood a chance

One of the humans barked out an order, and all I can remember after that is a deafening barrage of gunfire, a continuous roar of crashing guns---a few yelps of pain---the sound of bodies thudding to the ground---and then nothing but a terrible silence filled with the smell of gunpowder and death.

I cant write anymore.

Later on – after Ide finished writing and dozed in my chair for a few hours – I went over to Starrys house to see how he was doing. When his revolver had exploded at the beach, it could easily have blown his hand off, but hede been very lucky and all hede lost was the top half of his little finger.

He lives alone in a ramshackle 3-storey house that backs onto the beach, a rambling maze of winding stairs and dusty corridors and dozens of rooms filled to the brim with all kinds of bits and pieces. This vast collection of scavenged scrap includes just about everything and anything – from scraps of leather and coils of rope to iron railings and rusted hulks of machinery. Starry is the master of it all. Its his job, his duty. Hese both our Fisherman and our Scrapkeeper.

He was trying to repair his beloved old Colt Dragoon when I went to see him that afternoon. The remains of the revolver were laid out on his kitchen table, and he was sitting there poking through a box full of old pistol parts – his hand wrapped up in a grubby bandage – searching for a cylinder to replace the one that had exploded.

Its a good job you werent using a gun that actually works, I said, sitting down next to him. The only reason youve still got a hand is because that old pistol of yours was virtually falling apart anyway. If it hadnt been such a wreck it would have blown up properly.

Yeh, well, he replied, when I fix it this time, Ile make sure its strong enough to blow off my whole arm when it explodes.

Fix what? I said, gazing down at the wreck of the gun. Theres nothing left to fix.

He picked up the smokeblackened barrel and studied it for a few moments – holding it up to the light and squinting through the sights – and then, with a sigh of defeat, he put it back down on the table.

Damn it, he said wearily. Ime going to have to start looking for a new one now, arent I?

Guns are a precious commodity. Fighters have first priority on all available firearms, and any civilian who owns a gun considers it their most valuable possession. People will trade almost anything – food, tools, clothing, their homes – but the one thing everyone holds on to is their gun. Starry was going to have his work cut out to find himself a new pistol.

As he started picking up the remains of his revolver and putting them in the box full of old pistol parts, I noticed his heavy wooden walking crutch lying on the other side of the table. Hede made the crutch himself, laboriously carving it out of a 5-inch-thick branch of ironwood, and he was forever making modifications to it — adjusting the hand grip, improving the balance, trying different types of padding on the armrest. Hede even added a secret compartment to it. I dont know how he did it, but hede made it so that the armrest could be unscrewed from the main part of the crutch, and hede hollowed out the top 6 inches of the main part to form a hidden compartment that was virtually invisible when the armrest was screwed back on.

I dont know what he keeps in there, if anything, and Ive never asked. The way I see it, if he wanted me to know hede tell me.

So, he said to me, hows the account coming along? Have you started it yet?

I told him what Ide written so far, and that the next thing I was going to write about was my rehumanisation.

Right, he said, nodding thoughtfully. I dont think you need to spend too much time on the rehumanisation though---

He hesitated, looking at me.

Its up to you, of course, he said. Ime not telling you how to do it. I just think—

Its all right, I told him. I understand.

As he held my gaze for a moment, I could tell that he was feeling awkward, so I wasnt surprised when he nodded again, but this time with a sense of finality, as if to say the subject was closed.

He turned in his chair and pointed across the kitchen at a basket on the floor.

Do you mind taking that to Van Hesse on your way back? he asked me.

The basket contained 3 goodsized silver fish and a massive black crab.

Did you catch all that this morning? I asked him.

He nodded, his mind elsewhere.

Van Hesse is our Grocer, the man in charge of all the towns food and drink rations. Everything Starry catches goes to him.

I left Starry to his thoughts, took the basket to Van Hesse, and went back to my house.

Although dogchilds arent common, enough of them exist that over the years our people have developed a process for rehumanising the ones who are brought back from the wild, and after the trapping and killing of my pack that day, I was put through that process.

I dont remember much about the immediate aftermath of the massacre, but I know that I fought like Ide never fought before. I was wild with rage and grief at the slaughter of my family, and when the humans tried to restrain me I tore at them like a thing of madness. I no longer cared for my own life, I just wanted to kill them, every single one of them---I wanted to rip them apart, tear out their throats---I wanted to butcher them all. But although I fought like a demon, shedding their blood and making them scream, there were simply too many of them, and they had clubs and nets and chains and ropes, and eventually they overcame me and bound me up so tightly – wrapping my head and mouth with strips of leather – that I could barely move a muscle.

I was taken to a small stone building where they held me down and freed my head and my mouth but left my arms and legs tied, and then they locked me in and left me alone, and I lay on the dirt floor howling into the night.

The rehumanisation process takes a long long time. All dogchilds are savage and fearful of humans at first, so for the first few months – and sometimes more – theyre kept locked up in the stone building, chained securely to a post in the ground, and they stay that way until theyre considered safe to release. Throughout this period – however long it takes – the dogchild is fed and watered and never without human company. At this stage in the process the dogchild is accompanied by a different person every day. Its usually an Older or a Younger – but never another dogchild – and their only duty is to be there. They dont approach the dogchild, they dont attempt to communicate with it or comfort it in any way, they simply provide it with human company.

The idea behind this is that eventually the dogchild will learn that it has nothing to fear from humans, and for roughly half of those being rehumanised this is more or less what happens. But there are just as many cases when the dogchild simply fades away and dies. No one knows why. Its just the way it is.

Those that survive, and lose their fear of humans, are then allocated a mentor who stays with them for the rest of the rehumanising process.

My mentor was Starry.

He knew from the moment I was captured that I was his nephew, partly because I looked so much like my father, but mainly because of my birthmark – a small red crescent-shaped mark just below my right eye – which was impossible for Starry to forget because my mother, his sister, had an almost identical mark below her left eye. There was no question at all that I was Jeet, the 5-year-old son of Pooli and Kesra, and that Starry was therefore my uncle. He claimed that this gave him the right to be my mentor, and no one disagreed with him.

Ive never doubted Starrys reason for wanting to be my mentor – we were blood relatives, and it was his right to rehumanise and raise me – but Ime fairly sure that wasnt his only reason. Hese never stopped hating himself for running away when the wagon was attacked by the Wild Ones, and hese been eaten up with guilt and shame ever since. I dont think he believed that raising me would make up for his actions and absolve him of what he thought was his terrible sin – hese never going to forgive himself for that – but Ive always thought that as well as genuinely wanting to do his best for me, he also felt that it was his duty, his responsibility, his obligation.

That was partly why hede acted a little strangely when Ide told him I was going to write about my rehumanisation, but I dont think that was the only reason. Hese a very self-effacing man, and he knows how much he means to me, and how much I admire and respect him for making me what I am. Without Starry I would have been nothing. And its hard enough for him to hear that from me. The idea of it being committed to words that might one day be read by the rest of the world – if there ever is such a thing – is something that fills him with dread. But while I cant ignore that, I also cant ignore the truth. If Ime going to tell my story, Ime going to tell it as it is.

It took a very long time for Starry to rehumanise me, and for the first few months of his mentorship he did little more than just be with me 24 hours a day. He didnt try to change me or teach me anything – not in an obvious way anyway – he was just there in the stone building with me, all day and all night, week after week, month after month. He talked to me all the time, not expecting me to understand at first, just letting me get to know his voice, and very gradually I began to understand what he was saying. I still vocalised as a dog most of the time – barking, yelping, whining, howling---sometimes snarling and growling – but I also found myself beginning to mimic some of the sounds that Starry was making. Simple words – food, drink, good, bad, yes, no. I didnt sound very human at first, but Starry could understood what I was trying to say, and he was so patient and rewarding that it wasnt too long before we were capable of holding basic conversations. And it was once wede reached that stage that the teaching process began.

Starry taught me how to behave like a human – how to eat and drink, how to wash, how to carry out my bodily functions, how to walk as humanly as possible. He taught me that I wasnt dog, I was human. I was the same kind of creature as him.

I remember quite vividly the day he brought a looking-glass into the building – an almost-intact full-length mirror in a rickety wooden frame. He didnt say anything to me as he carried it in, he just leaned it up against the wall, stood in front of it, and let me see his reflection. He then gestured for me to join him. When I went over and stood beside him and stared at myself in the glass, the figure I saw – small and weak, stooped and bewildered – triggered something deep inside me, and all at once I let out a howl of rage and launched myself at the mirror, lunging openjawed at the throat of my reflection. The glass smashed, slicing open my face, and as the blood gushed from my shredded lips I threw myself down onto the shards of broken mirror and tore into them with uncontrolled savagery, ripping apart both the beast Ide become and the beast that had been taken away from me.

Starry grabbed hold of me, throwing his arms round my chest and dragging me away from the broken glass, and although I turned my fury on him – snarling wildly, clawing at his face and biting his arms – he didnt let go. He just kept his arms clamped tightly around me, silently enduring my attacks, until eventually I began to tire and the madness within me started to fade, and then everything inside me just went, and I slumped like a dead thing in Starrys bloodsoaked arms.

I looked up at him and tried to say sorry.

Thurru, I grunted. Um thurr– – –

Its okay, Jeet, he said softly. Dont worry. Everythings going to be all right.

My eyes were wet. I didnt know why.

Ide never cried before.

No one knows for sure how many dogchilds have been put through the rehumanisation process since our people settled here around 10 years ago, but from what I can tell – mostly from talking to Starry – 9 have been rehumanised, and at least the same number, if not more, have died during the process. 5 of those who survived were before my time – before I was taken back from the dogs – and of those 5, not one is still with us.

2 of them died from unknown diseases.

One disappeared – its generally assumed she either went back to the dogs or died trying.

And the other 2 simply faded away – one aged 14, the other aged 16 (the oldest known dogchild).

In the time Ive been here, 4 dogchilds (including me) have survived rehumanisation, and another 5 – that I know of – have died during the process. The other 3 survivors – 1 male, 2 female – are all roughly the same age as me. The male, Mose, is physically very capable – strong, tireless, a good Worker and an excellent Fighter – but hese never learned to speak at all, and one of the females, Prendy, has an extremely limited vocabulary. She can just about make herself understood, but thats all. The other female, Chola Se, can talk as well as me. Ive never actually spoken to her – although Ide very much like to – so I dont know if she can read and write, but Ide be surprised if she can. Reading and writing is a very rare ability among our people, and if it wasnt for Starry Ide be illiterate too.

He believed that in order for me to become human it wasnt enough to simply learn the basics of human behaviour, I had to learn how to use my mind. And, to him, that meant learning how to express myself, both verbally and in writing.

Words are the keys to the world, he told me.

I didnt understand him at the time, and even now Ime not entirely sure what he meant, but I had – and still have – so much faith in him that I never questioned his ways. I never complained when he spent hours and hours every day, for weeks and months and years, teaching me how to speak and read and write. There was very little reading material to learn from – the scant remains of a few ancient books, fragile scraps of yellowed pages – and writing materials were just as scarce. We had 2 very precious pencil stubs, and Starry had scoured the town for every scrap of useable paper he could find, which wasnt very much. But it was all we had, so we had to make the most of it. We also used anything else we could lay our hands on – bits of charcoal, wooden boards, sharpened flints, the bare stone walls---

Starry taught me everything he knew.

He told me about his father, who was one of the very last Storytellers, and his grandfather, who was both a Storyteller and a Poet. It took me a while to understand what a story was, and why people used to tell them and listen to them, and I found it even harder to grasp the idea of poetry. No matter how many times Starry tried to explain it – he even wrote some poems himself to show me what he meant – I just couldnt seem to make sense of it. It was, I suppose, just a step too far for the dog in me to take.

And that was the thing. However much I learned, however human I became – and however deeply I buried my past – my dogness was still there. Underneath it all, it is what I am.

It might seem as if our people spend an inordinate amount of time and effort in rehumanising dogchilds – often with little or no success – but the process serves a purpose. We have a very small and ever-dwindling population, so every addition to our number is incredibly valuable, a precious asset in our fight for survival, and our survival is all that matters.

Its gone midnight now. My heads emptied out and I need to sleep.

52

Here is The where and what of my world.

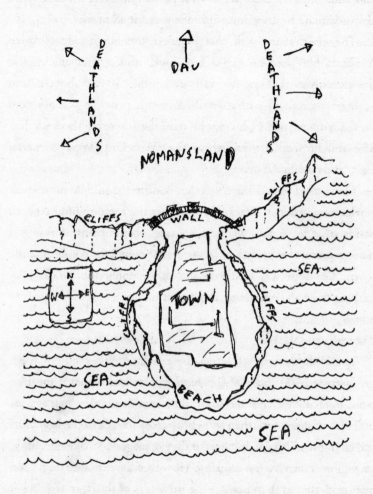

The town.

Apart from the Eastside, which is mostly in ruins – the houses and buildings reduced to piles of rubble, the narrow streets scarred with age-old bomb craters – most of the town is in reasonably good condition. The majority of the old stone buildings are still standing, and while most of them are at least partially derelict, theyre more than adequate to provide homes of a sort for all of us.

The great stone wall that protects the north side of town is about 600 feet long, 60 feet high, and 8 feet thick. The 5 watchtowers that line the wall rise another 30 feet above it, and each one is topped with a fortified turret, providing an allround view for the armed Fighters who man the towers 24 hours a day. The watchtowers are known as the West End, West, Central, East, and East End Towers.

There used to be a huge wooden door in the middle of the wall – which according to Starry was 4 inches thick and reinforced with bands of steel – but when it became obvious that it was too dangerous for our people to venture out beyond the confines of the town, the door was removed and the opening was blocked in, making the wall completely impregnable.

The cliffs and the sea.

The cliffs that stretch along the coastline either side of town are between 300 and 500 feet high, which means that if the Dau want to attack us from the south they have to climb down at least 300 feet of sheer rock then somehow cross the sea to the beach. Its not an impossible task, but even if they managed to make the climb, theyd never survive the crossing. However they tried to do it – on rafts or floats, even in boats – the monsters of the deep would get them---the jawfish, the wailfish, the eels, the great black squid.

The sea is no place to die.

The Dau know that.

Nomansland.

The only realistic way the Dau can get to us, and our only way of getting to them, is across the emptiness of Nomansland. Apart from a few jagged hillocks, Nomansland is just a flat expanse of harsh black glassrock, a barren strip of desert where nothing grows and nothing moves. Even the constant heat haze that hovers above the surface barely even shimmers. It just hangs there, motionless, like a mirror of black mist in the sun.

The Dau and the war.

The Dau compound is situated just half a mile away from us on the other side of Nomansland. It covers an area of about 25 acres and has evolved over the years from a temporary encampment of tents and wagons and trenches into a sprawling conglomeration of wooden buildings and fortifications. Unlike the town, the Dau compound isnt guarded by a wall, and it doesnt have the protection of the cliffs or the sea either, but although the Dau could probably construct a wall or a fence of some kind if they had to, the simple truth is that they dont need one. They have enough Fighters to guard their entire perimeter 24 hours a day, and because they outnumber us so heavily they know weare probably never going to launch a fullscale attack on their camp anyway.

Which is why they know that all they have to do is wait.

It wasnt always like this.

When Starry was rehumanising me, hede often tell me stories about how things were when the Long Walk finally came to an end. Hede tell me about the day our people first discovered the ancient walled town perched on a tiny peninsula that eventually became our home — telling me how empty it was, how devoid of all life---no people, no dogs, no birds, no rats – and hede tell me what he remembered about the weeks and months that followed, as the Dau settled into their stronghold on the other side of Nomansland and a war of attrition began – the Dau bombarding the town with heavy artillery almost every day, our Fighters shooting back with rifles and machine guns, theirs replying with heavier machine-gun fire and mortars---

It was a living hell, Jeet, Starry told me. People were dying every day, the town was being reduced to rubble---and it went on for months and months.

But eventually the Dau ran out of artillery shells, and both sides used up their stocks of small arms ammunition, and thats when things began to change.

Our people and the Dau learned very quickly how to manufacture gunpowder (saltpetre, charcoal, sulphur) and make replacement shells for rifles and handguns (using recycled shell cases and handcast lead), but although these handmade bullets were good enough to kill – just as they are today – they were far less powerful than authentic ammunition, so long-range combat became a thing of the past and the war evolved into a series of skirmishes and raids. But even though some of our early raids on the Dau were relatively successful, we soon learned that the losses we incurred outweighed any gains we made from our occasional victories, and after a time most of the raiding was carried out by the Dau against us, rather than the other way round. Theyd send out small war parties of up to 20 Fighters, usually at night, and theyd try to breach our wall or find some other way in. Most of the time they failed, but every now and then theyd manage to break into town and kill a few of us – or steal some of our females – before making a rapid retreat. But like us, they eventually realised they were paying too high a price for too few successes, and although their raids didnt completely die out, they became a very rare occurrence.

It was at that point, Starry told me, that the Dau finally realised they didnt actually need to do anything to destroy us. All they had to do was keep us under siege and wait.

For some unknown reason, females on both sides were becoming more infertile as the years went by, and the death rate of both populations was outstripping the birth rate – which is why females of breeding age became so highly prized. So both populations were slowly declining. But the Dau realised that because they had 5 times as many people as us, our people would either die out completely or wede become too small a force to defend ourselves long before the same happened to them. And they also had the added benefit of not being so cut off from the surrounding area as us, which meant they could hunt the land with relative ease, which gave them a much better diet than us.

Food.

Weare almost always short of food. Since the wall was blocked up and hunting trips outlawed, weve had to rely solely on the food we can produce ourselves, which is fairly limited, and whatever we can take from the sea and the beach. Our basic diet consists of fish and shellfish (mostly crabs), meat and eggs from our precious birds, cornbread (made from the small crop of corn our Farmers manage to grow), and various nuts, fruits, and vegetables (which again are provided by our Farmers). Once in a while a great wailfish or jawfish gets washed up on the beach – and very occasionally other sea creatures too, weird and terrifying beasts that presumably live in the ocean depths – and when that happens, everyone gets to work as quickly as possible, before the dead beast starts to rot in the heat. The carcass is immediately butchered and stripped of everything – meat, blubber, skin, bones – and the meat is cooked and salted and dried, and in some cases theres enough to keep us all fed for weeks. But thats a rarity, and most of the time our food is rationed – by Van Hesse the Grocer – and weare always hungry for more.

Even when food is extremely scarce though, we dont eat towndogs or their pups – in fact, the killing and eating of towndogs is strictly forbidden. This isnt because the townspeople care for the dogs, or even like them, because they dont. The dogs might live their whole lives in close proximity to humans, but they generally have very little, if any, contact with them. The people need the dogs as guards – to raise the alarm at the faintest sign of danger – and the dogs need the people for the food they provide, but thats as far as it goes. Theres no social interaction. The humans dont offer friendship, and the dogs dont seek it.

Water.

One more crucial difference between us and the Dau is that they have an unlimited supply of fresh water, and even if the small river that runs along the northside of their camp was to dry up, theyd still have access to the scarce streams and pools of the Deathlands. All we have is our spring – a small shallow pool that lies in the shadows of the West End watchtower.

And now even thats drying up.

The Deathlands.

Beyond the town and the Dau encampment – to the north, the

east, and the west – lies the endless expanse of the Deathlands. No one knows its true extent, but the dog in me knows every inch of the Deathland territory that my pack used to roam, an area of at least 50 square miles. I know the vast stretches of glassrock desert. I know the towering Black Mountains, with all their canyons and trails and streams and ridges and valleys. I know the plains. I know the young forests, growing up through the graves of their ancestors. I know the watering holes, the caves, the animal trails, the snake pits, the thornfields, the trees where the eagles nest. I know the skies, and what they mean. I know the wind, the air, the feel of the earth at my feet. I know it all. Its in me, part of me, its where Ime from. No matter how forgotten it is – how forgotten it has to be – my life in the Deathlands is still my life.

I dont know what time it is now, but I can feel a very faint rise in the temperature and I can smell the breaking dawn in the air. Ive been writing all night. The tiredness I felt earlier has gone though, and even if I felt like sleeping – which I dont – I know theres no point now. The new day is already beginning, and I still have so much to tell.

Our people.

Today, tonight, there are 156 of us.

This is who we are and what we do.

Our leader.

Weare led by our Marshal, Gun Sur, and his second-in-command, Deputy Pilgrim. Gun Surs authority is absolute. Hele take advice from his Deputy and the Council, and hele confer with the Fighter Captains on matters of security, but every decision that has to be made is ultimately made by Gun Sur alone.

The Council.

A committee of 6 men and women, mostly Olders, whose purpose is to advise on important concerns and make recommendations on matters of justice when necessary. The Council is directed by Deputy Pilgrim.

Fighters.

All ablebodied males become Fighters at the age of 12. When, and if, they reach 30, theyre either reassigned to other duties or kept on as Senior Fighters for another 5 years. All Fighters are compulsorily retired at the age of 35. An old man is too much of a liability as a Fighter – too slow, too weak, too dull-sensed.

Fighters have various everyday duties. Some man the watchtowers, some guard Gun Sur, others patrol the town and the perimeters or take the Youngers for Fighter training. Every one of them has to be ready at all times to defend the town against any form of attack and to carry out whatever actions Gun Sur demands.

All ablebodied females also become Fighters at the age of 12, and the same age rules apply to them as to the male Fighters. However, because of our declining population, all females are encouraged to have children as soon as they can – most of them have their first child at around 12 or 13 – and those who become mothers are relieved of their duties as fulltime Fighters until their child is 2 years old.

At the moment we have 49 Fighters in total — 30 male and 19 female.

Captains.

The Fighters are commanded by 3 Captains. 2 are female — Captains Luca and Kite — and one is male — Captain Glorian. The Captains command the Fighters and are responsible for putting Gun Surs military orders into practice.

Workers.

These are the townspeople who are either too old or not fit enough to be Fighters, but are not yet old enough to join the ranks of the Olders. They perform the basic tasks that help keep us all alive. Theyre Farmers, tending to the birds and growing crops. Theyre Fishermen, like Starry, mining the sea and trawling the beach for whatever food they can find. Theyre Builders, maintaining the security of the wall and the watchtowers and keeping the town buildings as useable as possible. Theyre Armourers, manufacturing gunpowder and ammunition, repairing and servicing weapons. Theyre Grocers, Nurses, Clothiers, Carpenters---and theyre Doctors too. Or at least one of them is. A man called Shiva. Doctor Shiva is the last in a long line of Doctor Shivas. He was taught medicine by his father, who in turn was taught by his father, who in turn was schooled by his father. Our Doctor Shiva doesnt have any children, but hese taken on 2 Youngers as apprentices, so that when he dies wele hopefully still have someone to treat our illnesses and injuries as well as possible with the very limited medical resources we have.

Youngers.

Youngers are those aged between 5 and 12. There are 27 of us at the moment – 15 male and 12 female – including 4 dogchilds. We dont have any specific duties – apart from Fighter training – but weare expected to do whatevers required of us whenever weare told. This can include almost anything – running errands, picking crops, helping out the Olders, scavenging the town for charcoal and lead and empty shell casings. Our official Fighter training begins at the age of 5, and we usually train for at least 4 or 5 hours every day, often longer. So by the time we reach the age of 12 we already have all the qualities we need to assume the duties of a Fighter.

Youngers are expected, and encouraged, to begin mating when they reach the age of sexual maturity, which is usually around 10 or 11.

Dogchilds.

Although the 4 of us are officially considered to be the same as everyone else – and as such weare expected to serve the town in the same way as everyone else – the reality is very different. Weare dogchilds. Weare not the same as everyone else. Weare different. Everyone knows it, and almost everyone treats us differently because of it. Some of them dont always show it in an obvious way, but its always there, just beneath the surface. We can feel it in them, we can sense it---

And I know its not just me.

Even though Ive never spoken to the other dogchilds about it – Ive never spoken to them about anything – I still know how they feel.

Dogchilds arent forbidden from socialising together or

becoming friends, but during the rehumanising process its constantly stressed that if we truly want to become human again we shouldnt mix with other dogchilds. So we dont. But that doesnt mean we dont know each other. Theres a connection between us that runs far deeper than anything wede get from simply being together, and we feel this bond in our guts every time we happen to see each other in the streets. The only outward sign of it though – if any – is a fleeting glance in passing, an almost imperceptible momentary raising of our lowered eyes.

We all know how we feel.

We see each other. We know each other.

We know what the humans feel about us.

Its a confusing mixture of fear and scorn and aggression. Weare the same as them, but not quite the same, and that frightens them. We frighten them. Because they know weare capable of ripping out their throats in a moment. So they keep their scorn and mockery well hidden, only calling us mongers and tykes and curs and bitches when they think we cant hear them.

We tell ourselves it doesnt matter---they cant help it---its as natural as the hatred between rival packs of dogs, or between warring humans.

Its just how it is.

Thats what we tell ourselves.

Olders.

Anyone over 40 is considered an Older. They can still work if they want to – as long as theyre deemed capable – but theyre no longer obliged to carry out any duties. Out of the 18 Olders we have at the moment, about half of them are still only semi-retired.

The oldest of them all is Lolo – a retired Fighter and mother of 3 – whose just turned 55. Most of those over 45 have some form of physical or mental impairment – blindness, deafness, some degree of madness – and all of them are cared for as well as possible. Whatever their state of mind or body, theyre revered and valued for their wisdom and experience. And as Starry had told me, theyre the only ones who know anything of our ancient history.

And thats why Ime going to go and see them now.

Most of The Olders live together in the Olders Home, a large 3-storey building in the centre of town that has dozens of separate rooms. Every Older has their own private room, but there are also several communal areas on the ground floor – including a dining room – where they spend a lot of their time together.

It was midmorning when I left my house and began heading across town towards the Olders Home. The skies were blue, the sun blazing down, and the air was free of dust. On some days the town is draped in clouds of fine dust that drift in the air like mist – the dust sometimes catching the light and shimmering with sheets of colour that ripple in the air like liquid rainbows – but today the dustclouds were nowhere to be seen and the air was still and clear.

The streets were quiet but not deserted. People were moving

around here and there, occasionally stopping to talk, but mostly just going about their business. I was so busy thinking about what I was going to ask the Olders that I barely noticed them. In fact, I was so deep in thought – and so familiar with the streets – that I wasnt watching where I was going, and as I turned the corner into Main Street I walked straight into someone. I wasnt walking very fast, and the other person had seen me coming and had stopped in their tracks, so it wasnt much of an impact, but it was enough to knock the writing book out of my hand.

Sorry, I said quickly, stooping down to pick up the book. I wasnt looking. Are you all right?

Ime fine.

I was just straightening up when I heard the voice, and for a brief moment I froze – still half stooped over – as if my body had suddenly seized up. It was a female voice, and although Ide only heard it a couple of times before, I instantly knew who it belonged to---and as the realisation sank in, I felt a strange tingling sensation in my belly, a feeling Ide never experienced before. After a moment or 2, I managed to unfreeze myself and start standing up again, and even though I knew who I was going to see before I straightened up and looked at her, the sight of Chola Se standing there right in front of me, gazing directly into my eyes, still took my breath away.

Ive always felt a special connection with Chola Se – something more than I have with the other dogchilds – but Ive never understood why. I dont know her. Ive never spoken to her. I dont know what it is that stirs within me whenever I see her or think of her---or when she sometimes comes to me in my dreams. I dont know what it is that she makes me feel, and I dont understand how I feel about it.

And I still didnt understand it in that breathless moment, when I stood there looking into her eyes.

Sorry, I muttered again. I didnt---I wasnt---I wasnt looking---

So you said.

Her voice was quiet and steady. It wasnt emotionless, exactly, but it had a sense of remoteness to it that gave her an air of not belonging.

Although Ide seen her hundreds of times before, Ide never been this close to her, and now that I was – and I was close enough to feel her breath on my skin – I could see that she looked exactly how Ide always imagined shede look if she was standing right in front of me. It was as if I already knew those large and sad-looking woodbrown eyes, that shaggy mop of bright black hair, that very slight crookedness to her mouth---

She had the same indefinable difference about her that all dogchilds have, and she had the same slightly crouched-over posture that we all have too. She was wearing a simple black smock with a leather belt, black moccasins, and a necklace of coloured stone beads. A long thin-bladed knife was tucked into her belt, and as far as I could tell that was the only weapon she was carrying.

Are you all right? she asked me.

I suddenly realised that for the last 5 seconds or so Ide just been standing there, staring dumbly at her like an idiot.

Uh, yeh---yeh, sorry, I mumbled, feeling stupidly tongue-tied.

Whats that? she asked, glancing at my writing book, which for some reason I was grasping closely to my chest.

I didnt know what to say at first. There was something inside me that wanted to tell her all about the account, and I cant deny that I couldnt help thinking – or, at least, hoping – that she might be impressed by the fact that Gun Sur had chosen me to write it. But at the same time I was wary of saying too much. Gun Sur hadnt specifically told me to keep the account to myself, and Ide already talked to Starry about it, but Starry was different. I knew him. And despite the connection I felt with Chola Se, I didnt actually know the first thing about her. So I thought it was probably best if I didnt tell her everything about the account. But I didnt want to appear rude either.

Its a---its a kind of project, I said hesitantly.

Whats a project?

Its like a task. A job Ive been asked to do---writing about things---

You can read and write?

I nodded.

Could you teach me?

To read and write?

Ive always wanted to learn.

All the time she was talking to me, I was closely studying her face, and I realised now that although shede never once smiled, the sadness that seemed so ingrained in her had lifted just a little. It was still there – and I got the impression that it was as much a part of her as her skin or her flesh or her bones – but it no longer seemed quite so intense as it had been.

I could try to teach you, I told her, trying to hide my childlike excitement. I mean, Ive never taught anyone before, but I could try—

Really?

Yeh.

When can we start?

When?

Yeh.

I shrugged. Tomorrow night?

Where?

Wherever you like.

Your house?

Well---yeh, okay. I live in that little street just off—

I know where you live.

Oh---okay.

Ile be there tomorrow night, before dark.

Right.

And then, without another word, she just walked off and disappeared round the corner.

All I could do for the next minute or so was stand there in a daze, replaying in my mind everything that had just happened. It somehow seemed almost unreal. But if I had any doubts over whether it had actually happened or not, there was no doubting the beating thump of my heart and the rush of blood in my veins.

I spoke to 5 Olders at their Home. 4 were residents, the other one just happened to be visiting. 3 of them were women – Leven Rai, Soyaan, and Lolo – and 2 were men – Cruke and Momid. Cruke was the nonresident. He was the youngest of the 5, around 41 or 42. Hede been a Fighter all his life – including 5 years as a Captain – and despite his age, he still looked as mean and tough as he always had. Hede lost his right eye many years ago when hede been hit by shrapnel in one of the last Dau artillery attacks, and although he was beginning to show the frailties of old age now, his battle-scarred face and empty eye socket still gave him an air of indestructability.

As I sat with the Olders in one of their communal rooms and explained what I was doing and why I wanted their help, a Younger called Raoul came over to us carrying a platter of cornbread and a jug of water. Theres always a Younger on duty at the Olders Home to help them with whatever they need, and for a lot of the Youngers its the task they least like doing. The Olders with physical and/or mental problems can be quite difficult to deal with sometimes, and some of the Youngers resent having to spend their time nursing sick old people when they could be out Fighter training or learning how to make ammunition. From the way Raoul came slouching over with the food and drink and almost threw it down on the table, it was perfectly obvious that hede rather be anywhere else but here, and that he didnt care who knew it.

He didnt bother trying to hide his contempt for me either.

He never does.

Most of the other Youngers are only openly hostile to dogchilds when theyre in a reasonably large group – theyre too scared to confront us on their own – but Raouls different. He hates us with a passion – especially me, for some reason – and he never tries to disguise it, whether hese on his own or not.

He didnt actually say anything to me as he put the food on the table, but he didnt have to – the mocking sneer on his face said it all. Whats a monger like you doing with these sick old fools?

But then Cruke spoke to him – You got a problem, boy? – and the sneer on Raouls face instantly disappeared.

Uh, no---he muttered, lowering his eyes. No problem---
I was just—

Go, Cruke said dismissively. Ile call you if I need you.

Raoul nodded, almost bowing, and as he turned and scurried
away there wasnt an ounce of arrogance left in him.

So, Cruke said to me, his voice slightly softened. What is it you
want to know?

The essence of what I wanted to know was how and why our world
was the way it was. Why and how had we come to be here? What
had there been before the Long Walk? What was the world like
back then? Had we always been at war with the Dau? And why?
Why did we hate each other so much that the war would never
stop until one of us had been annihilated?

The Olders tried their best to answer my questions, but the
truth is that although we talked for several hours, I was really no
wiser about the past when I left than I was when I first arrived.

The 4 resident Olders did most of the talking. I thought at first
that Cruke didnt have much to say simply because he was the
youngest, and as such didnt know so much about the past as the
others, but after a while I began to realise that it was more to do
with what he was, what hese always been, and what he still is. Hese
a Fighter, through and through. Thats what defines him, even now
hese retired – fighting. Its all hese ever done. Its his reason for
being – fighting the Dau, killing the Dau – and everything else is
irrelevant. The past, the reasons things happened, the history of
the war with the Dau---none of it means anything to Cruke. All
that matters to him is now.

So most of the time Cruke just sat there and listened as the others tried to answer my questions. He listened as Leven Rai told me that there were once hundreds of thousands of people, as many people as there are stars in the sky, and that the world was a thousand times bigger than it is today.

How long ago was this? I asked her.

Oh, hundreds of years ago, she said.

No, no, Lolo said, shaking her head. It was more than that, Leven. It was thousands of years ago---many thousands.

Leven Rai frowned at her. Are you sure?

Well---it was a long time ago, I know that. She smiled distantly. I remember my grandmother telling me about the great golden cities that floated in the sky, and the vast machines, as big as mountains, that kept everyone alive---and there was something else---something about---what was it?

The old woman faltered, her eyes blinking vacantly.

The silver men---? she muttered. Was that it? The silver men who lived on the moon?

Her mouth opened, then closed---she frowned---then her eyes suddenly widened.

No, no, she said quickly, it was the giants, thats it, the invisible giants, thats what I was thinking of, the Goods and Evils, the ones who could bring the dead back to life or burn the living in fires that never died---

She stuttered to a stop again, her mind adrift, lost in a confusion of memories.

There was magic, she said quietly.

Everything went quiet for a while then. Leven Rai and Soyaan picked awkwardly at crumbs of cornbread, both of them slightly embarrassed by Lolos strange little outburst, while Lolo herself just sat there, her mouth half open, staring at nothing. Cruke, meanwhile, just carried on sitting in his chair, upright and unmoved, not saying anything, just waiting to see how Ide react.

What happened to it all? I said eventually.

Soyaan looked at me. What?

This long-ago world, I said, all those people and cities and machines---what happened to it all?

The Dau destroyed it.

They poisoned the air, Leven Rai added.

What do you mean?

She shrugged. Thats all they said.

Who?

The Olders---our Olders.

They told you the Dau had poisoned the air?

She nodded.

How?

No one knows.

I looked at Soyaan. Did your Olders know why theyd poisoned the air?

To kill us all.

Why did they want to kill us all?

For the same reason they want to kill us all now. Because theyre Dau and weare us.

I glanced at Cruke, hoping he might have something to add, but although he met my gaze – his one eye staring steadily back at me – he didnt break his silence.

I turned back to the others.

Does anyone know when the war with the Dau first began? I asked them.

What do you mean? Leven Rai said.

When did the war start? A hundred years ago, 5 hundred years, a thousand---?

Soyaan and Leven Rai just stared at me, both of them frowning, as if they didnt understand the question.

Then Lolo spoke.

The war is just the war, she said to me. Asking when it started is like asking when the sky began.

But something must have started it, I said. There must have been a reason—

Does the sky have a reason?

I carried on asking my questions, trying to get some more realistic answers, but the longer I went on, the more vague and contradictory the Olders became. A thousand years ago became 50 years ago. The Long Walk was 200 miles, then 20 thousand miles. The Dau came from the other side of the world---they came from the sea, the moon, the stars. They used to be the same as us---theyve never been the same as us. Theyre not human, theyre alien, theyre Evils---monstrous beasts in human form---

Stories.

Myths.

Madness.

The truth, it seems, is all gone. Destroyed, rotted, turned to dust. Lost for ever.

The past, our history, is dead.

And as I sit here now, in the dead silence of the night, I wonder if it matters. Whatever the truth is about how we came to be here –

73

and how things used to be – nothing can change it. Reasons dont change reality. We are here. This is what we have. This is our world. And perhaps Crukes right to think that all that matters is now.

And maybe tomorrow.

Tomorrow---

Ime seeing Chola Se tomorrow. Shese coming here, tomorrow night. Shese coming to my house---

Ile have to clean the place up a bit.

Maybe make us something to eat.

Maybe---

Tomorrow.

I was woken the next morning by the sound of the town bell ringing. It wasnt the rapid clanging of the alarm bell, it was the slower and steadier ringing of the assembly call, but assemblies are usually called at midday, not first thing in the morning, so there was clearly something out of the ordinary going on.

Assemblies are held in the Quarterhouse Square, and as I left my house and joined everyone else heading along the streets towards the centre of town, I saw Starry hobbling along ahead of me. I caught up with him and asked if he knew what was happening.

He shook his head. No one seems to know anything.

The Square was already quite busy when we got there, and as we made our way through the milling crowds, I could feel the tension and uncertainty in the air – muttering voices, worried looks, uneasiness and confusion. The bell had stopped ringing now, and everyone was looking towards the Quarterhouse, waiting for Gun Sur to come out and speak.

The Quarterhouse is Gun Surs headquarters. Its a 4-storey whitestone building, with a belltower on top and a broad flight of steps leading up to the entrance, and its guarded 24 hours a day. All the windows have iron bars and metal shutters, and the heavy wooden doors are secured with locks and bolts. As Starry and I stopped near the front of the crowd, I could see that the main door was already open, and the 2 armed guards either side of it seemed even more vigilant than usual. A table and chair had been set up at the foot of the stone steps, and as I glanced at Starry I saw him peering thoughtfully at the table, trying to work out what it was for. I was about to ask him if he had any ideas when the murmuring crowd suddenly hushed, and as I looked up at the Quarterhouse I saw Gun Sur coming out through the open door. He was flanked by 2 Fighters, and behind him I could see 3 Councillors and Captain Kite. As Gun Sur moved to the top of the steps, one of the Councillors – a bearded Older called Ghauri – edged past him, went down the steps, and sat at the table.

Gun Sur just stood there for a few moments looking out over the assembled crowd. He was dressed as he always was – black robe, black skullcap, black boots. He carried a silver-handled sword in a scabbard on the right side of his belt, a 9mm Glock automatic in a holster on the left, and a long dagger in his right boot.

When he began to speak, his voice was strong and loud enough to carry across the Square, but at the same time it had a quiet calmness to it that somehow gave it an added sense of authority.

At some point during the night, he announced, our defences were breached and our town came under attack.

Gasps of surprise came from the crowd, followed by a rising murmur of worried voices. Gun Sur held up his hand and the voices went quiet.

As yet, he continued, we dont know exactly when the raid took place or how the attackers got in, and we cant say for sure who they were. Weare working on the assumption they were Dau, but we cant rule out the possibility that the Wild Ones have returned.

Gun Sur paused for a moment, lowering his head in thought, then looked up again and carried on.

The only thing we know for certain is that during the attack 2 of our people were killed and 3 more are missing, presumably taken by the raiders. The 2 fatalities are Aliaj and Berch, and 2 of those missing are the twin babies that Aliaj was raising following the death of her sister. The third missing victim is Chola Se.

At the sound of her name, everything inside me suddenly went numb, and for a few moments I couldnt seem to make sense of anything. Chola Se couldnt be missing---Ide seen her only yesterday---wede talked to each other---she was coming round to my house that night---

She couldnt be missing.

Not now---

It wasnt right. It couldnt be---

But I knew that it was. I might not want to believe it, but the gnawing ache in my belly and the coldness in my heart knew the truth.

Gun Sur was still talking. His voice had become meaningless to me in the last few seconds — just a hollow drone somewhere in the distance – but now that my initial numbness was fading, and my senses were beginning to come back to me, I knew that I had to listen to him. So I refocused my mind and concentrated on what he was saying.

---and if anyone saw or heard anything at all last night, no matter how insignificant you think it might be, its essential that you report it to Ghauri.

Gun Sur glanced down at the table where the old man was sitting, then looked back at the crowd again.

Ghauri, or another Councillor, will be available throughout the day – and all day tomorrow if necessary – so even if you dont remember anything right now, but something comes to you later, you can still report it immediately. Meanwhile I want everyone to start looking for answers. We have to find out how and where our defences were breached, and its vital that we find out as soon as possible to protect ourselves from another attack. So I want people checking every inch of the wall. I want people scouring the beach and the cliffs. And I want anyone with tracking skills to make yourselves known to one of the Fighter Captains so we can start making a search of the area around the homes of the victims.

Gun Sur waited a few moments, gazing sternly around the Square, making sure he had everyones attention. And then, with a cold determination to his voice, he said, All right, lets get to work.

Everyone started bustling around – some heading over to Ghauri, others seeking out one of the Fighter Captains to offer their services as trackers, while the rest began organising themselves into search parties. As Starry went off to join one of the search parties, I made my way over to the foot of the steps where a group of volunteer trackers were gathering around Captain Luca. Most of them were reasonably skilled trackers in human terms, but none of them could track like a dog. I was raised to hunt. I can read the stories of tracks and signs that humans cant even see. And I needed to know the story of what had happened to Chola Se. Ide never needed to know anything so much in my life.

But just as I was approaching Luca and the trackers, and before I had a chance to say anything, I heard someone calling my name. The voice came from the top of the steps, and when I looked up I saw Gun Sur staring down at me.

Come, Jeet, he said, beckoning me towards him. We need to talk.

I hesitated for a moment, torn between my instinctive reaction to obey Gun Sur and my overriding desire to get to Chola Ses house as soon as possible.

Did you hear me? Gun Sur said, his voice edged with hardness.

I knew I had no choice. If I disobeyed him and started heading off to Chola Ses house on my own, hede simply order his Fighters to come after me and bring me back, and then Ide have to apologise and explain myself, which would only delay things even more.

So I took a deep breath to calm myself, nodded dutifully at Gun Sur, and started climbing the steps towards him.

Until a few days ago, Ide never even seen Gun Surs private office, let alone been in it, but now here I was again, back in the room where Ide been ordered to write this account, back in the Marshals presence again.

His office is a large room on the first floor of the building. The door is always guarded by a heavily armed Fighter, and the windows are protected with bars and steel shutters on both sides. Apart from a massive oak table near the far wall, and other smaller tables and chairs dotted around the room, the room is mostly bare. No ornaments, no personal touches, nothing without purpose.

Gun Sur was sitting at the oak table when I was shown into the room, and Deputy Pilgrim was leaning against the wall by one of the windows, casually resting his foot on a chair. He didnt say anything to me when I glanced at him, he just stared back at me without even the hint of a greeting, but that didnt surprise me. Pilgrims a very capable man – an exFighter Captain, revered for his courage and loyalty, and according to Starry a highly intelligent and innovative thinker – but theres a coldness to him that sets him apart from others.

Hese quite a lot younger than Gun Sur – in his midtwenties, Ide guess – and he has a very distinctive appearance. Weather-worn skin, hard and leathery, deepset dark eyes, a beaklike nose, and a full black moustache. He wears a battered black hat with a wide brim, a leather singlet over his bare chest, and black trousers tucked into kneehigh heeled boots. Hese fairly short, and most people assume that he wears the heeled boots to make him look taller, but Starrys convinced that the real reason he wears them is that hese obsessed with an ancient race of gunfighting warriors called Cowboys.

An old friend of mine knows a woman who stayed with Pilgrim one night, Starry had told me once. And she said his walls are covered in faded scraps of pictures of Cowboys torn from the remains of old books, and he even has an almost complete storybook about them which hese read so many times he knows it off by heart. Thats why he wears those clothes – the heeled boots, the hat and

79

the vest – and that gunbelt too. He thinks they make him look like a Cowboy.

Pilgrim carries matching Colt 45s in lowslung holsters tied at the leg. He also carries a silver-gripped hunting dagger in a boot sheath, and he never goes anywhere without his prized MP40 submachine gun, which that morning was leaning against the wall beside him.

Sit down, Jeet, Gun Sur said as I entered the room.

I went over to the table and sat down opposite him.

Ime sorry I didnt come to you immediately just now, I said. I didnt mean any disrespect. I was just—

No matter, he said. Youre here now.

He looked down at the table for a second, then raised his eyes again.

Hows the account proceeding? he asked.

Fine.

No problems?

No.

Good. I heard youve been speaking to some of the Olders.

I nodded. I was trying to find out about our past.

Did they tell you what you wanted to know?

Well---they did their best.

He almost smiled, just a brief twitch of his mouth. Come and see me sometime when things have settled down a bit, he said. I know a little of our past.

That would be good, thank you.

He turned and gazed out of the window. The shutters were open, and I could hear the hustle and bustle from the Square below as the townspeople headed off to begin searching the town. The sound of their footsteps and voices fading into the distance was a stark reminder that while they were out there trying to find out what had happened, I was stuck in here, sitting at a table, doing nothing.

How well do you know Chola Se? Gun Sur said, turning back to me.

The question took me by surprise, and I couldnt help showing it.

What do you mean? I said, staring at him.

Its a simple enough question. How well do you know her?

I shook my head. I hardly know her at all.

You were seen talking to her yesterday.

I was beginning to feel uneasy now. Gun Sur had already told me that he knew Ide been speaking to the Olders, and now he was telling me that he knew Ide been talking to Chola Se. What else did he know about me? I wondered. And why was he asking me about Chola Se anyway? Was it something to do with her disappearance, or was he just trying to find out if I was guilty of ignoring everything Ide been told during my rehumanisation about mixing with other dogchilds? Whatever his reason for asking, I decided that the best course of action was to simply tell the truth.

Ive never spoken to Chola Se before yesterday, I told him. I was on my way to see the Olders and I bumped into her as I turned a corner. I dropped my writing book, and when I picked it up she asked me what it was.

Did you tell her?

No.

What happened then?

Nothing. I apologised for bumping into her, and asked her if she was all right. She said she was fine. And that was it. She carried on to wherever she was going, and I headed off to see the Olders.

As Gun Sur sat there, thoughtfully nodding his head again, I wondered why I wasnt being as honest with him as Ide meant to be. I hadnt intended to hide the fact that Ide arranged to meet Chola Se, and although I knew that Gun Sur wouldnt approve of it, I doubted if hede actually punish me. Mixing with other dogchilds might be socially unacceptable, but it isnt against the law. The worst Ide get for admitting to it was a stern rebuke and a reminder of what was expected of me as a human.

So why was I hiding it from Gun Sur?

I honestly didnt know.

Have you any idea why Chola Se might have been taken? he asked me.

I shrugged. Shese a young female. The Dau need young females as much as we do.

Any other possible reason?

Not that I can think of.

Do you have any thoughts about the attack?

What do you mean?

Does anything strike you as unusual about it?

I was about to say no when something suddenly dawned on me.

The towndogs, I said.

What about them?

Why didnt they make any noise?

I couldnt believe I hadnt thought of it before. Although Gun Sur hadnt actually said that the dogs hadnt raised the alarm, it was obvious from the fact that no one knew anything about the raid that they hadnt. And I knew they hadnt anyway, because I would have heard them. Even if Ide been sound asleep, and even if only 1 or 2 of them had barked from the far side of town, and for only a very short time---I would have heard them.

Why do you think the dogs didnt bark? Gun Sur asked me.

I gave this some thought before answering – not just to make sure that Ide considered everything, but also to make sure that I was comfortable sharing it all with Gun Sur.

There are only 3 possible reasons why the dogs didnt bark, I told him eventually. Firstly, there wasnt an attack at all, and Aliaj and Berch were either killed by one of us or they killed themselves.

Their throats were cut, Gun Sur said.

Okay, so they didnt kill themselves.

But if they were killed by one of our people, Gun Sur said thoughtfully, or more than one---whats happened to Chola Se and the babies?

I dont know.

Theres an obvious possibility though, isnt there?

I knew what he meant, I just didnt want to say it. But I knew that if I didnt, he would. And I didnt want to hear it from him.

Chola Se could have taken the babies, I said, emphasising the word could. She could have killed Aliaj and Berch, taken the babies, and somehow left town---but she didnt. I know she didnt.

How do you know?

I just do.

How can you be so sure? You said yourself that you hardly know her—

Shese a dogchild, I said, looking him in the eye. We know each other in ways you wouldnt understand.

Really?

He held my gaze, staring deep into my eyes, searching for the truth. And I just sat there in silence and let him see it.

All right, he said after a while, lets leave that for now. You said there were 3 possible reasons the dogs didnt bark. Whats the second?

They wouldnt have made any noise if they either knew the attackers, or if the attackers were with someone they knew.

Which would mean we have a traitor in our midst.

I nodded.

And the third reason?

The raiders had someone like me with them.

A dogchild?

Not necessarily.

I dont understand.

Someone with the ability to keep dogs quiet.

Gun Sur leaned forward in his chair, his eyes fixed on mine. Are you telling me that you can do that? You can silence dogs?

Yes.

Can other dogchilds do it?

I dont know. Ive never witnessed another one doing it, but that doesnt mean they cant. And the Dau might have those who can do it.

But youve never actually met another dogchild, or anyone else, who can do what you can do?

Not to my knowledge, no.

How do you do it? he said.

When I didnt answer immediately, he leaned across the table towards me, staring intensely into my eyes.

Ime not just asking out of idle curiosity, Jeet, he said, speaking softly. And Ime not accusing you of anything either. I know you didnt have anything to do with the raid. You wouldnt have told me about this ability of yours if you did. But what youve just told

84

me could be of great importance. It could help us find out what happened. And if Chola Se and the babies are still alive, it could help us to get them back. And it might even come to play a part in our very survival.

He waited a few seconds to let that sink in, his eyes never leaving mine, then he leaned in a little closer and spoke again, this time almost whispering.

I need to know what you can do, Jeet. I need to know if you can help us.

Ive never spoken about this ability of mine before, not even to Starry, and as Gun Sur leaned back in his chair and I began trying to explain it, I wasnt at all sure that I was doing the right thing. I knew why I was doing it – because Gun Sur had told me it might help Chola Se – but I also knew that he could be lying. I didnt trust him for a moment, and I trusted Pilgrim even less, but if there was any chance at all that by opening myself up I might find out what happened to Chola Se---

I had to open myself up.

I dont know how I do it, I told Gun Sur. But I can silence dogs if I want to.

You can stop them barking?

Yes.

He frowned at me. You must know how you do it.

I shook my head, remembering the first time it happened.

It was an unusually humid day, just over a year ago – the air thick and heavy, the skies bruised with thunderclouds – and I was heading down to the beach to see Starry about something. A group of 4 or 5 towndogs had been following me since I left my house, and as

85

usual Ide been ignoring them. They often followed me – just as they often followed the other dogchilds – and Ide become so used to it that I barely even noticed it most of the time. They usually kept their distance, never coming close enough to physically threaten me, and all they really did was make their presence known – constantly growling and snarling, and often keeping up an incessant chorus of yapping and barking. I knew it for what it was – a mixture of fear, curiosity, and anxious aggression – and I knew it was nothing to worry about. It happened all the time, and Ide lived with it so long now that it was nothing more than background noise, like the sighing of the wind or the distant clucking of birds.

But that day, for some reason, I was in a really bad mood, and as the towndogs began getting a bit too close – closer than usual – and their barking and yapping began getting on my nerves, something inside me just snapped. But instead of turning round and snarling back at them – as Ide done a couple of times before when theyd come too close – I just kind of did something---

I didnt know what it was.

I didnt know then, and I still dont know now.

Its hard to explain, I told Gun Sur. I just kind of---I dont know. I just do something, and something comes out of me---some kind of force or energy, like a wave of something. I dont tell the dogs to be quiet. Its as if I somehow become part of them, and they become part of me---and we just feel this sense, this feeling that we want to be quiet---

I paused, shaking my head, trying to find the right words. But it was impossible. There arent any words to describe this thing I can do. Its beyond words.

I can somehow just do it, I said. I can make the dogs quiet.

Can you make them do anything else?

They dont follow me if I dont want them to.

Is that it?

I dont know. Ive never tried anything else.

Why not?

Ive not had any reason to.

Can you do the same thing with people?

No.

Gun Sur looked thoughtfully at me for a few moments, then glanced across at Pilgrim. I didnt hear Pilgrim say anything to him – he hadnt made a sound from the moment Ide entered the room – and because he was sitting behind me, I couldnt see if he nodded at Gun Sur or gave him some kind of signal either, but when Gun Sur turned back to me, he looked as if hede made up his mind about something, so I guessed something had just passed between them.

Come with me, Gun Sur said, taking a pair of binoculars from the table drawer and getting to his feet. I want to show you something.

As part of our Fighter training we spend at least 2 or 3 hours every week in the turret of one of the watchtowers – familiarising ourselves with our surroundings, studying the layout of the Dau encampment, learning the basics of watchtower duty – so when I followed Gun Sur out of his office, and we left the Quarterhouse and crossed over to the wall, then entered the West Tower and climbed up into the turret, it was by no means the first time Ide been up there. Ive been in all the turrets, many times over. Ive spent hours and hours watching and waiting in watchtower turrets---

I know every inch of them.

Theyre all partially divided into 2 sections. The upper section – the lookout area – is protected on all sides by 5-foot-high battlements, with 4-foot-wide ledges spanning the base of each wall to form a perimeter walkway around the turret. The enemy can be engaged from the upper section if necessary, but the main combat area is the lower part of the turret. Each of the 4 walls in the lower section has a gunport – a narrow slit in the stonework thats wide enough for Fighters to shoot through, but not wide enough for them to be shot at – and because there are no other openings, and its not open to the elements like the upper section, the combat area is virtually impregnable to enemy fire.

The 2 sections are connected by a narrow flight of stone steps, and as I followed Gun Sur up the steps into the upper section – where Gun Sur relieved the guard – and we looked out over the battlements, the view was just as familiar to me as the layout of the turret. The vast wilderness of the distant Deathlands – the barren blur of the deserts and plains hazing into the wide blue skies – and directly below us, shimmering in the heat, the black emptiness of Nomansland stretching across to the Dau encampment half a mile to the north---Ide seen it all countless times before, both with and without the aid of a spyglass.

But when Gun Sur passed me his binoculars, and I put them to my eyes and focused on the distant compound, it was as if I was seeing it all for the very first time. The clarity was astonishing. I could see things as they actually were – the buildings, the pathways, the watchtowers, the people. The blurred figures I was used to seeing through the training spyglasses were now recognisable as individual people. I could see them perfectly clearly – Dau Fighters, Dau women and children, Dau Youngers – and now that I was seeing them properly for the first time, it was quite obvious how much fitter and stronger most of them looked in comparison to us. They didnt look hungry. They didnt look tired. They didnt look half dead.

Put the glasses down a moment, Gun Sur told me.

I did as he said.

He pointed out over the battlements. Do you see that wooden building with the red roof near the western edge of the compound?

I gazed in the direction he was pointing.

The one with the armed guard at the door? I said.

Thats it. Take a look at it through the glasses.

I raised the binoculars and focused on the building.

Have you got it? Gun Sur said.

Yes.

Tell me what you see.

Its a mediumsized log building with a painted metal roof. Metal shutters on the windows, a heavy wooden door with a bolt on it---

I adjusted the focus, concentrating hard on the bolt.

I think there might be a lock on it.

Anything else?

I carried on scanning the building and the guard through the powerful binoculars.

89

The guards armed with a semiautomatic rifle and a handgun, I said. I cant make out what kind of pistol it is, but I think the rifles an Armalite. The building looks fairly solid. Well-built, thick walls—

Do you think you could get into it?

I lowered the glasses and looked questioningly at Gun Sur.

Theres something we need in there, he explained. Ile tell you what it is later on. All you need to know at the moment is that if we dont get hold of it, our chances of winning the final battle will be severely jeopardised. So its absolutely vital that we get someone into that building to get what we need and safely bring it back to us.

Do you mean me? I said.

Youre one of a number of options Ime considering. Whether I choose you or not depends partly on you. If you think youre capable of doing it, and if you can think of a plausible way of doing it, I might decide youre the right option.

What are your other options?

Thats none of your concern, he said coldly. Your only concern at the moment, your only duty, is to stay up here and keep studying that building until youve worked out how youre going to get into it and get what we need. Once youve done that, come back to my office and wele talk some more. Is that understood?

What about Chola Se?

Did you hear what I just said?

Yes, but—

No more, Jeet. You have your orders. Do you understand them? Yes or no?

Yes.

He gave me a long hard look, reminding me of his authority,

and then – without another word – he turned away and headed off down the tower.

It didnt take long to work out how to get into the red-roofed building to get whatever it was that was in there. The difficult part was trying to figure out how to get to the Dau encampment without being seen. Crossing Nomansland was out of the question. The Dau have sentries posted all around their perimeter, both on the ground and in their watchtowers, and as well as having spyglasses and binoculars like our guards, they also have at least one nightvision scope. But even without it, theres so little cover in Nomansland that trying to cross it, even in the dead of a moonless night, would be fatal.

So, as far as I could tell, the only possible option was to take a much wider, encircling route – avoiding the flat and open glassrock terrain of Nomansland altogether – and approach the camp from its northwest flank, where the landscape around the compound provides at least some cover. Its still mostly desert, but its not quite as desolate and featureless as Nomansland. There are low ridges here and there, patches of shrubland and stunted trees, even a few dried-up river beds, and in some areas this relatively rugged terrain comes quite close to the camp perimeter, in places no more than a few hundred feet away. Ide still have to cross the wide-open stretch of ground immediately outside the perimeter – which the Dau keep meticulously clear of vegetation all the way round – but if I could get to within a few hundred feet of the camp without being seen, at least that would give me a chance.

The problem was how to reach the northwest flank of the camp in the first place. The Dau Fighters on lookout duty wouldnt just be keeping their eyes on Nomansland, theyd be watching out in all directions, scouring every inch of their surroundings for any signs of attack. Thered be dozens of them, positioned all around the camp – some on the ground, guarding the perimeter, others high up in their watchtowers – and between them all theyd be covering everywhere – the town, the Deathlands, the deserts, the mountains---

I gazed out to the west, imagining myself crossing the glassrock plains and heading up into the heart of the Deathlands---

It was a journey Ide made once before, a long long time ago – running back through the night with the pack, our jaws and my hands weighed down with plunder---

For a moment or 2 then, as I stood there in the watchtower looking out over the Deathland plains, it all came flooding back to me. That first exhilarating raid, the fear and the thrill of it all – crawling through the tunnel---rampaging through the town---running back through the night with the pack---then finally stopping to feast on our haul of plundered meat---gorging ourselves until we couldnt eat anymore, then lying down, our bellies bursting, to sleep without hunger for the first time in months. And then the horror of the second raid, the one we should never have made, the one my mother warned us against. I remembered the heavy crash of the metal grid as it dropped down and blocked our exit from the tunnel---the flaming torches in the darkness---the armed humans surrounding the cage---our futile efforts to attack them, flinging ourselves at the wire fences---the deafening barrage of gunfire, the yelps of pain, the sound of bodies thudding to the ground---and then nothing but a terrible silence filled with the smell of gunpowder and death---

I thought of my mother then, my dogmother, and I wondered – as Ive wondered many times before – if she was still alive. She was probably around 6 years old when I last saw her, which meant shede have to be at least 12 years old now, and I simply dont know if thats possible or not. I dont know how long Deathland dogs can live for. I dont recall seeing many – if any – old dogs when I was living with them, but that doesnt necessarily mean they cant have long lives. It just means that most of them – if not all of them – dont die of old age. They die of hunger, or thirst, or disease, or violence. So although its highly unlikely that my mother is still alive, it isnt impossible---

It was at that point, just as I was thinking about my mother, that an idea suddenly came to me.

I raised the binoculars and looked down to my left, focusing on a narrow strip of woodland that stretches out from the base of the West End Tower and runs along the edge of the westside cliff. Even though its not very big – maybe 100 yards long and 30 wide, narrowing even more towards the far end – Ive never understood why the woodland has been allowed to grow instead of being cut down and cleared away, in the same way that the Dau keep their perimeter free of vegetation. But Ide never had such powerful binoculars before, and now – as I focused the glasses on a patch of trees near the base of the wall – now I knew why the woodland hadnt been cleared. The fallen tree that had hidden the old animal burrow from sight all those years ago was still there, and although I couldnt actually see the entrance to the tunnel, I knew it had to be there. That was the reason the woodland was there – to keep the tunnel hidden from view.

At the same time as that realisation sank in, I suddenly realised how it might be possible to get to the northwest flank of the Dau encampment without being seen, and as I began thinking it over, it gradually dawned on me why Gun Sur had chosen me to carry out the raid.

It was gone midday now. The sun was high in the sky, glaring down with a blinding white ferocity, and I was hot and tired and mentally drained. I wasnt looking forward to going back to the Quarterhouse to tell Gun Sur my thoughts – I wasnt even sure I wanted to tell him anything at all – and if it had been up to me I would have stayed up there in the watchtower, scanning the Dau camp for any sign of Chola Se.

Ide been keeping my eyes open for anything that might tell me where she was all the time Ide been up there – anything that could be a prison, buildings with locked doors and barred windows, buildings with guards at the door. The problem was, at least half the buildings I could see were locked and barred or guarded, and Chola Se could be in any one of them. Or she could be in one of the countless buildings I couldnt see – the buildings inside the highwalled fort in the centre of the camp, for example – or in an underground cell in one of the many trenches that riddled the camp---

She could be anywhere.

Or nowhere.

She might not be there at all.

But I had to believe that she was.

If she was there, she was alive. If she wasnt---

She had to be.

And all I wanted to do was keep looking for her, but I knew

that I couldnt. If Gun Sur was right about the importance of this mysterious object in the red-roofed building – if it really was so crucial to our chances of winning the battle – then I had to forget about Chola Se for the moment and concentrate on following the Marshals orders.

There was no point in finding Chola Se if we were all going to die soon anyway.

Like it or not, I had to leave the watchtower now and go back to the Quarterhouse. I couldnt resist giving the camp a final quick scan through the binoculars though, just in case Ide missed something, but I knew in my heart that I wasnt going to find Chola Se now. Ide already searched everywhere. Ide already seen all there was to see. I knew I hadnt missed anything.

I lowered the binoculars, turned away from the parapet---
And stopped.

Ide seen something.

I thought about it for a moment, replaying the image in my mind, then I turned back to the parapet, raised the binoculars, and focused again on what Ide just seen.

It was a Dau Fighter, a guard. He hadnt just appeared – hede been there the whole time Ide been watching the camp – and he hadnt moved or changed in any way either. He was still in exactly the same position hede been in when Ide first seen him – standing guard at the far end of a large open courtyard in front of the fort. There was nothing different about him at all. The only difference was that Ide finally realised after all this time that he didnt seem to be guarding anything.

The courtyard – a flat expanse of sunbaked dirt – was about 50 yards long and 35 wide, and the Fighter was positioned at the opposite end to the fort, so he couldnt possibly be guarding the fort itself, and the only other building anywhere near him was a dilapidated wooden shack about 20 yards to his left which had clearly been abandoned a long time ago. Apart from that – and a pile of logs 15 yards to his right – he was surrounded on all sides by open ground.

So what was he doing there?

There was no doubt he was on sentry duty of some kind – standing in the same position for hours on end, a rifle on his shoulder, eyes on the alert - - - he was definitely guarding something. I scanned the area around him again, looking in more detail at everything, but I couldnt see anything suspicious or out of place. The courtyard was deserted, the wooden shack was definitely empty, the pile of logs was just a pile of logs. I focused the binoculars on the guards face, studying him closely in the hope that Ide see something, anything, that might tell me what he was doing there. And it didnt take long to realise that he seemed anxious about something – his eyes darting around, his face tense, his jaw tight. I kept watching. He licked his lips - - - once, twice - - - then wiped his mouth with the back of his hand. He glanced quickly over his shoulder, frowning to himself - - - then he began pacing around, muttering under his breath - - -

There was no doubt he was worried about something.

And then suddenly he froze, staring towards the fort, and it was obvious that he wasnt just anxious now, he was scared.

I followed his gaze to see what he was staring at and saw a fat old woman waddling across the courtyard towards him. She was wearing a grubby red turban, a necklace of bones, and a full-length brown robe that trailed in the dirt as she walked. She had a long spear in one hand, which she was using as a walking stick, and in her other hand she was carrying a wicker basket.

As I swung the binoculars back to the guard, I was just in time to see him turning his back on the woman and thumping the butt of his rifle into the ground. I saw his lips moving, as if he was talking to someone, and I got the impression that he was speaking in a loud and urgent whisper. He hammered the ground again, then stooped over – bending at the waist and lowering his head towards the ground – and spat out some more frantic words, his teeth bared in a mixture of anger and fear. It looked as if he was shouting at the ground---

I got it then.

I knew what he was doing. I knew why he was there.

As he straightened up and turned around, looking to see where the fat woman was, I focused the binoculars on the area of hardpacked dirt ground where the guard had originally been standing. It took a few moments, but eventually I saw what I was looking for – a heavy metal ring, about 4 inches in diameter, lying flat on the ground. It looked at first as if it was fixed into the ground, but as I studied the area around the ring I could just make out the outline of what it was actually attached to – a wooden hatch set in the ground. It was so well camouflaged, exactly the same colour as the dirt, that it was almost impossible to see, but from what I could tell it was about 5 feet long and 4 feet wide. It obviously led to something under the ground – a bunker or a tunnel perhaps – that for some reason needed guarding, and it was equally obvious that there was someone down there who the guard was trying to communicate with. I couldnt work out who it might be, and I didnt understand why the sentry was so fearful of the fat woman, but as she stopped in front of the hatch, and the guard stepped forward to meet her, I had a feeling I was about to find out.

It was immediately clear that the fat woman was the guards superior, and I could tell from the way she just stood there, barely even acknowledging his presence, that she was expecting him to do something – presumably open the hatch for her – and that she was expecting him to do it without delay and without being asked. When he didnt, but instead started talking to her – apologetically trying to explain something – she gave him such a withering glare that he immediately stopped speaking, his mouth hanging open, and just stood there, visibly shaken to the core. The fat woman barked an instruction at him, impatiently jabbing her spear in the direction of the hatch – OPEN IT! NOW! – and this time he didnt hesitate for a second. Whatever it was he was trying to hide from the fat woman, he knew the game was up. He scurried over to the hatch – keeping his head down and his eyes fixed to the ground – and stooped down to reach for the metal ring. Just as he was about to get hold of it though, the hatch began to open. The guard quickly stepped to the side, moving out of the way, and the hatch opened up and a dishevelled-looking man climbed out. His shirt was unbuttoned, his belt unbuckled, and he was breathing heavily and soaked in sweat. Blood was streaming from several deep scratches on the side of his face, and as he straightened up – stumbling slightly – I saw that he was carrying a large metal key in his hand. He seemed confused and disorientated – looking around, frowning and squinting, shielding his eyes from the sun. He saw the guard, started to hand the key to him, then froze – his eyes wide with fear – as he suddenly spotted the fat woman. She just stood there for a few seconds, staring impassively at him, then she slowly held out her hand. The man hesitated for a second, darting a quick glance at the guard, then he shuffled warily over to the woman – cowering away from her, as if he expected her to hit him any moment – and carefully placed the key in her hand. She nodded at him, her face quite calm, and he cautiously began to relax a little. I could see the relief in his eyes. She hadnt hit him. She didnt even seem that angry with him. Encouraged, he allowed himself the smallest of smiles, and with a casual shrug of apology – and a glint of amusement in his eye – he opened his mouth and began to say something.

The fat woman moved so fast that I barely saw it, swinging her spear up and round then hammering the blunt end into the mans head, all in one lightning-quick movement. He never saw it coming, and she hit him so hard that his legs instantly buckled and he slumped to his knees. Then, as he knelt there cradling his bloodied head, she stepped over, brought back her foot and – putting all her considerable weight into it – booted him hard in his groin. He doubled over in agony, curling up into a ball, and I could see he was struggling to breathe. The fat woman bent over him then, and as she put the blade of her spear to the underside of his chin, I saw her say something to him. There was no emotion in her face. She didnt shout or scream. She just spoke to him – calmly and quietly – in what I imagined was an icy whisper.

The man just stared at her, frozen in terror.

She dug the blade of her spear into his chin, drawing blood, and I saw his lips move as he whimpered in response. She forced him to his feet, keeping the spear pressed into his skin until he was standing up straight, then she took the spear away, spun it round in her hand, and raised it over her shoulder, as if to hit him with the blunt end again. But this time she paused for a moment, giving the man the chance to turn and run, and he took it without hesitation, running off as fast as he could, hobbling and bent over in pain.

The fat woman turned to the guard then. Hede moved back while she was dealing with the other man, and was standing about 10 yards away from her now – his face drained of colour, his eyes wide. The fat woman didnt say anything to him. She didnt have to. It was perfectly clear from the look she gave him that she held him responsible for letting the other man do whatever hede done, and that he was going to pay the price for it. But not just yet. Right now, she had more important things to do. She turned away from him and waddled over to the open hatchway.

Before she started climbing down, I quickly focused the binoculars on the basket she was carrying. I didnt have time to identify all the contents, but I clearly saw a chunk of dark bread, an earthenware bottle, and a hairbrush, and just before I lost sight of her I caught a brief glimpse of something pink – a piece of cloth perhaps, or maybe an item of clothing---

And then the fat woman was gone, squeezing her huge frame through the hatchway and disappearing under the ground.

She was down there for some time, so while I waited for her to come out again, I had plenty of time to think about what had just happened and what it might mean. There was no way of knowing for sure, but if I accepted that Chola Se was being held prisoner down there, then it wasnt that difficult to work out a fairly reasonable explanation of everything Ide just seen.

The guard had been told that only certain authorised people were allowed to visit the prisoner, and his orders were to make absolutely sure that everyone else was kept out. But for some reason hede disobeyed those orders and let the other man in. Perhaps hede been bribed, or threatened, or the other man was a friend of his, or his brother or something. Whatever the reason, hede let him go down there to do what he wanted with Chola Se. It was clear from the state of him when hede come out that shede tried to fight him off – and because shese a dogchild I knew she would have fought like a demon – but she was probably tied up or shackled to at least some degree, and the man was much bigger and stronger than her, so I couldnt be sure whether hede overcome her or not before hede been interrupted.

As for the fat woman, she was obviously a figure of some authority, but I doubted if she was of any great importance. If she was, she wouldnt have been tasked with giving food and drink to a prisoner. It was possible she was doing more than just that – Ide know more when she came out – but even so, she was still just carrying out orders.

An image came into my mind then – the fat woman forcibly brushing Chola Ses hair, forcing her at spear point to put on a pink dress---

I blanked the picture from my mind.

It was too sickening to imagine.

When the fat woman finally came out, the bread and the pink cloth (pink dress?) were no longer in her basket, but the hairbrush and the earthenware bottle were still there. I watched her as she waddled back across the courtyard to the fort, then I lowered the glasses, waited for the rage to leave my heart, and went to see Gun Sur.

Gun Sur and Pilgrim were standing together at the open window when I entered the Marshals office, both of them gazing out at the Square. Although it was only a few hours since Ide last seen Gun Sur, he looked a lot more tired now – leaning on the windowsill for support as if he was carrying a great weight on his back – and as he turned to face me, and I saw the exhaustion in his troubled eyes, I couldnt help wondering if age was finally catching up with him. He was an old man now – almost 40 – and seeing him this close up made me realise that he was beginning to show it.

Pilgrim, on the other hand, didnt looked worried or tired at all. In fact, if anything, he seemed even more energised than usual.

Gun Sur walked wearily over to the oak table, gesturing for me to join him. I went over to the table, waited for him to sit, then sat down opposite him.

Have you heard? he asked me.

Heard what?

He sighed heavily, then glanced at Pilgrim. You tell him, he said.

Pilgrim came over and perched himself on the edge of the table.

We know who killed Aliaj and Berch and took Chola Se and the babies, he told me. It was one of our own. A Fighter called Yael.

Yael? I said, astonished.

I know, Pilgrim said, shaking his head. I couldnt believe it myself at first. Ive always considered Yael to be one of our very best. Even when he was a Younger I thought he had it in him to be a Captain one day. But Ime afraid the evidence against him is overwhelming. He took Chola Se and the babies and he gave them to the Dau.

Why would he do that?

Pilgrim shrugged. Who knows? Hese still being interrogated at the moment, and so far hese maintaining his innocence. But wele get the truth out of him eventually.

But how could he have done it? I said. How could he have got them out of town without being seen? It doesnt make sense. Was there a breach in the wall somewhere?

Yael was on guard in the West End Tower last night, Pilgrim explained. We think he probably left the tower around 2 or 3 in the morning, killed Aliaj and Berch and took their babies, then broke into Chola Ses house and abducted her.

She wouldnt have just let him take her, I said. Shese a dogchild. She would have fought and screamed and howled—

Yaels a trained Fighter.

I know, but—

Hese one of the best Ive ever known, Pilgrim added. Maybe even the best of all. Trust me, I know what Ime talking about. Yael could have broken into Chola Ses house and incapacitated her while she slept and she wouldnt have known a thing.

I still found that almost impossible to believe, but there was a look in Pilgrims eyes that made me think it was best not to argue any further, so I kept my doubts to myself and let him carry on.

As far as we can tell, he continued, Yael went back to the watchtower with Chola Se and the babies, climbed to the top, tied them to a rope, then lowered them down to the ground. We dont know if the Dau were waiting at the foot of the tower, or if they were further away, perhaps at the far end of the woodland---in which case Yael would have had to climb down the rope himself, take Chola Se and the babies to the Dau, then return to the tower and climb back up---Pilgrim shrugged. It wouldnt have been too difficult, especially for someone as capable as Yael.

I glanced at Gun Sur – he was leaning back in his chair, his head bowed down, his eyes closed – then I looked back at Pilgrim again.

How do you know all this? I asked him. Did someone see Yael with Chola Se and the babies?

Pilgrim shook his head. We dont have any witnesses so far, but theres more than enough evidence to prove it was Yael. We found a bloodstained shirt and a hood hidden away in the cellar of his house, and his footprints were tracked from the watchtower to Aliaj and Berchs house, then across to Chola Ses, and back to the tower again. We also found some coloured beads both in the turret and on the ground directly below the tower. And as you probably know, Chola Se always wore a necklace of coloured stone beads.

In an instant my world was turned upside down. My initial belief that none of this made sense, that Yael couldnt possibly have done it, had suddenly been shattered. If Pilgrim was right about the coloured beads – and I couldnt see how he could be making it up – then that changed everything. It meant that Chola Se had been in the watchtower, and that she had been lowered to the ground, just as Pilgrim had said. And if that was the case, who else could have been responsible other than Yael?

Whats he saying? I asked Pilgrim.

Yael?

I nodded.

He says he cant remember anything. He claims that he went on duty as usual, and that at some point during the night he woke up and realised that he must have fallen asleep, but that he doesnt remember anything about it. He says its as if theres a big black hole where his memory should be. Pilgrim grinned. Its not exactly convincing, is it?

He was right, it wasnt convincing---and that didnt make sense either. If Yael was guilty, why would he come up with such a scarcely believable explanation? He wasnt stupid. He must have known how feeble it sounded. Why hadnt he come up with a better story?

Unless, of course---

So, Gun Sur said, interrupting my thoughts. Have you got an answer for me?

Sorry? I said, momentarily confused.

The red-roofed building, he said, slightly impatiently. The question I left you with this morning. Have you come up with an answer or not?

I paused for a few seconds to get my thoughts in order – switching my mind from Yael to Gun Surs question – then I looked directly at the Marshal.

Can I ask you a couple of questions first? I said to him.

A couple?

2.

Are they relevant to your answer?

Yes.

All right, go ahead.

Is it true that the Dau have nightvision spyglasses?

He nodded. We know for sure that they have a pair of binoculars and 2 rifles scopes with nightvision capability, but its quite possible they have more. Whats your second question?

Is the old animal burrow that goes under the wall still there?

Gun Sur just stared at me for a moment, and I could tell

he was deciding whether to answer me or not. But I already knew the answer now. The mere fact that hede had to think about it meant the tunnel was there.

Gun Sur glanced at Pilgrim, then looked back at me and nodded. We were going to fill it in, he told me, but we realised that it might come in useful one day, so we decided to keep it. As long as we could make it absolutely secure — out of sight of the Dau and only accessible to us — it gave us a way in and out of town that the Dau didnt know about, and it also provided an emergency exit should we ever need one. Its had quite a lot of work done on it over the years — we widened it to make it easier to use, added supports to make sure it doesnt collapse, and both ends have been secured with camouflaged cast-iron doors---

Does Yael know its there?

He nodded. All the Fighters know.

So why didnt he use it to get Chola Se and the babies out?

Is that relevant?

It might be, depending on the answer.

Gun Sur sighed. We dont post guards directly outside the townside entrance to the tunnel — because if we did, it would be obvious to everyone, including the Dau, that somethings there — but we always have at least 2 Fighters posted on the streets within sight of the entrance so that no one can get to it without being seen. So the only way Yael could have used the tunnel to get out was by killing both Fighters, and that would have been too much of a risk. And also, he didnt need to use the tunnel, because he didnt have to get out of town without being seen by the Dau. They were expecting him.

Gun Sur stopped speaking for a second and gave me a stern look.

Right, he said. No more questions. All I want from you now is an answer. Can you get to the red-roofed building in the Dau camp and get what we need or not?

Yes, I told him. I can do it.

I knew when Ide come up with the plan that it was far from flawless, but as I began explaining it to Gun Sur and Pilgrim, the process of putting it into words made me realise that it was even more full of holes than Ide thought. The only really positive thing about it was its simplicity.

My plan, in essence, was to leave the town by way of the tunnel and get to the Dau encampment without being seen by using a pack of Deathland dogs as cover. Although the dogs werent such a common sight now as they had been in the past – mainly because theyd learned over the years that it was best to keep away from humans – it still wasnt unusual to see packs of Deathland dogs crossing the distant plains. As long as they kept out of rifle range, which they nearly always did, neither our people nor the Dau paid them much attention. So the way I saw it, if I could make the journey across the Deathlands with a pack of dogs, rather than on my own, it wouldnt matter if the Dau guards spotted us – wede just be another pack of Deathland dogs---nothing unusual, nothing to worry about. Wede have to get a bit closer to the camp than the dogs usually did – in order to allow me to get to the relatively rugged terrain near the perimeter – so the Dau guards would probably start paying us a little more attention than usual, but I doubted if theyd be concerned enough to raise the alarm. And once Ide found cover, the dogs could leave me and head back into the distance again, and the Dau guards would hopefully relax.

It was at this point in my explanation that Gun Sur began asking me questions.

How do you know the dogs will help us? he said.

They wont help us, theyle help me.

All right then – how do you know theyle help you?

I dont, I admitted. But if my mothers still alive—

Your mother?

My dogmother. The one who raised me. She wasnt with us when you killed the rest of my pack. If shese still alive, and I can get in touch with her, I think shele agree to help me.

Youle need more than just her to help you.

She wont be alone.

She wont be anything, Pilgrim said bluntly. Shele be a pile of bones by now.

Youre probably right, I said, ignoring his disrespect. But that doesnt mean its not worth trying, does it?

He just shrugged.

And what if shese not alive or you cant get in touch with her? Gun Sur said.

Therell be other dogs out there that know me---ones that were young when I was there.

Didnt they all die in the raid?

Dogs dont always stay with the pack they were born into. Some of the pups I grew up with split off into other packs when they were older. They might help me if theyre still around.

And if theyre not, or they wont help you? What then?

Ile take my chances on my own.

Pilgrim let out a quiet snort of derision.

I ignored him again.

You realise theres a good chance youle never make it? Gun Sur said. Even if you take the long way round, youre still going to have to cross so much open ground that youre almost certain to be seen.

This item you told me about, I said, looking him in the eye, the one in the red-roofed building---you said that if we dont get hold of it our chances of winning the final battle will be severely jeopardised.

Thats right.

So what have we got to lose?

He thought about that for a moment, then simply nodded. All right, he said, lets say you can get to the camp without being seen, and that you can keep their dogs quiet, as you claim. How are you going to get past the guard and into the building?

Ile kill him and take his key.

Thats it?

I shrugged. Unless youve got a better idea.

Gun Sur just stared at me for a while, thinking hard again, then he looked up at Pilgrim.

What do you think? he asked him.

About the guard?

About all of it. Do you think theres a chance it could work?

Theres always a chance. But if you want my honest opinion, Ide say the chances of him pulling it off are somewhere between very slim and none at all.

Gun Sur nodded. Whats the situation with our other options?

Ime still working on them.

Are any of them ready to go?

Well, not yet, but—

We need to do this tomorrow.

I know.

Can you guarantee youle have something else ready by then?

Ime reasonably sure—

Can you guarantee it?

No, he admitted, a slight edge to his voice. I cant guarantee it.

Gun Sur just sat there for a while then – staring at the table, wearily rubbing his temples – until eventually he took a breath and sat up straight.

Show it to him, he said to Pilgrim.

Are you sure? Pilgrim replied. Dont you think we—?

Just do it.

Pilgrim went over to a cupboard in the far corner of the office. He opened it up, reached in and took something out, then came back over and placed it on the table in front of me. It was a rectangular metal box – about 8 inches tall, 6 inches wide, and 4 inches deep – with 2 small screw attachments and a T-shaped handle on the top. It was obviously very old, the dull brown metal casing battered and scratched and discoloured, but apart from a few patches of rust here and there, it wasnt in too bad a condition.

Do you know what it is? Gun Sur asked me.

No.

Its a detonator, he explained, for setting off explosives from a distance. Cables are connected to these screws – he indicated the 2 screws on the top – and the other ends of the cables are attached to fuses which in turn are embedded in the explosive. You prime the detonator like this – he held the box down with his left hand, took hold of the T-shaped handle in his right hand, and pulled it straight up until it stopped – and then, when you push the plunger back down – he leaned over the box and shoved the handle down – a mechanism inside the detonator produces an electric current which passes along the cables and sets off the explosive.

He looked at me.

Do you understand?

I gave it some thought for a moment, then nodded. I understood as much as I needed to.

Now if this was in good working order, Gun Sur continued, tapping the top of the detonator, it could generate enough power to set off explosives up to a mile away.

Right, I said, nodding again.

But unfortunately its not in good working order. In fact, it doesnt work at all. Theres something wrong with the mechanism that generates the current, and despite our best efforts we havent been able to fix it. However---

He stopped speaking, gazing at me with an expectant look, inviting me to finish his sentence for him.

The Dau have a detonator that works? I said.

He almost smiled. They actually have 3 detonators that work.

And they keep them in the red-roofed building.

Exactly. And as Ive already told you, its absolutely vital that we get hold of them.

Why?

I cant tell you that.

Why not?

If you know what we want them for, and youre captured by the Dau, theyle torture you until you tell them everything. We cant let that happen. Even if we dont have the detonators, its crucial that the Dau dont know what we want them for.

I wouldnt tell them anything. Whatever they did to me, Ide never talk.

You would. Believe me. The Daus cruelty to prisoners is beyond imagination. Everyone talks in the end---everyone. The only way we can guarantee you wont tell them anything is by making sure you dont know anything in the first place.

There was no point in pushing it any further. However much I tried to convince him that I wasnt the same as everyone else – that Ide never break under torture, no matter what – the truth was, his argument made perfect sense. The less secrets I knew, the better.

Do you know where the detonators are kept in the building? I asked him.

We dont know the precise location, but weare fairly sure theyre in a green canvas bag and that the bag isnt locked away anywhere. Its probably just in a cupboard somewhere.

I thought about asking him how he knew all this – and also why the detonators werent locked away, considering how important they were – but I guessed this was all information that I didnt need to know, so I kept my questions to myself---at least for now.

Ide better get going, I heard Pilgrim say.

I looked round and saw him standing in front of the open window looking across at Gun Sur. With the light of the lowering sun at his back, edging his figure in a pale red glow, there was something strangely dark about him – something I hadnt noticed before – and just for a moment I felt a shiver of coldness in my blood.

Gun Sur was looking back at him, and as they silently held each others gaze, it was clear there was something passing between them that they didnt want me to know about. Neither of them said anything or made a gesture of any kind, and after a few seconds Pilgrim just turned away and left the room.

Gun Sur waited for him to shut the door, then turned back to me.

Ile arrange for one of the Captains to meet you at the tunnel entrance at sundown tomorrow night, he said. Wele also have a Fighter posted on the outside by the exit. If theres anything you need—

I can go tonight, I told him. I dont need to wait til tomorrow. I can go right now.

Youle go tomorrow, he said simply.

I very nearly told him about Chola Se then. I couldnt bear the thought of her having to spend another night and day in that underground hell, and I was so desperate to get her out as soon as possible that I wanted to plead with Gun Sur to let me go now. But despite the desire in my heart, I forced myself to say nothing. If I told Gun Sur about Chola Se, hede know – or at least suspect – that Ide try to rescue her, and hede never sanction that because it might compromise my chances of getting the detonators. He might even decide that I couldnt be trusted with the mission at all. And I couldnt let that happen. Even if rescuing Chola Se did jeopardise my chances – and there was no doubt it would make the task of getting the detonators a lot more difficult – I had to get her out of there.

Whats on your mind, Jeet? Gun Sur said, leaning forward and looking me in the eye.

Nothing---

Have you got a problem with going tomorrow? Because if you have—

No, I said quickly, its no problem at all. I just meant that I could go right now if you wanted me to, thats all.

He carried on staring at me for a while, and then – seemingly satisfied that I was telling the truth – he leaned back and rubbed his eyes.

Whatever you need, he said wearily, guns, clothing, equipment---come and see me or Deputy Pilgrim tomorrow. At least one of us should be here most of the time, but if for any reason weare both unavailable, just sit tight and wait. You must not, under any circumstances, discuss this with anyone else. Is that perfectly clear?

Yes.

Good.

He got to his feet, and I took that to mean the meeting was over, so I stood up too. I thought he was going to say something – perhaps wish me luck – or maybe shake my hand, but instead he just nodded at me, a gesture so vague that it was impossible to tell if it was an expression of gratitude or a sign of dismissal. I waited a moment, not sure what to do, and as I stood there looking at him I gradually realised that although his eyes were still fixed on mine, he was actually gazing right through me, his mind somewhere else. And when I turned round and walked out, glancing back at him as I closed the door, he was still just standing there, his glazed eyes staring at nothing, totally unaware that Ide gone.

Ime back home now, back in front of the fire. Its not too late, only a few hours after sunset, but Ime tired and I need to get some sleep. I need to be rested and fresh for tomorrow. But at the moment my heads too busy to sleep. There are so many things to think about.

The first thing I did after leaving the Quarterhouse was head over towards the westside cliffs. I didnt go anywhere near the tunnel, I just walked around the streets where the 2 Fighters that Gun Sur had told me about were posted, the ones who kept an eye on the tunnel entrance. I knew where theyd be. Ide seen them countless times before, every time Ide ever been in this part of town, and Ide also noticed them looking over towards the earthbanks and thornbushes where the tunnel came out, but Ide always assumed they were just watching the cliffs as a whole rather than one particular part of them. When I walked past the Fighters on guard duty this evening though – taking care to make sure they didnt know I was watching them – it was perfectly obvious that their regular glances towards the cliffs were specifically directed at the area where the tunnel was. I couldnt actually see the entrance, but I could see the dense thicket of thornbushes that still hid it from view, and I could also see that Gun Sur was right – no one could get to the tunnel without being seen by the guards.

The sun was dipping down over the horizon by then, and I wanted to take a look around Chola Ses house before it got too dark to see anything, so I picked up my pace and headed back across town to the street where she lives.

I didnt know why I still wasnt convinced that Yael was guilty, and I didnt know what it was about Pilgrims story that kept nagging away at the back of my mind, all I knew was that there was something – possibly several things – that just didnt feel right about it. And as I walked through the darkening twilight towards Chola Ses house, I realised what one of those possible things might be.

Although it would have been fully dark when Yael abducted Chola Se and the babies and carried or dragged them to the watchtower – and at 2 or 3 in the morning the streets would have been empty, with most people asleep in their beds with their shutters closed and bolted – I still found it hard to believe that no one had seen him. Why hadnt any of the other guards spotted him? They couldnt all have been looking the other way. And even if they had been, why hadnt they heard anything?

It didnt make sense.

And neither did the hood. Pilgrim had told me theyd found a bloodstained shirt and a hood hidden away in the cellar of Yaels house. But why would he wear a hood? If someone had seen a hooded man abducting Chola Se and 2 babies, they wouldnt have ignored him just because they couldnt see his face. If anything, wearing a hood would have drawn more attention to him than not wearing one.

It made no sense at all.

I was still thinking about these things when I arrived at Chola Ses house. Aliaj and Berch lived in the same street, just a few doors down, and I was planning to take a look around their house after Ide checked out Chola Ses, but as soon as I got there I realised I wasnt going to find anything useful. Thered been so many people trampling around the house all day – trackers, search parties, Fighters – that any tracks the abductor might have left behind had now been obliterated. The ground was completely unreadable.

The house itself was all locked up, and a Fighter was standing guard outside the front door. I could easily have got in round the back, but the Fighter had already seen me – and was keeping a close eye on me – so I decided to leave it for now.

I headed off in the direction of the West Tower, scouring the ground for tracks as I went, but it was almost as trodden down and scuffed up as the ground around the house. There was actually a visible pathway leading to the tower where the ground had been worn down by trackers walking to and from the house, and as I followed the pathway I recognised some of the partial prints in the dirt. The bare footprints of Mose, the other male dogchild, were unmistakable – he never wears anything on his feet – and there was no mistaking the prints of Pilgrims heeled Cowboy boots either. I wasnt familiar with Yaels tracks, but what I was looking for were any prints that were deeper than usual – indicating the extra weight of a man carrying someone – or any continuous trails in the dirt that would have been made if the abductor had dragged Chola Se not carried her.

I didnt find any trails, and the only print I found with any unusual depth to it was a partial impression of Pilgrims left boot heel. It was about 20 yards from the tower, right at the point where the ground changes from hardpacked dirt to glassrock, and it looked to me as if Pilgrim had probably missed his step and slipped off the edge of the glassrock, his left foot taking all his weight.

The 20-yard band of glassrock extends all the way along the wall, and there was no point looking for any tracks in it because glassrock is so hard you can hit it with a pickaxe and barely leave a mark.

So I turned round and headed home.

And now here I am, struggling to keep my eyes open as I write these words. I know I should be thinking about the practicalities of tomorrow – what weapons to take, what to wear – but I cant seem to concentrate on practical matters, and I keep finding myself thinking about my mother. How am I going to feel if I see her? Or if I dont see her? Hows she going to feel about me? And I also keep asking myself why Ime actually doing this. Am I doing it for the good of our people, or simply for Chola Se? And if Ime doing it for Chola Se---?

What does that mean?

I dont have any answers.

I dont know---

Ime too tired.

Ive been asleep but now Ime awake again, woken by a mostly forgotten dream. All I can remember of it is an image of Chola Se in a ragged pink dress, her lips drawn back in a vicious snarl, her bared teeth red with blood.

I spent most of the next day getting hold of the things I needed for my journey to the Dau encampment. It was all fairly straightforward, and the only thing that needed much thought was whether or not to take a gun. It was highly unlikely that Ide get there and back without having to use a weapon, and it was tempting to take up Gun Surs offer and arm myself with a handgun or a rifle, perhaps even both, but in the end I chose to limit myself to the weapons I carry everyday – my knife and my sling. I know them so well theyre part of me, and Ime very good at using them. Thats not to say that I cant use a gun – everyones taught how to shoot during Fighter training, and Ime as good, if not better, than most – its just that I feel more natural using a knife or sling.

And guns arent silent either.

If I was going to get into the Dau camp without being seen, and safely get Chola Se and the detonators out, I had to do it without making a sound.

By midafternoon Ide got everything I needed and done everything I had to do, and now all I had to do was wait.

I lay down on the floor, closed my eyes, and let myself become a dog again.

The dying red glow of the setting sun was still shimmering over the sea when I arrived at the patch of thornbushes that hides the tunnel entrance from view. I couldnt see anyone waiting for me at first, but as I squeezed my way through the bushes, I saw the familiar figure of Captain Glorian standing beside the earthbank at the edge of the cliffs where Ide come out of the tunnel with the rest of the pack all those years ago.

Glorian is the oldest of the Captains, and by far the biggest too. Hese a beast of a man. Not that tall, but massively solid and strong. He must weigh at least 20 stone, and there isnt an ounce of fat on him. Just raw muscle.

Hede obviously heard me coming, and was just standing there, waiting patiently, his rifle cradled casually in his arms. The moment he saw me emerging from the bushes though, his attitude suddenly changed, and before I could take another step hede raised his rifle and was aiming it directly at my head.

Dont move! he barked at me. Hands in the air! Now!

Its me, Captain, I said quickly, holding up my hands to show him I was unarmed. Its me, Jeet---

He didnt move, but just stood there, still holding the rifle on me, staring hard, squinting and frowning, until eventually I saw the recognition dawn in his eyes, and he let out a sigh and slowly lowered the gun.

What the hell are you doing, Jeet? he said angrily. I didnt know who you were.

Sorry---

He cursed, shaking his head. You could have got your head shot off looking like that.

It was my fault he didnt recognise me. As part of my preparations, Ide changed my appearance to help me blend in with the dogs, and Ide forgotten to warn the Captain in advance. As well as hacking off all my long straggly hair – which made a surprisingly big difference to the look of my face – Ide also changed the way I was dressed. Instead of my usual clothing – hooded tunic and moccasin boots – I was wearing a long black heavy coat, buttoned up to the neck, and my feet were bare.

Beneath the coat I was naked.

As I approached Glorian, and he looked me up and down, taking in my appearance, his anger gave way to careless contempt. I dont know how much he knew about my mission, but he obviously knew I was heading into enemy territory, and it was clear he didnt think much of the way I was going about it.

He didnt say anything though.

And I didnt feel the need to explain myself.

I knew what I was doing.

I turned my attention to the earthbank behind him. It looked the same as it always had – a ridge of hardpacked rust-red dirt – and I knew the tunnel entrance was there somewhere, but at first I couldnt see it. It wasnt until Ide moved closer and was standing right in front of the bank that I finally spotted it. It was level with my chest – a circular metal plate, about a yard across, fitted flush into the bank. It was so well camouflaged – coloured the same shade of red as the dirt – that even as close as this I probably wouldnt have seen it if I didnt know it was there.

Are you ready? Glorian said.

I nodded.

He took 2 T-shaped metal handles from his pocket and stepped up to the metal plate. Each handle had a smaller crossbar at one end. He inserted these ends into matching slots on either side of the plate, and then – gripping them tightly – gave them both a half-turn outwards. I heard the sound of heavy bolts clunking open. Glorian then braced himself, took half a step back, and heaved out the plate. It was at least an inch thick, and clearly very heavy. I could see the muscles in Glorians arms and shoulders bulging as he removed the plate and carefully lowered it to the ground.

The tunnel was open now, and the underground smell of it – the air, the earth, the worms, the roots – immediately triggered a flood of memories. The raid, the pack, the thrill, the slaughter---

Are you all right? I heard Glorian say.

I looked at him, momentarily dazed, then I blinked, shutting down the memories, and nodded, letting him know I was fine.

He glanced upwards and signalled to the guard in the watchtower above us. The guard returned his signal, then moved out of view.

The other end of the tunnel is already open, Glorian told me. And theres a young Fighter on the other side waiting for you. Tomas. Do you know him?

I know who he is, yeh.

Make sure you call out to him before he sees you. He knows youre coming, but he doesnt know you look like that. And hese not as experienced as me. Do you understand what Ime saying?

Yeh, I get it.

Good. Off you go then.

Something flickered into my mind for a moment – a sense of a time to come – and then almost immediately it was gone. It was a strange feeling, like an unknown memory of something that hasnt yet happened, and there was something about it that felt like a warning---

But whatever it was, there was nothing I could do about it now.

I stepped forward and clambered up into the tunnel.

Although I can see in the dark much better than humans, it was so utterly pitchblack inside the tunnel that I couldnt see anything at all. I could still tell that the tunnel had been widened though – as Gun Sur had told me – because it was nowhere near as tight a squeeze as it had been before, and I was also well aware of the wooden supports that had been added to keep the tunnel from collapsing, because I kept bumping into them in the darkness.

As I crawled along on my hands and knees I was constantly

sniffing the earth and the air, hoping to find a trace of the pack from the last time wede been in the tunnel, but there was nothing left of them anymore. The tunnel smelled overwhelmingly of humans now. There was one particular scent that was fresher than all the others, and there was something naggingly familiar about it, but although I kept breathing it in, trying to work out who it belonged to, it just wouldnt come to me. I gave up trying in the end. It could have been almost anyone. I know the scent of most of our people, so whoever it belonged to it was bound to be vaguely familiar.

I could tell I was nearing the end of the tunnel when I began to smell the cold night air drifting in from outside, and a few moments later a circle of open-air greyness appeared in the underground blackness up ahead, and I knew Ide reached the exit.

I called out to Tomas to let him know I was there, waited for his reply, then crawled forward and scrambled out of the tunnel.

For the first time in over 5 years I was on the other side of the wall.

Is that really you, Jeet? I heard Tomas say.

I turned round and saw the young Fighter grinning at my appearance. It wasnt a disdainful or mocking grin, just a harmless look of amusement. Tomas isnt much older than me, and although I dont know him any better than I know anyone else – apart from Starry – I know him well enough to know that he has a decent heart.

I like it, he said, smiling at my shaved head and big black coat. It suits you.

Thanks, I told him, looking around to get my bearings.

The narrow strip of woodland stretched out ahead of me, the dark trunks of the young trees merging into the gloom of the night.

I breathed in, smelling the tang of vegetation in the ice cold air, and as the scent of the woodland flooded through me – bringing back more memories – I began to sense the first faint smells of the Deathlands – the deserts, the plains, the mountains, the past---

Are you okay there, Jeet? Tomas said.

Yeh---I muttered, smiling at him. Yeh, Ime okay.

He nodded.

Ide better get going, I said.

Be careful out there, he told me as I walked past him and headed off into the woodland.

I raised my hand in acknowledgement, then carried on into the wooded darkness.

The cover provided by the trees and shrubs wasnt as dense as I would have liked, but as long as I kept to the southside of the woods – but not too close to the cliffs – I was fairly certain I couldnt be seen from the Dau encampment. When I reached the far end of the woodland, I stopped about 10 feet from the edge and just stood there for a while, gazing out into the distance. Even in the darkness, the change in terrain was plain to see. There was no gradual merging of one landscape into another, the trees and vegetation of the woodland simply stopped, as if cut off by an invisible border, and beyond that there was nothing but glassrock – vast swathes of empty black nothingness stretching out into the distance. The ground wasnt totally flat, and here and there I could see starlight glinting on the ridges and hollows of the glassrock plain – like foam-topped waves in a frozen black sea – and although I couldnt see the distant Black Mountains themselves, I could just about make out the great jagged outcrops of the foothills that surround them---

And I knew that if my mother was out there, shede probably be somewhere in or around the mountains.

I was ready now.

Ready to call out to her.

I looked around for a good calling point, and saw it almost immediately – a great slab of rock near the edge of the cliff, sheltered behind a clump of young trees.

I went over to it and hopped up.

It felt right.

I stood there for a while – just breathing steadily, sucking in the cold night air---just waiting for the right moment – and then, when the moment came, I emptied my lungs, breathed in as deeply as I could, raised my head high to the sky, and howled long and hard into the night.

I cant fully explain the meaning of my howl – the sounds that dogs make have feelings rather than meanings – but in very basic terms I was simply telling my mother that I was here. If she was still alive, and she heard it, shede know it was me. And shede know it was safe for her to come.

As my howl faded away into the silence of the night, I waited for her reply.

It didnt come.

I closed my eyes, then threw back my head and called out again, louder this time.

Again my howl rang out into the distant mountains, and again it faded into the unseen darkness. But then, after perhaps 10 seconds, I heard a reply. It was very faint, almost inaudible, coming from a long way away – perhaps 10 miles – but there was no doubt at all it was the voice of my mother. I knew it in my bones, my blood---in everything I was.

My mother was alive.

I called out to her again, howling with all my soul, and she called back almost immediately. She was already a little closer.

She was coming.

My mother was coming to me.

I sat down on the rock, closed my eyes, and waited with the timeless patience of the dog that I was.

Assuming shede started around 10 miles away, and that shede be loping towards me, not running flat out, I guessed it would take my mother about 2 hours to get here.

2 hours was nothing.

I would have waited 2 days if Ide had to. 2 weeks, 2 months, 2 years---

Time was nothing.

Every so often I stood up and howled again to remind her of my location, and every time she howled back, her call was a little louder and clearer.

After the first hour had passed, I began getting ready, doublechecking all my preparations to make sure everything was still as it should be. I unbuttoned my coat and checked that my knife and sling were still held firmly in place – and completely covered – by the strip of cloth that Ide wrapped several times around my left thigh. Any sign of a weapon – even the faintest of distant glimpses – would be enough for a Dau guard to know that I wasnt a dog, and because Ide be naked when I was with the dogs,

I wouldnt have any pockets or clothing to conceal my knife and sling, so Ide bandaged my weapons to my thigh using a strip of cloth that Ide coloured a pale muddy brown to match the tone of my skin. The same reasoning lay behind my decision not to wear any clothes. Any kind of clothing would immediately stand out to a watching Dau guard, whereas being naked – and with my hair hacked off – my colouring and general body shape would at least be reasonably similar to that of a dog. My nakedness would also make me more acceptable to my mother and any other dogs she might bring with her. My mother had never seen me clothed, and clothing was such a human trait – and Deathland dogs hated humans so much – that wearing clothes would have put me at a disadvantage straightaway. The only reason I was wearing the big heavy coat was to keep out the cold until my mother arrived. Ide got it from Jemelata, the towns Clothier, and Ide asked her specifically for a heavy coat that hadnt been worn by anyone else for a long time, so as to lessen the scent of human on me as much as possible. The coat shede given me, the one I was wearing, was so thick and heavy – and uncomfortable and ugly – that as far as she knew, no one had ever worn it since it had been found in a house when our people had first arrived in the town. I knew I was going to feel the cold when I took it off, but once I got running Ide soon warm up, and being barefoot wasnt going to be much of a problem either. Like all dogchilds, I dont like wearing anything on my feet, but – unlike Mose – I eventually learned to put up with it. I still never wear anything on my feet when Ime at home though, and I still often forget to put on my moccasins when I go out, so although the soles of my feet are nowhere near as hard and leathery as they used to be, theyre still tough enough to cope with a night out in the Deathlands.

Being barefoot also gave me the advantage of silence.

After Ide checked my knife and sling, and was satisfied that they were both still secured, I buttoned up my coat and got to my feet. It was time to call out to my mother again. I raised my head and was just about to let out a howl when I suddenly sensed a presence behind me. I stopped, remaining motionless for a few moments, then slowly turned round---

And there she was.

My mother---sitting quietly, as still as a statue, gazing serenely at me.

I realise now that she must have skirted around me, ghosting through the woods to my right, before cautiously approaching me from behind, keeping herself out of sight until she was absolutely sure that she wasnt walking into a trap, and in hindsight I probably should have known that that was what shede do. She was a wise old dog. She wouldnt just walk into an unknown strip of woodland without first making sure it was safe, especially when that strip of woodland was right next to the town where her family was slaughtered---

I should have known that.

I should have realised---

But she was there now.

And at the time, that was all that mattered.

That was all there was – my mother, just sitting quietly, as still as a statue, gazing serenely at me.

The sight of her after such a long time was so overwhelming that all I could do for about 30 seconds was stand there, rooted to the spot, staring at her in awestruck silence. Shede changed a lot since the last time Ide seen her. Her glossy brown fur had lost its sheen and was flecked all over with silver and grey, and her face and muzzle were almost white. She wasnt as big and strong as I remembered either. She was thinner, less muscular, almost bony in places. But her true self, the essence of who she was, was still unmistakably there. I could feel it. It was there in her heart, her scent, her eyes, her spirit---I could feel it soaking into me, warming me, filling me with a sense of comfort and security that I hadnt felt in a very long time.

Ide thought about this moment for years – imagining how it would feel, wondering how Ide react – but now that it was actually happening, I didnt have any thoughts at all. I didnt need any thoughts. I was dog. I just did what I did. And the next thing I knew – without a thought in my mind – Ide scrambled out of my coat and jumped down off the rock and was running to my mother, just as Ide run to her all those years ago. I ran on all 4s, my head low to the ground, and I was moving so fast that I almost couldnt stop when I reached her, and as I tried to slow down I lost my footing and tumbled over, rolling into her like an overexcited pup. I was a lot bigger and heavier than I used to be, and she was a lot frailer, but she still barely moved when I stumbled into her. She just shuffled back a bit, absorbing the impact, somehow maintaining her grace and dignity, as she always had done. She also didnt seem to mind when my childhood emotions came flooding back to me and I began licking at her face and mouth, my body wriggling all over with joy and excitement, just as I used to do when she came back from a hunting trip---and just as shede put up with me then, she was putting up with me now – just sitting there, as calm and patient as always, letting me clamber all over her.

She didnt have to show her feelings for me to know they were there. I could sense them in her. I could feel them in her heart as clearly as if they were in my own – a mixture of deep contentment, relief, and a longheld sadness.

I finally settled down after a while, and for a few minutes we just sat there together, quietly smelling each other, getting to know each other again. She couldnt help her hackles rising in hate and rage at the smell of the human in me. Although she hadnt been there that night, she knew the humans had slaughtered her pack without mercy, and while she was just as savage and merciless as every other living creature – and she accepted without thought that we all kill to live – she still hated the humans for what theyd done, and I knew shede kill every one of them if she ever got the chance. But at the same time, despite the fact that Ide superficially become one of them, she neither considered me as truly human nor blamed me for becoming whatever it was Ide become. She understood why Ide done it, and as we sat there together she let me know – in a way I cant describe – that no forgiveness was necessary.

Ide done what Ide done to survive.

And survival is all there is. Not just for ourselves, but for our family, our bloodline, our species. We live to keep our ancient souls alive.

It didnt matter to my mother that my biological bloodline was human. I might not have come from her womb, but Ide become a dog in her heart. Shede passed on her ancient soul to me.

While the 2 of us were getting to know each other again, I gradually became aware that we werent alone. Shadowy shapes had appeared in the darkness of the nearby trees – silent presences, watching us from a distance.

My mother had come with her pack.

I knew I couldnt approach them first, but instead had to wait until they were ready to come to me, and slowly – step by soundless step – thats what they did. One by one, the dogs edged cautiously out of the trees and made their way over to my mother and me.

There were 8 of them.

A massive grey male, in the prime of his life, who was obviously their leader.

3 adult females.

2 almost fullgrown juvenile dogs.

And 2 young females, clearly sisters, about 6 months old.

One of the adult females had several features – the markings on her chest and lower legs, for example – that were almost exactly the same as my mothers, and I guessed she was a granddaughter, or possibly even a great granddaughter. I was also fairly sure that she was the leaders mate. All 8 of the dogs looked fit and healthy and reasonably well fed, with no obvious signs of disease or injury.

I watched them coming towards me, closely studying their positioning and posture in relation to one another, and by the time the leader was within a few feet of me, Ide instinctively worked out the basic hierarchy of the pack. As my mother moved aside, keeping close but allowing the big grey male to approach me, I could tell – without consciously knowing how – that my mother held a special position in the pack, one that Ide only come across a few times before. She was neither a leader nor a subordinate, but rather an esteemed Older, respected and revered by all the other dogs, including the leader, for her experience and wisdom, while at the same time being reliant on the others for sustenance and protection. Without them, she was too old and weak to survive. But without her, and the vast experience she had of living in the Deathlands, it was quite possible that they wouldnt survive.

Despite the respect she was held in though, I was realistic enough to know that I wouldnt necessarily be accepted – let alone helped – by the other dogs just because I was her adopted son. They knew I was a dogchild, but I was also a hated human. And if I wasnt accepted, which was entirely up to the leader, there was a reasonably good chance that Ide end up dead. But there was very little I could do to sway the grey males decision apart from being completely submissive to him, letting him know that I recognised and respected his dominance over me.

So thats what I did.

I lay down in front of him and rolled over onto my back, exposing my stomach and throat to him, at the same time turning my head to one side to avoid direct eye contact. And then I just lay there, perfectly still, and let him examine me – sniffing me all over, touching his snout to my skin, pawing curiously at the cloth wrapped around my thigh. At one point, he leaned over me and put his head so close to my face that I could feel the heat of his breath on my skin, and I almost flinched as a drool of warm spit dripped onto my cheek, but I forced myself to stay still. He growled then, a low and terrifying sound that came from deep within him, and for a moment or 2 I feared the worst. But after about 5 seconds – which felt like 5 years – I felt his head move away from me. I waited, not moving a muscle, until I heard him padding away, his steps almost silent despite his massive size, and then I finally let out the breath Ide been holding for the last few minutes.

When I cautiously raised my head and looked around, I saw the big male casually urinating against a nearby tree. The other 7 dogs were just milling around together, trying to appear equally casual – scratching, sniffing the ground, stretching and yawning – but I knew it was all just a show. Dogs dont like change – it makes them uneasy – and whichever way their leaders decision had gone, the pack had known that things were about to change. If the grey male had rejected or attacked me, my mothers relationship with him – and consequently the rest of them – would never have been the same. And if he accepted me – which he seemed to have done – thered be someone new for them to deal with. And just at the moment they were dealing with the newness of me by pretending they couldnt care less.

I got to my feet and gazed over at my mother. She was sitting on her own, away from the others, looking as quiet and composed as she always did, as if shede never doubted for a moment that everything would be fine.

I smiled at her.

She blinked.

In that moment, there was nothing I wanted more than to go over and just be with her. And as I imagined how that would be – remembering how she used to curl up around me to keep me warm as I slept – it suddenly struck me that there was nothing to stop me from being with her for the rest of her life. I could just leave with her right now, lope off into the Deathlands with her and the rest of the pack---just go, forget about everything else – Gun Sur, Pilgrim, the Dau, the detonators---

But then an image of Chola Se came to me again, and this time I saw her cowering on a filthy bed, trembling with fear and rage, her battered face streaked with bloodstained tears---

I couldnt forget her.

I carried on looking at my mother for a few moments longer, then I turned round and went over to meet the other dogs.

I cant explain how I let the dogs know what I wanted to do, and how – if they agreed – they could help me. I wasnt conscious of how I did it. But I didnt have to be. I was dog now, and for the most part dogs dont communicate consciously. It just happens, without us necessarily knowing that its happening or how weare doing it. Its not as precise or detailed as human communication, but it doesnt have to be, because our world, the dog world, isnt as complex as the human world. And as long as it works, thats all that matters.

And it does work.

After being with my mothers pack for about 20 minutes, they all had a basic grasp of where I wanted to go, and how I wanted them to help me. My reasons were of no interest to them at all. Once the big male had given it some thought, and decided – without explanation – that he and his pack would go along with me, thats all there was to it. We spent a few minutes readying ourselves for the journey – circling around, getting our bearings, emptying our bowels and bladders – and then we just left, trotting off at a steady pace, out of the woodland and across the wide-open stretch of glassrock.

We headed west at first, starting off at a parallel track to the cliffs before gradually angling away from them to begin crossing the open glassrock in a slightly more northwesterly direction. The pack kept closer together than they normally would – with the big grey male always at the front – and as long as I stayed on the left side of the pack, the tight formation provided me with plenty of cover against any watching Dau. I wasnt totally hidden from view, but the way I was running – crouched over, my upper body almost horizontal to the ground, my head held low – meant that most of the other dogs were bigger than me, and those that werent were roughly equal in size and height, so hopefully I wouldnt stand out.

It wasnt unnatural for me to run in this style. Ide spent the first year or so of my life with the dogs crawling and walking – and later running – on all 4s. I didnt know there was any other way. And although I could move much faster in this manner than any human child ever could, I soon learned that no matter how fast I could run on all 4s, I could never keep up with the other dogs. I was still no match for them when I eventually realised I could stand upright and run on 2 legs, but at least the difference in speed wasnt quite so massive anymore. I dont know why I adopted this crouched over running posture, but all the other dogchilds run – and walk – this way too. Perhaps we started doing it for the same reason I was doing it now – to help us blend in with the other dogs – but whatever the reason, it became so natural to us that even after wede been rehumanised none of us ever lost our crouch.

As I carried on running with my mothers pack across the seemingly endless glassrock desert, I began to feel at one with everything – the closeness of the other dogs, the hypnotic rhythm of our movement, the cold night air freshening the skin of my naked body. It felt how it was meant to feel, as if this was where I was meant to be – running with the Deathland dogs. The darkness all around us was so dense and black that at times it was impossible to separate the land from the sky, and with the mesmerising repetitiveness of our running – the same steady speed, the same terrain, the same direction – it was easy to imagine that there was no ground or sky, just a vast black nothingness, and we were making our way through it like ghosts being drawn into unknown worlds.

Eventually though, the barren flatness of the glassrock plains started giving way to the steepening terrain of the foothills, and as we headed into the rocky landscape, the towering heights of the great Black Mountains began to appear in the distance. At first they were nothing more than barely visible walls of greyness looming up into the blackness of the sky, but gradually – second by second, yard by yard – they edged their way out of the darkness and began to reveal their awesome form. Immense, soaring mountains, great jagged masses of rock, standing there with the brutal solemnity of giant stone kings whode ruled over this land since the beginning of time.

The mountains seemed quite close at first, but the nearer we got to them, the clearer it became that they were still a good mile or so away. But we were in the foothills now, in among the ridges and hollows, the ancient trails, the blackened stumps of longdead trees---

We were no longer out in the open.

No longer visible.

It was time to change direction.

We turned to our right, heading east---towards the Dau encampment.

As the pack thinned out – no longer needing to hide me from view – I dropped back to run alongside my mother.

I was concerned for her. She was a lot older than the rest of the dogs, a lot weaker and frailer than them, and I wasnt sure if she still had the strength and stamina necessary to keep up with them. But after trotting alongside her for a few minutes, I knew I had nothing to worry about. She wasnt as graceful a runner as she used to be, and she didnt have the elegant power she once did, but she was still perfectly capable of outrunning me.

I guessed we were about half a mile to the west of the Dau encampment now. We could follow the safety of the foothills for perhaps another 5 or 6 hundred yards, and then wede be coming to the most risky part of the journey – crossing the last 2 or 3 hundred yards of open ground to reach the more rugged terrain surrounding the camp perimeter. If the pack hadnt already been noticed, it definitely would be then. It was also the point at which the dogs would leave me and Ide carry on into the Dau camp alone.

In the 2 or 3 minutes it took us to reach the crossing point, I tried not to dwell on the possibility that this might be the last time I ever saw my mother. Once the dogs had gone, and shede gone with them--- once Ide done what I had to do in the Dau camp and had gone back to being human again---

I didnt want to think about that.

I just wanted to make the most of now – running side by side with my mother, together in our silence, our hearts alive with the simple joy of running---

Ide missed it all so much.

And now---

The pack was slowing to a halt behind the big male.

In front of him was a raised plateau of bare rock, about 6 feet high, and beyond it – about 200 hundred yards ahead of us – I could see flamelights flickering in the darkness. And in the faint glow of the torchlights I could see the outlines of several vague but unmistakable shapes – buildings, watchtowers, the fort. The lights were mostly concentrated around the centre of the camp, so I couldnt actually see the perimeter or any guards, but in my minds eye I knew exactly where they were. I could also picture the low covering of scrubland around the perimeter---

And that was all I could allow myself to think about now.

Not my mother anymore. Even as she nudged me forward, guiding me into my place in the pack as the dogs began closing up again, ready to hide me from view---I couldnt think about her anymore.

My place in the pack was at the back now, with the rest of the dogs ahead of me, shielding me as best they could from the watching eyes that would soon be directly ahead of us. My mother moved past me – brushing lightly against me as she went – adding her size to my mobile shield, and now we were ready to go.

The grey male raised his head and sniffed the air, and then – as one – we moved, stepping out from behind the plateau and loping off across the open glassrock towards the flickering lights.

There was no doubt we were being watched now. I could feel it, and I knew the rest of the pack could feel it too. What we didnt know was how many Dau were watching us. It could be just a single guard, cautiously monitoring our approach, waiting to see how close we came before alerting anyone else, or there could be scores of them watching us, maybe even more---

there could be hundreds of hidden eyes in the darkness watching our every step.

The dogs were on edge now.

Crossing open ground half a mile away from the Dau camp was one thing, but this was something else altogether. This was a brazen encroachment into enemy territory, and the dogs knew they didnt belong here. They werent afraid, but they were far from comfortable. And the closer we got, the more vulnerable they felt.

About halfway across the open ground, the glassrock began merging into a landscape of dust and ash. For the first 15 yards it was just as empty and flat as the glassrock, but then it began to change. Sparse vegetation began to appear – 1 or 2 groundhugging shrubs – and the ground itself started to become more uneven. It was still too open to provide any meaningful cover, but when I risked raising my head very slightly and glancing up ahead, I caught a glimpse of some denser cover about 20 feet to our right – a few clumps of rock perhaps, or maybe some bushes. Whatever they were, they looked big enough to hide behind. And that was all I needed.

The big male had obviously seen them too, and as he began leading the pack towards them I could sense the dogs communal anxiety beginning to ease a little. Their job was almost done now. Just a few more feet, a few more seconds, and then they could turn around and start heading back to where they belonged.

It was at that point that the shot rang out, and in an instant everything changed.

It was a rifleshot, a sharp crack that sliced through the night like a whipcrack, and even as its echo was still swirling in the air, the dogs were off and running. It seemed at first to be a chaotic reaction of pure panic, the dogs running wildly with no thought at all — some of them bounding off to the left, others to the right, while the grey male and his mate were inexplicably running towards the camp — and just for a moment I was struck with a sense of deep disappointment. My old pack wouldnt have panicked at the sound of a gunshot, running off in all directions like terrified rabbits---but in the very same moment, I felt a sudden hard shove from behind, and almost immediately I realised my mistake. The pack werent panicking, they were reacting in almost instantaneous unison to protect me — the big male and his mate leading me to cover, while the others flew off in all directions to acts as decoys and provide a distraction. And now my mother was shoving me from behind again, urging me to follow the grey male and his mate.

I set off as fast as I could, keeping so low that I was virtually scrambling on all 4s, and just as the 2 dogs ahead of me reached the cover — which I could see now was several thick clumps of claw bushes — I threw myself forward and dived after them. I hit the ground hard and half bounced, half rolled into the bushes, coming to rest on my side, with my face pressed up against a tangle of thorns. I could feel the barbs cutting into my skin, the blood trickling down my face, but I didnt move an inch. The dogs in the Dau camp had started barking now, and until I knew what they were barking at — and what was happening all around me — the best thing to do was keep perfectly still, keep out of sight, and let the dogs carry on barking. I could have stopped them if Ide wanted to, but if they werent barking specifically at me, there was no point in stopping them. In fact, if they were only barking at the Deathland dogs, it was better to let them carry on.

So I just lay there, as still as a dead man, and waited. One of the Dau guards had obviously seen something, but the question was whether hede just seen the dogs and fired at them to scare them away, or if hede seen me.

I lay there and listened.

Apart from the still-yapping dogs, I couldnt hear any other noises coming from the Dau camp – no shouting, no running boots, no sirens or alarms of any kind. That didnt necessarily mean that I hadnt been seen, but I felt reasonably sure that if Ide been seen as a human thered be a lot more noise coming from the camp.

I carried on waiting.

The Dau dogs were beginning to quieten down now.

They didnt know I was here.

And if the dogs didnt know, the Dau didnt know.

I waited a while longer, just to make sure, then I carefully began disentangling myself from the claw bushes. Once Ide got myself free, I started looking around for my mother and the rest of the pack, but there was no sign of them anywhere. Theyd gone, all of them, just melted away into the night as if theyd never been here.

I was alone again, and for a moment it felt as if something had been torn out of me, and in its place was a gaping hole deep in my flesh that was so cold and dark and achingly empty that I just wanted to lie down and die.

But then, from somewhere inside me, I heard my mothers voice.

Are you my son?

Yes, I muttered.

Are you dog?

Yes.

Are you a survivor?

Yes.

Then be what you are.

IT TOOK me almost an hour to get from the claw bushes to the area of cleared ground that ringed the camp perimeter. I had to inch my way through the darkness, most of the time crawling flat on my belly, crisscrossing the ground to get to whatever sparse cover I could find – low ridges and gullies, tree stumps, clumps of tall grass. Finally, when I came to a shallow basin in the ground shielded behind by a tangle of ancient tree roots – probably the dried-up remains of a small pool – I realised that was it. Ide run out of cover. All that was left between here and the camp was a broad stretch of wide-open ground – no bushes, no shrubs, no tree stumps, no rocks---just a flattened strip of hard black dirt.

There were no lights around the perimeter itself, but there was enough peripheral light coming from the torches inside the camp to let me see what I needed to see. The perimeter was marked by a low bank of packed earth – which, as far as we knew, was only there as a reference point for the Fighters, so they knew where to stand guard on perimeter duty. There were no fences, no trenches, no walls. A Dau Fighter was standing guard beside a tree just the other side of the bank. He looked fairly relaxed, and not especially vigilant, which suggested that the minor commotion caused by the sighting of the dogs had already been forgotten. He wasnt even carrying his rifle – it was leaning against the tree beside him – and he was paying more attention to what was going on inside the camp than outside it. Faint sounds of revelry were drifting in the air from somewhere inside the camp – music of some kind, singing, laughing, the occasional cheer – and I guessed the guard was wishing he was part of it rather than stuck out here on his own in the cold.

The view along the perimeter to his right was partially blocked by several small buildings, so I couldnt see anymore sentries that way, but I could just make out the figure of another perimeter guard about 100 yards in the opposite direction. I wouldnt have been able to see him if it wasnt for the lights of the camp behind him, and I doubted his nightvision was good enough to see me from where he was, even if I was out in the open. I couldnt bank on it though.

The basin I was in was about 2 feet deep, and the protective wall of roots added another foot or so of cover. It wasnt much, but if I hunkered down low there was enough room to do what I had to do in comparative comfort and safety.

I did what I had to do.

First of all, I untied the knot that held the strip of cloth wrapped around my thigh and began unwinding it. Ide bound my sling around my thigh beneath the strip of cloth, and once Ide uncovered that and the handle of my knife, I stopped unwrapping the cloth, then untied my sling and gave it a good stretch to straighten out any kinks.

Its a magnificent weapon – just under 3 feet in length, with a leather cradle and cords of braided flax – and Ive always been grateful to Starry for giving it to me. Hede inherited it from his father, and hede begun teaching me how to use it almost as soon as Ide been rehumanised. Ide taken to it so naturally that within a few months I was more accomplished with it than Starry, and one day, at the end of another long session of target practice, hede told me that the sling was mine to keep. Ide tried to refuse, but he wouldnt hear of it.

Its too good a weapon to be wasted on me, hede said.

Youre better than most with a sling.

I used to be before I lost my leg, but I dont have the balance for it anymore. And besides, I want you to have it, Jeet. You deserve it.

I laid down the sling now and pulled my knife from the cloth wrapping. The one disadvantage of the knife was its shiny reflective surface – if it caught even the faintest of lights, the resulting glint in the darkness could easily give away my position – so before leaving town that night Ide stained the blade with the black ink of several walnut husks, and now, while I still had the chance, I wanted to make sure that none of the blackness had rubbed off. It didnt take long to give the blade a good looking over, angling it this way and that, and when I was satisfied that the walnut ink was still doing its job, I slipped the knife back into the cloth wrapping, leaving the handle uncovered, and re-tied the strips of cloth, tightening them enough to hold the knife firmly in place against my thigh while at the same time allowing me to quickly unsheathe it.

I was almost ready now.

Just 2 more things to do.

The first was to find the right ammunition for my sling. Ide already noticed a number of goodsized rocks dotted around the basin, so all I had to do now was gather up a handful of the most likely looking ones and weigh them up against each other to decide which was best. The one I finally settled on was almost perfectly spherical, about 2 and a half inches in diameter, with a smooth pebblelike surface. Good and solid, hard and heavy, just the right size. I fitted it into the cradle of my sling, then turned my attention to the dogs in the Dau camp.

As Ide told Gun Sur, I dont know how I quieten dogs. I just do something, and something comes out of me, something that somehow brings us together, and when weare together we feel this sense, this feeling that we want to be quiet---

I dont know what it is or how I do it.

But as I got to my knees and cautiously looked out through the tangle of roots, I could already feel the dogs promised silence. Ide done what I had to do. Whatever happened when I entered the camp, whatever the towndogs saw or heard or smelled, they wouldnt raise the alarm.

The only thing I had to worry about now was making sure no one else did.

The perimeter guard was going through the motions of doing his job now – peering out into the darkness and scanning the surroundings – but it was obvious his heart wasnt in it. He was looking around so quickly and carelessly that I probably could have got to my feet and fired off my sling at him before he even noticed me. But I didnt need to take any risks. So I just kept still and waited, watching him all the time, and after a minute or 2 hede clearly had enough of gazing out into the darkness. He yawned, stretched, spat on the ground, then turned around and turned his attention back to the camp festivities.

I got to my feet.

Crouching down behind the roots, I shuffled across to the edge of the basin, watching the guard all the time, and then – as another distant cheer broke out from somewhere inside the camp, capturing his attention even more – I straightened up, stepped out of the basin, swung the sling in a lightning-fast arc and released the rock, all in one rapid but measured movement. The rock shot through the air like a bullet and caught the guard in the side of the head, just above his ear. The dull crack of rock on bone was barely audible, and because he crumpled instantly to the ground rather than toppling over, the sound of the impact was minimal. I was reasonably sure the other guard was too far away to hear anything, but I didnt want to wait and find out, so I was already off and running before the falling body hit the ground – sprinting across the open ground, leaping over the perimeter bank, and landing in a crouch beside the lifeless Fighter. The rock had cracked his skull – bone was showing beneath the blood. His eyes were open, but there was no life in them. He was probably dead before he hit the ground.

He was a young man – around 13 or 14, I guessed. He was wearing a thick coat with a high collar – the coat buttoned all the way up – with a fur hat and kneelength boots. A bayonet was tucked into the top of his right boot.

I wound my sling round my waist and tied it off to secure it, then I shuffled round behind the dead guard, took hold of his collar, and dragged him over to the tree. I reached over and got hold of the front of his coat, steadied myself for a second, then heaved his body into a sitting position and leaned it against the tree.

Anyone within a few yards of him would realise straightaway he was dead, but from a distance – and in the dark – he might just look as if he was resting.

I squatted down on the other side of the tree and gazed around the compound to get my bearings. The red-roofed building was clearly visible – about 20 yards ahead of me, just off to my right. It was facing away from me, so I couldnt actually see the Fighter guarding the door, but I could see the glow of a burning torchlight somewhere near the front of the building, so I knew the guard had to be there.

Apart from the fort, the camp was mostly quiet and still. I could see a few Fighters standing guard here and there, and the odd lone dog skulking in the shadows, but for the most part the compound was as lifeless as youd expect in the dead of night.

The fort was far from lifeless though.

The walls were ablaze with dozens of flaming torches, and from inside the fort a great fiery light was rising up into the darkness, filling the air with crackling sparks and plumes of orangey black smoke. Music was playing, people were singing---there was shouting and chanting and drunken laughter. Whatever was going on in there was hidden from view behind the high walls, but from the smell of burning wood in the air, and the mouthwatering scent of roasting meat, it was clear that some kind of celebratory feast was taking place.

I closed my eyes and pictured the scene Ide witnessed at the hatchway the day before – recalling the position of the hatchway in relation to the red-roofed building and the fort – and then, after a few moments thought, I opened my eyes again. The hatchway was about 150 yards east of here, and there were 2 different ways of getting there. I could either go via the red-roofed building and head directly towards the fort, or I could start from here and follow the perimeter around to the right then turn left and cut through a maze of small buildings, approaching the hatchway from the south.

I thought about the red-roofed building again. Getting the detonators was the easy part. Which was why, although my heart was telling me to find Chola Se first, and I was desperate to go along with it, my head was telling me otherwise. There was so much I didnt know about how and where Chola Se was being held – and I still didnt actually know if she was being held in the camp at all – but the one thing I did know, without any doubt, was that getting her out was going to be a lot more difficult than getting hold of the detonators, and if I was going to have any chance of achieving both, I had to take care of the easier option first.

The reasoning was simple. There was far less chance of the easier option jeopardising the more difficult option than the other way round, and if the easier option was as vital to our survival as Gun Sur claimed, Ide be putting Chola Ses life at risk – together with mine and 154 others – if I failed to secure the detonators.

I had to get them first.

I wished I didnt. I hated having to put my head before my heart. But it had to be done.

I scanned the camp and the perimeter again to make sure it was safe to get moving, then I got to my feet and began jogging towards the red-roofed building.

As I approached the red-roofed building I gradually increased my pace, and by the time I was within a couple of yards of it I was running so fast that all I had to do was take a flying leap at the back wall, and with a single bound I was up on the roof. There was no reaction from the guard at the front – I hadnt made a sound – but there was no harm in making sure, so for a minute or 2 I just crouched there on the roof, keeping perfectly still, and listened.

I heard the guard sniff a couple of times, and cough, and mutter something under his breath, but that was it. He didnt know I was there.

I crept silently across the roof, stopped at the front edge, and looked down. Just to the left of the building a small torch was fixed on top of a wooden stake in the ground, and in the light of the flames I could see the guard perfectly clearly. He was almost directly beneath me – standing still, in front of the door, with his rifle strapped over his shoulder and both hands deep in his pockets, trying to keep them warm. He was dressed very similarly to the other guard – heavy coat, fur hat, boots.

I glanced around the camp, checking that no one was watching, then I did what I had to do.

I untied the sling from my waist, took one end in each hand, and held it out lengthways in front of me – not stretched out tightly, but loosely, so it sagged down slightly in the middle. I then got to my feet, steadied myself for a second, and stepped off the roof. I dropped straight down, landing behind the guard and looping the sling over his head as I hit the ground. Before he had a chance to react, I twisted the sling round his throat and yanked it tight, cutting off his voice so he couldnt cry out, and then I wrapped the ends of the cords round my hands and began twisting and pulling as hard as I could, at the same time kicking his legs away and throwing myself backwards, pulling him down on top of me. He instinctively grabbed at the sling, trying desperately to get his fingers beneath it, but he didnt stand a chance. The sling was coiled so tightly round his throat now that it was cutting into his skin, and all the time I was twisting it harder and harder, slowly strangling the life out of him. After a while he realised that he was never going to get the cord off his neck, and he began trying to get me off him instead – kicking out at me, trying to butt me with the back of his head, jabbing his elbows at me, bucking up and down and rolling over in an effort to throw me off. But I just wrapped my legs round him and held on as hard as I could. As long as I kept him on his back, and stayed behind him, I knew he couldnt really hurt me, and it was only a matter of time before he ran out of strength. He was already beginning to weaken now, and it wasnt long before his frantic attempts to save himself grew more and more feeble, until eventually, after a final few twitches, his body went limp.

I kept a tight grip on the sling for another full minute, just to make sure, then I unwound it from his throat, rolled him off me, and began searching his body for the key to the building. I found it almost immediately – hanging from a loop on his belt – and after Ide unhooked it and got to my feet, I stepped over to the building, unlocked the bolt, and opened the door. I paused for a few seconds – retying the sling around my waist as I took a quick look around to make sure I hadnt been seen – then I went back to the guard, leaned down and took hold of him under the arms, and dragged his body into the building.

It was pitchblack inside – the shutters all locked – and I knew

Ide never find the detonators in the dark, so I went back out again and fetched the torch from the stake in the ground. When I went back in, shutting the door behind me and holding up the burning torch, I could see that the building was packed to the roof with all kinds of bits and pieces. Most of it was the same sort of scrap that Starry collects – broken tools, chains and ropes, cartwheels, crates, big metal drums – but it wasnt all quite so familiar. At the far end of the building, a metal table was piled high with hundreds of dried-out roots of a kind Ive never seen before – scaly black tubers, 2 inches thick and up to a yard long, some of them glistening with tiny red droplets oozing from splits in their skin – and on one of the shelves that lined the walls there were countless rows of jars and bottles filled with all manner of strange-looking concoctions – powders, liquids, dead insects and grubs, leaves, moss, tiny white bones---

I stood there for a moment, gazing around in the shimmering flamelight, wondering what it was all about---and then, with a quiet curse, I shut it all out of my mind.

It was all about the detonators and Chola Se, that was all.

The detonators.

And Chola Se.

That was all.

Gun Sur had told me that the detonators were probably in a green canvas bag and that the bag was probably in a cupboard somewhere. It was a fairly vague description, but as I raised the torch and began looking around, it soon became clear that there was only one piece of furniture in the building that could be described as a cupboard – a rusted metal cabinet, the paint flaking off, squeezed inbetween 2 sets of shelves in the far corner.

I went over and crouched down in front of it.

It wasnt locked – again as Gun Sur had said – and it didnt even have a handle. The door was just half hanging open. And when I pushed it back and peered inside the cabinet, I was relieved to see that all it contained was a large green canvas bag.

I pulled it out and opened it up. The 3 detonators inside werent exactly the same as the one Gun Sur had shown me – they were much newer-looking, for one thing, not a spot of rust on them, and they were slightly smaller too – but there was no doubt they were the detonators I was after. And now that I had them, I could get on with the job of finding Chola Se and getting her out of here.

The thought of that suddenly filled me with a feeling Ide never felt before, a feeling that overcame me, invading every cell of my body. It was neither a good feeling nor a bad feeling, neither right nor wrong.

It was simply what it was – a feeling beyond description.

I closed the canvas bag, looped the carrying strap over my head – adjusting the bag so it hung safely but unobtrusively against my back – then I left the building and locked the door behind me. I stopped and waited for a few seconds, looking and listening. The camp seemed the same as ever – the revelries still going on at the fort, the rest of the compound still deathly quiet, the dogs still keeping their promise---

I replaced the torch on the stake and set off towards the courtyard.

The Dau encampment doesnt have streets like the ones in town, but instead there are trails and pathways of hardpacked earth that have evolved naturally over the years as people have followed the same routes around the compound over and over again. One of these trails led directly – thought not in a perfectly straight line – towards the centre of the camp, and at first I thought it was the best route to take, but after Ide been following it for about 30 seconds I realised that although it was the quickest way to get to the hatchway, it was so open and visible that it was also the quickest way to get caught. So I moved off the path, heading down a narrow track to my right, then I turned left and started following a more indirect route – zigzagging through mazes of little alleyways inbetween buildings, sometimes even doubling back to find a safer way forward, keeping to the shadows as much as possible.

There werent that many Fighters about – I guessed most of them were positioned around the perimeter – but it wasnt just Fighters I had to avoid, I had to make sure that I wasnt seen by anyone at all, and although it was the middle of the night and most of the civilians were asleep, they werent all at home in bed. I saw an old man attending to a sow in a small pen, the sow either ill or giving birth, and at one point I almost bumped into a barefooted young man who seemed to be in some kind of daze. I just turned a corner and there he was – pacing around in the darkness, muttering madly to himself. I was sure hede seen me – he was staring right at me – but as I drew my knife and prepared to silence him, he just walked straight past me, as if I wasnt there. For a moment I thought about taking him out anyway, but from the weird emptiness Ide seen his eyes – the look of a broken soul – I was fairly sure I didnt need to worry about him. He would have been more trouble dead than alive. So I just left him to his own mindless world and continued my journey.

Eventually, after perhaps 15 minutes or so, I crept out from behind an empty building on the southside of the courtyard and scurried over to the pile of logs that was no more than 40 feet from the hatchway. A Fighter was standing guard by the closed hatch, and although his presence was going to cause me problems, I was relieved to see that he was there. It meant that Chola Se was probably still there too.

There were plenty of small gaps between the logs, which made it an ideal place for watching the guard without him being able to see me. There were no torches in the immediate vicinity of the hatchway, but the flames from the fort were still burning brightly, the orange light spreading across the courtyard with enough glowing radiance to cast a dim shadow behind the guard. He wasnt the same Fighter Ide seen from the watchtower, who no doubt had been relieved of his duties – and more than likely punished as well – for disobeying orders. The new guard was older, around 21 or 22, and he looked more experienced and capable than his predecessor, and because the hatchway was in a much more open and central location than the red-roofed building, easily within sight of the fort, I knew that the task of getting in – and safely getting Chola Se out – wasnt going to be as straightforward as stealing the detonators.

I could see that the watchtower inside the fort was manned, and there was no question that if the Fighter in the tower was looking this way he had a clear view of his colleague at the hatchway. The only upside was that the guard in the tower seemed as incompetent as the perimeter guard, and just like him he was more interested in what was going on in the fort than anywhere else. Almost every time I glanced up at him he was looking down, sometimes even shouting out to the revellers below, smiling and laughing along with them. The noise they were making – the music and singing and cheering – was louder now that I was nearer the fort, and hopefully that would work to my advantage too, covering up any sounds I might make that would otherwise have given me away.

Not that I planned on making any noise.

I untied the sling from my waist and began searching around for a suitable missile. To my surprise and annoyance there didnt seem to be any suitable rocks on the ground closeby, and even when I widened my search – crawling around on my hands and knees in the dark, running my hands over the ground – all I could find were a few small stones, not much bigger than pebbles. I cursed myself for discarding the handful of perfect rocks Ide found earlier in the shallow basin. If only Ide had the presence of mind to bring some of them with me, I thought. If only Ide---

And then suddenly I froze, all thoughts of rocks and if-onlys gone.

A lone figure was crossing the courtyard, heading towards the hatchway.

I quickly crawled back behind the log pile, making sure I was out of sight, then I leaned in close to a gap in the logs and peered out at the courtyard. The figure Ide seen was about halfway across now. I hadnt actually seen him coming out of the fort, but that was the direction he was coming from, and I could tell from the way he was stumbling and swaying that he was intoxicated. He was a stocky figure, about 18 years old, and even at a distance it was obvious he was a man of means. He was dressed in a long fur coat over what looked like a velvet tunic, with high-quality leather boots and a skullcap decorated with a band of jewels. I couldnt see if he had a firearm or not, but the goldtopped cane he was carrying looked like a swordstick, and he also had a magnificent cutlass in a silver scabbard attached to the belt of his tunic. He was leaning heavily on his cane as he walked, trying to keep his balance, and he was carrying a large pewter tankard which every now and then hede raise to his mouth and try to drink from, but he was so drunk that he spilled most of it down his chin. Despite his pathetic drunkenness, he still had the unmistakable swagger and confidence of a man who always gets what he wants.

And it wasnt hard to guess what he wanted right now.

The guard at the hatchway had seen him, and from the look of fear in his eyes – and the fact that he was suddenly standing to attention – it was clear that the drunk man was his superior. The drunkard was only about 10 yards from him now, and in a few moments he was going to tell him to unlock the hatch, and the guard would do it immediately and without question, and then the drunk man would be stumbling down into Chola Ses prison to do whatever he wanted with her---

I could see her down there.

Cowering on a filthy bed, trembling with fear and rage, her battered face streaked with bloodstained tears---

I had to force myself to stay still.

Stay calm.

I had to quieten my roaring heart.

And think.

Cold and hard.

Just think.

I looked over at the guard, studying his weapons – AK47 assault rifle, 9-shot Browning automatic, hunting knife in his belt. I glanced across at the fort. The Fighter in the watchtower was looking this way, grinning casually as he watched the drunk man. Just then I heard the slurred grunt of a voice, a low and ugly sound, and when I looked back at the hatchway I saw the guard hurriedly taking a key from his belt while the drunk man just stood there, his upper body wavering, waiting for his command to be obeyed.

Think.

My sling was useless without ammunition, which meant I was going to have to use my knife. But I couldnt rush the 2 men now. Even if I could reach the guard before he had time to arm himself with one of his guns, the sentry in the watchtower would see me and raise the alarm, and that would be the end of it.

All I could do was wait.

I waited as the guard opened the hatch and the drunk man stepped down inside, almost immediately losing his balance and lurching sideways. The guard quickly stooped down and grasped his arm to stop him falling, but once hede helped the drunk man straighten up again, the only thanks he got was a drunken curse – get your hands off me! – and a flailing arm thrown at his head, which he leaned away from and easily avoided. I carried on waiting, watching as the drunk man continued his awkward descent, until eventually his head disappeared below the surface and the guard peered down after him to make sure hede gone, and then – with a roll of his eyes and a shake of his head – he closed the hatch again. As he straightened up and looked across at his colleague in the watchtower, ostentatiously shrugging his shoulders, I followed his gaze and saw the guard in the watchtower grinning back at him and giving him a mock salute. I waited, trying not to think about what was happening under the ground just a few yards away from me---

Chola Se cowering---trembling---

No.

Her lips drawn back in a vicious snarl---

No.

She was dog. Shede fight. Shede give me time.

I waited, my gaze alternating between the 2 guards – the one at the hatchway, the one in the watchtower – waiting for the right moment – hatchway, tower---hatchway, tower---hatchway---

A loud crash came from the fort, followed almost instantly by an outburst of cheering and laughing, and the guard in the tower immediately turned away and looked down, his attention drawn to whatever it was that was going on down below. At the same time, the hatchway guard relaxed for a moment, turning his back on me as he raised his arms behind his head and stretched his back.

This was it, the moment Ide been waiting for.

I drew my knife, stepped out from behind the logs, and began racing towards the guard. Within a few seconds I was already halfway there, but just as I was beginning to think that I might make it all the way without being seen, the guard suddenly spun round. I dont know what alerted him – I hadnt made a sound – but somehow hede sensed my presence. I was still a good 7 or 8 yards from him now, and hede reacted so quickly that he already had his rifle raised to his shoulder and was about to pull the trigger. If hede relied solely on instinct and fired without hesitation I wouldnt have stood a chance, but instead he made the fatal mistake of pausing for a fraction of a second to steady his aim before taking the shot, and a fraction of a second was all I needed. Without missing a step or even slowing down, I whipped back my arm and threw the knife.

It spun through the air and thudded almost silently into the guards chest, just missing his heart. An inch or 2 to the right and he would have died instantly, but it was still a serious wound – the knife buried deep in his flesh – and as the rifle fell from his hands and he dropped to his knees, clutching his chest, I knew he was badly injured. But I also knew that it wasnt over yet. It wouldnt be over until he was dead.

I carried on running, risking a quick glance at the watchtower – the sentry was still distracted – and a moment later I was bearing down on the wounded guard. The life was visibly draining out of him – his skin deathly pale, his eyes glazed over – but he wasnt giving up without a fight, and by the time I reached him hede already fumbled his pistol from his holster and was raising his arm to shoot. I lashed out with my foot, kicking the gun from his hand, but just as I was swinging round to kick him again, this time in his head, he whipped out his hunting knife with his left hand and plunged it into my leg. The shock of it numbed the pain, but the impact knocked me off balance, and as I stumbled sideways he lunged at me with the knife again. I leaped back just in time, avoiding the slashing blade by inches, and in the same movement I leaned down and scooped up his fallen rifle. He went for me again, swinging wildly with the knife, but his strength was fading rapidly now and he missed me by a long way. As his flailing arm threw him off balance, I sprang forward and hammered the rifle butt into his head. I put all my weight into it, clubbing him so hard that I heard the dull crack of bone, and as he fell to the ground I knew he was dead.

I quickly looked across at the watchtower again. The guard was engrossed in trying to catch a bottle that someone below was throwing up to him. He kept missing it, either because it wasnt thrown high enough, or it was too far away for him to reach. Each time he almost caught it, a cheer from below turned into a groan.

I stooped down over the dead guard, rolled him over, put my foot on his chest and yanked my knife from his body. Then I dragged the body over to the hatchway, laid it down again, and opened the unlocked hatch. A steep flight of wooden steps led down into some kind of chamber about 10 feet below. I couldnt see all of it, just the section of dirt floor and bare walls directly below, but there was clearly more to it than I could see because a torchlight was burning somewhere out of sight, and I could hear muffled sounds coming from further back, ominously ugly sounds – a slurred curse, a savage grunt, the sudden dull slap of a violent blow---

I pulled the guards body over to the hatchway and heaved it down into the chamber. As it clattered and thumped down the steps, I stood up straight, positioned myself on the edge of the hatchway, and jumped.

The moment I hit the ground everything suddenly froze, and in that frozen moment I was nothing but dog. I could see and hear and smell and feel every tiny detail of everything there was – all together, all at once.

And its all still with me now.

The doorway ahead of me at the far end of the chamber, the

heavy wooden door wide open, showing the cramped and squalid cell behind it, dimly lit by the flamelight of a torch on the wall. The big iron key in the lock of the door, the small square window cut in the wood about threequarters of the way up, secured with a grid of iron bars. And inside the cell, the filthy little bed in the corner – just a dirty scrape of blanket thrown on the ground – and the overturned water bowl beside it---and in the opposite corner the shallow tin bucket almost overflowing with human waste, filling the stale underground air with the sickening stink of degradation. And the other smells too---all mixed up together in the used-up air thats been breathed too many times – blood, alcohol, sweat, vomit, sex---odours of human brutality.

And I can see Chola Se---

I can see her---splayed out on the ground, almost naked, the ragged pink dress ripped and torn and hanging off her in bloodstained shreds---her manacled wrists chained to an iron stake fixed to the ground in the middle of the cell---her face battered and bruised, bleeding from a fresh gash on the side of her head---her upper lip split open, her eyes blackened, one of them swollen shut---

And her body---so beaten and abused---

The only part of her that isnt beaten is her spirit. I can see it in her vicious snarl, the snarl Ide imagined so many times – her lips drawn back, her bared teeth red with blood – and most of all I can see it in her eyes---the fire, the ferocity, the will to keep fighting as long as shese still alive, the willingness to die before giving herself up to the drunk man---

I can still see him too.

Standing over her, naked from the waist down, his goldtopped cane raised above his head, ready to strike her again---his slobbering mouth, his twisted grin, his glazed eyes sick with lust---

I moved then, stepping over the guards crumpled body, and the frozen moment burst into life.

There was no fear in the drunk mans eyes when he saw me hurtling towards him, just a momentary flash of surprise and a glare of imperious outrage. He had the look of a man whode always been so feared, so protected by his position, that he simply couldnt comprehend what was happening. No one ever interrupted him. No one even approached him without his permission. The notion of being attacked was so alien to him that he didnt know how to defend himself – hede never had to – and it wasnt until I was a few yards away from him, and getting faster all the time, that it finally dawned on him that I wasnt going to stop, that I really was attacking him, and all at once his swagger and arrogance cracked.

Hey, just a minute, he began to say, taking a step back. What do you think youre—?

And that was the last thing he ever said.

I dont remember if I had my knife in my hand or if Ide left it sheathed on my thigh, but I never had any intention of using it anyway. I was as unhuman now as Ide ever been, and when I launched myself at the drunk man, leaping through the air at him, I only had eyes for his throat. At the very last moment he raised his arm in front of his neck in a futile attempt to protect himself, but I was flying at him with such savage fury that there was nothing he could do to stop me, and I didnt even feel his arm as I lunged the last few inches and sank my teeth into his throat.

He fell back under my weight, grabbing at my head in a desperate attempt to free himself from my grip, but Ide bitten into him so deeply that he didnt stand a chance, and by the time he hit the ground, with me still astride him, Ide already ripped open his jugular vein and he was rapidly bleeding to death.

I jumped off him, leaving him writhing and gurgling on the ground, clutching in vain at the streams of blood spurting from his throat, and I ran over to Chola Se and crouched down beside her.

How bad is it? I asked, quickly scanning her injuries. Can you stand up?

She nodded, wincing painfully as she got to her knees. She held out her manacled wrists.

Get these off me, she said.

Her wrists were red raw, the skin scraped off by the rough metal shackles, which I could see now were bolted together so tightly that Ide need a hacksaw or boltcutters to get them off. I got to my feet and went over to the iron stake in the middle of the cell. The chains were fixed to the stake as securely as the manacles, and when I tried pulling the stake from the ground I couldnt move it an inch. It was either buried right down into the hardpacked dirt, or it had been set into the ground with concrete. Which meant the only way to free Chola Se was by breaking the chains themselves.

I looked around the cell for some kind of tool. At first I couldnt see anything – the cell was bare, stripped of everything – but then I spotted the drunk mans fur coat and some of his clothes piled in a heap near the far wall, and from the bottom of the heap I could see the silver tip of his scabbard poking out. I hurried over, drew the cutlass from it, and went back over to Chola Se. Shede already guessed what I was doing and was kneeling down with her arms stretched out flat on the ground in front of her.

Turn your head away, I warned her.

As she turned to one side, I raised the cutlass over my head, holding it in both hands, and brought it down with all my strength on one of the chains. The chain broke with a harsh metallic crack, and a bit of the cutlass blade snapped off and flew up into the air, only just missing my face. I raised the cutlass again and hammered it down on the other chain, and this time the cutlass blade completely snapped, but the chain burst open too.

Chola Se was free.

The manacles were still bolted to her wrists, with short lengths of broken chain still attached to them, but she was no longer chained to the stake.

She cautiously got to her feet, and for a few seconds she just stood there, swaying slightly, staring over at the drunk man. He was lying perfectly still now, his eyes wide open, his head resting in a pool of blood, and it was plain to see that he was either dead or very close to it. From the way Chola Se was looking at him – her eyes burning with hatred – I thought for a moment that she was going to take her revenge on him, whether he was still alive or not, and I was torn between letting her do whatever she wanted – and probably needed – to do, and just getting her out of there as quickly as possible.

In the end I didnt have to make the decision, because just as I was trying to make up my mind, she turned away from the drunk mans body and began walking out of the cell, limping heavily, calmly removing the ragged remains of the dress from her body as she went.

The stab wound in my leg was about 6 inches above my knee, and I was beginning to feel the full effect of it now. The pain wasnt the problem, I could deal with that, but the leg was starting to stiffen up, and if it got any worse it was going to make things difficult. At the moment though, I was still a lot more mobile than Chola Se, who – despite her best efforts to ignore her injuries – was clearly in a really bad way.

As I led the way up the hatchway steps, turning round every now and then to help her up, she gently took hold of my foot and told me to stop.

We need to bandage that wound in your leg, she said.

Its all right, I told her.

No, its not. Youre losing too much blood.

I glanced down at the wound and saw that she was right. So much blood was streaming down my leg that Chola Ses face was covered in it.

Sorry, I said. I didnt realise.

She wiped her face and smiled at me, wincing at the pain in her swollen lip.

Ile go back and get something to use as a bandage, she said.

No, I told her, reaching down to take her hand. We dont have time. Theres 3 missing guards out there, and eventually someones going to notice theyre gone. We have to get out of here before that happens. Ile deal with my leg once weare safe.

Chola Se looked up at me, thought for a moment, then nodded.

I didnt think we stood much chance of getting all the way out before the alarm was raised, but I was hoping wede make it at least part of the way. It was a hope that didnt last very long though. As I cautiously inched my head up through the open hatchway to check if it was safe for us to leave, the first thing I saw was 3 Dau Fighters striding across the courtyard towards us. They spotted me immediately – they must have had their eyes on the hatchway – and all 3 of them suddenly stopped, the one in the middle pointing right at me, and a moment later they all started running, their guns at the ready as they raced across the courtyard towards us.

I cursed.

What is it? Chola Se said.

3 Fighters, I said quickly. Stay where you are, okay?

She nodded.

I scrambled out of the hatchway, then immediately dropped to the ground as gunshots split the air. I darted over to my left, snatched up the dead guards rifle, then turned and fired back at the rapidly approaching Fighters. They were easy targets – upright and out in the open – and I hit 2 of them straightaway, one in the chest, the other in the head. As they went down, and I fired off another round, the third one threw himself to the ground and took cover behind one of the fallen bodies. Now I was the one out in the open, and I could see the third Fighter resting his rifle on his dead colleagues shoulder and calmly taking aim at me. I let off 4 quick shots, and as the bullets thudded into the body in front of him, the Fighter ducked down out of sight. I jumped up and ran back to the hatchway, stooping down to pick up the dead guards pistol as I went, and just as I reached the hatchway and leaped back into it, slamming the hatch closed behind me, I heard the third Fighter opening fire again, his shots ploughing into the ground just above me.

I passed the pistol to Chola Se.

I got 2 of them, I told her. But the third ones still out there and hese got us covered.

We cant stay here, Jeet, she said. Listen---

I kept still and listened. Ide been so focused on the gunfight with the 3 Dau Fighters that I hadnt heard what I was hearing now – the revelry at the fort had stopped and the whole camp was coming to life. Shouting voices, the clatter of running boots, a bell ringing, dogs barking. I must have lost the silence of the dogs when I was caught up in the chaos of the gunfight, and for a moment I began setting my mind to quieten them again, but I quickly realised there was no point. We were trapped in a cellar in the middle of the Dau encampment, surrounded by enemy gunmen and hundreds of hostile people – the sound of a few barking dogs wasnt going to make any difference.

The perimeters about 50 yards from here, I told Chola Se. If we can get there in one piece and get out into the Deathlands we might just make it. Can you run?

I can run.

I glanced at the pistol in her hand.

Are you okay with that? I asked her. Or do you want the rifle?

This is fine, she said, thumbing a switch on the guards Browning. The magazine slid out. She checked it was fully loaded, then slapped it back in and racked a round into the chamber.

The Browning was a Mark 3, which held 13 rounds. The guards AK47 had a 30-round magazine, and Ide already fired 7 shots, so – assuming it had been fully loaded to start with – I had 23 rounds left.

We had 36 shots between us.

I looked at Chola Se. Are you ready?

She nodded.

Ile lead the way, okay?

She nodded again, then reached up and and took hold of my arm.

Before we go, she said quietly. I want you to promise me that you wont let them take me alive.

I hesitated, not sure what to say.

She gripped my arm, squeezing so hard that her nails drew blood.

Listen, Jeet, she said. What they did to me down here---it was just---She shook her head. I cant go through that again. Do you understand? Ide rather die. So I need your word, okay?

Okay.

Say it.

I wont let them take you alive.

Thank you, she said, letting go of my arm. Ime ready now.

Okay, lets go.

I was half expecting to see dozens of Dau Fighters surrounding me when I inched open the hatch, but although the fort doors were wide open now and 6 or 7 Fighters were running out – and I could also hear shouts and running boots in the near distance all around us – the closest Fighter to us was still the one behind the dead body. He started firing as soon as he saw the hatch opening, and as the shots crashed all around me – some of them blowing holes in the hatch – the temptation to duck back down was almost irresistible. But I knew I couldnt. We had to get out of there before more Fighters arrived, and the only way to get out without being shot was to take out the one who was shooting at us.

So I stayed where I was – keeping my head down as low as possible, my eyes just above the hatchway – and as I forced myself to ignore the shots screaming all around me, I steadied the AK47 and carefully took aim at the Fighter. He was still well hidden behind the body in front of him, and the only part of him I could see was the very top of his head. I took my time – breathing steadily, gripping the rifle firmly but not too tightly, waiting patiently until the V of the rifle sight was perfectly still, fixed precisely on the small patch of thinning brown hair that was the only visible part of the Fighters head – then I slowly breathed out and pulled the trigger.

There wasnt much to see, just a burst of red spray, then the Fighters head disappeared from view and his rifle clattered to the ground.

I glanced quickly at the group of Fighters running across the courtyard and saw that they were nearly halfway across now, and 1 or 2 of them were already raising their weapons, preparing to open fire.

I jumped up out of the hatchway, then leaned back down, grabbed hold of Chola Ses hand, and pulled her out.

The crack of a rifleshot ripped through the air, followed by another, then all the Fighters began firing. They were shooting on the move, their shots hurried and wild, but we had to get moving before they got any closer.

This way, I told Chola Se, heading for the log pile.

I was planning on taking the shortest route to the perimeter – cutting back through the maze of small buildings to the south – but before wede even reached the log pile, a group of Dau civilians emerged from the darkness directly ahead of us. There were at least a dozen of them, all of them armed, and as soon as they saw us they opened fire.

I fired back, hitting 2 or 3 of them and scattering the rest, but I knew theyd soon regroup. And I knew wede never make it past them to the perimeter. There was only one option left.

This way! I yelled to Chola Se as a volley of gunfire came from the Fighters to our left.

We turned to our right and sped off along the well-worn pathway that cut through the centre of the camp – heading west now, back towards the red-roofed building. Although we were both limping badly, we were still outrunning the Fighters, and it wasnt long before we were beyond the effective range of their rifles. We were still far from safe though. The problem was, there was virtually no cover at all on the pathway – we were completely out in the open – and the western perimeter was at least another 150 yards away, and although we were gradually getting away from the Fighters behind us, more and more Dau were appearing all the time – civilians as well as Fighters – and they were all doing their best to kill us. We were being shot at from everywhere – from distant buildings and unseen trenches, from the doorways and windows of nearby houses – and although our speed made us hard to hit, and we were firing back as we ran, making it even harder for anyone to get a good clean shot at us, we were rapidly running out of both energy and ammunition.

By the time the red-roofed building came into view, we were down to our last few rounds. But at least the perimeter was in sight now. Wede almost made it, just another 30 yards to go---

We were about 10 yards away from the red-roofed building when a Dau Fighter suddenly appeared from behind it and opened fire on us with a Thompson submachine gun. Its an awesome weapon, fitted with a drum magazine that carries 50 rounds, and the Fighter wasnt even trying to take us out with well-aimed shots, he was just shooting from the hip, spraying dozens of rounds in our general direction, knowing that hede hit us eventually. As we both instinctively threw ourselves to the ground, Chola Se let out a sudden cry of pain, and instead of diving to the ground she just dropped like a sack, hitting the dirt hard and lying still. I started scrambling towards her, but a salvo of machine-gun rounds slammed into the dirt in front of me and I had to roll away. I kept rolling, as fast as I could, then abruptly stopped and changed direction, rolling to my left. The Dau Fighter was good, calmly adjusting his aim each time I rolled in a different direction, but just as he thought he had me, I flung myself back in the opposite direction and fired back at him. My first shot missed, thudding into the wall of the building just to his right, and when I corrected my aim and pulled the trigger again, the rifle clacked emptily. I immediately tried again, but even as my finger tightened I knew what I was going to hear.

The rifle made the same dull clack.

The Dau Fighter smiled, realising I was out of ammunition, and he began walking towards me – still smiling, in no great hurry, just strolling along with his machine gun swinging casually in one hand, intent on savouring his moment of triumph---and then, all of a sudden, the smile left his face and he stopped in his tracks, scrabbling desperately to raise the gun. Hede only just got hold of it in both hands when a shot went off from somewhere behind me and a bullet ripped into his chest. He staggered back, just about managing to stay on his feet, but a moment later a second shot hit him in the head and he instantly dropped to the ground.

I turned round and saw Chola Se lying flat out on the ground, her arms outstretched, her pistol held in both hands. Blood was trickling from a black-edged bullet graze on the side of her head. The wound was so shallow that it had barely broken her skin, but I guessed the impact must have knocked her out for a few seconds.

I was just about to ask her if she was all right when a salvo of shots rang out from behind us, and we both turned to see the group of Fighters and a large mob of civilians bearing down on us. We looked at each other for a moment, and without saying a word we knew what we had to do. We both jumped to our feet and ran, not towards the the perimeter – because we knew wede never make it without weapons – but towards the red-roofed building.

As Chola Se headed straight for the dead Fighter, stooping down to snatch up his Thompson and quickly searching him for spare magazines, I carried on over to the red-roofed building, stopping by the door where the guard Ide strangled had dropped his rifle. The Dau were closing fast now, no more than 30 yards away, and their shots were getting closer and closer all the time. I heard Chola Se fire off a long burst from the Thompson, and straightaway the incoming gunfire stopped. As I picked up the rifle and grabbed the burning torch from the stake in the ground, the Dau started shooting again, but their gunfire was more tentative now, and they were no longer charging towards us.

I stepped over to the door, smashed open the lock with the rifle, and went inside. The guards body was still there. I lay the torch on the floor and quickly began searching him for more weapons. I found a Colt automatic with 2 spare magazines in one pocket, and another 3 magazines for the rifle in another. The torch had set the wooden floor alight now, and the flames were spreading rapidly. I put the spare magazines in the green canvas bag and hurried back out to join Chola Se.

Shede found another 50-round magazine for the Thompson on the dead Fighter, so now we had enough firepower and ammunition to at least give ourselves a chance. And for the next few minutes we just stood there together, side by side in the light of the burning building – Chola Se with the submachine gun, me with the rifle and pistol – and we didnt stop shooting until every last bullet was gone.

The Dau werent expecting us to stop running and make a stand – we werent expecting to either – and the shock of it worked to our advantage. While we were at least partly shielded by the burning building, most of them were out in the open when we started shooting, and we took out at least a dozen of them before they had a chance to retreat and take cover, either killing them outright or wounding them badly enough to put them out of action. Now that the odds werent so much in their favour, the fight went out of most of the civilians, and they rapidly dropped back out of range, leaving their Fighters to deal with us. They fought hard, holding their ground as well as they could, but by the time wede emptied our guns theyd retreated enough to give us what we needed – the time and space to make a relatively free run to the perimeter and the safety of the Deathlands beyond.

We dropped our empty weapons and ran.

The distance to the perimeter was only 20 yards, but wede barely taken half a dozen steps before we realised that it might as well be 20 miles. 3 Dau Fighters had suddenly appeared directly ahead of us – 2 moving in from the right, the other one from the left – and it was clear from the way they were confronting us, neither hurrying nor bothering to take cover, that they knew we were unarmed. They must have been watching us, waiting for us to run out of ammunition. And now they were just standing there, line abreast, their rifles levelled directly at us. We had no choice but to stop. They were 10 yards away. And there was nothing incompetent or overly triumphant about these 3. They had the cold hard faces of seasoned Fighters. They knew exactly what they were doing.

Without taking his eyes off us, the one in the middle spoke quietly to the other 2.

He wants them both alive, he said.

They nodded.

But kill him if you have to.

Then he raised his voice and spoke to us.

On your knees, he said.

Jeet? Chola Se whispered. Remember your promise.

I drew my knife.

All 3 rifles turned on me.

Drop it, the one in the middle said calmly. Right now.

I thought I had a reasonable chance of throwing the knife before they could all pull their triggers, and I was fairly sure that if I did manage to throw it, one of them would die. But that still left the other 2. And I knew that no matter how fast I moved, theyd shoot me down before I got anywhere near them. And that would mean breaking the promise Ide made to Chola Se. If they killed me, I couldnt stop them taking her alive.

Youve got 3 seconds to drop the knife, the middle one said. 1---

Jeet? Chola Se whispered again. You promised---

I tightened my grip on the knife.

2---

Please, Jeet---

I saw their fingers tightening on the triggers.

I had to do it now.

I took a breath and was just about to make my move when 3 silent shapes flew out of the darkness behind the 3 Dau Fighters, slamming into them with such brutal power that all 3 men hit the ground without firing a shot. I barely had time to recognise the shapes as the big grey male and 2 of the adult females before theyd taken the Fighters skulls in their massive jaws and crushed them like eggs.

There was a moments silence as the 3 dogs just stood there, licking their bloodied lips and looking expectantly at Chola Se and me, and we just stood there looking back at them, both of us struck dumb---

Then a shot was fired from behind us, followed a second later by a sudden barrage of shouts and yells and barking dogs and more gunshots, and our senses came back to us and we ran for our lives – leaping over the 3 dead Fighters, crossing the perimeter, and following the 3 dogs out into the Deathland darkness.

My mother and the rest of the pack were waiting for us in the rugged terrain beyond the perimeter, and as we all headed off into the Deathlands together, I thought at first that wede easily outrun the pursuing Dau and soon be far enough ahead of them to stop for a while to rest and tend to our wounds.

But it wasnt that simple.

Chola Se was so exhausted from the beatings and abuse shede suffered – and still dazed from the bullet that had grazed her head – that she could barely keep running in a straight line, and my wounded leg was getting worse all the time. As well as losing a lot of blood, which was weakening me by the minute, the leg was seizing up badly, which was seriously slowing me down. We both needed to stop and rest, if only for a while. But we didnt have time. Our injuries were hindering us so much that the dogs had to keep stopping to let us catch up, and instead of putting distance between ourselves and the Dau, we were losing ground to them all the time. Every time I glanced over my shoulder I could see the lights of their torches getting closer and closer. At this rate it wouldnt be long before they caught up with us.

Come on, Jeet, Chola Se said breathlessly, taking hold of my arm. Weve got to keep going.

I kept going.

We were following the trail of a shallow gully that cut through the glassrock plains, and in the darkness up ahead I could see that the pack had stopped again to allow us to catch up with them. Theyd already put themselves in considerable danger by coming back to the camp and saving us from the 3 Dau Fighters, and while I didnt doubt my mothers willingness to carry on risking her life for me, I had no right to expect anything more from the rest of the pack. And as Chola Se and I wearily approached them, Ide already made up my mind to tell them not to wait for us anymore. They should go---go back to their world and leave us to it. Theyd done more than enough for us as it was.

But before I had a chance to do anything, my mother took hold of my hand in her mouth and led me over to the bank of the gully. It was only 3 or 4 feet high, and she hopped up with such ease that she didnt even have to let go of my hand. She gave me a gentle tug, letting me know that she wanted me to follow her, and as she helped me clamber up the bank – pulling me up by my hand – I saw the big male nudging Chola Se with his flank, quietly – but firmly – telling her to join us. My mother waited as Chola Se came over and climbed out of the gully, then she led us both over to the blackened trunk of a longdead tree jutting up out of the glassrock beside the bank. The crown of the tree had broken off a long time ago, and all that remained now was a hollow pillar of fossilised black wood, about 8 feet tall and 30 inches across, the top cracked open like a splintered bone. The texture of the wood – like frozen black iron – was so similar to that of the glassrock that the trunk seemed part of the ground itself, as if a mutant outgrowth had sprouted from the rock in misformed memory of the trees that had once grown there.

My mother lowered herself down at the base of the trunk, carefully positioning herself with her head laid flat on her outstretched front legs, her snout just inches from a thick tangle of roots. As I crouched down beside her, following her gaze, I realised what she was showing me. The tightly twisted roots were fused into the glassrock, forming an impenetrable wall round the foot of the trunk which sealed off the hollow interior, but on the side of the trunk nearest the gully – just where my mother was lying – a section of glassrock had broken off, taking the roots with it, leaving a narrow gap in the wall. It wasnt much of a gap, and at least half of it was below ground level, making it even more awkward to get through, but my mother obviously thought that Chola Se and I could make it, and Ide never known her to be wrong.

My mothers ears suddenly pricked up then, and as she jumped to her feet and stared back along the gully, I heard the distant sound of rapidly approaching running boots. The big male let out a low growl, and when I looked across I could see that the pack was desperate to get going – circling around, their tails raised, their instincts telling them to run.

Go, I said to my mother, at the same time moving aside and guiding Chola Se down towards the gap in the roots.

My mother didnt move. She just stood there, staring at the big male, silently telling him what to do. He stared back at her, concentrating intently, and a moment later he turned away, glanced at the pack, and they all took off into the darkness.

The bootsteps were closing fast now.

I knew my mother wouldnt leave until she knew I was safe, and I knew there was no point in trying to tell her otherwise, so I just crouched there, watching and waiting as Chola Se crawled through the gap, wriggling and twisting through the roots, and as soon as her feet had disappeared inside the hollow trunk, I scrambled after her – burrowing into the gap and squeezing my way through the roots as fast as I possibly could. I was about halfway through when I suddenly became stuck – unable to move either forwards or back, no matter how hard I tried – and at first I couldnt work out what was stopping me. It felt as if I was caught up on something, but I wasnt wearing any clothes---there was nothing to get caught up. But then I remembered the green canvas bag on my back, the bag with the detonators in---it must have got stuck. The strap must have snagged on a broken root or something. I tried reaching round to unhook it, but I was stuck in the narrowest part of the gap, squeezed inbetween 2 thick roots, and I couldnt twist round far enough to get hold of anything.

I felt Chola Se taking hold of me then, gripping me firmly by the arms, and when I looked round I saw that shede managed to wriggle round inside the trunk so that she was sitting on the ground, facing towards me.

Push yourself as hard as you can, Jeet, she said. And Ile pull you, okay?

She tightened her grip on my arms, and as I dug my feet in and shoved with all my strength, she leaned back and pulled. For a second or 2, nothing happened – I was still stuck fast – and however hard we pushed and pulled, I couldnt break free. But then all at once – as Chola Se braced her feet against the trunk and yanked even harder – there was a sudden dull snap, like the solid crack of breaking rock, and I went flying through the gap into the base of the hollowed-out trunk, sprawling face down on the ground.

There was very little room in there, and the easiest way for both of us to fit in was by standing up straight, which Chola Se did as soon as I was safely inside. I was just getting ready to join her – removing the canvas bag from my back so it didnt get in the way – when I heard a strangely familiar sound coming from outside the trunk. It was the soft rhythmic sound of a lapping tongue. I knew it was my mother – I know every sound she makes – but I couldnt understand what she was doing.

What is it, Jeet? I heard Chola Se ask. Whats going on?

Just a second, I told her, shuffling over to the gap in the roots.

When I looked out through the gap and saw my mother licking the glassrock around the base of the trunk, it still took me a moment or 2 to work out what she was doing. I could see her well enough in the starlit darkness – or at least well enough to see what she was doing – but the glassrock itself was just a blur of black, and it wasnt until Ide got to my knees and moved closer to the gap that the realisation suddenly hit me.

I still couldnt see what it was that my mother was licking from the ground.

I just knew.

It was blood.

My blood.

I hadnt stopped bleeding since the Dau guard had stabbed me – I could feel blood trickling down my leg right now – and what Ide just realised was that as well as leaving a trail of blood all the way from the Dau encampment, I must also have left at least a few more spots, if not more, between the gully and the tree trunk. So when the Dau got here – and theyd be here any second – my bloodtrail would lead them directly to our hiding place.

Which was why my mother was getting rid of it.

Shede cleared the area around the trunk now, and as she began backing away from it, licking up every spot of blood she could find, I couldnt help smiling to myself at her thoroughness. I shouldnt have been surprised really. I should have known shede think of everything. She always did. Thats why shede lived so long – she wasnt just knowing and strong, she was wise. She used her mind to survive.

The Dau were so close now that I could feel the stomp of their boots through the ground, and as I carried on watching my mother – silently urging her to hurry up and leave before the Fighters arrived – I saw her do something even more amazing. Shede finished clearing up my blood now and was just standing there, looking around and sniffing, making sure she hadnt missed any drops. Satisfied that she hadnt, she raised her head, pricked up her ears, and listened to the approaching Dau for a moment, and then – to my astonishment – she sat down and lowered her head to her underbelly, as if she was going to lick herself clean. But instead of licking herself, she bit herself. It wasnt a hard bite, just a quick nip with her front teeth, but it was enough to cut into the soft skin of her belly and draw blood. She sat there for a moment longer, watching as the blood began to run, then she stood up, waited for the blood to start dripping to the ground, then calmly loped off into the darkness.

She wasnt just wise, she was a genius.

Shede not only cleared away the trail of blood leading to the trunk, she was now laying down a new trail of blood for the Dau to follow, leading them away from the trunk and out into the Deathlands.

And shede done it just in time.

As Chola Se took my hand and helped me to stand up straight, we heard the Dau Fighters stomping along the gully outside – heavy bootsteps, the rattle of gunbelts, the dull clank of cold metal. We froze, holding our breath and listening hard as the bootsteps passed by, and then almost immediately they began to slow down, and within a few moments the Fighters had come to a halt. They were no more than 15 feet away.

Looks like they stopped here, one of them said, breathing heavily.

Whered they go?

Over there, look---theres more blood on top of the bank.

They must have left the gully.

Theyre heading into the mountains.

All right, lets go. They cant be that far ahead of us now.

We heard them clambering up the bank, onto the glassrock, and then they were off again — their boots clattering on the hard rock as they headed off into the Deathlands, following the trail of blood my mother had left for them.

We stayed where we were — not moving, not breathing, not making a sound---just listening to the Fighters as they clattered off into the distance — until eventually, after 2 or 3 minutes, we couldnt hear them anymore. And then, at last, we both breathed out.

We were safe.

At least for a while.

Safe and together.

We were very much together — standing up straight, our backs against the trunk, our faces just a few inches apart. But even at that distance we could barely see each other. The top of the trunk was blocked up with something — a birds nest maybe, or just debris built up over the years — so there was virtually no light in there at all, but we didnt have to see each other to be aware of each other. We could feel each others breath, smell each others naked bodies, sense each others every movement.

That was your dogmother, wasnt it? Chola Se said quietly.

I nodded. I didnt have to ask her how she knew. She was a dogchild. She would have known the moment shede seen us together.

What was she doing just now when you were watching her? she asked.

I told her how my mother had cleaned up my blood and laid a false trail for the Dau to follow.

Thats why the Fighters left the gully and ran off towards the mountains, I explained. They were following my mother.

How long do you think theyle keep following her?

It wont just be her theyre following. The rest of the pack will have been waiting for her somewhere out in the Deathlands. Once shese joined up with them, theyle probably keep heading for the mountains for a while, but at some point theyle veer round towards town to make the Dau think theyre taking us back. Theyle keep going at a fairly slow pace as well.

As if weare still holding them up, Chola Se said.

Yeh, but they wont let the Dau get too close, because once theyve gone far enough to convince the Fighters theyre taking us back to town, theyle turn back again, pick up speed, and head off to the mountains.

And then the Dau will give up and go back to their camp.

Yeh.

So wele have to stay here til then.

It probably wont be too long. A couple of hours maybe.

What if they go back another way? We wont know theyve gone back unless they pass us, will we?

I hadnt thought of that. There was no reason the Fighters had to come past us on their way back, and depending on where they started from – which could be almost anywhere – it was quite possible they wouldnt come anywhere near us. And on top of that, I realised, I didnt actually know where we were anyway.

Wele give it til just before sunrise, I said, trying to sound more confident than I was. If they havent passed us by then, wele leave anyway.

Okay.

I heard her sigh then, and as her breath brushed my skin I could feel the depth of her exhaustion. I wanted to ask her how she was, or to at least try to do something to comfort her, but after the horrors shede been through it seemed utterly meaningless to ask her how she was, and I didnt have the faintest idea how to comfort her. Ide never comforted anyone in my life. Ide never had to. I didnt have a clue how to do it.

Ide better fix your leg, she said matter-of-factly. If it carries on bleeding, youle be dead before sunrise.

As she began lowering herself – bending her knees to one side and sliding down – the broken chains on her manacles rattled against the trunk.

It took her a while to get into a position where she could work on the wound without being too uncomfortable, but once shede found it – kneeling on the ground in front of me, with a knee on either side of my legs – she didnt waste any time. After quickly but carefully locating the stab wound, she unsheathed my knife from the cloth wrapping on my left leg, passed the knife to me, then loosened the wrapping and tore off a short strip of cloth. She licked the cloth to moisten it, then set to work wiping away the worst of the blood and dirt from the wound. Once shede got it as clean as she could, she put the cloth down, made a slight adjustment to her position, and began examining the punctured flesh.

The initial lack of pain when the guard had stabbed me was hard to remember now – every time Chola Se touched the open wound it felt like a red-hot knife slicing into my leg. She did her best to be careful, but she was working blind, relying on touch alone, so the only way she could assess the damage was by probing the wound with her fingers. I tried not to show any pain, but no matter how careful she was, I couldnt help gasping every now and then.

Sorry, she said, but I cant help it. Its going to hurt.

Its okay, just do whatever you have to. Can you tell how bad it is?

Its quite deep, and its going to need a lot of stitches, but I dont think the bleedings coming from an artery. Hold still, Ime going to clean it up inside now.

She gently took hold of my wounded leg in both hands, leaned forward, and began licking at the open cut. To anyone else but a dogchild this would probably seem quite strange, but to us it was perfectly natural. Wede grown up having our wounds licked clean, and wede learned to do the same for others. It was the only way we knew, the only way we had.

Right, she said after a while, I think that should do it. The bleedings nearly stopped now. Is it all right if I use the rest of this cloth for a bandage?

Yeh.

She tore off another strip, wadded it up into a compress, and placed it over the knife cut.

Hold that there for me, she said. And keep it pressed down.

While I did as she asked, she unwound the rest of the cloth from my left leg, then started bandaging the wound. She worked calmly and methodically, carefully winding the cloth round my leg, constantly checking to make sure it wasnt too tight, but that it was tight enough to keep the compress in place.

Youre obviously not going to tell me, are you? she said after a while, rewinding a loop of cloth that had become twisted.

Tell you what?

Why youre not wearing any clothes.

I hadnt actually forgotten I was naked, it was just that with everything that had been going on, and the fact that Chola Se was naked too, Ide just kind of got used to it. But now, as she tied off the bandage and slowly straightened up, I suddenly realised how odd it must seem to her. I also realised – as her body momentarily brushed against me – that now shede made me aware of my nakedness, Ide begun to feel awkward and embarrassed about it. And as I began telling her the whole story – the mission to steal the detonators, the way Ide used the dogs to help me, and why Ide decided not to wear any clothes – I was only too glad to have something to take my mind off the confusing and unsettling feelings that were rising up inside me---feelings that I neither wanted nor understood.

By the time Ide told her everything though, up to the point when Ide entered the underground chamber, the feelings had all but gone.

So Gun Sur didnt tell you to find me and bring me back? Chola Se said when Ide finished.

No, I admitted. My orders were just to get the detonators.

He wont be expecting me to come back with you then.

Not unless he guessed what I was going to do.

Do you think he did?

I dont know. You know what hese like – its hard to tell what hese really thinking.

What about Pilgrim?

Pilgrim? What about him?

Did he know what you were doing?

He knows I went after the detonators.

Are you sure?

Yeh. He was in Gun Surs office when we were talking about it.
Why do you——?

So he definitely knew you were going to break into the Dau
camp and go after the detonators?

Yeh.

Chola Se went quiet, and I could tell from the tremor in her
breathing that something was wrong. I could sense it in everything
about her – the tension in her body, the slight tremble of her skin,
the fear and anger in the scent of her sweat---

Why are you asking me about Pilgrim? I asked quietly.

He was there.

Where?

With the Dau.

What do you mean?

He was with the Dau, in their camp.

How do you know?

Because he was the first one, the one they kept me for---

I waited for her to go on, but all I could hear was the sound of
her breathing – fast and shallow, shaking with emotion – and for
a moment or 2 I had no understanding at all. What did Pilgrim
have to do with any of this? And what did she mean by the
first one---the one they kept me for? It didnt make any sense. But
then all at once something shifted inside my head – like the sudden
lifting of a cloud – and with a terrible feeling of dread, it began to

187

dawn on me what she was saying.

What did he do to you, Chola? I said quietly. What did Pilgrim do?

He raped me. He beat me up, held a knife to my throat, and raped me.

I didnt know what to say. I just couldnt think of the right words---I didnt know if there were any right words.

Ime so sorry, I muttered. Ime just---I dont know---

They dressed me up for him, she said, her voice cold and empty. There was this woman---a big fat woman---she came down into the cell after one of the Dau tried to take me. She was all smiles and niceness at first, telling me how pretty Ide look if I brushed my hair and put on a dress---but she wasnt so nice anymore when I told her what she could do with her stinking dress. I didnt think I had anything to worry about at first. She was just a fat old woman. Even with my hands chained up, I was sure I could deal with her. But she moved so fast, Jeet---I couldnt believe it. She had me down on the ground before I knew what was happening. And she was so strong, and so incredibly heavy---I just couldnt do anything to stop her. She hit me so hard I didnt know where I was, and by the time Ide come to my senses shede forced me into that damned dress and ripped half my hair out with the hairbrush. And before she left, she told me that if I wasnt wearing the dress when my special visitor arrived – thats what she called him---my special visitor – shede come down here when hede finished with me and rip out my heart with her bare hands.

And the special visitor was Pilgrim?

Yeh.

He didnt try to hide his face or anything?

No. He wanted me to know who he was.

She didnt say anything for a few seconds, and I heard her breathing in deeply through her nose, holding it for a moment, then letting out a pained sigh.

I thought I could handle him, Jeet, she said, shaking her head at the memory. He was so drunk he could hardly stand up---I really thought I could fight him off. And I did for a while. I waited for him to come at me, and then I just threw myself at him – clawing, kicking, biting, screaming---he didnt know what had hit him. He was all over the place – stumbling around, trying to stay on his feet, trying to get away from me---and then, I dont know---I dont know if he tripped and fell over, or if I pushed him---all I remember is seeing him on the ground, lying on his back, and then I was on him---sinking my teeth into his face and tearing out a big chunk of flesh---

I sensed a brief smile from her then. But it quickly faded.

And that was it, she said emptily. He just kind of exploded then – like something inside him had suddenly erupted – and before I knew it, hede thrown me off him and was battering me to a pulp – punching me, kicking me, flinging me around the room---and then he got me down on the floor and started smashing my head into the ground---and I think I must have blacked out---

She shrugged.

And that was it---he had me.

She went quiet again, and although there were so many things I wanted to say to her, I stayed silent too. I tried to distract myself by focusing on the practical questions – why was Pilgrim there, and what was he doing with the Dau? – but my head was bursting with so many uncontrollable feelings that I could barely think at all, let alone focus on anything.

Do you know who took you and the babies that night? I asked quietly.

Babies?

The twins. Whoever abducted you took the twins as well. And they killed Aliaj and Berch.

Oh no---

Do you know who it was?

She shook her head. All I can remember is going to bed as normal, and the next thing I knew I was waking up in that horrible stinking cell. The rest of it, whatever happened inbetween---I cant remember a thing. Theres just nothing there, no memory at all, just a blank space.

They think it was Yael.

Yael? The Fighter?

Yeh. They think he must have done some kind of deal with the Dau.

Yael would never do that.

Thats what I thought. But he had a bloodstained shirt and a hood hidden away in the cellar of his house, and they found some of your necklace beads in the turret of his tower—

My beads?

Her voice had suddenly become frail and choked with emotion, and as her hand moved to her throat, feeling for the necklace that was no longer there, it was as if something had finally cracked in her, and at last she could let herself cry.

And thats what she did.

I didnt know what to do. Ide never been alone with someone in tears before – I didnt know what I was supposed to do, what Chola Se might want me to do, or even what I felt like doing. Should I hold her? Should I say something? Should I just keep quiet and wait? I didnt even know how long she might cry for---

Ide never felt so useless in my life.

In the end, she didnt cry for long – a minute or 2 at the most – and as soon as shede stopped, with an abrupt sniff and a sudden hard swallow, she immediately began talking again, only now her voice was emotionless, as dead and empty as the desert night.

Pilgrim was just the first, she said. A few hours after hede finished with me, another one came down. I think he was their Marshal. He had 2 other men with him – bodyguards, servants---I dont know. They just followed his orders. They got me ready for him, made sure I couldnt hurt him. Then they turned their backs and left him to it.

She sniffed again.

I think the next one was probably their Deputy. He didnt have any bodyguards or servants with him, but he didnt need any. Ide had it by then. I could barely even stand up, let alone put up a fight---

She hesitated, clearing her throat. Then she sniffed yet again and started rubbing her eyes.

You dont have to do this, I said. You dont have to tell me—

Yes, I do, she said, quietly but firmly. I need to get it all out. I need to tell you everything, Jeet. I need you to know what happened.

Okay.

Theres not really much more to tell anyway. After the Deputy had finished, they left me alone for the rest of the night. I didnt get any sleep. I tried to – I was so tired – but I kept thinking another one was going to come down---I just lay there all night, listening and waiting---but no one else came. The fat woman brought me some food in the morning, but I couldnt eat it. And that was it really. Nothing else happened and no one else came down until that drunk pig you killed tonight. He was the Marshals son, by the way. You ripped out the throat of the Dau Marshals son.

Ile do the same to his father if—

What was that? she whispered suddenly.

Ide heard it too, a faint sound in the distance. We both kept quiet and listened. I couldnt make out what it was at first, but as it drew closer — moving in from the west — it gradually became clearer — bootsteps, dull rattles and metallic clinks---

The Dau Fighters were coming back.

It seemed to take them a long time to get here, and when they finally arrived — heading towards us along the gully — it was clear they were struggling to keep going. They sounded exhausted — walking slowly, dragging their feet, barely saying a word — and as I pictured them trudging along, I felt a growing sense of cautious relief. They sounded like men whode been led on a long and ultimately futile chase, and while I couldnt be certain that my mother and the pack had all escaped unharmed, the despondency of the Dau Fighters was a good sign that they had.

The Fighters were very close now.

We held our breath as they approached the trunk — clomping, clanking, grunting, shuffling — and then, for a few long moments, they came alongside us, close enough for us to smell them---and then, at last, they passed us by, their heavy bootsteps slogging away into the distance.

We waited.

The minutes passed, the bootsteps faded.

Silence.

They were gone.

We were safe again.

Safe and together.

Together---

I still dont know how I feel about what happened next – whether it was right or wrong---whether Chola Se was so broken that she didnt know what she was doing---whether I should, or even could, have refused to go along with it---

I dont know.

All I know is, however I feel about it, it happened.

And nothing can change that now.

It began shortly after the Dau had come and gone. Wede decided to wait a while before leaving the trunk and heading back to town – just to make doubly sure it was safe – and while we were waiting, Chola Se had asked me how my leg was feeling.

Its fine, Ide told her.

Good, shede said. Ide better take a look at it before we get going though, just in case its started bleeding again.

As she lowered herself down, her hair brushed against my nakedness, and within a few moments I realised that Ide become physically aroused. I was ashamed of myself. Not just because of the awkwardness and embarrassment – I could have lived with that – but because it felt so wrong. It was ugly, insensitive, sickeningly inappropriate---everything about it was wrong. But as I stood there in the darkness, with Chola Ses hands gently feeling my leg, there was nothing I could do about it. No matter how much I tried, I couldnt make it go away.

The bandage feels okay, Chola Se said. Nice and dry. Theres no sign of any fresh bleeding. I dont think youre going to die after all.

As she started straightening up, I pushed myself as far back against the trunk as I could, trying desperately to keep myself away from her, but I didnt succeed. I dont know if she stumbled a bit as she stood, or if she just happened to lean against me, but however it happened, our bodies came together, and she couldnt fail to notice the state I was in.

Oh, she said, moving back.

Ime so sorry, I muttered, turning sideways and twisting away from her. I didnt mean to---I mean, I dont want---it just happened. I know its unforgiveable, but please—

Its all right, Jeet, she said softly. Its all right.

I felt her hands on my hips then, and a moment later I felt her gently pulling me round towards her.

Listen, Jeet, she said quietly, moving closer to me. Ive killed my feelings. You understand that, dont you? Weve both had to do it ever since we were taken back from the dogs – kill all our memories and feelings, bury them deep inside us, forget them. We have to do it every day, every hour, every minute. And thats what Ive done with the things those men did to me. Ive killed the Chola Se they did them to---killed her and buried her. Shese gone, dead. And now Ive become a new emptiness.

She moved even closer, putting her mouth to my ear.

You were going to kill me, werent you? Back at the camp, facing the 3 Dau Fighters---you were going to keep your promise and not let them take me alive.

194

I didnt answer. I couldnt speak.

Well, now Ime asking you to kill something else, she breathed. I want you to kill what Pilgrim and the others put inside me.

I dont understand, I managed to mumble.

They put their sexblood in me. They might have given me a child---and I cant let that be. I cant carry a child of theirs. But your blood is stronger than theirs, Jeet---strong enough to kill it.

No, Chola, I dont think—

I want you to kill the bad blood in me, Jeet. Youre special—

Ime not—

You are. Youre strong. You have a destiny. I want you to do this for me.

She held me then, she made us one, and we moved together in the whispered breath of the cold night air.

It was still dark when we left the tree trunk.

Although we didnt know exactly where we were – and we couldnt see any landmarks to guide us – we knew the Black Mountains were over to our right, so all we had to do was keep heading west and eventually the town would come into view somewhere to the south of us. I knew the Dau would be looking out for us from their camp, but I wasnt overly worried. We were too far away for them to get a good shot at us – especially in the dark – and I doubted if theyd risk sending any Fighters after us because the sun would be up soon, and by the time they reached us theyd probably be in shooting range of our Fighters. There was no point in taking any chances though, so we kept out of sight as much as possible, and every now and then we stopped for a while and stood perfectly still, listening out to make sure we werent being followed.

It wasnt long before the first light of dawn began reddening the eastern sky, and a few minutes later, as the burning edge of the morning sun crept up over the horizon, we crested a low ridge and saw the welcoming sight of town. It was just over to our left, no more than a quarter of a mile away.

We looked at each other and smiled.

Wede made it.

We were cold and tired, weak, hungry, exhausted. My leg was throbbing, the stab wound bleeding freely again, and Chola Se was battered and bruised from head to toe and had been through a living hell---

But wede survived.

We were still alive.

Wede made it.

We couldnt relax yet though, and as we set off towards town – heading towards the far end of the woodland – we talked again about our plan for dealing with Pilgrim. Wede already discussed it at some length while we were walking in the foothills, and wede come to the conclusion that the only option we had was to tell Gun Sur. If Pilgrim was a traitor – and we couldnt think of any other reason why hede be with the Dau, or why hede do what he did to Chola Se – then Gun Sur had to know, and he had to know as soon as possible. The problem was going to be how to make him believe us. Pilgrim would obviously deny everything, and ultimately it was going to be his word against ours – the word of Gun Surs loyal Deputy against the word of 2 dogchilds – so it wasnt going to be easy. But wede come up with a few ideas, and we were fairly sure that once Gun Sur had listened to our side of the story, hede know we were telling the truth.

The sun had risen by the time we entered the woodland, and it didnt take me long to find the slab of rock near the edge of the cliff where Ide left the thick heavy coat. I helped Chola Se put it on – to keep her warm and cover her nakedness – then I jumped up onto the rock, threw back my head and cupped my hands to my mouth and let out a howl. I was calling out to my mother again, letting her know that wede made it back, and that we were both okay, while simultaneously asking her if she and the others were safe. I didnt have to wait long for a reply. It came almost immediately, and from surprisingly closeby. She couldnt have been more than a few miles away, and I realised she must have been keeping an eye on us. Her answering call was partly a simple acknowledgement – letting me know that shede heard me, and that she and the others were all safe and well – but at the same time it was both a personal and public affirmation of our relationship – telling me and the rest of the world that she would always be my mother and I would always be her son. And as the echo of her cry faded away, I heard the rest of the pack calling out – all 8 of them – singing out to me in ragged unison, letting me know that I was one of them now. It was a sound that filled me with a deep sense of belonging---and a deep sense of sadness too.

I was leaving them, leaving their world---a world that could be mine.

Tomas was waiting for us when we approached the tunnel entrance – the same young Fighter whode been there when Ide left – and the tunnel was already open, so I guessed the watchtower guards had seen us coming and passed on the news. It was clear from the look on his face that Tomas realised we were both in poor shape, and as he came running over to help us, he was already taking off his coat to give to me.

Thanks, I said, putting it on.

Although he was obviously surprised to see Chola Se with me – he couldnt help glancing at her every few seconds – he didnt say anything or ask any questions, he just led us over to the tunnel and flashed a quick signal to the guard in the West End Tower.

The other ends open, he said to me. Theyre already waiting for you.

They? I said.

Captain Kite, the Marshal, and Deputy Pilgrim.

Pilgrims there?

Yeh.

I looked at Chola Se. Her face was blank.

Ile go first, I told her. You stay close behind me, okay?

She just nodded.

I lowered myself into the tunnel, crawled forward a few yards, then stopped and waited for Chola Se.

Hese been through here, I heard her say from behind me.

What?

Pilgrim. I can smell his scent in here.

She was right. I recognised it now. It was the smell Ide noticed before when Ide come out through the tunnel, the scent Ide thought was familiar but couldnt put a name to. It was definitely Pilgrims.

Listen, Chola, I said. When we come out of the tunnel, dont say anything to Gun Sur about Pilgrim, okay? Its better if we wait until we can talk to him on his own.

But whats Pilgrim going to do when he sees me? she replied. He wont be expecting me—

Yeh, he will. The guards in the watchtower will have told him youre with me. Thats probably why hese come to meet us. He wants to be there in case you tell Gun Sur about him.

Whats he going to do if I dont?

I dont think hele do anything. Hese not going to bring it up if you dont. Just keep quiet for now, okay? Wele work out what to do about it later on.

All right.

She sounded calm and composed, but as we crawled on through the tunnel I couldnt help worrying how she was going to react when she saw Pilgrim. It was asking a lot for her to keep quiet when she came face to face with the man whode done such terrible things to her, and although she claimed to have killed her feelings, I was fairly sure that just wasnt possible. Hide them, yes. Bury them, fine. But kill them?

There are some things you just cant kill.

I still wanted to believe in Chola Se though. I wanted to think shede be okay.

She can deal with Pilgrim, I told myself. Shese strong. Shele deal with it.

But I was wrong.

For the first few seconds after wede stepped out of the tunnel, I thought everything was going to be okay. Gun Sur and Pilgrim were waiting for us directly outside the tunnel exit – standing side

199

by side – and Captain Kite was just off to the left of Pilgrim. The Deputys face was heavily bandaged, and even with the bandage I could see that Chola Se hadnt been exaggerating when shede told me shede bitten a big chunk of flesh from his face. It was obviously a serious wound – his whole cheek was swollen out of shape, the skin reddened and badly bruised – and he must have been in a lot of pain, but you wouldnt have known it. His eyes showed nothing at all – no pain, no fear, no surprise, no concern. He didnt even look at Chola Se at first, he just stood there staring dead-eyed at me, his face completely unreadable. I could sense the tension in Chola Se as she stood beside me, but she seemed to be keeping herself under control, and I was beginning to think that maybe she was going to get through this after all. It was only when Pilgrim turned his eyes on her, and a mocking smile flickered briefly across his face – too quick for anyone else to see – that I realised I was hoping for the impossible. I heard the quiet snarl in her throat, and a moment later I felt the tension inside her suddenly explode, and before I could do anything to stop her shede launched herself at Pilgrim – her teeth bared in silent rage as she lunged wild-eyed for his throat. She moved so fast that I was sure there was nothing Pilgrim could do to stop her. But as fast as she was, he was even faster. His hands were a blur as he reached for his guns, and by the time Chola Se was within a few feet of him, hede drawn both his Colts and had them levelled at her head in his outstretched arms. I didnt doubt for a moment that hede use them, and even in her murderous fury Chola Se could see the killing look in his eyes, but she only just managed to stop herself in time, stumbling to a halt just as her head came face to face with the pistols. For a couple of seconds the 2 of them just stood there, frozen like statues, staring into each others eyes.

Then Gun Sur spoke – what the hells going on? – breaking the spell, and Chola Se slowly began backing away.

Its not what she thinks, Pilgrim told Gun Sur, keeping his guns on her.

Whats that supposed to mean?

Its complicated, Pilgrim said, still watching Chola Se. We need to talk.

Gun Sur glanced at Chola Se, then looked at me. Do you know what this is about?

I nodded.

So tell me.

The Deputys right, I said. Its complicated---I think it might be best to leave it for now.

Gun Sur was clearly incensed, but one of the reasons hese been our Marshal for so long is that hese good at making decisions under difficult circumstances, and as I watched him standing there, quietly shaking his head in dismay and disbelief, I could tell he was already thinking ahead.

Did you get the detonators? he asked me.

I took the canvas bag from my shoulder, removed my knife – which Ide put in there when we left the tree trunk – and passed the bag to Gun Sur. He opened it up, looked inside, nodded, then closed it again.

Any trouble? he said.

A bit.

All right, you can tell me about it later. He glanced at Chola Se, taking in her battered condition. Right now you both need to get yourselves fixed up. Go and see Doctor Shiva, and when hese done what he can for you, I want you both to go home, clean yourselves up, get something to eat, and get some rest. Wele meet in my office tomorrow morning, and then youle tell me everything that happened. And I mean everything. Understand?

We both nodded.

He looked at Chola Se again. Its good to have you back.

Thanks, she muttered, her head bowed down.

Its sometime in the early hours of the morning now.

Weare staying the night at Starrys house. We both desperately needed to get some sleep, and if wede gone back to my house or Chola Ses we would have had to take it in turns to stay awake just in case Pilgrim decided to try anything, and I wasnt sure we could manage that. So after wede seen Doctor Shiva we came straight here and explained the situation to Starry, and he was more than happy to give us his bed and act as our guardian for the night.

Shiva did his best for us — stitching and bandaging my stab wound, fixing up the worst of Chola Ses multiple injuries — but there was little he could do for her innermost wounds. He knew what had been done to her, and he examined her thoroughly to make sure she hadnt suffered any physical damage, but he didnt question her about it too much.

I dont think you have any internal injuries, he told her, but if you feel any sudden pain or you start bleeding a lot, come back and see me immediately, okay?

Shede just nodded.

She was so utterly exhausted when we got to Starrys house that she went straight to bed as soon as we arrived. I was bone-tired too, but after cleaning myself up a bit and having something to eat, I didnt feel quite so bad. And I knew I wouldnt sleep until Ide cleared my head anyway. So while Chola Se slept, I sat down with Starry in his big old clutter-filled living room and told him the whole story.

I told him everything, from the moment Gun Sur had called me into his office to the moment Chola Se had attacked Pilgrim at the tunnel. The only part I left out was the togetherness Ide shared with Chola Se in the hollowed-out trunk. It wasnt that I was embarrassed about it or didnt want Starry to know, I just didnt think it was right to tell him without Chola Ses knowledge. Or maybe there was more to it than that---maybe part of the reason I didnt tell him was that Ime still trying to work out how I feel about it myself---

I dont know.

Apart from that though, I told Starry everything I could remember in as much detail as possible.

He listened carefully, only interrupting very occasionally when he wanted me to clarify or explain something, and when Ide finally finished he just sat there in silence for a full 5 minutes – staring blindly out of the window, thinking things through, trying to piece it all together.

Pilgrim must have taken her himself, he said eventually.

You think he took Chola Se?

Starry nodded. She told you she couldnt remember anything about her abduction, didnt she?

Yeh, she said there was just nothing there, no memory at all, just a blank space.

And didnt Yael say something very similar?

I thought back to what Pilgrim had told me about Yael, trying to remember his exact words.

Yael claimed that he went on duty as usual, I said to Starry, and that at some point during the night he woke up and realised that he must have fallen asleep, but that he couldnt remember anything about it. He said it was as if there was a big black hole where his memory should be.

Starry just looked at me. He didnt need to say anything. Blank space, black hole? The similarity was too close to be a coincidence.

What do you think it means? I asked him.

Pilgrim must have given them both something, some kind of potion that knocked them out and wiped their memories. He probably got it from the Dau.

Have they got potions like that?

Theyve got potions and poisons you wouldnt believe.

I remembered the things Ide seen in the red-roofed building at the Dau encampment – the scaly black roots, the jars and bottles filled with strange-looking concoctions---powders, liquids, dead insects and grubs, leaves, moss, tiny white bones---

Pilgrim planted all the evidence too, Starry said. The bloodstained clothing in Yaels cellar, the beads, the footprints---

But why? I said. Thats what I dont get. Why go to all that bother if all he wanted was Chola Se? And why did he have to kill Aliaj and Berch and take the babies as well as taking Chola Se?

He wasnt just after Chola Se, Jeet, Ime sure of that. Ime afraid shese just a pawn in their game.

What game?

The game Pilgrims playing with the Dau – the traitors game. He gave them Chola Se and the babies to prove his worth.

But they gave her back to him---they saved her for him.

Thats how the game works. You give something to the enemy, you get something back in return. In this case it just happened to be the same thing.

It was sickening to have to think about Chola Se in this way – as a thing, a token, a gift---something to be used, something to be traded, something to do whatever you wanted with---

I knew thats how it was, and always had been, and probably always would be---and up until then Ide never really given it much thought. Ide always just accepted it as a reality – neither good nor bad, just the way things were. But things were different now. I was different. The way things were wasnt the same anymore.

Is Yael still under arrest? I asked Starry.

Hese dead.

What?

He was found dead in his cell last night. Hanged himself--- couldnt live with what hede done. At least, thats how its supposed to look. Pilgrim must have decided it was too risky to let him live, and by making his death look like suicide he made Yael seem even more guilty.

A sound came from upstairs then – the muffled murmur of quiet sobbing. There was nothing hysterical or uncontrollable about it, and it didnt last very long – fading back into silence after just a few minutes – but somehow that made it seem worse.

Hows she been since you got her back? Starry asked me.

Ime not sure, I admitted. She told me shede dealt with it by killing the Chola Se it had happened to and becoming a new self---a new emptiness was how she put it. But when she saw Pilgrim waiting for us at the tunnel, and he gave her a nasty little grin, she just went for him. She would have killed him if he hadnt been so quick with his guns.

Starry nodded thoughtfully. And what about you, Jeet? How are you managing?

Managing what?

Well, you went through a lot at the Dau encampment, didnt you? You had to kill people---I mean, I know weare all trained to fight and kill the Dau, but training for it isnt the same as doing it.

I spent 5 years killing to survive, I reminded him. Its nothing new to me.

So it doesnt affect you at all? It doesnt make you feel anything?

I shrugged. Does a starving dog feel anything when it hunts down and kills a deer?

Thats different—

No, its not.

A dog doesnt know any better.

Nothing knows any better. We all just do what has to be done. What do you think would have happened if Ide thought better of killing the guard at the hatchway or the drunk man who was about to rape Chola Se? What do you think would have happened if Ide given any thought to their lives and tried to incapacitate them rather than kill them?

Starry said nothing.

I wouldnt be here, I said. Thats what would have happened. I wouldnt be here, and neither would Chola Se. And we wouldnt know that Pilgrims a traitor either, which might just mean that we dont lose the battle thats coming---the battle that could mean the end of us all.

I stared hard at Starry.

So, no, I told him. I dont feel anything about the killing I had to do. I had to do it. Just like the starving dog has to kill the deer. Its how it is – kill or be killed. Feelings dont come into it.

I cant write anymore now. I need to get at least a few hours sleep before we meet with Gun Sur at the Quarterhouse.

Ime sharing Starrys bed with Chola Se.

I wasnt sure how Ide feel about it at first – Ive never shared a bed with another human before, and Ive only really known Chola Se for less than a day – but as I sit here in the candlelit darkness, scribbling quietly in my writing book while Chola Se sleeps fitfully beside me, it feels perfectly natural – as if this is how its always been – and its hard to imagine there was ever anything else.

Wede assumed that Gun Sur would be talking to us in private when we met him the following morning, so when we entered his office and saw that Pilgrim was there, it stopped us both in our tracks for a moment, especially Chola Se. They were talking to each other as we opened the door – Gun Sur sitting at the oak table, Pilgrim in a chair just off to one side – and as soon as Chola Se laid eyes on the Deputy, it was as if shede been turned to ice. She stopped dead, frozen to the spot---her body rigid, muscles tensed, her face suddenly drained of colour. I thought for a second that she was either going to attack Pilgrim again or simply turn round and leave, but when the Marshal got to his feet and gestured for us to join him at the table, she just gave me a quick look – telling me she was okay – and we carried on into the room.

Pilgrim didnt stand up to welcome us. He just sat there, looking completely at ease – leaning back in the chair, his legs crossed, his submachine gun resting in his lap – idly watching us as we came over and sat down in the 2 empty chairs waiting for us at the table. I glanced at him as I sat down. He nodded at me, barely moving his head, but made no attempt to acknowledge Chola Se. She didnt look at Pilgrim or Gun Sur as she sat down in the chair beside me, but instead kept her eyes fixed firmly on the floor.

It wasnt just Pilgrims presence that was making her uncomfortable. This was a totally new experience for her, just as it had been for me when Ide been called into the Marshals office for the first time. We werent used to formal settings, they made us feel out of place, and as she sat there beside me I could feel the tension bristling inside her.

She was desperate to run.

But she was equally desperate to stand her ground.

First of all, Gun Sur began, speaking directly to Chola Se, I want to say how sorry I am for the traumatic experience youve been through. I cant imagine what it must have been like, and I give you my word that the Dau will suffer for what they did to you.

And what about him? Chola Se said quietly, forcing herself to look up and glance briefly at Pilgrim. She turned to Gun Sur. Is he going to suffer for what he did to me too? Or hasnt he told you about that?

Deputy Pilgrim has told me everything, Gun Sur said. And I understand how you must feel about it. But theres a reason why he did what he did—

He did it because he wanted to, Chola Se interrupted, her voice hard but steady. Thats why he raped me — because he wanted to. And because hese a traitor, and because the Dau—

Ime not a traitor, Pilgrim said calmly.

No? she snapped. And I suppose you didnt rape me either?

I had to.

You had to?

I had no choice.

Chola Se was genuinely dumbstruck, so stupefied that all she could do was sit there staring at him, her mouth half open, utterly lost for words.

Weve been working on infiltrating the Dau for years, Gun Sur said, leaning forward and lowering his voice. Theyve always been superior to us in just about every aspect — numbers, equipment, location, health, food and water supplies — and we realised a long time ago that unless we found an alternative way of fighting them, it was only going to be a matter of time before they destroyed us. And in the end we came to the conclusion that the only way to beat them was by fighting them from within, and the only way to do that was by infiltrating their ranks at the highest possible level. We had to make them believe that one of us was a traitor, willing to betray our people and work for them instead. We werent sure how we could use this to our advantage if it worked, at least not at first, but the more we thought about it, the more we realised that it was our only viable option.

Gun Sur looked briefly at Pilgrim, then turned back to us.

It was a very long process. It took almost 6 months from the first tentative contact before the Dau agreed in principle to meet with Deputy Pilgrim, and another 4 or 5 months after that until the meeting actually took place. And even then he was blindfolded the whole time he was in their encampment. But that was nothing compared to what happened on his second visit, just a month or so later. As soon as he arrived at their camp, he was beaten unconscious and thrown in a cell, and they kept him there for the next 2 weeks, torturing him to within an inch of his life until they were finally convinced he was telling the truth.

And what was his truth supposed to be? I asked.

Deputy? Gun Sur said, glancing at Pilgrim again, this time inviting him to answer my question.

Pilgrim took his time – slowly uncrossing his legs, sitting up straight, carefully adjusting his MP40 in his lap – and once he was sure that he had everyones attention, he finally began to speak.

The story we came up with, he said, was that Ide had enough of serving as Gun Surs Deputy and that I wanted, and believed it was my right, to take over the leadership of our people. I was a bitter man. Ide always been loyal to the Marshal, even when he didnt deserve it, but my loyalty had never been recognised. I believed I was a better man than him – younger, wiser, stronger – and Ide grown to hate him for holding me back. Ide had enough of it all – it was time for Gun Sur to go, and I wanted the Dau to help me get rid of him. And in return, once I was Marshal, wede strike a deal that benefitted us both.

Pilgrim looked me in the eye.

That was my truth, he said, with absolute confidence. And I stuck to it.

And they believed you?

They almost killed me every day for 2 weeks, and I never changed a single word of my story. In the end they couldnt fail to believe me.

So youre saying that youve infiltrated the Dau, and they think youre working for them, but youre actually still true to us?

Pilgrim nodded. I tell them whatever they want to know about us – our supplies situation, our guard duties, patrol times, the health of our people, our battle plans. Most of its accurate enough to make it both believable and provable, but none of its significant enough to seriously put us at risk. And they dont have the faintest idea of what weare actually planning.

And at the same time, Gun Sur added, every time the Deputy visits their camp, we learn more about them – their capabilities, the way they think, the way theyre likely to behave---

I dont go there too often though, Pilgrim explained. We need to keep up the pretence of my betrayal, and if I really was a traitor, Ide want to keep our meetings to an absolute minimum. So most of the time we communicate using coded light signals—

But you were there the other night, Chola Se said.

There was a moments silence then. Pilgrims expression didnt change, but I could sense his annoyance at Chola Ses interruption.

There was a big celebration, he said calmly, looking her in the eye for the first time. I was invited. In fact, I was the guest of honour. He shrugged. So I went---I had to, to preserve my cover. And I joined in with the celebrations too, for the same reason. At some point during the night, Hensch came up to me – hese the Dau Marshal – and told me they had a special gift for me, a reward for my services—

211

And that was me, wasnt it? Chola Se said coldly. I was your special gift.

I had to go along with it, Pilgrim told her. I had to behave like the man I claimed to be – the man they believed me to be – and that man would never have turned you down. If I hadnt accepted their offer, my cover would have been blown. I had to do what was expected of me.

No, Chola Se said firmly, shaking her head. No, you didnt. You could have just pretended to go along with it. You could have come down into the cell, told me the truth, waited a while, then gone back to them as if youd gone through with it—

And what if Ide been found out? What if Ide been sitting down there in the cell with you, just pretending to go along with it, and Hensch had sent one of his Fighters to check up on me?

Why would he do that? If he trusts you as much as you say—

Hensch doesnt trust anyone. Hese so wary of everyone and everything that his caution verges on paranoia. But it works. It keeps him in power, and it keeps him alive. So it was entirely possible that hede ordered someone to follow me to your cell to make absolutely sure that I did what I was expected to do. And I had no way of knowing if I was being watched or not. I dont know if you noticed it, but theres a spyhole in the roof of the cell, so anyone can look in from outside without being seen.

He leaned forward in his chair, his eyes fixed on Chola Ses.

I had to assume I was being watched. I had to do what I did to you. If I hadnt done it, and Ide been caught out---

He paused, glancing at Gun Sur for support.

The Marshal looked uncomfortable now. He seemed hesitant, unsure what to say, and I wondered if he simply felt awkward because of the subject matter, or if there was something more to it. We were all watching him now, waiting for him to say something, and for a few moments he just sat there – his eyes lowered, staring at the table, seemingly unable to make up his mind – then he took a breath, raised his head, and looked across the table at Chola Se.

I cant take your pain away, he said to her, getting to his feet. But I can show you something that might help you understand it.

The storehouse that Gun Sur took us to is on the edge of the Eastside ruins. Its a large stone building with heavy double doors and solid metal shutters on the windows, and unlike most of the buildings in Eastside its in reasonably good condition. Its a secure facility – authorised access only – and as Gun Sur led us across the yard at the front of the building – with Pilgrim walking alongside him – I couldnt help feeling a tingle of expectation. Every time Ide ever passed the storehouse Ide wondered what secrets it could be hiding – Ide asked Starry once and even he didnt know – and now it seemed I was about to find out.

As we approached the building, Gun Sur nodded at the Fighter guarding the doors, and as she began opening them – after calling out to someone inside – Gun Sur stopped and turned to us.

Before we go inside, he said, you both need to understand that what youre about to see is of the highest confidentiality. You cannot – and you will not – share this experience with anyone else. He paused, staring hard at me. And that includes Starry. Understood?

Yes, I said.

He looked at Chola Se.

She nodded.

He carried on looking at her.

Yes, she told him. Understood.

We heard the heavy groan of the doors opening then, and a moment later we were following Gun Sur and Pilgrim into the storehouse.

The interior of the building was just a vast open work area – no separate rooms, no hallways or corridors, just wall-to-wall open space – and because all the shutters were closed, the whole place was illuminated with dozens of burning torches. The walls were lined with workbenches and tables, and everywhere I looked there were piles of scrap – metal sheets, wooden boards, rods and axles and chains – and all kinds of mechanical equipment. There were 5 or 6 Fighters working away at the benches and tables – hammering, sawing, cutting, drilling – and over to our left, Captain Luca and another 2 Fighters were pounding away with sledgehammers at what looked like the remains of a steel cabinet, trying to hammer it flat.

In the midst of all this activity though – standing alone in the centre of the room – was the one thing it was impossible to take your eyes off.

It was some kind of vehicle, I was fairly sure of that, but it was unlike any wagon or cart Ide ever seen. In fact, the only feature I recognised – and the only reason I guessed it was a vehicle – was its wheels. There were 8 of them – 4 on either side – 8 solid wooden cartwheels with metal rims, each of them almost as tall as me. The vehicle itself was essentially a massive rectangular box, a bit like an elongated covered wagon. It was at least 40 feet long, and maybe 10 feet wide and 12 tall. The 4 wheels at the front were closer together than the 4 at the rear, and there was an enclosed compartment at the front which I assumed was the drivers position. I could just about make out 2 seats and a control wheel of some kind, but it was hard to see clearly because, just like the rest of the vehicle, it was almost entirely encased in a patchwork covering of scrap metal – old steel doors, tin panels, sheets of corrugated iron---all cobbled together and fixed to the body of the vehicle with a mixture of screws and plates and tightly bound cables and wires.

As I stood there staring at this gigantic contraption, one of the Fighters came over to it carrying a large metal plate with holes drilled round the edges. He held up the plate against a gap in the patchwork – checking it fitted – then he took out a screwdriver and began fixing the plate into place.

I realised then that whatever this monstrous thing had once been, it was now being turned into an armoured vehicle.

Its an ancient motorised wagon called a truck, Gun Sur explained. We discovered it when we first arrived here. Most of us had never seen one before, and we only found out what it was from the Olders. According to Soyaan, there used to be millions of them.

What happened to them all? I asked.

No one seems to know, but they were powered by oil-based fuel, and its possible that at some point in the past the reserves of oil ran out, making the vehicles redundant as a means of travel. So over the years, most of them may well have been stripped down and their parts used for other purposes---but for some reason this one was left mostly intact.

Does it still work?

Wele come to that later. This is just---well, this is just a small part of what I wanted to show you, and it will make more sense when youve seen the rest. Its this way---

As he set off towards the far end of the building, and Pilgrim went with him, I waited a moment then turned to Chola Se.

Are you okay? I asked her.

I dont know, Jeet. I dont understand whats going on---

We can go if you want.

I dont know what I want. I just---I dont know. I suppose we might as well see what he wants to show us.

Are you sure?

No. She shrugged. But weve come this far---

As we followed Gun Sur and Pilgrim across to the far end of the building, I couldnt work out where they were taking us. There was nothing obvious where they were heading – no doors, no windows, just an empty space at the end of the storehouse. But then, as they slowed down and stopped a short distance from the far wall, I noticed 2 lengths of heavy chain stretched out on the ground at their feet. The chains were about 10 feet apart, and as we got closer to them I could see that they were attached to a large slab of metal lying flat on the ground, and I suddenly realised it was some kind of hatch. It was a lot bigger than the one at the Dau camp, and it didnt look very much like it, but it was still a hatch--- an opening to the underground.

I looked at Chola Se.

Her face was blank, her eyes cold and empty.

Are you all right? I asked her quietly.

She just nodded.

Gun Sur and Pilgrim had taken hold of the chains now, and as they began walking back, pulling the chains as they went, I watched the metal hatch slide open. It was obviously very heavy, and it sounded as if it was rolling back on some kind of wheeled mechanism that allowed it to slide back beneath the floor. And as it rolled back it revealed what lay below it – a ramp, cut into solid rock, sloping down into a torchlit tunnel 20 feet below.

We discovered this when we first arrived here too, Gun Sur told us.

Where does it lead to? I asked.

Youle see when we get there.

He turned to Chola Se then and was about to say something to her when he saw the piercing coldness in her eyes. He blinked – momentarily taken aback – and from the corner of my eye I saw a flicker of amusement in Pilgrims face. It was gone in an instant, and Gun Sur was totally unaware of it. But I wasnt. And neither was Chola Se.

Wede both seen Pilgrims truth.

The slope down to the tunnel was quite steep, but from the way Gun Sur and Pilgrim walked down it – with the thoughtless ease of familiarity – it was obvious theyd been down here many times before. I looked at Chola Se again, checking to see if she still wanted to carry on. She didnt say anything, just nodded, and we followed Gun Sur and Pilgrim down the ramp and into the tunnel.

It was nothing like the old animal burrow beneath the wall. It was much larger for one thing – easily big enough to walk through without stooping – and while the tunnel under the wall was dug out of packed earth, this one was carved out of solid rock. It wasnt pitchblack either – there were torches on the walls every 30 feet or so – and in the light of the flames it wasnt hard to tell that the tunnel had been constructed a long time ago. The massive wooden support beams were so blackened with age that they were almost indistinguishable from the surrounding rock, and as we passed along the tunnel, I kept seeing primitive drawings and ancient graffiti etched into the walls, the writing of a kind Ide never seen before.

Apart from an almost imperceptible humming sound, which I guessed came from a ventilation system – the air was noticeably cool and fresh – the tunnel had an overwhelming sense of silence to it. It was the kind of silence that seems to quieten everything else – including the air – and as the 4 of us made our way through the hollowed-out rock, we barely made a sound.

The tunnel seemed to go on forever, and as we carried on through it – with the silence continuing – I found myself gazing around, studying everything I could see, trying to work out how the tunnel had been made. It appeared at first sight to have been carved out of the rock all around us, but the more I thought about it, the more unbelievable it seemed. Everything was pure black solid rock – the walls, the roof, the ground – and I simply couldnt understand how the rock could have been excavated to create a tunnel of this size. It didnt look as if it had been dug out by hand – there were no pickaxe or sledgehammer markings, no telltale signs of digging or carving – and the overall size and shape of the tunnel was far too uniform for it to have been blasted out with explosive.

It didnt make sense.

Then I began to notice that every now and then the solid blackness of the rock was broken up with patches of a slightly paler colour – a dark brownish grey – and as I passed one of these patches and ran my finger over it, I realised that it was soft enough for my finger to leave a line on the surface. And when I examined the

218

residue left on my fingertip, rubbing at it with my thumb, it didnt feel like powdered rock. It wasnt actually soft, but it wasnt rockhard either. It had a grainy kind of hardness to it, a hardness that I could imagine digging through.

An idea began forming in my mind – a possible answer as to how the tunnel had been constructed – but just as I started rubbing at the residue on my fingertips again, Chola Se suddenly appeared at my side.

What is it? she whispered, looking down at my hand. Have you found something?

No, I said, wiping my fingers on my shirt. No, its nothing.

And it was nothing, I realised.

Whatever it was, whatever my idea had been, it was of no relevance whatsoever. It meant nothing. It was nothing. It was human thinking – a complete waste of time. I should have been thinking, or nonthinking, like a dog.

Ime in a tunnel. Where does it go?

Any other thoughts were meaningless.

It was hard to keep track of distance in the underground silence, but by the time we began nearing the end of the tunnel, I guessed wede probably travelled about 250 yards, maybe a bit further. Gun Sur and Pilgrim had stopped up ahead of us and were waiting by an opening at the end of the tunnel that led into some kind of large open space. I couldnt tell what it was, but the closer we got to it – and the more I could see of it – the more I realised how huge it was. When we finally reached Gun Sur and Pilgrim, and they stepped aside to let us see through the opening, we were both so amazed that we couldnt help letting out quiet gasps of astonishment. It was a massive chamber, an enormous cavern –

roughly cube-shaped – that must have been at least 150 feet across. The roof of solid rock towered so high above us that we had to angle our heads back to look up at it. It was easily 100 feet high.

Burning torches lit up the cavern with a bright orange glow, and in the light of the flames I could make out dozens of little caves and ledges cut into the rock walls – from ground level up to about head height – and every one of them was crammed full of tools and equipment – drills, sledgehammers, pickaxes, spades---metal drums and canisters, coils of rope, countless spools of cable---

One of the caves, just over to our right, was larger than all the rest, and it was piled high with large wooden crates. Ide seen the remains of similar crates before – splintered fragments half buried in the rubble of the Eastside ruins – and Ide also seen the ruined remains of what the crates had once contained. If these were the same, and their contents werent spoiled---

Do those crates contain what I think they do? I asked Gun Sur.

My voice echoed eerily around the cavern.

What do you think they contain? Gun Sur replied.

Explosive.

That would be something, wouldnt it? he said. Especially if the explosive was still viable.

Is it?

Come and have a look.

We followed him over to the cave, then stood back and watched as he picked up a crowbar from a ledge and prised open the top of one of the crates. I knew I was right about the explosives now, but when Gun Sur stepped aside to let me see, and I went over and looked inside the crate, it was still hard to believe my eyes. The wooden box was filled to the brim with bright orange rectangular bars, each one about 5 inches by 3 inches. Foreign lettering was printed in black on the front of each bar.

ТРОТИЛОВАЯ
Шашка
Вес 200гм

Ide seen the lettering before – on the crumbled remains of similar bars scavenged from the ruins. I didnt know what the words actually said, but I knew what they meant. They meant that the orange bars were TNT, a powerful high explosive.

Is this where the old TNT in the ruins comes from? I asked Gun Sur.

He nodded. We think this must have been the main stockpile. The crates were here when we discovered the cavern, piled up in this cave exactly as they are now. We knew what was in them, of course, but although the crates themselves seemed to be in mint condition – unopened and undamaged – we didnt think there was much chance of the TNT still being viable.

Why not?

Because it was ancient, like everything else down here, and TNT degrades with age. Thats why every scrap of TNT weve ever dug out of the ruins has been useless.

He shrugged, gazing thoughtfully at the pile of crates.

We just assumed that all this would be useless too. But it turned out we were wrong.

He reached into the crate and took out a bar.

As far as we can tell, every one of these is in perfect condition – no degradation at all. Its probably something to do with the atmosphere down here. The airs very dry, and it never gets too hot or cold---it seems to prevent things from decaying.

He turned and gazed around at the cavern.

Everything stored down here is still useable, he continued. Weve got gunpowder, fuses, blasting caps, cable---the only thing we found that didnt work properly was the faulty detonator---

He turned round and looked at me.

But thanks to you, thats no longer a problem.

How many crates are there? I asked him.

116, with 150 bars in each crate – enough to blow up a small mountain.

I gazed around at the vastness of the underground chamber, wondering if thats how it had been made – blown out of the solid rock by huge amounts of TNT – but in the same way that the tunnel hadnt looked as if it had been blasted out with explosive, neither did the cavern. But it didnt look natural either. I thought about asking Gun Sur if he knew anything about it – whether or not the cavern was manmade, and if so whode made it, and how, and why, and when---but then my thinking suddenly switched again – from human back to dog – and, just like before, I realised that the history of the cavern was irrelevant. It didnt matter how it had been made, or whode made it, or how, or why, or when---

It was a cavern. It was here.

And thats all there was to it.

What are those holes for? I asked Gun Sur, pointing up at the roof.

I couldnt see the actual holes, but I could see the tiny rays of daylight streaming in through the rock that told me the holes were there. At first I could only see 3 or 4 of them, but as I carried on looking I realised there were dozens of them spread out all over the roof.

The rock up there is only about 6 inches thick, Gun Sur explained. Its incredibly hard – even harder than the surface layer of glassrock – but we managed to drill through it with a diamond-tipped bit that we found among all the mining equipment down here. It took us a long time, but by drilling the holes and inserting marker sticks through them we were able to work out the exact location of the cavern in relation to the landscape above.

He raised his hand and pointed at the lefthand corner of the cavern roof.

If you put a marker stick through a hole up there, he said, it comes out directly in front of the Central Tower. And if you put a stick through a hole over there – he indicated the opposite corner of the roof – it comes out in front of the East Tower.

He moved his hand again, this time pointing straight up at the roof directly above us.

And if you put a marker stick through one of the holes up there, he continued, it comes out about 50 yards south of the wall, in the open ground between the wall and the ruins.

He lowered his hand.

So basically the cavern lies beneath a roughly square-shaped stretch of ground that begins at the wall – directly inbetween the Central and East Towers – and runs for about 50 yards in the direction of the Eastside ruins.

He looked at us.

Are you with me?

I nodded – visualising the ground above us – but when Gun Sur turned to Chola Se, expecting her acknowledgement, she just stood there staring back at him.

You told me you were going to show me something that would help me understand my pain, she said to him.

She glanced at Pilgrim, then turned back to Gun Sur.

I dont see what any of this has got to do with what he did to me.

Perhaps it would be best if I let Deputy Pilgrim answer that, Gun Sur told her.

There was a slight coldness to his voice, and I sensed – not for the first time – that although Gun Sur believed Pilgrims side of the story, he wasnt entirely comfortable with it, and he didnt like having to defend it. And as Pilgrim began speaking, I also sensed a growing air of impatience in the Marshal, as if he felt there were far more important things he should be doing than this – whatever this was – and that he held Pilgrim responsible for putting him in this situation.

The reason the Dau were celebrating that night, Pilgrim told us, was that Ide finally given them the information theyd been waiting for – the full details of our battle plan. Ide already told Hensch that we had a stock of TNT – and Ide given him a few samples to prove it – but he didnt know exactly how much we had or what we were planning to do with it. But that night I told him everything.

Pilgrim glanced across at Gun Sur, as if doublechecking that it was okay for him to tell us the full story, but the Marshal wasnt paying any attention to him. He was just standing there, staring at the ground, deep in thought.

Pilgrim turned back to us and carried on.

I told Hensch that we had a fully operational armoured truck, and enough TNT to blow the Dau encampment to pieces. I told him that at a certain time on a certain day we were going to blast a hole in our wall, then drive the truck through the gap and across Nomansland into their camp. The truck would be packed full of TNT, and once it reached their fort, the explosive would be detonated. The blast would be so powerful that the entire camp would be obliterated, and anyone within a quarter-mile radius would be killed or seriously injured. Immediately after the explosion, our Fighters would enter the camp and finish off any survivors.

As he finished speaking, Pilgrim kept his eyes on us, waiting for our reaction.

Thats the battle plan? I said to him.

Its what I told Hensch.

And he believed you?

He believed me as much as he ever believes anyone. He wont be fully convinced until hese seen the truck himself, and seen that its just as I told him – in full working order, and capable of being driven across Nomansland and into their camp. But thats not a problem. Weare already making arrangements to put his mind at rest, and in the next few days or so hele not only see the truck with his own eyes, hele see it in action. Pilgrim grinned. Or at least, thats what hele think hese seeing.

What do you mean? I said.

Weve arranged a display—

We need to get back to the storehouse now, Gun Sur said bluntly, interrupting the Deputy. Wele tell you whats really going to happen when we get there.

When we got back to the storehouse, and Gun Sur and Pilgrim led us over to the armoured truck, the first thing I noticed was that most of the armour was fake. The reason I hadnt noticed before was that we hadnt been so close to the truck before, but now that we were standing right next to it, the deception was obvious. Some of the thinner metal panels were real, but most of the armour was actually wooden panelling that had been painted to look like metal. It was an impressive piece of work, and unless you were as close as I was – which obviously the Dau were never going to be – it looked like genuine armour plating.

The second thing I noticed was that most of the trucks original bodywork – at least the parts of it that were still visible – were eaten away with rust, and some parts were so paper-thin and peppered with holes that it was a miracle they were still in one piece.

As youve probably guessed by now, Gun Sur said, the battle plan that Deputy Pilgrim gave to the Dau was a fantasy. If we packed this truck with TNT and tried to drive it across Nomansland, it would fall apart before it got anywhere near the Dau camp. And thats if it had an engine.

He nodded at Pilgrim. The Deputy went round to the front of the vehicle and lifted up a large metal lid just in front of the drivers compartment.

This, Pilgrim explained, stepping aside to let us see, is where the engine that drives the truck should be.

We went over and looked down into a large empty compartment. It clearly wasnt meant to be empty, but whatever was supposed to be in there was gone. All that was left was a few struts of rusted metal, some equally rusty springs, and dozens of frayed wires and cables sticking out all over the place.

Without an engine, Pilgrim said, the trucks totally useless.

So hows Hensch going to see its in full working order? I asked.

I told him that its being moved out of the building on Friday night to check the brakes and gears. Its only going to be a very brief test – just in and out of the building – but Hensch knows the exact time and location, so all he has to do is find somewhere that gives him a reasonably clear view of the storehouse, and with his nightvision glasses hele be able to see everything he needs to. All we have to do is make it look real.

Whats the point? I said. If the trucks useless, and we cant use it, whats the point of making Hensch think we can?

Pilgrim glanced at Gun Sur.

Gun Sur nodded – go ahead, tell him.

Ive promised Hensch that on the night of the attack Ile disable the guards in our watchtowers. When I signal him to let him know that its done, hele give the order for his people to cross Nomansland and gather outside our wall. And thats all of his operational people, by the way---not just his Fighters, but anyone whose capable of firing a weapon. So that means therell be close to 700 of them waiting on the other side of the wall – well away from the section thats going to be blown apart – and what Ive told Hensch is that as soon as the hole has been blasted in the wall, Ile detonate the TNT in the truck. The massive explosion will kill or maim scores of our people, and meanwhile the Dau can simply stream in through the hole in the wall and finish off whoevers left---

Pilgrim grinned.

All except me, of course. I wont be anywhere near the truck when it goes off. And once the Dau have secured the town, and its safe for me to show myself, Ile be welcomed with open arms and given my due reward. Thats what Hensch has promised me anyway. In return for my services, hese not only going to make me his second-in-command, but I have his word – and the word of his people – that when he finally retires, or upon his death, Ile be made Marshal. And since the Dau will have wiped us all out by then, that means, in effect, that Ile be the leader of the entire human race.

Very appropriate, Chola Se muttered.

Pilgrim smiled at her.

She didnt smile back.

I knew she didnt trust a word that he said, and that she could barely bring herself to speak to him, but while I didnt trust him either – and I found it sickening to have to talk to him – I thought it was best, for both of us, to keep our feelings to ourselves and play along with him, at least for now.

So whats really going to happen? I asked him.

Again, he glanced at Gun Sur before answering, and again Gun Sur gave him the nod.

Instead of packing the TNT into the truck, he said, turning back to us, weare going to plant it all around the edge of the cavern roof. The rest of the plan – from the Dau point of view – will go ahead as arranged. Wele let them cross Nomansland and wait outside the wall, and wele blast the hole in the wall at the prearranged time. At that point, of course, theyle be expecting me to detonate the TNT in the truck, and when that doesnt happen theyre going to realise that somethings gone wrong. They wont know if Ive simply been unable to trigger the explosion for some reason, or if Ive betrayed them, but theyle quickly realise that it doesnt make any difference.

Theyre all already there, all 700 of them, and theres a massive hole in our wall. And whether Ive betrayed them or not, they still outnumber us 5 to 1. Theyre never going to get a better chance of annihilating us. So theyle carry on as planned, and when Hensch gives the order, all 700 of them will come swarming in through the fallen wall – guns blazing, war cries splitting the air – and meanwhile wele be waiting for them, hunkered down in our defensive positions, just watching and waiting---and wele wait until as many of them as possible are directly above the cavern, and then wele detonate the TNT in the roof. The initial blast will take out a lot of them straightaway, but at the same time the ground beneath their feet will collapse into the cavern, and anyone within the blast area – dead or alive – will go down with it. Wele have our Fighters – and everyone else who can fire a gun – strategically positioned around the outskirts of town to pick off any stragglers who manage to remain above ground, but the rest of those who survived the explosion will be trapped inside the cavern, with no way out, and nowhere to hide.

What about the tunnel? I said. They could escape—

The tunnel will be blocked off. They wont be able to use it. And you saw the walls of the cavern, didnt you? Theyre far too steep to climb. So basically weare going to end up with all the surviving Dau trapped in a massive hole in the ground, completely at our mercy.

No one spoke for a while. Pilgrim didnt have to spell out what would happen to the surviving Dau. Wede do exactly what theyd do to us in the same situation – take their young children and their women of childbearing age, and slaughter the rest. And once wede taken care of those in the cavern, wede deal with those left behind at their camp – the oldest of their Olders, their sick, their babies and mothers---

Wede obliterate the Dau once and for all.

Wede exterminate them.

I remembered then what Starry had said when Ide told him that Gun Sur was planning the final battle.

Whatever you think of him, hede told me, and theres many who think hese had his day, the Marshals no fool. Hele have a plan. Hese probably been working on it for months, maybe even years. Its just a matter of what it is and whether it stands any chance of working or not.

And as I stood there now, thinking about what Pilgrim had just told us – running the plan through my mind, imagining the reality of it, trying to find any obvious faults – I knew Starry was right. Gun Sur wasnt a fool. His plan wasnt flawless, obviously. No plan is guaranteed to work. There are always unforeseen circumstances, unexpected problems, things that dont go the way theyre supposed to. And there were plenty of things about this plan that I could easily imagine going wrong. But it wasnt impossible to imagine it working either.

I could see it---

It could work.

But then I looked at Chola Se, wondering how she was feeling and what she was thinking about, and as we held each others gaze for a moment – and she let me see beyond her emptiness – I knew that I was wrong.

Gun Surs plan could never work.

I could see that now---

I could see the truth in Chola Ses pain.

Wede never destroy the Dau.

Gun Sur cleared his throat then – ending the silence – and as we turned our attention to him, he spoke directly to Chola Se.

Ime sure youre aware that weve been running out of water for some time now, he said to her. But what you probably dont know is that if things carry on as they are, weve only got enough water to last us another 4 or 5 weeks. If it doesnt rain before then, the only way we can avoid dying of thirst is by finding our drinking water elsewhere, which means sending people out into the Deathlands. And you know whats going to happen if we do that, dont you?

The Dau will get them.

Gun Sur nodded. It doesnt matter how many we send out or how well armed they are, the Dau will always outnumber us. And they know where all the water is too. So all theyle have to do is sit tight and wait for us to come looking for it, and then theyle pick us off at will. And while weare losing more and more people every day, the rest of us will be getting weaker all the time, slowly dying of thirst, until eventually wele be too weak to defend ourselves. And that, Ime afraid, will be the end of us. So you see, we have to do something before that happens. We have to eliminate the Dau before they eliminate us. And the only way we can do that is by infiltrating their ranks and luring them into a trap. Which is why---

He hesitated, not sure how to say what he wanted to say.

So Chola Se said it for him. Which is why Pilgrim had to do what he did to me.

Yes, Gun Sur said. He had to preserve his cover in order to preserve our plan. If hede given himself away, that would have been the end of it.

231

The end of our people, Chola Se added.

Thats right. And thats why its so important that the plan goes ahead without any unnecessary complications. He paused, his eyes still fixed on Chola Se. Nothing can be allowed to jeopardise our survival---do you understand what Ime saying? Nothing matters more than our people.

Chola Se held his gaze for a second, then lowered her eyes and stared thoughtfully at the ground.

I glanced at Pilgrim, wondering if he was going to say anything, but from the way he was just standing there – gazing around the storehouse, idly picking at his teeth – it was plain to see that not only did he have nothing to say, but it hadnt even occurred to him that he ought to have something to say.

Thank you, Chola Se said quietly to Gun Sur. I appreciate your honesty.

He nodded. Ime sorry it had to happen.

Me too, she said, looking over at Pilgrim.

The Deputy carried on ignoring her – pretending to watch as a Fighter fitted a new panel to the truck – but Chola Se wasnt going to back down, and she just kept standing there, staring blankly at him, waiting for him to look back at her. He made her wait a few more seconds, then turned casually – as if hede only just realised she was looking at him – and finally met her gaze. I thought at first that she might be seeking an apology from him, or at least some kind of expression of regret, but I should have known better. She wasnt after an apology – she knew it wouldnt have been genuine anyway – she simply wanted him to hear what she had to say, and she wanted to make sure he was looking her in the eye when she said it.

I can smell your heart, Pilgrim, she said as their eyes met. I can smell it now, and I could smell it in the dungeon.

Yeh? he said dismissively. And what does it smell of?

The truth.

When we got back to Starrys house, we found him sitting at the kitchen table stripping down and cleaning a doublebarrelled shotgun.

I got it from Cruke, he told me. He heard I was looking for a new weapon, and there were a couple of bits and pieces he needed that he thought I might have, so he came over yesterday to see if we could trade. He had the shotgun and a Luger – he wouldnt say where he got them from – and I ended up taking the shotgun.

I thought you wanted another pistol? I said.

I did---but to be honest, Jeet, my aims not so good these days. I think my eyesights going. When I shot at the eel the other day, I missed it by miles.

He picked up the shotgun.

Its almost impossible to miss with this. All you have to do is point it in the general direction of the target and pull the trigger---

His voice trailed off and he glanced across at Chola Se. She was standing quietly by the window, gazing out at the distant sea, her face a picture of troubled thoughts.

Youre both welcome to stay here as long as you like, Starry

said, turning back to me. There are 2 empty rooms upstairs which I never use. Feel free to have either of them, or both of them---whatever you need, okay? And if you need—

Pilgrims lying, Chola Se said.

We both looked over at her. She was still staring out of the window.

He wasnt acting when he was with me in the dungeon, she continued, her voice cold and distant. He wasnt just playing a part to preserve his cover. He loved it – the violence, the humiliation---

She turned from the window and looked at me.

He liked hurting me, Jeet. He didnt do it because he had to, he did it because he wanted to. Ive never been so sure of anything in my life. The mans a monster.

I know, I told her.

And hese lying about everything else too. Hese not just pretending to be a traitor, he is a traitor.

Is that what he told you? Starry said. That hese only pretending to be a traitor?

She nodded.

And Gun Sur confirmed it, I added. He said its all part of his battle plan—

Gun Sur told you his battle plan?

Yeh---but I cant tell you what it is.

Why not?

Gun Sur told us not to. He gave us a direct order not to share it with anyone else, especially you, and I gave him my word that I wouldnt.

Starry smiled. And he believed you?

I didnt feel any guilt – or any sense of wrongdoing at all – when I sat down with Chola Se at the kitchen table and we went ahead and told Starry everything. Ive always recognised and accepted Gun Surs authority, and Ile never usually question his orders, but my relationship with Starry is on another level altogether, and the notion of keeping any secrets from him is as meaningless as keeping them from myself.

When Ide finished telling him everything that Gun Sur had told us, laying out all the details of the battle plan, I was fully expecting Starry to confirm what we both thought – that the plan stood no chance of working because Pilgrims betrayal was genuine. It was Starry after all whode suggested the Deputy was a traitor in the first place. But now it seemed he wasnt quite so sure anymore.

Ime not for one moment saying that Pilgrims a good man, he told Chola Se. Youre absolutely right about him – hese monstrous. What he did to you is the most abhorrent thing that any human being can do to another. But Ime afraid it doesnt prove hese a traitor. He would have done what he did to you whether hese a traitor or not. So while I realise how difficult it must be for you, we have to look beyond that.

Its not difficult, Chola Se said. I hate him for what he did, and Ile kill him if I ever get the chance, but Ime not the Chola Se he did it to anymore. Shese still part of me somewhere, but Ime not living her pain anymore.

Starry nodded, accepting her words without question, but I knew him well enough to know that he wasnt convinced. He knew as well as I did that Chola Se was still very much living her pain.

Theres no doubt that Pilgrims a degenerate and dishonourable man, he continued. And I dont doubt for a second that hese capable of turning traitor. But hede have to be either completely stupid or delusional to believe that the Dau would reward him for betraying his own people.

Why wouldnt they reward him? Chola Se asked.

Starry looked at her. The Dau detest betrayal as much as we do. Theyre perfectly happy to seek it out and encourage it in their enemy, and to make the most of it in whatever way they can, but no matter how useful a traitor might be to them – and no matter how much he or she might profess to have changed their allegiance – the bottom line for the Dau is that a traitors always a traitor. And Pilgrim knows that. He knows what the Dau will do to a traitor whose outlived his usefulness.

Theyd kill him?

No question. Theyd string him up from the nearest tree.

And Pilgrims not an idiot, is he? I said.

No, Starry agreed. Hese a psychopath, and a self-obsessed savage, but hese definitely not an idiot.

What about being delusional? You said hede have to be either completely stupid or delusional to believe that the Dau would reward his betrayal.

Starry shook his head. I think hese probably delusional enough to genuinely believe he has all the qualities to be our Marshal, but I dont think hese so out of touch with reality that he doesnt know what happens to traitors when they no longer serve any purpose.

So do you think hese telling the truth? Chola Se asked. Do you think hese really just pretending to be a traitor?

Starry frowned. I honestly dont know. Its certainly possible. And if he is deceiving the Dau, and his deception works---well, you have to admit its not a bad plan. And who knows – with a bit of luck, it might even succeed.

But what if youre wrong? Chola Se said. What if Pilgrim is working for the Dau?

Starry sighed. Youre right. We need to find out one way or the other. Its no good just guessing. We need hard facts---or at least some kind of evidence. If Pilgrims a traitor, we need to be able to prove it somehow. We need something we can take to Gun Sur---

Like what?

I dont know. I need to look into it---Ile do some digging around, see what I can find out.

What kind of digging around? I said. You cant just go round asking questions about Pilgrim, or poking around in his—

Ile be careful, okay? He grinned. Do I look like a man who doesnt know what hese doing?

Yeh, you do, I said, glancing down at the grubby bandage that was still wrapped round his recently wounded finger.

He smiled. At least I didnt get stabbed in the leg.

We all gazed around at each other then – a ragtag collection of damaged misfits, battered and bruised, tired and confused, none of us really knowing what we were doing---

And we started laughing.

It was a sound that filled me with a wonderful sense of warmth and belonging, and – for the moment, at least – it made everything seem all right.

Later that night, as we lay together in Starrys bed – while he stayed up and kept guard – Chola Se asked me how it had felt being with my dogmother again. The room was dark and quiet, just a faint

237

crackling of embers in the fireplace, and as I gazed up at the ceiling, recalling the moment in the woodland when Ide turned round and seen my mother, the feelings came flooding back to me.

Do you remember how you used to feel when you were in the den and your mother and the rest of the pack came back from a hunt? I said.

Yeh, she muttered.

Thats how it felt when I first met my mother again. I was so excited that when I went running up to her I fell over my feet and crashed right into her.

I sensed Chola smiling.

It was all so---I hesitated, trying to think of the right word. It was all so natural. And so immediate too. The moment I was back with my mother, all the human stuff in my head instantly disappeared and everything was just how it used to be – instinct, feeling---the sense of simply being there. It felt---I dont know. It just felt right.

What about the other dogs? Did you know them?

No, Ide never met any of them before. It was a bit unsettling meeting them at first, especially the leader, the big male, but even that was a familiar kind of uneasiness, you know, the way it always was meeting new dogs. And once theyd accepted me, and wede set off into the Deathlands---

As I stared up into the silent blackness, I remembered how it had felt that night – the hypnotic rhythm of our movement as we loped across the glassrock desert, the closeness of the other dogs, the cold night air on my naked skin, the darkness of the ground and the sky merging together into a vast black nothingness---

I felt at one with everything, I said.

We lay there in silence for a while then, not saying anything, just breathing softly in the darkness, alone with our thoughts but together in our solitude.

It felt right.

Just being there.

They saved our lives, didnt they? Chola Se said quietly. The 3 dogs who killed the Fighters at the Dau camp---they saved our lives.

Yeh, they did.

Even though theyd only just met you, and they didnt know me at all, and weare both humans—

They did it for my mother.

She must mean a lot to them.

Shese a special dog.

Just like you.

I turned and saw Chola smiling.

It lifted my heart.

What about your dogmother? I asked her. Do you know if shese still alive?

She shook her head. She died soon after she took me. Ive only got a very vague memory of what happened – I was just a baby at the time – but I think there must have been a fight with a rival pack. All I can really remember is the noise – ripping and snarling, cracking bones, howls of pain---and the smell of blood. There was so much blood---it was everywhere. My mothers fur was soaked, all sticky and wet---and I remember her whimpering quietly for a while---and then nothing, just a dead silence. And her coldness---

Chola went quiet.

What happened to your human parents? I asked her.

My mentor told me they were both very sick when the dogs took me, and they died soon afterwards. She looked at me. What about yours?

The dogs got them.

She nodded. The dogs didnt touch mine. Didnt even wake them. They didnt find out I was gone til they woke up in the morning and I wasnt in the wagon.

Where did it happen?

About 30 miles north of the Black Mountains. My packs territory was way out in the heart of the Deathlands.

Thats a hard place to live.

I liked it out there.

Why?

I dont know---theres just something about all that emptiness, the endless nothingness of the glassrock desert---the way it makes you feel.

How does it make you feel?

Like youre the smallest thing in the world and as big as the world itself, both at the same time.

Like youre everything and nothing?

Yeh---

We carried on talking about our dog lives long into the night, both how wede lived them and how wede lost them.

I told Chola Se the story of how my pack had been trapped and slaughtered, and she told me how hers had been wiped out by disease when she was 6 years old, leaving her to wander the Deathlands alone for days on end, almost dying from the sickness herself, until eventually shede been spotted in the foothills by one of our watchtower guards and a team of Fighters had been sent out to rescue her.

But eventually our tiredness got the better of us and we gradually stopped talking and just lay there together in the pitchblack silence, our weary breaths misting in the cold night air.

I thought Chola Se had fallen asleep – and I was just dozing off myself – when I heard her say, Why dont we just leave, Jeet?

What?

Leave here. Go back to the Deathlands, back to the dogs.

I was too taken aback to say anything at first. It wasnt the question itself that surprised me but simply the sheer suddenness of it, the way it had come out of nowhere. The idea of leaving here and going back to live with the dogs didnt shock me at all. Ide been thinking the same thing myself from the moment Ide seen my mother.

We dont belong here, do we? Chola Se went on. We never have. And no one would miss us if we left, would they?

Starry would.

Yeh, but hese the only one. The rest of them wouldnt care if they never saw us again. They probably wouldnt even realise wede gone.

Its not that bad—

Yeh, it is. You know it is.

She rolled over on her side, her face inches from mine.

Do you really want to be here when everyone starts killing each other? she said. Its going to be a bloodbath, Jeet. Whichever way the battle goes, its going to be a massacre. And what do you thinks going to happen when its over?

I dont know. It depends who wins, I suppose.

It doesnt matter who wins. You know that as well as I do. Whatever the outcome is, wele either be dead or living the same dead life weare living now.

I considered pointing out that our life wouldnt be exactly the same if we won – wede have all the drinking water we needed, more food, no enemies, no need to wall ourselves in – but I knew that wasnt what she meant. She meant wede still be outsiders, still not accepted, still nothing more than curs and bitches.

And she was right.

She was right about everything.

And I wanted to leave as much as she did. Ide wanted it from that moment in the woodland when Ide smiled at my mother, and shede blinked, and Ide remembered how she used to curl up around me to keep me warm as I slept---and it had suddenly struck me that there was nothing to stop me from being with her for the rest of her life, that I could leave with her right there and then, just lope off into the Deathlands with her and the rest of the pack---just go, like Chola was saying now---just go, forget about everything else---Gun Sur, Pilgrim, the Dau---just go.

So what was it that was holding me back?

If youre worried about Starry, Chola Se said. Ime sure he wont—

No, its not that, I said, although I think I knew, deep down, that Starry was at least part of the reason for my hesitancy. I just need a bit more time to think about it, thats all. Is that okay?

Yeh, of course. She smiled. Weve been here half our lives. Another day or 2 isnt going to make much difference.

She shuffled up closer to me then, and as we curled up together to keep warm – and almost immediately began drifting off to sleep – I couldnt help feeling that we didnt have as much time as she thought, and that maybe I was making a big mistake---maybe we should just get up and go right now, before it was too late---

But even as the thought came to me, and I began to think about telling Chola Se, I felt myself sinking down into the mindless comfort of sleep.

It's Thursday now, 5 days since since Ive written anything, and so many things have happened I barely know where to start.

I suppose it all began at midday on Sunday, when the assembly bell started ringing and Chola Se and I made our way across town to the Quarterhouse Square. Captain Kite must have been waiting for us – together with a Senior Fighter called Muqatil – because as soon as we got there, the 2 of them took us aside and escorted us into the Quarterhouse and up to Gun Surs office. Captain Kite wouldnt tell us what was going on – just that our presence was required – but when we were shown into the Marshals office, Gun Sur himself was nowhere to be seen. In his place, sitting alone at the big oak table, was Deputy Pilgrim.

Despite all the clamour and commotion of the assembly, and the unmistakable sense of anxiety in the air, Pilgrim was as calm and composed as ever – leaning back in his seat, his legs crossed loosely, his MP40 looped over the back of the chair. The only thing about him that didnt look comfortable was the bite wound on the side of his face. But although his cheek was still heavily bandaged, and still badly swollen and bruised, even that didnt seem to bother him too much. Or if it did, he didnt show it. He looked perfectly content, as if this was where he belonged---here, in the Marshals office. This was where he should be.

Sit, he said to us, giving a cursory wave at the 2 chairs across the table from him.

The shutters on the window behind him were open – it was a searingly hot day – and as we crossed over and sat down, I could hear the anxious murmurings of the gathering crowd in the Square down below as they waited for Gun Sur to come out and address them. Pilgrim paid no attention to it, instead focusing on us, watching our every movement with the cold-eyed curiosity of a snake.

His voice, when he spoke, was blunt and indifferent.

The date of the battle has been brought forward, he said. Thats not what Gun Sur will be telling everyone out there, but thats why weare all here.

Pilgrim leaned his head back, adjusted his hat, and carried on.

The decision was made this morning. Instead of taking place a month from now, as originally planned, the battle will be fought a week from today.

Next Sunday? I said.

He nodded. An hour after sundown.

Why?

2 reasons, he said. Firstly, at sunrise this morning, when Van Hesse went to the spring to collect the days water rations, he found it completely dried up. And not just on the surface either. He tried

digging down, hoping it was somehow just blocked or something, but the ground was bone-dry as far down as he could dig.

Maybe he didnt dig far enough, I suggested.

Pilgrim shook his head. We put a team of Fighters onto it as soon as we found out. They dug all the way down to bare rock, about 8 feet below ground, and they didnt find a hint of moisture anywhere.

So whats happened? I said. We were told the water wouldnt run out for weeks yet.

Pilgrim shrugged. Everything was fine last night. The water level was a bit lower than normal, but its been hotter than normal over the last few days, so that was only to be expected. As I said, everything seemed fine. But then---He clicked his fingers. This morning its all gone.

Why?

We dont know.

Could the Dau have done something to it?

Possibly.

Or maybe its got something to do with the tunnel and the cavern. I mean, if youve had people drilling into the rock—

Did I ask for your opinion? he said suddenly, cutting me off.

I was just saying—

Well dont. He leaned forward, giving me a cold hard stare. I didnt bring you here for a discussion, Jeet. Ime just telling you what the situation is. And Ime only doing that because Gun Sur seems to think you need to be kept informed. If it was up to me---

He hesitated, realising that maybe hede said too much.

Just keep quiet and listen to me, all right? he said. If I want your opinion, Ile ask for it. Is that understood?

I nodded.

Good. He sat back, closing his eyes for a moment to steady himself, then he carried on. Now, as you know, weve already been rationing our water to make it last as long as possible, but now that the springs completely dried up weare going to have to make drastic changes. Van Hesse has got a certain amount of water put back for emergencies, and Gun Surs going to announce a series of measures that should give us a bit more time, but even on survival rations weare only going to last a week at the most, especially if this heat continues. So we dont really have a choice. We have to bring the battle forward. If we dont, weare all going to die of thirst.

At that point, Gun Sur began speaking to the crowd outside, and as Pilgrim looked over his shoulder and listened for a few moments, I turned to Chola Se. She hadnt said a word since wede come in, and Pilgrim hadnt looked at her once the entire time hede been talking, not even the slightest glance. It was impossible to tell how she felt about anything though because her face was as blank as stone.

Is she all right? I heard Pilgrim say.

I turned to look at him. He was doing a reasonably good job of appearing genuinely concerned, but he knew he wasnt fooling us, and from the glint of amusement in his eyes it was perfectly clear that he wasnt trying to. He still didnt look at Chola Se, just kept his eyes fixed on mine, waiting to see how Ide react. But I didnt rise to his bait. I just sat there in silence, holding his gaze, showing him nothing. He wasnt fazed by my lack of reaction though, and as he sat there staring back at me, there was something in his eyes, some measure of inner strength, that made me realise that whatever he was – monster, traitor, or just a man – he wasnt to be taken lightly.

You said there were 2 reasons for the battle being brought forward, I said to him. Whats the second?

You.

What do you mean?

He was smirking now – his coldness gone – and the change in character had been virtually instantaneous. It was as if he was 2 different people – the grinning carefree warrior who was looking at me now, and the more sinister creature hede been a few moments ago. They were both him, and he was both of them – the devilish and the devil.

The Dau you killed when you rescued her, he said – and for the first time he flicked a quick glance at Chola Se. The one whose throat you ripped out with your bare teeth, he went on, looking back at me. Remember him?

What about him?

His name was Skender. He was Henschs son. You killed the Dau Marshals only child.

So what?

Pilgrim laughed. Actually, thats probably what most of the Dau thought when they heard about it, including his father. The Dau arent renowned for their pleasantness – its not a quality they value that much – but even the worst of them would admit that Skender was an aberration. No one liked him, not even his own family, and if hede been anyone else he would have been murdered years ago. But he wasnt anyone else – he was the Marshals son. And the Dau Marshal is allpowerful. So no matter how much his son was reviled, no one dared say a word against

247

him. If you valued your life – and the life of your loved ones – you pretended to like and admire Skender. You welcomed his presence, you laughed at his terrible jokes, and you put up with his depraved desires. Whatever he did to your daughter – or son, come to that – you just had to accept it. He was the Marshals son – he could do whatever he wanted.

So why should anyone care that I killed him? I said. If everyone hated him so much – and it sounds like they all thought he deserved to die, which he did – whats the problem?

The problem is exactly what Ive just been telling you. He was Henschs son. It makes no difference that the Marshal despised him as much as everyone else – and was relieved to finally be rid of him – he still has to avenge the death of his son. If Hensch were to let an enemy dogchild get away with the brutal murder of his only child, his reputation would be ruined. No one would fear or respect him anymore, not even those who had most reason to abhor his son. Unless he publicly vowed to hunt down and execute Skenders killer, his leadership would be over.

I still dont see what thats got to do with the date of the battle, I said.

Pilgrim sighed, as if tired of having to explain so much.

Ide already given Hensch all the details of the battle before you killed his son, he told me, and hede already told his people about it. Thats what they were celebrating that night, remember? So when you killed his son, and he realised that he couldnt let you get away with it, he decided that the easiest way to appease his people was by making use of the battle. He wouldnt just avenge his sons death by killing his sons killer, he promised them, hede kill every one of us. The only problem with that though was that it meant waiting another month, and it seems that his people arent happy with that.

Why not? I asked.

Theyre Dau. Pilgrim shrugged. They want strength and action from their leader, not patience and caution. They want him to make you pay for what you did, and they want him to do it now, not in a months time. So Hensch is under a lot of pressure to bring the battle forward. And if he doesnt do something about it, its quite possible he might be overthrown, and we cant take that risk. The only way we can beat the Dau is if the battle goes to plan and they fall into our trap. If Hensch is overthrown and the new Marshal just launches an all-out attack, we wont stand a chance. Theyle lose a lot of people – which is why Hensch hasnt gone ahead with an all-out attack himself – but theres no question theyle overwhelm us in the end. So even if the spring hadnt dried up, wede still have to bring the battle forward.

Pilgrim gave me a long hard look.

Do you get it now? he said wearily.

Yeh, I told him. I get it.

Good.

But thats not what Gun Surs telling everyone about, is it?

Pilgrim grinned. You know what the Marshal thinks about sharing information. The less people know, the less they can talk.

So whats he telling them?

That weare running out of water, and that from now on weare all on emergency rations.

What about the battle?

Pilgrim cocked his head towards the open window, listening to Gun Surs voice as it reverberated around the Square.

---everything will be explained in due course, the Marshal was announcing sombrely, and I can assure you that when the time comes, you will all be told exactly whats happening and what your duties will be. Until then, however, your only responsibility is to follow your orders without question and carry them out as if your lives depended on it. Because, believe me, they do. Our survival, the future of us all, is in your hands.

Despite Gun Surs refusal to reveal anything about the battle, everyone knows its coming – theyd have to be stupid not to. They might not know when its happening – or how or where or why – but they know the time has finally come. Its the only thing that makes sense. And if they had any doubts at all when Gun Sur addressed them on Sunday, they certainly dont have any now, because ever since then everyone whose physically capable has been put to work preparing the town for war.

There are teams of people planting TNT in the roof of the cavern, others fixing up the truck, others working on the explosives in the wall. There are at least a dozen people working with the Armourers – repairing and servicing every available weapon, manufacturing as much ammunition as possible – and others have been assigned to various engineering tasks – providing ladders and scaffolding, preparing gun positions, cobbling together whatever straps and brackets and mountings are required to fix everything together. Those who arent so physically capable are helping out too – providing food and (rationed) drink for the Workers, assisting Doctor Shiva, running errands, delivering messages---

The town has never been so busy.

And, unfortunately, its never been so hot either. The temperature is rising all the time, and every day the blinding white sun blazes down from a cloudless sky making the air almost too hot to breathe, and every day our water supply dwindles---

And every night I lie in bed with Chola Se wondering why weare still here.

Weare living at Starrys house permanently now, having taken up his offer to move into one of his spare rooms. As well as making us feel safer, it also just felt like the right thing to do. We feel comfortable here. We feel at home.

The news that weare living together didnt take long to get around, and it didnt take long for us to realise that almost everyone disapproves. Weare dogchilds, and dogchilds arent meant to socialise, never mind live together as mates. Apart from the other Youngers, most people arent actually saying anything to our faces, but theyre not trying to hide their feelings either. Everywhere we go we see people whispering to each other, making overly loud tutting noises, glancing slyly at us, then rolling their eyes and shaking their heads. The Youngers dont bother with sly looks or whispers though, they just come right out with it, yelling out all kinds of insults and obscenities. They still keep their distance when theyre doing it though, and although its often quite threatening as well as being abusive – especially towards Chola Se – we know theyre too scared of us to actually do anything.

Its just noise, I told Chola Se. It doesnt mean anything.

Its ugly noise, she said. We shouldnt have to put up with it.

This was late Monday night, early Tuesday morning. We were lying in bed together, both of us tired out after a hard days work, and both of us dirty and sticky and sweaty because there isnt enough water to wash.

You know its not right, dont you? Chola Se said.

Lots of things arent right.

Yeh, but this is one we can do something about. We dont have to put up with it anymore, Jeet. We can get away from it if we want. Theyre never going to change, are they? Unless we leave, weare going to have to put up with their ugly noises forever.

Forever might only be another few days, I reminded her.

Its still going to be forever.

I knew she was right, and I still didnt know what it was that was holding me back. Was it some twisted sense of loyalty? Did I simply think it was wrong to leave right now, just when the town desperately needed everyone to stay together and fight? Did I feel Ide be letting them down if I just upped and left them to it?

I didnt know.

I honestly didnt know.

What would your mother want you to do? Chola Se said quietly.

Shede want me to leave. Shede want me to be with her.

Would she care about the people you left behind?

No, she hates them. Shede like to see them all dead, the Dau too. Shese the same as every other Deathland dog – shede like to see every human wiped from the face of the earth.

You have to decide what you are, Jeet, Chola Se said.

What?

You have to decide if youre human or dog.

Ime both, I said without thinking.

You cant be both.

I know.

We almost missed Starry on Tuesday morning. Wede woken early, before first light, and as we went downstairs to the kitchen to get something to eat before leaving for work, Starry was heading along the hallway towards the front door — his crutch under one arm, his shotgun slung over his shoulder, his fishing gear in his other hand.

I called out to him, and he came back in and joined us while we ate.

Neither of us really felt like eating, but we knew we had a long day ahead of us and would need the energy later on, so while we sat there talking to Starry, we filled ourselves up with as much bread and fruit as we could, and washed it all down with our mornings ration of water — half a cup each.

Take some more fruit with you, Starry told us. Its not that fresh, but its better than nothing when youre thirsty. And it looks like its going to be even hotter today.

Are you fishing all day? I asked him. Or have they got you working on the battle preparations?

I shouldnt be going fishing at all really, he admitted. Ime supposed to stay here all day to provide whatever bits and pieces are needed. He sighed and shook his head. The thing is, Jeet, Ive gone fishing first thing every morning for as long as I can remember, and when I woke up this morning knowing that Ide been ordered to stay here---He smiled awkwardly. I just couldnt do it. It was like---I dont know. I just had to go fishing. He shrugged again. Ile only be gone a couple of hours. Ile leave the door open while Ime gone. If anyone needs anything, they can find it themselves.

Youd better hope Pilgrim doesnt find out, I said.

Starry grinned. Whats he going to do if he does? Lock me up? Courtmartial me?

He locked up Yael, Chola Se said quietly. And look what happened to him.

I know, Starry said, nodding thoughtfully. And Ive had some thoughts about that---

His voice trailed off and he just sat there, staring blindly into space.

And? I said.

What?

You said youd had some thoughts about Yael. Do you know what happened to him?

I cant prove anything, he said. Not yet anyway.

Prove what?

Ile know more about it by the time I get back tonight, he said, standing up and reaching for his crutch. Ile tell you everything then.

Get back from where? I asked him as he picked up all his fishing gear and went to leave. Starry? Where are you going tonight? What are you---?

Ile see you later, he said.

Hold on, Starry---just a minute. Starry?

But he wasnt going to tell me anything else, and all I could do was sit there and watch as he hobbled wearily out of the kitchen with his precious fishing poles clutched in his hand. I listened to the familiar sound of his crutch clomping along the hall, then I heard the front door opening, a brief pause, then the quiet thud of the door being closed.

You love him, dont you? Chola Se said simply.

Her words slammed into my heart like a sledgehammer. Love him? Was that it? Was that what it was that I felt for Starry? I had no idea. All I knew was that the feeling in my gut right then was a kind of sickness Ide never felt before, a howling sickness deep down inside me that hurt so much I wanted to scream.

I dont know if a conscious decision had been made to keep me and Chola Se apart, or if we just happened to be assigned different tasks in different parts of town, but thats how it ended up. While Chola Se was put to work with the team laying cables for the explosives in the wall, I was assigned to a handpicked group who were working on the truck in the storehouse on Eastside. There were lots of other Workers in the building – some of them working on the truck itself, others helping out with the preparations in the cavern – but my team was kept apart from all the others, working in a sectioned-off area behind makeshift walls so that no one else could see what we were doing. There were only 4 of us in the group – me, 2 Senior Fighters (Muqatil and Ovan), and Captain Kite – and the reason we were working on our own was that we were the only ones in the storehouse who knew all the details of the battle plan, and it was one of those details we were working on.

The Marshal is perfectly aware that the battle is common

knowledge now, Captain Kite had told us when wede first got together. And hese also aware that everyone wants to know more. But its vital that the specifics – such as this one – remain confidential, and its your job, your duty, to make sure that happens.

Our job was to get the truck ready for the public display that would convince Hensch the vehicle was in full working order. Pilgrim had told the Dau Marshal that on Friday night, an hour after sunset, the truck would be given a final test drive in order to check the gears and brakes. It wouldnt last long, hede told him, just a quick circuit of the yard at the front of the storehouse, but it would be enough to prove that the truck was capable of carrying out its mission. So we knew that Hensch – together with his Captains – would be watching closely through their nightvision glasses that night, probably from either one of their watchtowers or a carefully chosen elevated spot somewhere out in the Deathlands – and we knew we had to provide a convincing display for them. The entire battle plan depended on the Dau believing that the truck was operational, and although Pilgrim had told us that Hensch would see what he wanted to see, it was obvious he had his suspicions. If he wasnt totally convinced by what he saw, if he had any doubts at all, he wouldnt go along with the plan. As Captain Kite kept reminding us, we couldnt leave anything to chance. If Hensch – or any of his people – saw anything at all on Friday night that was in any way slightly suspicious, we were all as good as dead.

So the question was, how do you make a massive empty shell of rusted metal look like – and behave like – a fully functional engine-powered vehicle?

It was the kind of work that requires a lot of hard thinking – discussing different ideas, trying things out, solving practical problems – and although I did my best to forget about everything else and concentrate on what I was supposed to be doing, for my own sake as much as anything, I simply couldnt do it. No matter how hard I tried, I just couldnt get everything else out of my mind – me and Chola Se, staying or leaving, my dogmother and the pack, Starry, Pilgrim, Yael, the Dau---it was all tangled up inside my head, all of it crashing and whirling around like a thousand crazed birds caught up in a roaring wind.

I tried to listen to what the others were saying, and every now and then I somehow managed to say something myself, but I might as well have not been there at all. And in my mind, I wasnt.

Muqatil and Ovan didnt seem to care about my lack of engagement – or if they did, they didnt show it – but it was obvious that Captain Kite was aware of it. She seemed to be watching me all the time, and although I tried not to let it bother me, it wasnt easy to dismiss her from my thoughts. If it had been anyone else, I probably could have just shrugged it off, but Kites not like anyone else. You can feel it when shese staring at you – like cold knives slicing into your skin – and when she looks away, it feels as if shese left something inside you---

Something of her.

Shivering like a parasite in your bones.

Its a disturbing experience, and what makes it even stranger is that despite the sense of menace that Kite can impart just by looking at you, there isnt anything obviously malicious about her. But then there isnt anything obviously anything about her. She doesnt seem to like or dislike anyone---or anything at all, for that matter. She has the same blank emptiness about her that Chola Se sometimes has, only with Kite its there all the time. She never smiles, never gets angry, never looks sad or content or dismayed about anything. Its as if theres nothing inside her, no feelings at all, just an overriding drive to achieve something – something that only she knows.

Or maybe she doesnt know.

Maybe shese just like a jawfish – she has to keep moving all the time, keep striving, keep going---because if she doesnt, if she stops for even a moment, shele sink down into the depths and die.

Maybe thats all it is – the desire to survive.

But whatever it is – whatever Kite is – she wasnt always like this.

There was a moment that morning when Ide felt Kites eyes on me again, and this time, rather than trying to ignore her, Ide found myself looking up and meeting her gaze instead, and it was just then – as our eyes came together – that a remembered image suddenly came to me.

It was the image of a much younger Kite, a Kite who was actually smiling.

It was a memory from a long time ago, an almost-forgotten moment from the final stages of my rehumanisation process, when Starry was first introducing me to the town. As far as I could remember, hede taken me to the Grocers with him to hand in his mornings catch, and while he was busy talking to Van Hesse about something, hede let me wander around on my own for a few minutes. I didnt go far. It was one of the first times Ide been anywhere without Starry being right next to me all the time, and every few seconds I found myself looking around to see where he was, just to make sure he was still there, and at one point – after a brief moment of panic when I thought Ide lost him – I realised that hede finished talking to Van Hesse and had moved across to the doorway to talk to a woman whode just come in. I didnt know who she was at the time, and it was only now – as I stood there in the storehouse momentarily gazing into the Captains ashgrey eyes – that I realised it was Kite. All I could remember thinking at the time was that she was about the same age as Starry, maybe a year or 2 younger, that she was obviously a Fighter, and that although she was kind of nice-looking in a way, there was something a bit strange about her too---something slightly disturbing. She had a very pale face, oddly small features, and her skin was so smooth that it looked almost unnatural. She reminded me a bit of a childs doll Ide once seen. Her face was expressionless as Starry talked to her, and even when she made eye contact with him, it seemed to me that she was gazing right through him.

But then something changed.

Starry still had his basket of fish with him (for some reason he hadnt yet handed it in) and as he carried on talking to Kite, I saw him reach into the basket and pull out a goodsized fish, and then – without so much as a pause or a smile – he held up the fish and pretended to make it talk to her. And as he stood there with the fish head in his hands, opening and closing its mouth while he continued speaking to Kite – presumably in a funny voice – her blanked-out face suddenly broke into a beaming smile, and in that moment it was as if shede become a different person. The smile didnt just light up her face, it totally transformed her entire being, and just for a few seconds she wasnt a coldhearted Fighter anymore but a wondrously joyful child.

But then Van Hesse called out to Starry, and as he turned to answer him, momentarily forgetting the fish, everything suddenly changed again. In the short time it took for Starry to answer the

Grocer and turn his attention back to Kite, her smile had disappeared and the joy had gone from her eyes. And although Starry made a halfhearted attempt to bring it back – pretending to have a conversation with the fish – it was clear he was wasting his time.

The moment had gone, and it wasnt coming back.

And now, all those years later, as I held the Captains gaze for a few seconds more – wondering if that was the last time shede ever smiled – the moment was broken again, this time by Kite herself.

Did you want something, Jeet? she said coldly.

I shook my head.

Well get on with your work then.

I got on with my work.

Or rather, I got on with pretending to work.

I was fairly sure by now that although Kite was keeping an eye on me, she didnt actually care whether I did anything useful or not. I wasnt there to work, Ide realised. I was there because Pilgrim wanted me to be there. And he wanted me there for 2 reasons. Firstly, because I had to be somewhere, and I had to be seen to be doing something, and being with Kite meant that he knew where I was and what I was doing. And secondly, by putting me with a team that was working in secret, he was letting everyone else know that I was one of the privileged few who knew exactly what was going on, which gave them all the more reason to dislike and distrust me.

And I knew thats what he wanted.

He wanted me to be hated, despised, discredited---

He wanted to make sure that whatever I might accuse him of, no one would believe me.

I knew it.

But at the same time I couldnt help wondering if I was wrong. Maybe I was just being paranoid? Maybe there was nothing going on here at all? Maybe it was all just me, my mind mixed up with too many things I didnt understand, my head full of too much chaos---like a thousand crazed birds caught up in a roaring wind---

But then along came Cruke.

And that changed everything.

It was midafternoon by then, and I was standing at a workbench, supposedly experimenting with different types of cable – trying to figure out which of them was strongest for its size – when I heard someone behind me calling out my name. The storehouse was a hive of activity – lots of people working and talking, lots of loud hammering and thumping – and in all the noise I didnt recognise the voice at first, but when I turned round and saw the unmistakable figure of Cruke – the one-eyed Older and Councillor – I knew straightaway it was him whode called out. He was about 20 feet away, walking slowly past me, carrying a heavy-looking wooden crate in both arms. He was heading towards the tunnel entrance at the back of the storehouse, so I guessed he was delivering something to the Workers in the cavern.

As I caught his eye, he called out again.

Can you spare a second, Jeet?

I glanced round, looking for Kite, but she wasnt there. I looked all around, trying to find her, but I couldnt see her anywhere.

Wheres the Captain? I asked Muqatil, who was standing beside me dipping a length of cable in a pot of black paint.

Gone, she said without looking up.

Where?

Muqatil shrugged. She didnt say.

Did she say how long shede be?

Half an hour.

When was that?

When she left.

Her voice was blank – neither spiteful nor amused – and when I looked at her for a moment and saw the same blankness in her eyes, I knew I wasnt going to get anything else out of her. I glanced around again, scanning the whole storehouse for any sign of Kite, then I walked off and went over to Cruke.

Hede stopped now and was waiting for me, but before I reached him he started moving again, carrying on across the storehouse. I increased my pace and caught up with him, and as we walked side by side towards the tunnel entrance, he awkwardly reached into the wooden crate – briefly holding it with just one arm – and brought out a spool of fuse wire.

Just make out like weare talking about it, he said, passing me the spool.

What?

Pretend weare talking about the fuse wire, okay?

I took the spool from his hand and unwound some of the wire as we walked, studying it closely as if Cruke had asked me a question about it.

Whats going on? I started to say. What do you want—?

Now now, he said. Wait til weare in the tunnel. Just keep looking at the wire.

We didnt speak again until wede reached the bottom of the slope that leads down into the tunnel. Although we were only 20 feet below the surface, the cacophony of noise from the storehouse above suddenly sounded a long way away, and in the relative silence of the tunnel, the ringing in my ears – which I hadnt been aware of before – was deafening.

The tunnel up ahead of us was empty.

Cruke glanced over his shoulder, then began to speak.

Slow down a bit, he said quietly. I want to get this finished before we get to the cavern.

We both slowed our pace to a steady walk, then Cruke got straight to the point.

You know Ime a Councillor, dont you? he said.

I nodded.

Well, you need to know that representations have been made to the Council about you and Chola Se, he continued. The townspeople dont like you being together, and a lot of them have made official complaints.

What dont they like about us being together ? I asked.

Come on, Jeet, dont be stupid. You know what Ime talking about.

I just want to know their exact words, how they actually put it.

Cruke sighed. Youre dogchilds. Dogchilds shouldnt mix. And they certainly shouldnt breed. Its not only not right, and unhuman, its dangerous.

Dangerous?

You could go wild again. You could go back to being dogs. He looked at me. Thats what theyre saying, all right?

I nodded.

He glanced over his shoulder again, then carried on.

When representations from the public reach a certain level, the

263

Council is legally bound to act upon them. In some cases this means that a Councillor will table a motion on the subject, and then all 6 of us have to debate the motion and vote on it.

He paused for a moment, looking slightly awkward, perhaps even embarrassed.

In this case, he went on, clearing his throat, the motion calls for sexual relationships and/or cohabitation between dogchilds to be made a crime.

There wasnt any doubt in my mind who would have put forward this motion, but I asked Cruke anyway, just to make sure.

It was tabled by Deputy Pilgrim, he answered. And the vote was a tie – 3 for, 3 against.

Really?

You sound surprised.

I am.

Weare not all as bad as you think, Jeet, he said. Some of us still have the guts to stand up for what we think is right. The trouble is – and this is really what I came here to tell you – because the vote was tied, we now have to continue the debate until someone changes their mind and we get a majority vote either way, and Deputy Pilgrim has made it perfectly clear that if the motion isnt carried, those who continue to oppose it will face serious consequences.

And I suppose that means it will be carried? I said.

He nodded. Pilgrims threats dont bother me, but Solarin and Talmud – thats the other 2 who voted against the motion – theyre not going to stand against the Deputy.

He shrugged, and I got the feeling that part of him despised them for their weakness, but another part of him felt sorry for them and didnt want to hold them to blame.

Anyway, he said, I just wanted to warn you really. Theres going to be another vote in a day or 2, and theres no doubt Pilgrim will get his way.

So that means that if I carry on living with Chola Se, we could both be locked up for breaking the law?

Its worse than that, Ime afraid, Cruke said. All it would take to have you arrested is an allegation of a sexual relationship. And once Pilgrims got you locked up- - -

I looked at him, wondering if he knew about Yael, or if he was just saying that Pilgrim was capable of anything. It was hard to tell. There was something about him – something that only the dog in me could sense – that made me think he was hiding something. It was too deeply hidden to tell what it was, but whatever it might be – good or bad, right or wrong – I got the feeling that he was shaped by it. I was almost certain it had nothing to do with Yael though, and even if I was wrong, there was no time to think about it anyway. I could hear the sound of people working in the cavern now – an echoed swirl of hammering and drilling – and when I looked up I realised wede almost reached the end of the tunnel.

Why are you telling me all this? I asked Cruke.

Does it matter?

Yeh, I said, it does.

We stopped at the opening to the cavern.

Ime a Fighter, Cruke said simply, lowering his voice and glancing around the massive underground chamber. I might be retired now, he went on, but Ime still a Fighter. Its what I am, what Ile always be. And thats why I respect you for what you did.

He turned and looked me in the eye.

You went into the Dau camp, alone, and you brought back one

of our people. That takes some doing. And it deserves respect.

He shook his head, and I could see the pent-up anger in his eyes.

The town should be thanking you, not treating you like dirt. Its wrong, whichever way you look at it. Its just wrong.

He took a deep breath, then let it out slowly.

I wish there was more I could do to help put it right, he said. And I promise you that Ile do whatever else I can, but for now---well, at least you know whats going on. Its not much, I know. But its better than nothing.

I was just about to thank him when he reached across, took the spool of fuse wire from my hand, and started moving off into the cavern.

Watch yourself, okay? he said, looking back over his shoulder.

You too, I told him.

He smiled, and just for a moment I saw the hidden truth in his eye. And then he was gone, into the echoing clamour of the cavern.

After Ide left Cruke, all I wanted to do was go and find Chola Se and leave town straightaway. We couldnt stay here anymore – if we stayed, we were dead – and there was no way I wanted to stay anyway. The townspeople were making official complaints, Cruke had said. They didnt like us being together--- they were worried we might breed---we might go wild again---

we might go back to being dogs---

Well, to hell with them, I muttered, heading back through the tunnel. To hell with them all.

By the time Ide reached the exit though, the storm of rage crashing through my head had begun to die down, and as I climbed the slope back up to the storehouse, I was thinking clearly enough to realise that if I left with Chola Se right now, almost immediately after meeting with Cruke, Ide be as good as sentencing him to death. Pilgrim was going to find out that Cruke had talked to me – there was no doubt about that – and if I left with Chola Se straightaway, Pilgrim would know that Cruke had tipped me off about the vote. He wouldnt be able to prove it, but Pilgrim doesnt need proof. He just needs to know. And hede know. And Cruke would pay the price.

I couldnt let that happen.

So instead of rushing off to find Chola Se, I just walked back through the storehouse to the sectioned-off area, and went back to work as if nothing had happened. Captain Kite had returned from wherever shede been, and 5 minutes after Ide come back, she came over to me and asked me where Ide been.

I was helping Cruke with something, I told her.

Cruke?

I didnt like telling her the truth, or at last part of the truth, but I knew shede already know about Cruke – Muqatil or Ovan would have told her Ide left with him – so there was no point pretending I hadnt been with him. I just had to make up a reason why.

There was a problem with some fuse wire, I told her. Cruke asked me to help.

What do you know about fuse wire?

I know all sorts of things, I said, smiling at her. Youd be surprised.

It was a stupid thing to say, and I probably shouldnt have said it, but later on that night, when I was telling Chola Se what had happened, it had made her smile, so it was worth it in the end.

We were in our room at Starrys house, sitting on the floor in front of the fire. Chola Se had cleaned up my stab wound again – licking away all the dried-up blood – and once shede examined the cut and was satisfied it wasnt infected, she began rebandaging my leg with a fresh strip of cloth.

Tell me what Cruke told you again, she said. The bit about the vote.

I knew she didnt actually need me to go over it all again – shede taken in every word the first time – and I guessed her real reason for asking me to repeat it was to make sure I understood what it meant to us. She neednt have worried though. Ide already been over it so many times – endlessly replaying Crukes words in my head – that I knew what it meant to us as well as Ide ever known anything. There was only one thing it could mean. As long as Cruke was telling the truth, and I couldnt think why he wouldnt be, we had no choice but to leave town as soon as possible.

What else could we do?

There was no doubt that Pilgrim was going to get his way, and once the vote was passed – making relationships between dogchilds a crime – wede be arrested and thrown into prison. And we both knew what that meant. Wede end up like Yael – found hanged in our cells.

So if we wanted to carry on living, and carry on being together---

We have to leave, dont we? Chola Se said. We cant stay here anymore.

I looked at her. Her face was pale in the light of the flames, and despite the fiery determination that burned in her eyes, I knew she was just as frightened as I was.

We should have gone when you said, I told her. Ime sorry. I should have listened to you.

You did listen. And I listened to you. Thats the way it works, Jeet.

Yeh, but I was wrong, wasnt I? I should have—

It doesnt matter what we should have done. All that matters is now, okay?

Yeh.

Weare going, arent we?

Yeh, I said, taking hold of her hand. Weare going. We have to.

We smiled at each other then.

We were going---

At last.

We were going home.

When Chola Se had finished bandaging my wound, I got up and walked around the room, testing my leg. It was still quite stiff, but it felt strong enough, and there was virtually no pain at all.

What about Cruke? Chola Se said, throwing the old bandage on the fire. Pilgrims still going to find out he talked to you, isnt he? In fact, he probably knows already. So as soon as we leave, hese still going to know that Cruke tipped us off.

I know, I said. But what can we do? The only way we can keep

Cruke safe is by staying here.

And if we stay here, weare dead.

Exactly.

She went quiet for a while then – crouching down in front of the fire, staring thoughtfully into the flames – and I think she was beginning to realise that there was more to us leaving than just what it meant to us. It affected other people too. It had consequences.

What about Starry? she said quietly.

Hele understand.

Thats not what I meant.

I looked at her, wishing that I didnt have to talk about Starry, but knowing I couldnt avoid it.

Ile miss him, I said. Hese everything to me---Ile miss him so much I cant even imagine it. But he cant come with us, can he? The dogs would never accept him. And even if they did, hede never survive out there. He can manage well enough here with one leg, but out in the Deathlands---I shook my head. He wouldnt stand a chance. So he cant come with us, and we cant stay here--- and thats it really. I dont like it, but thats how it is.

We dont have to go tonight, Chola Se said. I mean, if you want to spend a bit more time with Starry before we go—

No, I said firmly. We have to go tonight. We cant leave during the day, so if we dont go tonight wele have to wait another 24 hours, and a lot can happen in 24 hours. We cant risk it. We need to get going as soon as we can. Starry will be back soon anyway, and weve still got to work out how weare going to get out of here. So at least wele see him before we go---

He should be back already, shouldnt he? Chola Se said. Hese not usually this late.

I went over to the window and opened the shutters. It was an icy black night, the heat of the day a distant memory, and way out across the sea a bloodred moon was hanging low on the horizon. It was nearly full, just a sliver missing from one side, and the air around it was ringed with a crystal-white halo. The sea was so still and flat that the moons crimson reflection barely shimmered on the surface.

It was gone midnight, I realised. And Chola Se was right. Starry was usually back by now.

Do you think hese all right? she asked.

I remembered him telling us the day before that he was going to do some digging around to see what he could find out about Pilgrim, and only that morning hede said something about Yael – I cant prove anything, hede told us, not yet anyway---Ile know more about it by the time I get back tonight---Ile tell you everything then---

I was beginning to feel something now.

Not fear exactly. But something very close to it.

He didnt say where he was going, did he? Chola Se said.

No.

Maybe hese visiting friends or something, she suggested. Is there anyone he sees regularly? Someone close to him maybe?

I shook my head. He mentions an old friend of his sometimes, and I think he might see them every now and then, but hese never told me who it is. I dont think theyre close though. And he wouldnt be visiting them tonight anyway.

Why not?

Because he promised hede tell us what hede found out about Yael tonight. He wouldnt just forget about that. He wouldnt leave

us waiting here while he went off to see some old friend of his---
he just wouldnt do it.

Maybe hese just out delivering something? Chola Se said.
Theyre working round the clock on some of the battle
preparations---maybe someone needed something from Starrys
scrap collection, and instead of coming round to pick it up, they
ordered Starry to bring it to them---

Hese been gone for hours, I pointed out.

Maybe they put him to work on something when he got there.

Yeh, maybe---

Ime sure hele be back soon, she said.

I nodded, but without much conviction. I wanted to believe
it was as simple as that, but something inside me was telling
me it wasnt.

I can usually sense a coming presence.

Whenever Ime waiting for someone, I can usually imagine how
its going be when they arrive – the door opening, the look on their
face, the sound of their voice---I can picture it all as clearly as if it
had already happened. But that night, waiting for Starry, I couldnt
see anything. No matter how hard I tried, I just couldnt picture
him coming through the door.

What is it, Jeet? Chola Se said. Whats the matter?

Nothing, I said, gazing out at the icy darkness. Its just---
its nothing.

I closed the shutters and turned to face her.

We need to start working out how weare going to get out of
town, I said. Any ideas?

What about the tunnel we used when we came back from the
Dau camp---the little one that goes under the wall?

I shook my head. There are Fighters watching it all the time. Its impossible to get to it without being seen.

The sea? The cliffs?

Wede never make it.

Its going to have to be the wall then, isnt it?

As she closed her eyes, her brow furrowed in thought, I wondered if she was just thinking things through – the practicalities of going out over the wall – or if she was thinking back to the night of her abduction, trying to access her vacant memory---

Had she really been taken out over the wall that night, as Pilgrim had claimed? Or had Pilgrim taken her out through the tunnel? And was that why the tunnel was still fresh with his scent?

I assume theres some rope in the house? Chola Se said, her eyes open again.

Yeh, I told her, down in the basement---theres miles of it.

Right, she said confidently, its simple really. All we have to do is climb up to the top of one of the watchtowers – the West End Tower is probably the best – then fix the rope to the battlements in the turret, throw it over the side, and climb down.

What about the guard in the tower?

Wele just have to deal with that.

Deal with it?

I dont mean permanently.

Okay.

So what do you think? she said.

I thought about it for a moment, running it all through in my mind, then nodded.

Lets go and find some rope, I said.

As we went down into the basement and started sorting through

Starrys vast selection of ropes – looking for a piece that was long enough, strong enough, but lightweight enough to carry out of sight – Chola Se asked me why I thought Pilgrim was so desperate to get rid of us.

I know it doesnt actually matter now because weare leaving anyway, she said, but I just dont get it.

Neither do I, I admitted. Hese up to something, Ime sure of that. But I cant work out what it is.

Do you think hese a traitor?

Everything points to it. Did you see how he was in Gun Surs office?

She nodded. Like he owned the place.

Starrys right though, I said. If he is a traitor, the Dau will kill him as soon as hese no use to them anymore. And Pilgrim knows that. He must know. But if hese not a traitor, whyse he doing all this to us – turning everyone against us, making our lives impossible, forcing us out---I sighed, shaking my head. None of it makes sense.

Yeh, well, she said, whatever hese up to, by this time tomorrow night it wont matter, will it? Wele be long gone by then.

As we carried on searching through the piles of ropes, I couldnt help thinking about what Chola Se had just said – by this time tomorrow night it wont matter – and I kept trying to imagine how tomorrow night would be – out in the Deathlands with my mother and the pack, sleeping beneath the stars---

It was there, I could see it---but it wasnt quite how it was supposed to be. I couldnt work out what was wrong with it at first, but then all at once it dawned on me. It was too far away. The picture was there. The reality was there. But it wasnt tomorrow. It was too far away to be tomorrow.

Once wede found the right length of rope and gathered together the few belongings we wanted to take with us – weapons, spare clothes, my writing book and pencils – we went downstairs and waited for Starry in his cluttered old living room.

The time seemed to pass both too slowly and too quickly – the minutes like hours, the hours like minutes. Every now and then Ide go over to the window and open the shutters, and every time I looked out, the bloodred moon had moved further across the sky, bringing the morning ever closer. By the 4th or 5th time I looked out, I knew that Starry wasnt coming back.

He just wasnt there.

In my head, my heart---

In the air.

In the time to come.

He wasnt there.

But we carried on waiting all the same.

It was too late for us to leave now anyway. The sun wasnt up just yet, but away in the distance I could already see the pale light of dawn beginning to break, and I knew that even if we left right now, the sun would be rising by the time we reached the top of the watchtower, and the chances of us getting down over the wall without being seen would be close to nonexistent.

Wede just have to wait.

Try again tomorrow.

And who knows? I told myself, as I gazed out at the fading red eye of the moon. Maybe Starry might be back by then---maybe everything Ime feeling about him is wrong---maybe hese just—

Everything stopped then – my thoughts, the silence, the world---it all stopped dead as 2 shattering gunshots ripped through the night. They came from the beach, just a few hundred yards away---2 shots in quick succession, the second just an instant after the first. BA-BANG!

The unmistakable twin blasts of a shotgun.

What was that? Chola Se said, jumping to her feet.

Starry, I told her, already halfway out of the window. Its Starry.

I've never run so fast in my life as I did that night – racing along the beach, bare feet pounding the sand, heart hammering hard, sucking in lungfuls of icy air. I wasnt the only one whode heard the gunshots, and as I sped across the sand I was vaguely aware of the town behind me coming to life – barking dogs, shouts, running boots – but it was all just a background blur to me. My conscious mind was gone. I couldnt think, didnt want to think. I just had to keep running---faster, harder---faster, harder---running blindly through that terrible bloodred night.

I remember every wretched moment.

The feel of the sand beneath my feet – cold, grainy, dry then moist – and the smell of the sea – salt and oil and rotting fish – and the black chemical stink of the mud. I remember the reddened darkness of the air, everything veiled in the inbetween halflight of the rising dawn---

And the silence.

A deadness.

And running forever – faster, harder – my feet barely touching the ground, and the colours of the sand flashing through my mind – gritty brown, patches of black, gravelly grey and white---

And broken memories of Starrys voice.

What does it feel like?

What?

Everything. What does it feel like to you?

Like its all I know---like its dying.

I remember it all.

The grey and white gravel meant I was nearing the base of the old sea wall where Starry always fished from, and now I was slowing down, cautiously easing up, and I remember wanting to keep going, wanting to keep running, because I knew if I kept running Ide never see anything, and I didnt want to see anything, I didnt want to see what had happened to Starry---

I stopped at the old sea wall.

Silence.

I could still hear all the background noise – barking, shouting, running – and I knew it was getting closer. I could hear people coming down the beach now. Fighters, I assumed. But the noise they were making was in a different world. This world, right here, was perfectly silent. The sea was motionless, the air was still. The only sound I could hear was the terrified thumping of my heart.

I remember---

This world was death.

I was about 15 feet from the base of the wall, and although I couldnt recall drawing my knife, I was holding it in my hand---gripping it so tightly that the grain of the bone handle was searing into my skin. The sky was still dark – the sun just beginning to rise – but the red light of the moon was clear enough to show that something terrible had happened here.

I could smell the violence.

It hung in the air like a cloud of flies.

There was no sign of Starry himself at first, but there was no doubt hede been here. His shotgun was lying in the sand just a few feet away from me, his crutch a couple of yards to the right of it, and the remains of his fishing pole were scattered all over the place – broken bits of the wooden pole, the handle, the smashed-up reel---there were bits on the wall, others on the beach, some nearby, others yards away. And as I looked around at the splintered fragments, wondering what had happened, thats when I began to see it – the churned-up gravel and sand, like monstrous whirlings in the ground, the trails, slitherings, the copper-red bloodstains---

The signs of a massive struggle.

I breathed in deeply, tasting the scent of blood and violence---the smell of the beast---sour and sharp, a scent of ammonia---

I could see it all now.

Dawn was breaking, its pale light spilling across the beach, and I could see the trail of the giant eel – a feathered line in the sand, from the stinking black mud of the shoreline to the base of the wall---and another trail going back, a parallel line – this one a little deeper – leading back to the oily black depths of the mud.

From the corner of my eye I could see the approaching Fighters now – 4 or 5 of them maybe, less than 30 yards away, running down the beach towards me. One of them was calling out to me, shouting out some kind of order – Dont move! Stay where you are! Dont touch anything! – something like that. But they were still in a different world. They had nothing to do with me.

And Ide seen something now.

Something that had stopped my heart.

Ide seen it.

It was right at the base of the cliff, just lying there in the sand---like something unwanted, abandoned, a discarded toy.

I wished it was.

I wished it more than anything else in the world.

But of course it wasnt.

It was Starrys severed hand, bitten off at the wrist.

There was no question it was his. Ide grown up with that hand, Ide seen it a million times – holding his fishing pole, offering me food, carefully turning the pages of ancient books – and the bandaged little finger proved it beyond doubt.

It was Starrys hand.

I didnt want to look at it, but I couldnt tear my eyes away. The sand beneath it was soaked black with blood, the deadwhite skin crawling with flies---and all around it, already drawn to the feast, were dozens of tiny scavengers – white crabs, sandworms, yellowbacked beetles---

I sank to my knees and howled.

It didnt seem to take any time at all for the 2 worlds to come together. One moment there was just me and Starrys savaged remains, alone in our bubble of silence, and the next thing I knew the bubble had burst and our world was swarming with people. Pilgrim and Kite were there – it was Pilgrim Ide heard calling out to me – and I could see Captain Luca bustling around, and Ghauri and Doctor Shiva and Tomas and Ovan and dozens of other Fighters---and further up the beach – behind a cordon of yet more Fighters – crowds of townspeople were watching on, desperate to see what was happening. I knew Chola Se was among them – I could sense her presence – and as I looked up for a moment, and our eyes met across the beach, everything else melted away.

She mouthed a question at me – Is it Starry?

I nodded.

I saw her eyes close.

I looked away.

Pilgrim had taken control of the situation as soon as hede arrived – setting up the cordon, forming a line of Fighters to guard against eel attacks – and the first thing hede told me, the only thing hede told me so far, was to stay exactly where I was and wait for him while he examined the scene.

And so far thats what Ide been doing – just sitting there on the beach, too dazed and broken to get up---just sitting there like a dead thing, staring hopelessly at the remains of a life---

But the sun was up now – the heat already rising – and in the bright morning light I could see everything with a lot more clarity than before, and I was beginning to realise that some of those remains werent as they should be.

The remains of the fishing rod, for example – the broken bits of wooden pole, the crushed and buckled reel, the snapped-off handle---they werent the remains of one of Starrys rods. The handle was made of cork, for one thing. And while Starry had a lot of fishing poles, with handles of all different kinds – hardwood, cane, bamboo, metal – none of them had a cork handle. He didnt like the feel of cork, hede told me once. And cork handles had a tendency to crack. He liked something more solid – walnut, bitterroot, maple, cherry---anything but cork. And the reel wasnt his either. It only had one handle. Starry always used a twinhandled reel.

As I was thinking about these discrepancies, trying to work out if I was absolutely sure I wasnt mistaken, I found myself staring at Starrys severed hand, and as I wiped a bead of sweat from my brow, then leaned forward – shielding my eyes from the sun – to get a better look, a question suddenly struck me.

Why was it there?

Why had the eel bitten off Starrys hand and just left it there?

It was meat, food.

Eels dont waste food.

And now that I could see it more clearly, there was something else about the hand that wasnt right---

Something.

I couldnt quite see it.

I needed to get closer.

I got to my feet and started walking towards the hand.

What are you doing, Jeet? I heard Pilgrim call out. I told you not to move.

I ignored him and carried on.

Hey!

I could see it now---I could see what it was that was bothering me about the hand. I picked up my pace – wanting to get closer, to make absolutely sure – but then all of a sudden the massive figure of Captain Glorian appeared out of nowhere, blocking my way. He

281

didnt say anything, just stood there – solid and immovable – holding his rifle across his chest, staring at me as if I was nothing. I reached instinctively for my knife – which Ide sheathed when Pilgrim and his world had arrived – but Glorian moved so fast that I never got anywhere near it. A quick dip of his shoulder, half a step forward, and he hammered his rifle butt into my belly. It wasnt much more than a short sharp punch, and Ive no doubt he didnt put all his strength into it, but it still felt like Ide been hit with a sledgehammer. My lungs emptied instantly and a wave of pain ripped through me, knifing upwards into my heart and down into my legs, turning them to jelly. I crumpled to the ground and doubled over in agony.

As I knelt there in the sand, groaning and gasping for breath, I was dimly aware that Glorian had stepped to one side to let Pilgrim through, and now the Deputy was standing over me in silence, waiting patiently for me to finish wheezing and coughing and moaning. It took me a while – as well as struggling to breathe I was also doing my best not to be sick – and I remember fixing my gaze on Pilgrims ridiculous Cowboy boots in an attempt to distract myself from the waves of nausea that kept surging up into my throat. And as I stared at the boots, something suddenly clicked – a faint and faraway click, somewhere a long way away, buried deep in the back of my mind---

But a click nonetheless.

One of the Cowboy boots moved – Pilgrim shifting position – and as the heel dug into the sand, setting off more distant clicks, I heard the Deputys voice from above.

Ime sorry for your loss, Jeet, he said blandly. I know how much Starry meant to you, and I can only imagine how terrible you must be feeling at the moment. If theres anything I can do to help—

How about shutting your mouth? I said, looking up at him. That would help a lot.

He stared back at me, a mask of sympathy frozen to his face.

Get up, he said.

I turned my head and spat in the sand.

I dont have time for this, Jeet, he said wearily. I just want a quick word with you in private, okay? 5 minutes at the most. You can either get up and come with me of your own accord, or Ile have to ask Captain Glorian here to give you a hand. Whats it to be?

Ile come with you on one condition, I said.

Youre in no position to lay down conditions.

I want Starrys shotgun and his crutch.

What?

Ime the only family Starrys got, so everything he owns belongs to me now, including his shotgun and crutch. I want them.

Youle get them when weare finished with them.

I want them now.

Pilgrim just stared at me for a while then, his eyes shot through with a mixture of disbelief and pure venom, and for a moment or 2 I honestly thought he was on the verge of drawing one of his Colts and shooting me in the head. And the strange thing was – although it didnt seem strange at the time – I didnt really care if he killed me or not. I didnt actually want to die, but I wasnt too bothered about living either.

It was just a life---I could take it or leave it.

And so could Pilgrim.

But after a while, I saw the poison fade from his eyes and he just laughed and shook his head.

Youre something else, Jeet, he said. Ile give you that.

I didnt know what he meant, and I didnt want to know.

He called out to a nearby Fighter – I think it was Ovan – to bring the shotgun and crutch over to him. Ovan did as he was told, and then Pilgrim just stood there for a while, with the shotgun in one hand and the crutch in the other, studying them with a mixture of curiosity and disdain. There was a hint of wariness in his eyes – as if maybe, just maybe, I had an ulterior motive for wanting them – but I dont think he really believed it. The overriding feeling I got from him was a sense of idle contempt, as if he simply couldnt understand why anyone would want such things. Eventually, after a final frown and a quick shake of his head, he passed the shotgun and crutch to me.

Thank you, I said, getting to my feet.

Happy now?

I didnt dignify that with a response.

This way, he said, turning his back on me and walking off.

I followed Pilgrim up the beach to another section of the old sea wall. Kite was waiting for us there, sitting on a slab of rock at the base of the wall. She stood up when we got there, and Pilgrim told me to sit down.

Ime all right standing, thanks, I said.

Sit down, he repeated.

I didnt want to do what he said, but I was suddenly beginning to feel a huge weight of tiredness bearing down on me, as if the air itself was a solid mass of rock, pushing down on my shoulders, and I could already feel my legs starting to buckle.

I sat down on the rock.

Pilgrim glanced at Kite.

She gave him a brief nod.

He turned back to me.

Look at me, Jeet, he said.

I wearily raised my head. It weighed a ton.

Do you know where Starry was last night? he asked me.

What?

Do you know where Starry was?

I shook my head. I dont understand—

Listen, Jeet, he said, leaning down towards me. Weve pieced most of it together now, okay? We think we know what happened to Starry. But there are still a few loose ends that need tying up, and because you knew Starry better than anyone else, you might be able to help us. Do you understand that?

I nodded.

Right, so Ile ask you again. Do you know where Starry was last night?

No.

Pilgrim glanced at Kite.

She stepped closer to me.

Starry was with me last night, she said.

You?

She nodded. Weve been friends for a long time. Starry didnt like other people knowing his business, as Ime sure youre well aware, so we kept our relationship very much to ourselves. I dont know if he told you about it---

She gave me a questioning look, but I didnt say anything. If she wanted to ask me a question, she was going to have to ask it outright.

Well, she said, tight-mouthed, Ime guessing from the look on your face that this is the first youve heard of it. But Ime sure youle correct me if Ime wrong.

Is there a point to all this? I said. I mean, why did you ask me if I knew where Starry was when you knew the answer anyway?

We need to know if anyone else knew where he was, Kite said. Look, Ime just trying to tell you what happened, thats all. I assumed youd want to know. Ime quite happy to stop if you dont.

I looked at her, not sure what to say. I knew she was lying, and part of me didnt want to hear anymore. It was the same part of me that didnt want to be here anymore either, the part that wanted to go home and go to bed and stay there forever. But there was another part of me, the vengeful part, that wanted to know what Pilgrim and Kite were up to, and the only way to do that was by staying here and listening to their lies. Thats where Ide find the truth – in the nature of their lies.

Tell me what happened, I said to Kite.

Starry left my house at the usual time, she told me. About an hour before dawn. As you know, he always went fishing first thing in the morning, and thats why he kept a few fishing rods at my house, so he could go straight to the beach when he left---

She frowned for a moment, pretending to think.

Were you aware that he didnt come home last night?

No, I said, not knowing why I was lying. I went to bed around midnight and didnt wake up til I heard the gunshots.

Was Chola Se with you?

Does it matter?

I wouldnt ask if it didnt.

Yeh, she was with me.

All night?

Yeh.

You just said you were asleep from midnight onwards.

So?

So how do you know she was there all night?

What are you trying to say? You think she had something to do with Starrys death?

Do you?

I sighed. This is ridiculous.

Kite stared at me for a few seconds, then turned to Pilgrim. Shede said her piece, it seemed, and now it was his turn.

The way it looks, he told me, is that Starry was fishing from the old sea wall, and at some point, for some reason, he climbed down onto the beach. We dont know why. Maybe he dropped something and was picking it up---his crutch perhaps, or maybe his shotgun. Pilgrim shrugged. It could have been anything. But whatever it was, there must have been an eel waiting in the mud, and when Starry climbed down onto the beach, it either saw him or felt the vibrations of his movement---and it must have moved so fast that Starry didnt have time to get back up onto the wall. He obviously managed to get off a couple of shots, but its impossible to tell if any of the blood on the beach is the eels, so we dont know if he hit it or not. But even if he did, he could only have wounded it, otherwise it wouldnt have been able to take him down and drag him back to the mud.

Pilgrim paused, idly rubbing the back of his neck.

And thats about it really, he said, not bothering to hide his lack of concern. As I said, wele probably never know exactly what happened, but everything points to it being nothing more than a tragic accident. Starry either made a mistake or he simply ran out of luck.

I looked at Kite. Is that what you think happened?

She nodded.

Nothing to do with Chola Se then?

I didnt say it was. All I meant was—

Why do you think the eel left his hand behind? I said, turning back to Pilgrim.

What?

Why would it bite off Starrys hand but not eat it? Why leave it there?

Pilgrim just shrugged.

I stared at him. Its a good job it did leave it behind really.

Whyse that?

Its the only thing that proves beyond doubt it was Starry.

The last Time I saw Starry at the old sea wall, I told Chola Se, was the day after Gun Sur asked me to write the account. I had no idea how to do it, and I wasnt even sure I was capable of doing it. So I did what I always did when I didnt know what to do – I went to see Starry.

I closed my eyes for a moment, picturing the scene at the beach that day – the early-morning light, the air already thick with heat, the smell of the ocean drifting across the beach.

Caught anything yet? Ide asked Starry.

And hede shaken his head and said, Its getting harder every day, Jeet. Everything out there is dying.

I opened my eyes.

It seems like a lifetime ago, I said. A different world, a different me---a different everything.

Every days a different everything, Jeet.

It was early afternoon now, some 7 or 8 hours after Starrys death, and we were talking quietly in our room. I was lying on my back on the bed – my eyes half closed, my hands behind my head – and Chola Se was sitting crosslegged at the foot of the bed with her back to me, facing the closed door. In the half-seen haze of the afternoon light she looked like a creature of dreams--- a shimmering vision in a long white dress – her breast crossed with a leather bandolier, Starrys shotgun resting in her lap, her black hair edged red in the light, her head silhouetted against a galaxy of sunlit dust---

It was hard to believe she was real.

A door slammed downstairs---

That was real.

Now that the house was officially uninhabited – and there was no longer a Scrapkeeper on the premises – wede been ordered to leave the front door unlocked at all times so that everyone still had access to Starrys bits and pieces. Wede appealed against the order – how could we keep ourselves safe if we couldnt lock the door? – but Gun Sur himself had upheld it, leaving us with only 2 options.

Move somewhere else.

Or stay here – unofficially – and spend most of our time locked in our room.

We werent going anywhere else.

Not yet anyway. This was where we lived now, officially or not. Until we left for the Deathlands, this was our home.

We werent going anywhere else.

Chola Se had taken hold of the shotgun at the sound of the door slamming, but thered been no more noises since then – no sound of anyone coming up the stairs – so shede lowered the gun, and now it was resting in her lap again. When Ide given her the shotgun – assuring her that Starry would have wanted her to have it – Ide told her that if she looked in the little storeroom at the end of the landing shede probably find some ammunition for it. When shede come back from the storeroom, she not only had 4 boxes of homemade shotgun shells, shede also found an old bandolier – a leather shoulder belt with loops for carrying cartridges – which she was wearing with the cautious delight of a child whose just found a brand-new toy but isnt sure if theyre allowed to keep it or not.

I just thought Ide try it on, shede said awkwardly. I know its not mine—

Yeh, it is, I told her. Its as much yours as anyone elses. It looks good on you. You should keep it.

Shede adjusted it to make it fit better, then contentedly loaded it up with shotgun cartridges, and shese been wearing it ever since.

I glanced at her now – sitting upright, straightbacked, alert, cradling the shotgun in her lap – and I didnt know what Ide do without her.

She made me feel like living.

I wasnt purely sad anymore. My eyes were tired and bloodshot from crying, my chest ached – it felt as if my ribs had been crushed in a vice – and there was a desolation inside me that seemed to come from everywhere, as if the world itself was in mourning – the blue light of day, the heat, the air, the sounds of the town drifting in through the open shutters---it all seemed hushed and funereal. It was a strange feeling – neither good nor bad, just there. It was a feeling that told of the missingness in my heart.

When I was at the beach with Starry that day, I told Chola Se, he taught me how to take everything in – how to see things and hear things – and then how to put those things into words.

Chola nodded silently.

I closed my eyes then, remembering Starrys words.

Close your eyes, hede said. Now tell me everything you can hear and feel and smell and taste.

He told me not to think about anything, I said, my eyes still closed. He told me that all I had to do was take all the feelings from my heart and mind and put them into words.

Did it work?

I nodded, opening my eyes. And thats why I have to do it again now.

I dont understand.

I need to take myself back to the beach this morning and live it all again. I need to see and hear it all again, smell and taste it all again, then put it all into words. Its the only way Ime going to find out what really happened to Starry.

I could see the concern in Chola Ses eyes, and I knew she was worried about my state of mind. Ide been a mess when Ide come back from the beach – crying, shaking, freezing cold, violently sick – and she didnt want me to go through all that again. But at the same time, she knew that I had to. I could see that in her eyes too. She knew that I had to go back and live it all again.

Close your eyes, she said. Tell me everything.

I closed my eyes and saw it all again.

I saw the shattered fragments of fishing pole scattered all around like windstripped branches after a storm. I saw the cork handle, the handle that Starry would never use, and the singlehandled reel that hede never use either, crushed and buckled into a misshapen glob of metal---and I heard Kites flat and empty voice again – Starry was with me last night---he kept a few fishing rods at my house, so he could go straight to the beach when he left – and I still didnt believe a word of it.

And I told Chola Se everything.

Why would Kite lie? she said.

Because shese with Pilgrim.

What do you mean? With him how?

Shese with him in whatever hese doing, whatever he did. She was with him when he arrived at the beach. And they were the first to get there too. They turned up just a couple of minutes after me.

So?

So how did they get there so quickly?

Chola Se thought about that for a while, then said, Are you absolutely sure that Starry wasnt seeing Kite?

He wouldnt be with someone like her.

Why not?

He just wouldnt. Shese everything he wasnt---everything he despised.

You dont have to like someone to desire them, Jeet. Sometimes people cant help themselves. And we dont know what Kites really

292

like anyway, do we? We only know what we see of her. Maybe she was different with Starry---its not impossible, is it?

I thought back to the time when Starry had made Kite smile with the talking fish, and as I was thinking about it, wondering if it meant anything, I suddenly remembered him telling me how hede found out about Pilgrims obsession with Cowboys – an old friend of mine knows a woman who stayed with Pilgrim one night – and that made me wonder even more---

But then something dawned on me.

Even if Starry was seeing Kite, I said to Chola Se, she was still lying about the fishing pole. And I know that for a fact. He didnt use poles with cork handles. So why would he keep a corkhandled pole at Kites house when he never used them? I shook my head. She was lying. And if she was lying about that---

I closed my eyes again, and this time I saw Starrys severed hand – the deadwhite skin crawling with flies---the sand beneath it soaked black with blood – and I saw again the thing about it that had bothered me, the thing that wasnt as it should have been---the thing that Glorian had stopped me from seeing close up. But now – in the darkness of my closed eyes – I could see it quite clearly. It was the open wound that was wrong – that pink and white sand-dusted slice of flesh and bone where the giant eels jaws of needlelike teeth had hacked through the hand at the wrist---

My mind flashed back to another memory – a memory as vivid as the bluest of skies – the remembered vision of the remains of a little girls body lying in the sand---2 little legs and 2 little feet, perfectly unharmed, attached to a bottom and waist that had been severed from the torso with such massive power that it looked as if it had been sheared off with a giant sword---

Starrys hand didnt look like that.

Thats what was wrong.

Starrys hand had been hacked off, the wound ragged and imprecise. There were little nicks all round the edge, little cuts — sharp, angular, jagged — like tooth marks. Or like someones idea of how toothmarks should look.

I told Chola Se everything.

This time her face visibly paled.

If an eel didnt take off his hand, what did? she said quietly.

A heavy knife, machete---maybe an axe.

And the little nicks?

I think whoever did it was worried that the hand was cut off too cleanly for an eel attack, so they messed it up a bit, tried to make it seem more natural-looking.

Chola Se went quiet, staring blankly at the floor, and I guessed she was trying to comprehend how anyone could do such a thing. I felt like telling her she was wasting her time, that these kinds of things are beyond understanding, but I didnt have the will or the energy.

I closed my eyes again.

I was seeing things with an unnatural clarity now, things Ide only half-seen before, things Ide seen but hadnt consciously registered, like the unmistakable bootprint halfway up the old sea wall. Ide seen it that morning, but hadnt recognised it for what it was. It had almost come back to me when Ide been staring at Pilgrims Cowboy boot, when Ide heard that faint and faraway click from somewhere deep in the back of my mind, but then Ide lost it again. But now it was back. And I could see it quite clearly — half a bootprint, just a heelprint really, in a small patch of hardpacked

294

sand in a gap between 2 rocks in the wall. The rocks in this part of the wall jutted out slightly from the rest, forming steps that led up to the top, and the bootprint was at least halfway up, nowhere near the ground, so whoever it belonged to had been climbing to the top of the wall for some reason.

And it belonged to Pilgrim.

There was no question about it. It was a print from the heel of his Cowboy boot. Ide recognise it even if I hadnt seen it before, but I had. Ide seen it the day after Chola Se and the babies were abducted, when Ide followed the trodden-down path of the trackers from Chola Ses house across to the West Tower. Ide been looking out for any prints that were deeper than usual, indicating the extra weight of a man carrying someone, and the only one Ide found with any great depth to it was an imprint of Pilgrims left boot heel. It was about 20 yards from the tower, right at the point where the ground changes from packed dirt to black glassrock, and Ide assumed its depth was probably caused by Pilgrim missing his step and slipping off the edge of the glassrock, his left foot taking all his weight.

But Ide been wrong.

I told Chola Se everything.

Youre sure its the same bootprint? she said.

I nodded. And he definitely didnt climb up the sea wall when I was there. So he must have been there before.

Why would he need to climb the wall?

I dont know.

And what about this other bootprint, the one by the glassrock at the tower---?

She hesitated, lowering her eyes and looking away from me, as if she couldnt quite bring herself to finish the question for fear of hearing the answer. I waited, not saying anything, and after a few moments I saw her shoulders rise and her back straighten as she took a deep breath to compose herself, then she breathed out slowly, turned her head, and looked me in the eyes.

Yael didnt abduct me that night, did he? she said quietly.

No.

It was Pilgrim.

I closed my eyes again, and this time I didnt plan on opening them until Ide seen everything there was to see – every act, every word, every movement, every memory---every piece of the picture. There were so many pieces still missing that I knew Ide never find the answers to everything, but I didnt stop looking. I didnt give up on the black silence of my closed eyes. I couldnt. It was all I had. I knew it was a kind of madness – a madness of grief – but I also knew that it was keeping me from a greater madness, and if thats how it had to be, so be it. So I just kept going, searching for everything I could see, and bit by exhausted bit, the picture kept growing, until eventually I realised that something had clicked into place and all of a sudden the entire picture made sense.

I opened my eyes, got up off the bed, and crossed over to the corner of the room where Starrys crutch was leaning against the wall. I picked it up and went back over to the bed, then sat down beside Chola Se and began removing the padded leather covering that Starry had fixed to the top part of the crutch, the part that went under his arm.

It stopped the wood rubbing against his skin so much, I explained to Chola Se.

Right---she said, looking bemused. Are you going to tell me what youre doing, Jeet?

Youle see in a minute.

The hollowed-out compartment was so well made that even when Ide removed the leather covering it was still virtually invisible. I could only just about make out the telltale join myself. But if you didnt know it was there, youd never see it. So unless Pilgrim and Kite had made Starry tell them---

I couldnt think about that.

I was sitting on the edge of the bed holding the main part of the crutch between my knees now. Ide never opened the compartment myself before, but Ide seen Starry do it, and I was just trying to copy his technique. Knees gripping the crutch, holding it still---hand gripping the top, pressing down and simultaneously twisting to the right---

The top turned, I felt a dull clack of wood on wood, and when I gave it a quick firm tug, the top section came away in my hand, revealing the hollowed-out compartment in the main part of the crutch.

I glanced at Chola Se.

She wasnt bemused anymore, just totally engrossed, staring wide-eyed at Starrys secret hideaway.

I placed the top section of the crutch on the bed and brought the other part closer, angling it towards us for a better look. There was definitely something in there, but whatever it was, it was wrapped up tightly in a piece of black cloth. I reached in carefully, got hold of the package with my finger and thumb, and gently pulled it out. I could feel something solid beneath the cloth – some kind of cylinder, maybe. Not that big, about 4 inches long, and not that heavy.

What is it? Chola Se whispered.

I think its what got Starry killed.

I put the crutch down, then shuffled along a bit to make enough room to unwrap the package on the bed between us. It didnt take long, and even before it was fully unwrapped I knew I was right, and as I peeled away the last layer of cloth to reveal a small cylindrical blueglass bottle, I knew it was the answer to Chola Ses question.

It was the kind of glass phial thats used for medicines – no more than half an inch wide, and with a cork stopper – and it was about half filled with a clear liquid.

I dont get it, Chola Se said. What is it?

I picked up the phial, held it up to the light for a moment, then very carefully pulled out the cork stopper. The smell hit us almost immediately – a strong chemical odour, gaseous and acrid – and Chola Ses reaction was instant. Her mouth fell open, the colour drained from her face, and her eyes stilled with a look of horrified realisation.

I remember it, she whispered, her voice frail with shock. That smell---She raised her eyes and gazed emptily out of the window, desperately trying to remember more. I still cant get hold of it, Jeet, she said, shaking her head. All I can remember is that burning stink in the back of my throat when I woke up in the dungeon that night.

Pilgrim drugged you, I said, staring at the liquid in the phial. He gave you some of this.

She just stared at me.

He drugged Yael to get him out of the way and frame him, I told her, then he drugged you, got you out of town somehow, and handed you over to the Dau.

Why?

I dont know.

How did he drug me? How did he get the liquid into me without me knowing?

I dont know that either.

What about the babies and Aliaj and Berch---?

I dont know, Chola, I said. The only thing I know for sure is that Starry thought Pilgrim was behind your abduction, and he went after him looking for proof. And this – I held up the blueglass bottle – this is what he found. I dont know where he found it, or if he had anything else on Pilgrim, but Pilgrim obviously caught him in the act – although not before Starry had time to hide the bottle – and once the Deputy realised that Starry knew everything, he must have decided he had to get rid of him.

But why didnt he just kill him? Why go to all the lengths of staging his death to look like an eel attack? He must have known wede suspect it was him.

He wants us to know it was him. He knows we cant prove it, and thats the whole point. He wants us to know that he can kill people at will and get away with it.

Do you think Kite helped him?

I nodded. He couldnt have done it all on his own. He had to keep Starry subdued while he worked out what to do with him--- he had to get hold of a fishing pole from somewhere, get Starry to the beach---I swallowed hard and cleared my throat. Then one of them would have had to stand guard, watching out for eels, while the other one killed Starry and chopped off his hand---and after that they would have had to set up his body, leaving it like bait, and wait for an eel to come out and take it, then fire the shotgun to alert me---

I stopped then.

Tears were streaming down my face.

I couldnt go on anymore.

I was still lying on the bed when the sky outside started fading to grey and a cool evening breeze began drifting in through the open shutters. Chola Se had laid with me for a while – comforting me while I cried, then holding me in her arms until Ide fallen asleep – but now she was back at the foot of the bed again, her eyes on the door, the shotgun in her lap.

I hadnt slept very long – an hour or so at the most – and I hadnt got much rest. My dreaming mind kept taking me to places I didnt want to be. In the last few hours though Ide gradually settled down into a semiconscious state that was somewhere between sleeping and not sleeping – a twilight world with no dreams and no reality, where all I had to do was lie there and breathe and let time pass by.

It was a good enough place to be, safe and uncomplicated, and it would have been easy to stay there forever, but I knew that I couldnt. There were things that had to be done.

When Chola Se stood up and went over to the window to close the shutters, I breathed in deeply – preparing myself for the return to reality – and sat up straight on the bed. Chola Se turned at the sound of my movement.

Sorry, she said, I didnt mean to wake you.

Its all right, I told her. I wasnt asleep.

As she turned back to the shutters to finish closing them, I got up off the bed and stretched the stiffness from my back. My body felt numb, slowed, too heavy. I ran my fingers through my hair (forgetting for a moment that it wasnt long anymore), rubbed the sleep from my eyes, then sat down on the edge of the bed.

You know I cant leave now, dont you? I said to Chola Se.

She turned and looked at me.

I still want to, I told her, and Ime still going to. But I have to stay here and deal with Pilgrim first.

What do you mean – deal with him?

I dont know yet.

She came over and sat down beside me.

You can still go, I said to her. Ile help you get out tonight, if you want. Then Ile join you as soon as I can. I dont know how long its going to take—

Weare dogs, arent we? she said.

What do you mean?

She took hold of my hand. Look at me, Jeet.

I looked at her.

Weare dogs, she said simply. Dogs pair for life. That means weare one now. Do you understand? Weare one and the same thing. We live together, fight together, die together. So whatever you have to do, Jeet, and however long it takes, we do it together.

Half an hour later, after Ide been downstairs and found us something to eat – a few scraps of bread and some dried meat – and wede sat together in our room and quietly filled our empty bellies, we were resting on the bed again, comfortable in our silence, when we heard the sound of bootsteps coming up the stairs.

We both froze, listening hard.

Sounds like 2 of them, Chola Se whispered.

I nodded. One of them sounds familiar.

She looked at me.

Theyre on the landing now, I said, getting up and drawing my knife. Cover the door. Make sure its locked.

As Chola Se went over and checked the door, I quickly pocketed the blueglass bottle then picked up Starrys crutch and fixed the 2 parts back together again. I was just leaning it against the wall when the bootsteps stopped outside the door. Everything went silent and still for a moment. I stood there, motionless, gripping my knife. Chola Se stayed by the door, her back against the wall, shotgun at the ready. The silence hung in the air, waiting. And then it broke, and the stillness crashed, as a heavy fist hammered twice on the door.

Who is it? I called out.

Deputy Pilgrim.

What do you want?

Open the door, Jeet.

What do you want? I repeated.

Silence. I heard him muttering something, then a mumbled reply from the other one. Then Pilgrim called out again.

I just want to talk, Jeet, okay?

I looked at Chola Se, asking her what she thought.

She shrugged, as lost for an answer as me.

I stared at the door, thinking things through, and it suddenly dawned on me that the answer was obvious. We either stayed in here and kept hiding away from Pilgrim, or we opened the door and faced up to him.

I stepped forward, unlocked the door, and cautiously inched it open. Pilgrim was standing there with Captain Glorian. Pilgrim, as always, was armed with his twin Colts and his MP40 submachine gun – which was slung over his shoulder – and Glorian was carrying the same rifle hede slammed into my belly at the beach, a big old bolt-action Mauser.

You can come in, I said to Pilgrim, glancing at Glorian. But not him.

You dont need to worry about the Captain, Pilgrim said. Hese not going to—

Ime not worried about him. Ime just telling you hese not coming in. Its either you on your own or nothing.

They both just stood there staring at me – Pilgrim thoughtfully, Glorian with a look of disdain – then after a few seconds, Pilgrim shrugged and turned to Glorian.

Wait here, he told him.

Glorian nodded, still staring at me.

I stepped back and opened the door.

As Pilgrim came in, Chola Se kept her eyes on Glorian, ready to act if he tried anything. I was wary of the big man too, remembering how fast hede moved at the beach, and as soon as Pilgrim was through the doorway I closed the door behind him – shutting it in Glorians face – and locked it again.

When I turned back from the door, Pilgrim was standing in the middle of the room, facing Chola Se. Shede stepped away from the wall now and was holding the shotgun at her hip, with the barrels aimed at Pilgrims belly and her finger resting on the trigger.

Youre not going to need that, he said to her, trying to sound casual but at the same time glancing nervously at her trigger finger. Why dont you put it down, eh? Or at least take your finger off—

Shut up, she told him. Sit down over there.

The nervousness left his eyes then, replaced by a sudden flash of anger which almost immediately turned to contempt.

You know youre both dead if anything happens to me, dont you? he said. You wont last 5 minutes.

That will be 5 minutes longer than you though, wont it? Chola Se replied.

He nodded slowly, allowing himself a smile, then began backing over to a chair against the wall. We both waited until hede lowered himself into the chair – watching him very carefully as he removed his MP40 and slowly rested it in his lap – then we moved across the room towards him. I sat down on the edge of the bed, directly in front of him, while Chola Se stood by the wall about 6 feet to his right. I still had my knife in my hand, and Chola Se was still covering him with her shotgun, so if he tried anything – no matter how fast he moved – at least one of us should get him.

As he settled himself into the chair, crossing his legs and leaning back to show us he wasnt intimidated, I saw his eyes flick downwards, drawn to something on the floor by the bed. I followed his gaze and saw the leather casing from Starrys crutch, and I silently cursed myself for forgetting it. When I looked back at Pilgrim, I caught him glancing across at the far wall where Ide leaned the crutch, before quickly turning his attention back to me. There was nothing in his face to tell if hede worked out the significance of the leather casing or not, but there was just something about him – a feeling, a sense – that he knew. He knew wede found the phial. And if he knew that, then he had to know – if he didnt before – that we probably knew everything else.

What do you want? I said to him.

He glanced at the knife in my hand. Ide feel a lot happier if you put that away.

Ile put it away if you give me your Colts and your MP40. Hows that?

He said nothing, just smiled.

Right, I said, Ile ask you again. What do you want?

He didnt answer immediately, and I got the feeling that he was forcing himself not to react to the way I was treating him – telling himself to stay calm, ignore the disrespect, dont rise to the bait, just do what you have to do. I watched as he lowered his eyes for a few seconds, composing himself, then he sat up straight, sniffed hard, and looked me straight in the eye.

Whatevers going on here, Jeet, he said solemnly, it needs to stop. And it needs to stop right now. The battles just a few days away, and unless we all pull together and do whatevers necessary to ensure our victory, weare all going to end up dead. You know that, dont you? We cant lose this fight. We have to succeed. Its the only thing that matters. Everything else – our feelings and desires, our own personal battles – its all utterly meaningless. Do you understand what Ime saying? Both of you?

He glanced over at Chola Se, then turned back to me.

Whatever differences any of us may have, he continued, we cant afford to let them endanger our survival. If we arent fully committed to this fight, the Dau will destroy us. And when the streets are running red with blood, where will our differences be then?

He stared sternly at both of us in turn – taking his time, stretching out the silence – then he leaned forward in his chair until his face was inches from mine.

Theres been enough death, Jeet, he said quietly. Theres no need for anymore.

He carried on staring at me in silence for some time, until eventually – with a very slight nod of his head – he broke his gaze and slowly sat back in the chair.

I glanced across at Chola Se. She hadnt moved. She was still standing there, still covering Pilgrim with the shotgun, utterly unmoved by his words.

I turned back to him.

Is that it? I said. Is that what you came here to tell us?

Youd do well to listen to me, Jeet, he said, staring calmly into my eyes. Youle be sorry if you dont.

Is that a threat?

Its what will be.

Its the early hours of Friday morning now. Its still dark outside, the sun yet to rise, and Ime sitting in bed writing this in the low light of a candle. Chola Se is sleeping soundly beside me – her head resting on her hands, her knees drawn up to her chest, breathing the breath of sleep. A while ago I had to wake her from a nightmare. It had started as a dream, a doglike reverie of twitching legs and quiet yelps, but it had quickly deteriorated into a crazed panic of desperate jerks and stifled sobs, and Ide had to wake her as gently as possible and hold her in my arms until she stopped shaking, and eventually shede drifted off back to sleep.

Ive been wide awake since then.

My head spinning with too many thoughts.

Unwanted thoughts, memories, pictures I dont want to see.

Unanswered questions.

Pilgrim?

I cant think about him anymore. Ive thought him to death. And I still dont have any answers.

I need to clear my head.

I know what I need.

I need to go fishing with Starry. I need to get up at the crack of dawn and walk the empty streets with him, like I used to when I was a child — carrying our fishing poles together, side by side, heading down to the beach---clambering up onto the old sea wall as the day begins to break, the pink light glinting through the early-morning haze---casting our lines, the silver threads twinkling as they disappear into the mist---

I need to just sit on the wall with him and fish.

We dont have to talk. Weve got the rest of forever to talk. For now all we need is to be together.

I cant actually do it, of course. I cant leave Chola Se on her own. And if I took her with me, I wouldnt be alone with Starry. But I can go fishing with him in my mind. I can go wherever I want in my mind. And thats where Ime going now. Ime going to put down my pencil and close my eyes and spend a long morning sitting on the sea wall with Starry.

Friday morning.
The day after Starrys death.
The first day of life without him.

By the time the morning sun was high in the sky – the burning white light slicing in through the shutters – Chola Se and I had already been talking for hours. Wede woken together at the break of dawn, and we were still sitting in bed now, still trying to work out what to do.

We knew that Gun Sur would dismiss our accusations against Pilgrim, and we knew there was nothing we could do to make the Marshal believe us. It wasnt enough that we knew – without doubt – that Pilgrim was guilty of murder and rape and corruption (and possibly treason), we had to be able to prove it, and prove it beyond question. And we couldnt. The only evidence we had was circumstantial at best – a couple of partial bootprints (which probably werent even there anymore), the wrong kind of fishing rod, a phial of clear liquid which could be anything and could have come from anywhere---

It was all useless.

None of it proved anything.

All we had was our belief, our feelings, our personal experience of what Pilgrim had said and done---and none of it meant a thing. It would be our word against his. The word of 2 dogchilds – whode soon be deemed criminals – against the word of Deputy Pilgrim, the Marshals trusted second-in-command.

It wasnt hard to guess who Gun Sur would believe.

So what was the point of taking our accusations to him? What purpose would it serve? All wede be doing was wasting our time, and wasting the Marshals time, and possibly turning him against us---

Hese not going to appreciate it, is he? Chola Se said. I mean, I dont think he actually likes Pilgrim that much, but hese going to like us even less if he thinks weare making up stories about his Deputy, especially now, just a couple of days before the battle. Even if he believes us – which he wont – the last thing he wants right now is another problem to deal with.

Hele have a much bigger problem to deal with if we lose the war because we didnt tell him about Pilgrim.

But hese not going to listen to us, is he? So it wont make any difference.

We still have to try.

Why?

I dont know, I said, looking at her. I just think---

What?

I sighed. I dont know, Chola. I dont know what I think anymore. I just---I just dont know. Everything feels wrong. I dont know what to do.

She put her arms round me then, and for a while we just sat there together – not saying anything – just holding each other in the silence.

It doesnt matter, does it? Chola Se said eventually, letting go of me and getting up off the bed.

What do you mean?

She went over to the window and opened the shutters. The light surged in, filling the room with a rush of white heat.

It doesnt matter what Gun Sur thinks, Chola Se said. If he believes us or not, if he likes us or not---it doesnt make any difference in the end. It wont change anything.

It might, I said. It might change everything.

Yeh, but not us, she said, turning from the window and smiling at me. It wont change us, will it? Nothing can change us.

Friday morning.

The first day of just the 2 of us.

Everything seemed to be floating as we walked across town to the Quarterhouse – the streets, the buildings, the people, the light---everything seemed weightless and slow, hushed, stilled, not bound to anything – and everywhere we went there was an uneasy sense of expectancy hanging heavily in the air. It was as if everyone was just waiting now, waiting for the final battle. They all knew it was coming, the armies gathering on the horizon, but that was all that most of them knew. They didnt know how it was going to be, or why it was coming now---they didnt know when it was going to be, or where, or why they were being kept in the dark about it---and because they didnt know anything about the battle, they had no way of knowing if they had any chance of surviving it. All they knew was that it was going to be everything – it already was everything – and to them its everythingness overshadowed everything else---

Including Starrys death.

The shock and drama of yesterday morning – and what little true sadness thered been – had all but gone now, overwhelmed by a communal fear that hung over the town like a great black cloud.

But although Starrys death – in itself – had mostly been forgotten now, its consequences were still very apparent.

At least to me anyway.

His death had changed things.

I knew it. I could feel the difference as we walked the streets---the way people reacted to us, they way they perceived us. There was more distance between them and us now – both physically and socially – as if we were even less a part of them than we had been before. But at the same time – for reasons I didnt understand – they didnt seem quite so hostile towards us. I dont know if this was something to do with my grief – a collective fear of some kind, as if I was somehow tainted with death, and if they got too close it might infect them – or if it was simply the case that now Starry was gone – my mentor, my master – Ide become something else to them, something that was no longer owned, no longer restrained, no longer humanised---

A lone dog.

Something to avoid.

Whatever it was, I could see it all around us as we entered the Quarterhouse Square – furtive glances, shielded whispers, people moving out of our way. This wasnt unusual in itself – as dogchilds wede always been viewed with fear and suspicion – but there was something different about it now---something had changed. There was no overt hatred from anyone, not even from the

Youngers, but somehow that only added to our sense of exclusion. It was as if we were so insignificant now that we werent even worth their abuse.

When I mentioned this to Chola Se as we started climbing the Quarterhouse steps, she told me not to worry about it.

Theyre just frightened, she said. They dont know whats going on anymore. And whatever it is, they dont know if weare involved in it or not. People do strange things when theyre frightened.

Theyve forgotten about Starry already, I said.

She stopped and turned to me, putting her hand on my shoulder and looking me in the eye.

Lifes too short to mourn the dead, Jeet. Its different for you because you loved him.

Its still not right.

Are you still in mourning for Aliaj and Berch? Or Yael? Or Sheren?

She was right, of course. I might not have completely forgotten about Aliaj and Berch and the others, but I certainly wasnt mourning them anymore. Theyd lived, theyd died, and that was that. And as I stood there on the steps with Chola Se, with her hand on my shoulder and her eyes stilling my mind, I found myself wondering why I felt so differently about Starrys death---

What made it different?

Why did it hurt so much?

Why did loving him——?

Jeet?

The sound of Chola Ses voice brought me back to reality, and as my focus came back, I realised that instead of looking at me she was staring up the steps at someone whode just come out of the

312

Quarterhouse. There was little doubt who it was — I could tell from the hate in her eyes — and when I followed her gaze and saw Pilgrim staring down at us from the top of the steps — flanked by 2 massive Fighters — I knew straightaway that Gun Sur was never going to listen to us now. Pilgrim had just made sure of it---I knew it. I could see it all over him. It was in his eyes, his face, his self-satisfied smirk---hede guessed we might go to Gun Sur, and while he must have known we had virtually no chance at all of persuading the Marshal to believe us, hede decided to play it safe and make absolutely sure. I didnt know how hede done it, but the glory in his eyes told me he had.

As he began heading down the steps towards us, the 2 Fighters came with him — staying close by his side, their rifles at the ready, their eyes fixed on us. I knew who they were. It was impossible not to know them. Theyre brothers, Diedle and Sweet, and theyre both enormous — well over 6 feet tall, with great bull heads and arms as thick as my waist — and as I watched them coming down, I wondered what they were doing with Pilgrim. Were they guarding him? Protecting him? And if so, who were they protecting him from?

From us?

Maybe he wasnt so sure of himself after all---

And just for a moment, as he stopped in front of us, and Diedle and Sweet moved to edge past him — to shield him from us — thats how it looked. And Pilgrim knew it. The moment the 2 brothers moved, he instantly ushered them back — not making a big show of it, but making it clear that he was in charge, and that he was perfectly capable of dealing with us on his own.

Jeet, he said, smiling casually. Good to see you.

He glanced at Chola Se, gave a her a quick nod, then turned back to me.

If youre looking for the Marshal, he said, Ime afraid youre out of luck. Hese not seeing anyone today. Hese so busy he could only spare 10 minutes for me. So unless youve got an appointment---

He let that hang in the air, looking expectantly at me, waiting to see how Ide respond. When I didnt say anything, but just stood there staring back at him, his casual smile began to tighten.

Is there anything I can help you with? he said.

Like what?

As he leaned in a little closer to me, I realised that something had suddenly changed in him. There was no obvious physical sign of it – nothing in his face or his eyes had changed – but something had risen in him, something that became him – a cruelness, something vile---crawling like worms under his skin.

Youre suffering, Jeet, he said quietly, his voice as cold as his eyes. Youve been through a traumatic experience---you both have. You and Chola Se---youre both victims of terrible tragedies—

Youre unbelievable, I muttered, shaking my head.

Ime just trying to help, Jeet, he said softly. I know youre both—

Come on, I said to Chola Se. Lets go.

We turned away and started to leave.

I just wanted you to know that you dont have to worry about Gun Sur, thats all.

We stopped and turned back to him, as he knew we would.

What? I said, staring at him.

You dont have to worry about the Marshal, he repeated, unable to prevent a sick smile coming to his face. Ive talked to him---he understands now.

Understands what?

That youre both suffering.

He waited a moment, enjoying our confusion, then carried on.

Its not that the Marshals coldhearted or anything, he said, its just that he has to detach himself from the emotional side of things in order to do his job properly, and sometimes he needs reminding that not everyones as strong-willed as him. And thats all Ive done, Jeet — Ive just reminded the Marshal of the awful things that trauma can do to our minds---how it can play tricks on us, distort our perceptions, distance us from reality---Ime sure you know what Ime talking about. Anyway, as I said, Ive talked to Gun Sur now, Ive explained your situation to him — how youve both been through terrible experiences recently — and he understands, he knows what to expect from you. So if you ever feel the need to share anything with him, anything at all, no matter how unacceptable or outrageous it might seem---

I wasnt aware that I was reaching for my knife until I saw the sudden alarm in Diedles eyes, and in the same instant — just as he was about to make his move — I felt Chola Ses hand gripping my wrist and pulling my arm away.

Its all right, she said quickly, holding her hand up to Diedle. Hese not going to do anything.

Of course hese not, Pilgrim said, smiling at her as he casually waved Diedle back. And neither are you, are you?

There was no point in going to see Gun Sur now. We both knew it. Pilgrim had convinced him that we were both out of our minds — traumatised, delusional, paranoid — so whatever we told him about the Deputy, no matter how compelling we were, he was never going to believe us.

We waited in silence, watching as Pilgrim and the 2 brothers left the Square and walked off together along Main Street, then we headed down the steps and began making our way home.

We're only been gone for just over an hour, so when we got back to Starrys house and found that our room had been ransacked – the door kicked in, the lock smashed to pieces – we knew that whoever had done it must have been watching the house, waiting for us to leave. And although there was no question that Pilgrim was behind it, we knew he couldnt have done it himself. Hede only just left us about 10 minutes ago, and the damage to the room was so extensive it must have taken a lot longer than that. Everything had been torn apart – the bed, the walls, the floor – and everything we owned, which wasnt much, lay scattered in pieces all around the room---our clothes ripped to shreds, our crockery smashed, our personal things – ornaments, mementos---our cherished nothings – vandalised, wrecked, destroyed. Even Starrys crutch had been demolished, the lovingly carved ironwood staff split open and hacked to pieces.

We just stood there in silence for a while, looking around at the carnage, not knowing what to say. It wasnt so much the act itself that shocked us – wede always known there was a chance it would happen – it was just the sheer brutality of it, the needless violence, that left us lost for words.

The only consolation was that wede been prepared for it, and wede taken precautions, and as we went back downstairs – checking all the rooms to make sure no one was around – I could only hope our precautions had worked.

Once wede made sure that the house was empty, and that all the shutters were closed, we locked the front door, lit a torch, and went down into the basement. It didnt look as if anyone had been down here, and as we crossed over to the far side of the room, I could see that the pile of boards wede left leaning against the wall were still in place and hadnt been disturbed. I crouched down, slid the boards to one side, then drew my knife and carefully prised out 2 loose bricks, revealing a small space behind the wall. I reached into the space, felt around for a moment, then pulled out the sturdy metal box that wede placed in there earlier that morning. I already knew now that it hadnt been found, but I opened it anyway just to make sure.

The blueglass phial and my writing book and pencils were still there, just as wede left them.

I took them out, put the box back, and replaced the loose bricks. I doubted wede need the hiding place again, but there was no harm in keeping it, just in case. I slid the boards back in place, then we went back upstairs and started cleaning up our room.

By the time wede finished clearing up as much of the mess as we could, the day was almost over and the evening light was beginning to fade. Tonight was the night of the truck display. An hour after sunset, the great rusted hulk was due to be moved out of the building in such a way as to make it look as if it was a fully functioning vehicle. I hadnt been back to work in the storehouse since Starrys death, so I didnt know how Kite and the others had finally solved the problem, but I didnt doubt that they had. The display was a key part of Gun Surs grand deception. Hensch would be watching, and he had to believe that the truck was capable of being loaded with TNT and driven across Nomansland into the Dau encampment. If he didnt believe it, if he had any doubts at all, then Gun Surs plan would fail.

Which was why wede decided to wait until the display was over before we killed Pilgrim.

Wede talked it through while we were clearing up, and wede come to the conclusion that killing the Deputy was the only option left to us. Hede drugged and abducted and raped Chola Se. Hede killed Aliaj and Berch, stolen the twin babies and given them to the Dau. Hede framed Yael and had him killed. Hede murdered Starry and mutilated his body, and hede threatened to kill me and Chola Se if we didnt back off. And on top of all that, he was almost certainly a traitor.

He had to die.

It was as simple as that.

We just have to do it, Chola Se had said. You know that, dont you? We either do it or we dont. Theres no inbetween.

He knows weare coming after him, I told her. Thats why hese got Diedle and Sweet with him. Its not going to be easy.

Its him or us, Jeet. Even if we do back off, hese not going to let us live. He doesnt even have to come after us, does he? All he has to do is wait for the law against cohabiting dogchilds to go through and he can do whatever he wants with us. Weare dead whatever we do.

Not if we leave, I said.

She looked at me. You said you couldnt leave until youd dealt with Pilgrim.

Maybe I was wrong.

No, she said, you werent wrong.

She wiped a sheen of sweat from her face and leaned against the wall, suddenly looking exhausted. She rested there for a few seconds, staring into space, then she slowly slid down the wall and lowered herself to the floor, sitting with her head bowed down and her knees pulled up to her chest.

He haunts me, Jeet, she said emptily. Hese in my head all the time---every moment of every day, every time I try to sleep---hese always there, always hurting me, humiliating me---She let out a long sigh, a tired breath from deep inside her. I know I said all those things about killing my feelings, burying them, forgetting them---and I wasnt lying. I honestly thought I could do it---I thought I could kill myself, my old self---the Chola Se from the dungeon---I thought I could kill her, bury her---but I couldnt. I tried, Jeet, I really tried. But she wouldnt go away.

Shese you, I said. You cant kill her.

I know. But if I cant kill her---

You have to kill him.

She nodded. Ile never get rid of him if I dont. And running away to the Deathlands wont make any difference, because hese in here — she tapped her head — and I cant run away from that.

Will killing him get him out of your head?

She looked up at me. Its the only way Ile know for sure that he can never hurt me again.

When we arrived at the storehouse that night, I was surprised to see that most of the town had turned up to watch the display. Ide assumed it was going to be kept as quiet as possible, but either news had leaked out or someone had decided that a crowd would give the display an added sense of authenticity. The fact that a cordon had been erected around the yard to keep people from getting too close to the truck — and the cordon was guarded by dozens of Fighters — suggested to me that the audience was planned.

As we looked around for a suitable vantage point — close enough to see the display, but not so close that we couldnt leave in a hurry if we had to — I wondered if Pilgrim was expecting us. We hadnt seen any sign of him yet, but we knew he was going to be here.

He had to be.

We were banking on it.

We found ourselves a reasonably good place to watch from — a pile of rubble in the backyard of a bombed-out building just across the road from the storehouse — and we settled down to wait for the display.

It was fully dark now — the heat of the day almost gone — and although it would still be a few hours before the iciness of the night began setting in, we were both dressed up as warmly as possible. I was wearing the thick coat Ide got from Jemelata the Clothier, and Chola Se was wearing the coat that Tomas had lent me when wede returned from the Dau camp. Wede also brought all the rest of our clothing with us — the few remaining things we could find that hadnt been torn apart — together with everything else we thought we might need. Wede decided it wasnt safe to leave anything at Starrys house anymore, not even in the hiding place in the basement, so wede gathered together everything of any value – our clothes, my writing book and pencils, the glass phial, spare shotgun shells – and brought it all with us in a knapsack that Starry used to use for his fishing gear.

Although there was no sign of the truck coming out of the storehouse yet, and the double doors were still firmly closed, there was definitely activity inside the storehouse. Torchlight was visible through the shutters, and every now and then we could see shadows moving around in the flamelight.

There was no lighting in the yard, which surprised me at first, but then I remembered that Hensch would be watching through nightvision glasses, so hede get a better view without lights than with them. And there was no doubt that wherever he was watching from – a watchtower, an elevated spot somewhere out in the desert, maybe even up in the Black Mountains – hede get a good view.

It was a clear night – jetblack and cloudless, the moon almost full – and from where we were sitting we could see for miles, all the way out into the vast darkness of the surrounding Deathlands. We could see the eastern deserts stretching out into the distance beyond the cliffs to our right, and over to our left we could see the endless emptiness of the glassrock plains leading up into the foothills of the mountains. The mountains themselves werent visible – too black and too far away – but I could see them in my mind, and just for a moment, as I found myself gazing evermore deeply into the faraway world of blackness, all sense of time seemed to fade away – not just stopping, but actually ceasing to exist, as if time had never been – and in that timeless moment I could see myself out there in the mountains---sitting in the shade of an old blackwood tree---the early-evening sun high and white in the

321

sky---a cooling breeze fluttering in the tall grasses scattered sparsely around the hillside---

What was that?

The vision disappeared and time restarted at the sound of Chola Ses voice, and as I turned to her – blinking the afterimage from my mind – the world of now came back to life.

Did you feel it? she said to me.

Feel what?

I dont know---it was like something in the air---something happened to it---

Happened to what?

The air itself---it changed---She shook her head, frowning. I dont know---maybe it was just me---She looked at me. Are you sure you didnt feel anything?

I didnt know if the vision Ide just seen and the strange sense of timelessness had anything to do with whatever it was shede felt, and I wasnt sure I wanted to know either. But as it was, I never got the chance to find out anyway, because just at that moment – just as I was trying to work out what to say – the silence of the night was suddenly broken by a massive rumbling sound coming from the storehouse.

Ide never heard anything like it before.

It was a huge sound – low and heavy, like a roll of thunder or a continuous roar of gunfire – and it was getting louder all the time, filling the air all around us, crashing around our heads---and when it reached its peak – so loud now that lots of people were covering their ears, unable to bear it – the deafening roar began to pulse--- up and down, up and down---like the sound of storm waves crashing on the shore---before eventually settling to a steady –

but still massive – booming rumble.

The towndogs were barking and howling, crazed with fear, and as the roar carried on throbbing away, shaking the ground under our feet, I suddenly realised what it was‑‑‑or at least what it was supposed to be.

It was all part of the deception.

The truck was supposed to be engine-powered, and presumably a trucks engine would make a lot of noise. The throbbing roar was that noise – the sound of the trucks engine – and as the storehouse doors swung open, and the truck began to appear, I could see how the noise was being made. It was coming from a drum mechanism of some kind that had been set up on a metal frame near the doorway. The drum itself was a heavy-looking metal cylinder, about 5 feet in diameter and 7 feet long, with large metal handles on each end. It was fixed to an axle, allowing it to turn, and there was a Fighter at each end working the handles, spinning the drum. Metal struts had been fixed lengthwise along the drum so that when it rotated the struts clattered rapidly against a series of tightly sprung metal rods jutting out from the frame, and it also sounded to me as if there was something inside the drum – hundreds of metal bolts perhaps – rattling around as it turned. The crashing metallic clatter was being amplified and whirled around by the hollow cylinder, with the volume and tone being controlled by how fast and hard it was being spun. As the truck edged slowly out of the storehouse, for example, the 2 Fighters were spinning the drum quite steadily, but as the truck moved out into the yard and began to pick up speed, the Fighters worked faster, increasing both the volume and power of the engine roar.

I had no idea how realistic the sound was – Ide never heard a truck engine – but I doubted if Hensch had heard one either, and if he could hear the roar of the drum from wherever he was – and it was easily loud enough to be heard from miles away – it could only help to convince him.

The truck itself was even more convincing.

Even at this distance it looked perfectly believable. It probably didnt look anything like a truck was supposed to, but as it rumbled along the far side of the yard, it looked to me as if it was more than capable of being driven across Nomansland into the Dau camp, and it also looked sufficiently well armoured to protect it from rifle and machine-gun fire. It wasnt moving at any great speed, but it was moving fast enough, and – most importantly of all – it seemed to be moving under its own power. It had a driver, of course – a Senior Fighter called Herron – who was sitting up at the front, seemingly controlling the direction and speed of the truck, but there was no sign at all of any ropes or cables, or any other external means of propulsion, and there were even plumes of oily black smoke billowing out from a pipe attached to the engine compartment. As the mutant vehicle carried on lumbering around the yard, and the night air shook with a great rumbling roar, it wasnt hard to imagine that the truck had somehow been fixed and really was working properly.

I knew that was impossible though.

I knew it had to be an illusion.

But it still took me a while to work out how it was being done.

Eventually I realised that if the truck wasnt being pushed or pulled from the outside – and I was absolutely sure now that it wasnt – then it must be being propelled from the inside, and when I refocused my attention on the body of the truck and studied it closely for a while, I finally figured out how it was being moved.

The answer was so simple it was almost childish.

There were people inside the shell of the truck, pushing it along as they ran.

There was no way of telling how many there were, but from the speed it was going there had to be at least 8 or 10 of them, if not more – and theyd no doubt be Fighters, chosen for their strength and fitness – and I guessed they were lined up 2 abreast, as centrally as possible, to avoid their feet being seen, and that they were probably harnessed to some kind of framework securely fixed to the body of the truck---

It was ridiculous really.

But it worked.

And the Fighters inside were as good as invisible. Even though I was actively looking for them, all Ide seen was a very brief glimpse of moving bare flesh through a tiny gap in the false armour plating, and Ide never have seen that if Ide been any further away. I certainly wouldnt have seen it if I was watching from a distance through nightvision glasses.

The truck had stopped at the far end of the yard now. The engine pipe was still puffing out smoke – which I assumed was being controlled by Herron – and although the engine noise had dwindled to a low steady rumble, it hadnt completely stopped. 3 men came running out of the storehouse then, all of them carrying a variety of tools – large spanners, screwdrivers, hammers. They crossed over to the truck, spoke briefly to Herron as he leaned out of the drivers compartment, then they split up and began examining the vehicle. One of them lowered himself to the ground, rolled over onto his back, and slid in underneath the truck. Another one opened up the engine compartment and pretended to work on something with a spanner. And the third one knelt down beside one of the giant cartwheels and tapped at the hub with a hammer.

We knew what the 3 men were doing because Pilgrim had told us – they were pretending to check the brakes and gears – but as I gazed around at the crowds of townspeople watching from behind the cordon, I knew that most of them, if not all of them, didnt have a clue what was going on. In fact, now that the engine noise wasnt so thunderous, I could hear their confusion and frustration as well as see it, and I could hear it rising too – low mutterings getting louder, voices turning angry, 1 or 2 shouts beginning to cry out. Their frustration and anger was understandable. Here they were, witnessing this fantastical machine being paraded around the yard to the sound of a roaring drum, and they didnt know the first thing about it. No one had told them anything – what it was, what it was for, what it meant to them. It made me wonder how much longer Gun Sur could get away with keeping the battle plan secret.

There he is, look, Chola Se said, nudging me and nodding her head in the direction of the storehouse.

I thought she meant Gun Sur at first, but although the Marshal was visible when I looked over at the storehouse, it was Pilgrim she was talking about. He was standing with Gun Sur and a group of others watching the truck display from the doorway. All 3 Fighter Captains were there – Kite, Glorian, and Luca – together with Dr Shiva and 5 of the 6 Council members. The missing Councillor was Cruke. Diedle and Sweet werent part of the group, but they werent that far away – standing together about 10 yards further back in the storehouse – and it was clear they were aware of our presence.

Both of them were looking directly at us.

As the roar of the drum started up again, and the truck began moving – clumsily at first as it turned around, then more freely as it started heading back towards the storehouse – I saw Sweet approach Pilgrim and speak in his ear. Pilgrim listened, not taking his eyes off the truck, then he casually looked up at us, fixing our position straightaway. He turned back to Sweet and said something to him, and after a brief nod of acknowledgement, Sweet went back to Diedle. As he began talking to his brother, I saw Gun Sur saying something to Pilgrim. It looked like he was asking him a question – Whats going on? Is there a problem? Pilgrim shook his head and waved his hand, assuring Gun Sur that everything was fine. Gun Sur didnt look totally convinced, glancing over his shoulder at Diedle and Sweet, but then Councillor Ghauri spoke to him, pointing at the truck, and the Marshal turned his attention back to the display.

Chola Se nudged me again, wanting to draw my attention to something, but Ide already spotted it myself. Diedle was no longer standing beside his brother. Hede sidled away while Gun Sur was talking to Pilgrim. And now we could both see him coming out of a side door of the storehouse and making his way around the cordon, heading in our direction.

We could have easily taken him on – it was 2 against 1, and we could see him coming all the way – but he was a Fighter, Deputy Pilgrims personal bodyguard---he was a figure of authority – and we were just dogchilds. If wede taken him on there and then, in front of the Marshal and his Captains and Councillors – and most of the towns population – wede never have got away with it.

We both knew what we had to do.

We climbed down off the pile of rubble, moved quietly out of the yard, and disappeared into the Eastside ruins.

There are so many places to hide in the ruins that once Diedle had realised thats where wede gone, he didnt even bother coming after us. We hadnt gone far – wede taken shelter in the ruins of an outbuilding about 50 yards from the storehouse – and wede seen Diedle arriving at the pile of rubble. Hede stopped in front of it, looked around, then shouldered his rifle and drawn a revolver from a holster at his belt. It was a massive handgun – a Colt Python 357 Magnum with an 8-inch barrel – and even in Diedles huge hand it looked like a miniature cannon. Holding the gun at his side, he clambered up the pile of rubble, then stood at the top gazing across at the ruins, trying to work out where wede gone. After a minute or so he frowned to himself, scratched his head, then lumbered back down to the ground again. Intelligence wasnt his greatest asset, but he was smart enough to realise that if he followed us into the ruins he almost certainly wouldnt find us, and there was a reasonably good chance that he wouldnt come out again.

He stood there for a few more minutes, halfheartedly looking around, but when the roar of the truck engine from the yard suddenly died, the unfamiliar crash of silence seemed to spur him into action, and he holstered his Colt, turned on his heels, and began heading back the way hede come.

We waited quietly, watching him every step of the way until he was no longer in sight, then we carried on watching and waiting for another minute or so just to make sure he wasnt coming back.

Do you think hese gone back to the storehouse? Chola Se said.

Probably---for now anyway.

She nodded, and we both went quiet again.

We couldnt see the storehouse or the yard from where we were hiding, but we could see that the townspeople were beginning to leave now, heading back along the streets towards the centre of town. There was still a lot of heated discussion going on – people complaining about not being told anything – but there were lots of Fighters around, and while they werent doing anything more than making their presence known, it was enough to keep the atmosphere relatively calm.

We should go, Jeet, Chola Se said.

She was right.

We checked a final time to make sure Diedle wasnt around, then we left the demolished outbuilding and headed off into the night.

Although we were reasonably confident that we werent officially outlaws yet – because Pilgrim would rather deal with us quietly if he could – we still couldnt be absolutely sure of our safety, so as we made our way across town to the Quarterhouse we kept to the backstreets as much as we could and made ourselves scarce whenever we saw any Fighters.

When we got to the Quarterhouse – approaching it from a little alley on the east side of the Square – the Square and the streets all around it were completely deserted. The only sign of life we could see was a pair of Fighters – not Diedle and Sweet – standing guard at the main entrance, and a glint of candlelight showing through the shutters of a room on the second floor.

Apart from that, there wasnt a soul in sight.

We waited in the alleyway entrance, keeping our eyes on the Quarterhouse.

Do you think theyre already in there? Chola Se said.

I shook my head. They would have had to leave the storehouse straight after the display to get here before us, and there were too many angry people around for them to do that. I think they probably waited until the streets were clear before leaving. Theyle be here soon.

What if Pilgrims not with them?

I was just about to answer when we heard voices over to our left, and a moment later we saw Gun Sur and Pilgrim and the 3 Fighter Captains approaching the south side of the Square. We edged back into the darkness of the alley and watched as they crossed the Square and headed up the steps. As before, Diedle and Sweet werent actually part of the group but were following along behind them, and when the others went inside the Quarterhouse, the 2 brothers waited at the foot of the steps.

We made ourselves as comfortable as possible, sitting on the ground with our backs against the alley walls – Chola Se facing the Quarterhouse, me facing her – and we settled down to wait.

An hour later, we changed position.

The towndog appeared half an hour later.

It was a lone male, quite young, and it came from somewhere

behind the Quarterhouse. He seemed unusually friendly for a towndog – perhaps because he was still just a juvenile – and instead of ignoring Sweet and giving him a wide berth as most dogs would, the young male began sidling up to the big Fighter. It was a very cautious approach, and clearly submissive – circling around, head low to the ground, tail between his legs – but there was no question the dog had friendly intentions. I could see the tip of his curled-up tail wagging, and his facial expression was that of a young dog seeking affection from a dominant elder.

Sweet was having none of it though.

First of all he swung a lazy boot at the dog, and when that didnt work – the dog scuttling away, then trying again – Sweet went a step further, lunging at the dog and swinging his rifle at him like a club. The dog dodged the blow with ease, skipping away from it with no trouble at all, but hede learned his lesson now and didnt try approaching the big Fighter again.

Unfortunately, as he trotted off across the Square, glancing over his shoulder to make sure Sweet wasnt coming after him, the young dog caught our scent.

He was almost level with the alley when it happened. I saw him freeze for a moment – a front leg half raised, his head turned our way, his snout angled upwards as he breathed in our scent and pinpointed its location – and then, with an added purpose to his movement, he was off again, this time heading straight for us.

I glanced over at Sweet, hoping that he hadnt seen the dogs sudden change of direction, but I was out of luck. Although the Fighter showed no sign of alarm or suspicion, and was clearly only watching the dog out of boredom, the mere fact that he was watching it spelled trouble. The dog was about 20 yards from us now – close enough to see us – and while his growing excitement and curiosity probably wasnt obvious to Sweet just yet, it was only a matter of time before the young dogs reaction to us became so animated – circling us, yapping, bowing and prancing – that Sweet and Diedle were bound to suspect something.

I couldnt let that happen.

I dont know how I did what I did then.

Whatever it was though, it came from the same place inside me – the same sense, the same part of me – that allows me to silence dogs, only this time when it came out of me and took me into the dogs heart, the feeling we had together wasnt just that we wanted to be quiet, we also wanted to keep away from the alley.

And it worked.

The young dog slowed to a halt and looked slightly puzzled for a moment – frowning to himself at his unexpected change of heart – and then, after a quick look around, he shrugged off his confusion, turned to his right, and started loping off towards the far end of the Square.

How did you do that? Chola Se said quietly.

I turned to her. Do what?

You know what. She stared at me. I felt it happen, Jeet. I felt it coming from you. It was like---I dont know---like a ripple in the air, but in a different part of the air, a part that we dont usually see---She shook her head in quiet disbelief, and her voice lowered to a whisper. What did you do?

Before I could answer her – or more likely not be able to answer her – our attention was suddenly drawn to the sound of the Quarterhouse door opening. Chola Se quickly shuffled over to my side of the alley, and we watched together as the 3 Fighter Captains came out of the building and headed down the steps. They were discussing something as they came down – Captain Glorian gesticulating with his hands, explaining some kind of manoeuvre – and as they neared the foot of the steps, where Diedle and Sweet were waiting, Captain Kite noticed the brothers and shot them a piercing look. Even from a distance the contempt in her eyes was unmistakable, and as the 2 Fighters dutifully shuffled away to a more respectful distance, she didnt give them a second glance.

The 3 Captains carried on talking for a while when they reached the foot of the steps. The night was icy cold now, and as they stood there huddled together, with their shoulders hunched and their breath clouding in the frosted air, I tried to make out what they were saying. Their voices were just about audible, and I could tell that most of the talking was coming from Kite and Glorian, but apart from 1 or 2 words I couldnt hear enough to make sense of anything.

They didnt talk for long – 2 or 3 minutes at most – then Captain Luca said goodbye to the other 2 and walked off towards the eastside of the Square, and a few moments later Kite and Glorian moved off together in the opposite direction, before turning left at the corner of the Quarterhouse and disappearing around the side of the building.

In the stillness of the night, the 3 sets of footsteps took a long time to fade away, but eventually we couldnt hear them anymore. We watched Diedle and Sweet resume their position at the foot of the steps, then we settled back and carried on watching and waiting.

An hour later we heard the now familiar sound of the Quarterhouse door opening again, and this time – finally – we saw Pilgrim coming out. Diedle and Sweet were immediately on the alert – rifles at the ready, eyes on the lookout – and as Pilgrim came down to the foot of the steps they fell in beside him, one on either side, and the 3 of them moved off together, heading for the westside of the Square.

There was no point in following them – at this time of night, with no one else around, they would have spotted us straightaway – but it didnt matter because following them was never our intention anyway.

As our second-in-command, Pilgrim had certain privileges – although hede call them requirements – one of which was having more than one home. He had 3. One just off Main Street, another on the Beach Road, and a third on Long Avenue. And all we needed to know – all wede been waiting to find out – was which of these homes he was using that night. And as we watched him leaving the Square and heading off down a broad street of large and virtually undamaged houses, we finally had our answer.

The street hede just entered was Long Avenue.

Diedle and Sweet were still with him, and there was little doubt theyd be staying with him for the rest of the night. It was highly unlikely theyd be staying in the same room as him while he slept though, and there was a good chance they wouldnt be inside the house at all, but would spend the night standing guard outside. And if they were outside, that meant that Pilgrim would be alone in the house – unprotected, probably asleep, as vulnerable as he was ever going to be.

This was the moment wede been waiting for – waiting for hours in the freezing cold, hiding away in ruins and alleys, patiently biding our time – but now that it had finally arrived, I suddenly found myself beset with questions and doubts.

Why were we doing this? Why were we risking so much to end the life of this man? And why were we even still here? We could have been far away from all this by now – out in the Deathlands, where we belonged, running with the dogs through that vast black nothingness---but instead we were here, crouched in an alleyway, cold and tired, our hearts weighed down with murder.

It didnt make sense.

But as I turned to Chola Se to voice my thoughts, and I saw the desperation in her eyes, everything came back to me. I remembered her words – he haunts me, Jeet---hese in my head all the time---every moment of every day, every time I try to sleep---hese always there – and I remembered seeing her in the dungeon – splayed out on the ground in a bloodstained dress, chained to a stake, battered and bruised, beaten, abused – and I remembered Starry too, or what was left of him – his severed hand on the beach, the deadwhite skin crawling with flies, the sand beneath it soaked black with blood---

I remembered now. I remembered why Pilgrim had to be killed.

It made perfect sense.

Are you ready? I said to Chola Se.

She nodded.

Okay, lets go.

335

Pilgrims house was a large detached building set back from the street behind a 6-foot-high stone wall. Heavy wooden gates led through to a large open courtyard in front of the house, and when we took a quick look through a gap in the gates we saw Diedle standing guard in a pillared porchway at the front door. There was no cover in the courtyard, and the moonlight was bright enough to give Diedle a reasonably clear view, so even if we could have climbed over the wall without being spotted – which was unlikely – wede never have made it across the courtyard unnoticed.

Lets try round the back, Chola Se whispered.

We moved away from the front gates, carried on down to the end of the road, then doubled back along a series of narrow backstreets and pathways that eventually brought us round to the rear of Pilgrims house. There was a wall here as well, and at first sight it seemed just as solid and impenetrable as the wall at the front – with the added security of having no gates or doors – but after searching every inch of it, we found a section near one end where the stonework was beginning to crumble away, and once wede got to work on it – silently clawing out the stones – wede soon made a big enough gap to squeeze through. Chola Se went first, sniffing the air as she cautiously edged through the hole, and I followed immediately after her.

The yard at the back of the house was at least as big as the courtyard at the front, if not bigger, but it wasnt so wide open. There was scrap and clutter all over the place – discarded furniture, rusted machinery, piles of timber and stone – and both sides of the yard were lined with the remains of tumbledown outhouses. Parts of the yard were overgrown with thornbushes and weeds, and dotted around here and there were dozens of ancient stone statues

– carved figures of strange-looking men and women, some almost intact, others with heads or limbs missing. In the icy moonlight the statues resembled ghostly sentinels, frozen in time, forever watching and waiting---their sightless eyes never seeing, their senseless minds never knowing.

We took cover behind a tangled thicket of brambles and gazed through the frosted branches at the back of the house.

A short flight of stone steps led up to the back door, and we could see Sweet sitting wearily on the top step. He clearly wasnt happy with the job hede been given – hunched over, his head in his hands, his rifle in his lap – but he was doing his best to stay alert, and every few minutes hede straighten up, stretch his back, rub his eyes, and gaze around the yard.

There were no lights showing in the house, and we couldnt see inside because all the shutters were closed, but we knew Pilgrim was in there. Diedle and Sweet wouldnt be guarding the house if he wasnt.

He had to be in there.

Can you see any sign of him? I whispered to Chola Se.

She shook her head.

Do you want to wait? I asked her.

What for?

Its a big house. He could be anywhere in there. If we stay here and keep watching, we might see something that tells us where he is.

She looked at me. Weve been waiting all night, Jeet.

I held her gaze for a moment, then nodded and reached for my sling.

There were plenty of rocks and stones around, and it didnt take long to find one that was just right. I fitted it into the cradle of the sling, checked the balance, then squatted down again and peered through the brambles at Sweet. He was only about 40 yards away – an easy enough target – but there was a walnut tree directly in front of the brambles, its branches blocking my line of fire. I crawled over to the edge of the thicket, away from the tree, then took another look. There was nothing in my way now. I had a clear shot.

As I closed my eyes for a moment to steady myself, I wondered briefly if I should hold back a little when I fired the rock at Sweet. He didnt mean anything to me, and I knew he wouldnt think twice about killing me if he had to, but he wasnt my enemy. I didnt want to kill him unless it was necessary. But at the same time, I knew I couldnt afford to think like that. He was a big strong man, and if I held back even slightly – trying to incapacitate him without actually killing him – I might not hit him hard enough to knock him out. And if I didnt take him out with the first shot, I probably wouldnt get a second chance.

It was him or us.

I opened my eyes, took a final deep breath, then stood up, stepped out from behind the brambles, and whipped the rock from the sling. It was a low flat shot – fast and hard – and the rock cracked into Sweets head with barely a sound. It caught him square in the forehead, right between the eyes, and the effect was instantaneous. His head lurched back with the impact, he wobbled for a moment, then his body crumpled and slumped to the ground. There was a dull thump as his massive bulk hit solid stone, and although it wasnt as loud as it would have been if hede fallen from a standing position, it was still a fairly heavy thud. And if we could hear it, there was a possibility that Diedle had heard it. I stepped back behind the thicket, squatted down beside Chola Se, and for the next minute or so we just waited — not moving, not making a sound — until we were as sure as we could be that no one else had heard anything. Only then did we creep out from behind the brambles and cautiously make our way across the yard to the steps.

Sweet wasnt dead. He was unconscious, and badly injured — his head almost split open — but he was still breathing. There wasnt much chance of him waking up any time soon, and even if he did, I doubted hede be capable of doing anything. But just to be sure, I took the blueglass phial from my bag, knelt down beside him, opened his mouth, and poured a few drops of the liquid into the back of his throat. While I was doing that, Chola Se quietly tried the door.

Its locked, she whispered. But I dont think its bolted.

I started looking through Sweets pockets, hoping that Pilgrim had given him a key so he could open the door in a hurry if he needed to. I found a 9mm Beretta automatic in one of his coat pockets, and a pearlhandled switchblade in another — both of which I transferred to my pockets — but I didnt find any keys.

Whats that? Chola Se said, pointing at Sweets neck.

I looked closer and saw what she meant. A length of string was looped round his neck, most of it tucked out of sight beneath his shirt. I reached across and pulled it out, then lifted the string over his head and held it up for Chola Se to see. She smiled at the sight of the heavy iron key dangling from my hand.

I got to my feet and passed her the key. She carefully inserted it in the keyhole, and turned it slowly. After a few moments there was a muffled clank, and Chola Se turned to me and nodded.

I drew my knife.

She took hold of her shotgun.

I thought about taking Sweets Beretta from my pocket, but quickly decided against it. We were heading into an unknown darkness, with no idea where we were going or what we might find. The last thing I needed was an unfamiliar weapon in my hand. It was there if I needed it, but I felt more comfortable with my knife.

I turned to Chola Se. She had the shotgun in one hand, the door handle in the other, and her ear pressed up to the door.

Can you hear anything? I whispered.

She shook her head. Maybe hese not in there.

Hese in there.

How are we going to find him?

I dont know, I admitted.

She looked at me. Weare just going to have to go in and see what happens, arent we?

Unless youve got a better idea.

She lowered her eyes for a second, thinking things through, then she looked up again and shrugged.

Ime okay with seeing what happens if you are.

I smiled.

Ready? she said.

I nodded.

She took a breath, ran her hand through her hair, and slowly opened the door.

The darkness inside the house was close to absolute, and if it wasnt for a few chinks of moonlight creeping in through gaps in the shutters – and our more-dog-than-human nightvision – we wouldnt have been able to see our hands in front of our eyes. As it was though, after wede stood in the sheer blackness for a few minutes with our eyes closed – allowing them to adjust to the darkness – we could see just enough to give us a vague idea of our immediate surroundings.

We were in a large corridor. It had a stone floor, a high ceiling, and it looked as if it led off towards the front of the house. To our right was a flight of stairs – broad stone steps, metal railings, paintings on the wall. As Ide said to Chola Se, it was a big house, and Pilgrim could be anywhere – upstairs or down – but we had to start somewhere, and the most likely place hede be at this time of night was upstairs.

As we cautiously made our way up the stone stairs – taking them one at a time, and pausing every few steps to listen – we were both instinctively sniffing the air as we went. It didnt smell good. Damp, mould, unwashed clothes, sweat, excrement, urine---the sickly stink of foul things.

The smell grew stronger as we reached the top of the stairs, and I could see Chola Se wrinkling her nose and covering her mouth to stifle a retch. A corridor stretched out ahead of us. There were 2 doors on the left, and 2 on the right. All of them closed. We stood still and listened again, hoping to hear something that would tell us where Pilgrim was – breathing, snoring, dreaming---anything.

The house was deathly silent.

It didnt feel right.

You can tell when a house is empty – it has an unmistakable lifelessness to it, a tangible lack of presence – and this house didnt feel empty. But it didnt feel like a house with a man sleeping alone in it either. We should have heard something by now. This silence was too silent.

I looked at Chola Se, and I could see she felt the same. She could sense the wrongness too.

This isnt right, is it? I said quietly.

She shook her head.

Do you want to go back?

Do you?

I think its too late for going back.

She nodded. Lets get it done then.

We tried the nearest door on the right first. It wasnt locked, but when we inched it open and cautiously looked inside, it was clear straightaway that Pilgrim wasnt in there. One of the shutters had a number of broken slats, and in the faint light of the moon we could see that the room was packed from top to bottom with all sorts of unbelievable things – paintings, sculptures, ornaments, books, furniture, clothing, jewellery, weapons---there was even a boxful of writing books and pencils---a whole boxful. There must have been at least a dozen writing books in there, all of them as good as new.

The room was a treasure trove – Pilgrim had clearly been plundering for years – and it was tempting to arm ourselves with as many weapons as we could carry, but apart from a collection of swords and lances leaning against the wall to our right, all the weapons were stored on the far side of the room, and we would have had to clamber over everything else to get to them.

There wasnt time for that.

The boxful of writing books was right in front of us though, and

I couldnt resist helping myself to 6 or 7 books and a handful of pencils. I wasnt sure why I was taking them – I had no idea what I might use them for, or even if Ide ever get the chance to use them at all – but just as I was putting them in my knapsack, the memory of the timeless vision came back to me – the image Ide seen of myself in the mountains – and this time, when I saw myself sitting in the shade of the old blackwood tree, I could see that I had a writing book open in my lap---

I was writing.

And I could see something else too---I could see my mother, my dogmother, stretched out asleep on a patch of sandy ground in front of a cave---and in the background I could hear the faint sound of playful laughter---

I blinked, dismissing the vision from my mind.

Whatever it was, and whatever it meant – if anything – it didnt matter right now. The only thing that mattered now was finding Deputy Pilgrim. And he definitely wasnt in here.

We left the room, closed the door, and quietly padded along the corridor to the next door. Again, it wasnt locked. But this time, the moment we quietly eased it open, we knew wede finally found him.

We could smell his scent in the air – strong, fresh---right here. We could smell his breath, his sweat, his being. And as Chola Se opened the door a little wider – slowly, warily, inch by inch – and we leaned in carefully and peered into the room, we saw him.

He was asleep – lying motionless in a massive bed, the sheets drawn up over his head. His submachine gun and hat lay on the bed beside him, and one of his Cowboy boots was clearly visible poking out from beneath the sheets at the foot of the bed.

The reason we could see all this was that the shutters in the window over the bed were half open – letting in the moonlight – which struck me as being a bit strange. Why would he leave the shutters open at night? No one ever leaves their shutters open at night – its always too cold, too dangerous. It also seemed strange that hede sleep with his boots on---

And I should have given these things more thought. I should have realised what they meant the moment I saw them. But before Ide had a chance to think about anything, Chola Se had stepped through the doorway and begun crossing the room towards the bed. Shede become something else now, something savage, like a hunter closing on the kill – measured steps, silent, determined---the shotgun at her hip---her eyes fixed intently on the figure beneath the sheets. I dont know what my intentions were as I set off after her, moving as fast as I could without making any noise. I dont know if I planned to stop her, join her in the kill, or just be with her. But whatever it was, Ide left it too late.

I was a couple of steps behind her when she stopped beside the bed. I knew what she about to do. I could see it coming. She wanted to see Pilgrims face before she killed him, and she wanted him to see her. She wanted him to know he was about to die. I saw her left hand letting go of the shotgun, and I saw her beginning to lean over the bed and reach out for the sheet---but that was as far as she got before the room suddenly erupted in a burst of light and a crash of shouting voices.

DONT MOVE!

DROP YOUR WEAPONS!

PUT THE GUN DOWN!

Everything seemed to happen all at once then. In the same

moment that I spun round at the sound of the voices and saw 4 armed figures emerging from the darkness at the back of the room – one with a blazing torch in his hand – there was a sudden deafening boom from Chola Ses shotgun and the room was instantly filled with a billowing cloud of smoke and feathers and straw. I just had time to see the figure with the torch waving it to clear the air, then stepping back and covering his face as the swirling cloud caught fire, and the next thing I knew there was another blast from Chola Ses shotgun – the second barrel – followed immediately by a crash of splintering wood and a sudden gust of icy air that whipped up the burning cloud of feathers and straw into a swirling frenzy of smoke and flame, then Chola Se grabbed hold of my arm and started pulling me across the room.

This way, Jeet! she yelled. The window!

The window on the far side of the room was wide open now, the shutters blown apart by Chola Ses shotgun, and as we ran towards it – side by side, crouched down low – I could hear the panicked shouts of the figures behind us.

STOP THEM!

NO! HOLD YOUR FIRE!

I CANT SEE ANYTHING!

We were both pure dog now, and in the last few moments, just before we jumped, everything became perfectly clear to me. I could see the night sky through the gaping window – the stars, the moon, the sleeping town stretched out below – and I could see in my mind the 30-foot drop from the window into the backyard beneath it. I could see all the clutter in the yard – the heaps of building materials, the discarded furniture, the ghostly statues, the thornbushes and weeds – and I could see in my memory a pile of timber planks stacked up in an unsteady block almost directly beneath the window.

I sheathed my knife without breaking stride, took hold of Chola Ses outstretched hand, and we launched ourselves into the air and dived headfirst through the open window.

The crack of a gunshot followed us out, and I felt the air scream as the bullet shot past my head, missing my ear by inches, and then we were falling, dropping down through the darkness together, and just for a second the world slept in silence. There was nothing – just a gentle rush of cold black air, the soundless sound of falling, and the quiet flapping of our clothes, as hushed as the wings of settling birds---

Ide never felt so free in my life as I did in those few fleeting moments. It was as if the world had ended and all we had to do for the rest of forever was fall through the silent darkness together. No more fighting, no more killing, no more living or dying – all we had to do was hold hands and fall through the sky, and nothing would ever stop us---

The bonejarring impact as I slammed down into the pile of timber ripped all thoughts from my head, and in an instant the world came alive again. The silence exploded in a crash of collapsing timbers, and for a moment all I was aware of was Chola Ses hand being torn from mine as the falling planks swept us apart like a great wooden wave, and then – for what seemed like an age – I was engulfed in an avalanche of tumbling planks, the heavy wooden boards battering into me as I rolled and twisted among them.

At one point I found myself lying on my back, sliding headfirst towards the ground, and for a fraction of a second I saw 2 familiar faces staring down at me from the window wede just jumped from

– Pilgrim and Captain Kite. Pilgrim had his submachine gun in his hands, and as Kite suddenly spotted me and reached out of the window to point me out – There he is! – Pilgrim put the MP40 to his shoulder and calmly began firing. The machine gun spat flame, and just as a rapidfire hail of bullets began ripping into the timbers around my head, peppering my face with needlesharp splinters, I felt my shoulders hit solid ground. I rolled backwards, landing in a crouch, then leaped to one side and threw myself to the ground, taking cover behind the base of a large stone statue. Pilgrim kept shooting, spraying the statue with dozens of rounds, and I could hear the bullets ricocheting off the stone with a highpitched scream, but I knew I was safe for the moment.

I looked around for Chola Se, but couldnt see her anywhere.

Chola Se! I yelled. CHOLA!

Over here, Jeet.

Her voice was closeby, and as I peeked around the righthand edge of the statue I saw her lying flat on the ground beside the collapsed pile of timber, calmly reloading her shotgun. The pile of boards was between her and the house, and as long as she kept low and close to the heap, Pilgrim and Kite couldnt see her.

Are you okay? I called out in a loud whisper.

She gave me the thumbs up. You?

I raised my thumb in return.

The machine-gun fire had stopped now – I guessed Pilgrim was either saving his ammunition or had run out and was reloading – and in the momentary quiet I heard the heavy clomp of running boots coming from inside the house.

We need to get out of here, Chola, I said.

Have you got still got Sweets pistol?

Yeh, I said, reaching into my pocket and pulling out the Beretta. How many rounds have you got?

I slid out the magazine and saw that it was fully loaded.

15, I called back to Chola Se, snapping the magazine back in.

You take the door, she said, Ile take the window. The moment they take cover, we run. Okay?

I nodded, holding her gaze for a second, then I turned towards the house, racked a round into the chamber of the pistol, and levelled the gun at the door. I could see Sweets lifeless figure slumped on the ground where wede left him, just a few yards from the door---directly in my line of fire. I couldnt tell if he was alive or not, and I didnt have time to dwell on it. The bootsteps had stopped now, and I could sense a presence behind the closed door.

I hadnt seen the 4 figures in the room clearly enough to identify them, but I was fairly sure that Pilgrim hadnt been one of them, so it was possible there were 5 people in the house altogether, maybe even more. And if Pilgrim and Kite were still upstairs, that meant there could be as many as 3 Fighters preparing to burst through the door, if not more.

I waited, keeping perfectly still – arms outstretched, hands gripping the pistol, finger on the trigger – with the V of the gunsight fixed steadily on the door.

Nothing happened for a good 30 seconds, and I began to wonder if the bootsteps had been a diversion, a distraction to keep our attention from the real point of attack, but just as I was about to take a quick look around to make sure we hadnt been fooled, the door crashed open and 3 Fighters came rushing out, all of them firing rifles, and at the same time I heard the deafening clatter of Pilgrims MP40 opening up from the window, raining down fire on the statue, followed almost instantly by the ear-splitting boom of Chola Ses shotgun.

I started firing the instant I saw the Fighters, letting off shots as fast as I could. One of the Fighters went down almost immediately – hit in the chest as he charged down the steps – and the other one didnt get much further, making 10 yards at most before clutching his shoulder and reeling sideways, then spinning back round again and sinking to his knees as I caught him with a second shot in the leg. As I swung the Beretta back towards the door, I saw the third Fighter running back into the house and slamming the door shut behind him, and at the same moment I heard the thunderous crash of the shotgun again, followed almost instantly by a sharp cry of pain from the window, then a sudden ringing silence as the roar of the machine gun stopped.

The silence was our signal to move, and a split second later we were both up and running – streaking silently through the darkness, swerving around trees and statues, leaping over piles of rubble---we were in our element now, running wild, and we knew that nothing could stop us. Even when the shooting started up again – machine-gun fire and rifleshots coming from the house – and we could feel the bullets slicing through the air all around us, we knew we were safe as long as we kept running. And as we approached the wall at the end of the yard, thats all I had in my mind – dont stop, dont even slow down, just keep on running---

We could see the opening in the wall now, the narrow gap wede made in the loose stonework on the way in, and as we veered towards it, and Chola Se instinctively began slowing down – preparing to squeeze through the gap – I increased my pace, edging ahead of her, and then I just put my head down and ran, racing straight at the wall, and at the very last moment I lowered my shoulder, leaped into the air, and launched myself at the gap. The thick cloth of my coat cushioned most of the impact, and the stonework was already so weakened there was hardly any resistance anyway. The hole in the wall cracked open like an egg, the crumbled stonework breaking away and falling to the ground in heavy chunks, and as I stumbled through to the backstreet on the other side – my momentum almost sending me sprawling – I looked back and saw Chola Se following me through the newly gaping hole.

The smile on her face was something Ile never forget. It made me want to run through the wall again.

Nice work, Jeet, she said. But why didnt you do that on the way in? It would have saved us a lot of hard work, wouldnt it?

I was about to answer when a bullet thwacked into the wall behind her, and as she quickly threw herself to the ground, I saw the third Fighter taking aim at us from halfway down the yard. He must have come back out of the house again while we were running. I raised the Beretta and let off a couple of shots at him, and as he took cover behind a limbless statue, we set off running again.

The third Fighter tried following us – we could hear him clomping along the streets behind us for a short while – but he never got close enough to take another shot, and within a few minutes wede left him way behind and were jogging along the empty backstreets and alleyways on the southside of town. For the moment we were safe, but we knew it was only a temporary reprieve. The gunshots had woken the whole town, and as we loped along through the early-morning darkness we could see more and more torchlights flickering all around us. The town was coming to life, getting louder and brighter and busier by the second – voices calling out, dogs barking, bootsteps running – and I knew it wouldnt be long before everyone knew that Deputy Pilgrim had been attacked in his own house, and that the would-be killers – the dogchilds Jeet and Chola Se – were on the run. And once everyone knew that, we wouldnt just be on the run from the Fighters, wede be on the run from the entire town.

Which way, Jeet? I heard Chola Se ask.

Wede reached the end of a highwalled alleyway at the back of some empty buildings near the Beach Road. Another narrow alley led off to the left – towards the road – and there was a patch of scrubland to our right that led across to the top of the beach.

We were both breathing heavily now, and as we stopped and looked around, trying to decide which way to go, we took the opportunity to get our breath back and check our weapons. As Chola Se reloaded her shotgun, and I counted the rounds left in the Beretta – 5 – I found myself wondering if it really made any difference which way we went. Left or right, towards the road or towards the beach---what did it matter? There was no escape. The townspeople were everywhere. Whichever way we went, theyd get us in the end.

OVER THERE!

The sudden shout came from our right, and as we looked across we saw torchlights in the darkness beyond the scrubland. We didnt wait to see who it was or if theyd actually seen us or not, we just turned to our left and took off down the alley.

We were dogs again now.

No worries, no doubts, no need to think.

The future didnt exist.

There was nothing but now. And now was nothing but running.

By The Time the sky was beginning to lighten with the pink glow of dawn, wede just about run ourselves to exhaustion. Wede stopped and laid low a couple of times – once in a corn shed on the westside of town, another time in the basement of an abandoned house – but on both occasions wede almost been discovered, and wede had to make our escape before wede had time to rest. The town was out in force now – Fighters, Youngers, Workers---everyone was out and about looking for us – and although wede managed to avoid them all so far, I knew we couldnt keep going forever. We hadnt slept or eaten for a long time. We were thirsty. We were running out of energy. We needed to rest.

We were back on the southside of town now, close to the beach again. For the last few minutes wede been running from 2 Fighters whode spotted us coming out of a house a few streets away – wede broken into it in the hope of finding some water – and wede finally given the Fighters the slip by throwing ourselves into a ditch that runs along a strip of wasteland between the beach and the edge of town. The ditch was no more than 3 feet deep, but as long as we kept our heads down we couldnt be seen, so after the Fighters had passed us by – close enough for us to hear them talking – we just slumped down together and took a few moments to rest our legs.

Do you think theyve gone? Chola Se said.

For now, yeh. But they could be back any minute. And weare not safe from the eels here either.

We cant keep running, Jeet. Its nearly daylight. We need to find a place to hole up for a while, somewhere they wont find us.

I know, I said, glancing up at the sky.

The sun was rising rapidly now, the dark of the night fading by the second.

What about Eastside? Chola Se suggested. The ruins arent far from here, are they? I know theyre going to be looking for us there, but theres lots of places that most people dont know about, especially around Dog Town.

Dog Town is a bombed-out area near the Eastside cliffs where all the houses are totally demolished. Its known as Dog Town because the female towndogs use it as a den site, and the reason they like it there is that beneath all the rubble are dozens of old cellars and vaults which make perfect dens for raising their pups. And Chola Se was right – theyd make perfect sanctuaries for us as well. As long as we could get to them without being seen.

If we can make it across the Beach Road without being spotted, I said to her, we could follow that track that leads through the thornfield to Dog Town.

The track the dogs use?

Yeh.

She thought about it for a moment, picturing the route in her mind, then turned to me and nodded. She looked exhausted – pale, gaunt, drained--- her lips cracked, her eyes glazed, her face streaked with dirt and covered in scratches.

Wele be there soon, I told her. And then we can rest properly, okay?

Yeh.

I shuffled round onto my knees then straightened up and cautiously peered out over the top of the ditch. I could see the flamelight of torches moving around all over town, but I couldnt see any nearby. The wasteland directly in front of us was empty and quiet, and in the dim morning haze I could just make out the Beach Road beyond it. I watched the road for a while, looking for any signs of life, but it too was empty and quiet.

Chola Se was sitting up now. I reached down and gave her a hand, and a moment later she was kneeling beside me, gazing across the wasteland at the road. The morning sun was brightening, the haze beginning to lift. If we left it any longer we wouldnt stand a chance.

We have to go, I said to Chola Se. Can you make it?

She just nodded again.

We looked around for a final time, then scrambled out of the ditch and set off across the wasteland.

Wede nearly reached the Beach Road when we heard the gunshots. They came from our right – rifleshots at first, then a ragged volley of pistol fire – and when I looked across I saw a group of Youngers heading towards us from the east. There were about 6 or 7 of them, and as they charged towards us – whooping and shouting and shooting their guns off – I could see the bloodlust in their eyes. They were firing so wildly that most of the shots were sailing harmlessly over our heads, but they were closing fast – less than 40 yards away now – and some of them were beginning to find their range.

Keep going! I yelled to Chola Se. We can still get across the road!

But as we leaped over the stone wall that borders the road we saw 3 Fighters heading towards us from the north, blocking our way to the thornfield. They were running hard, alerted by the gunfire, and the moment they saw us they dropped to their knees, raised their rifles, and opened fire. Unlike the Youngers, they knew what they were doing, and if we hadnt thrown ourselves to the ground and taken cover behind the wall across the road, we would have been cut down where we stood.

The Fighters had us pinned down now – rifleshots cracking into the wall and splitting the air above our heads – and the Youngers were still closing in. As I glanced over to our right, I saw one of them standing in the middle of the road no more than 30 yards away, pointing at us and calling out to the others, and a moment later the rest of them appeared and started clambering over the wall onto the road.

Chola? I said.

Yeh, I see them.

We both ducked down for a moment as a shot from one of the Youngers smacked into the wall just above our heads, and then we just gave each other a quick look – and a brief nod of agreement – and did what we had to do.

We made our moves simultaneously – Chola Se springing up into a sitting position and blasting the shotgun at the Youngers, while I swung my arm over the wall and let off 3 rapid shots at the Fighters – and a split second later we were up and running again, keeping low and shooting as we went. One of the Fighters was already down, and I think Chola Se winged another one when she let loose with the second barrel of the shotgun, and when I glanced over my shoulder at the Youngers I saw that one of them was on the ground and another one was bent over double, holding his bloodied head in his hands. The rest of them were still coming on fast though.

The one in front was Raoul – the Younger whode been on duty at the Olders Home when Ide visited – and it was clear from the way he was urging the others on, yelling and waving his gun around, that he was the leader of the group. I let off a quick shot at him and got lucky, hitting him in the arm, and as he screamed in pain and dropped his gun, the others slowed up and began backing off a bit. The 2 Fighters still on their feet were keeping their distance now too, and although they kept firing at us as we raced away up the road, we were moving so fast they were unlikely to hit us.

The problem was, we were heading the wrong way now – towards the centre of town where most of the townspeople were – and because of all the gunfire, everyone knew we were coming. And we no longer had the cover of darkness to help us. The sun was up now, burning down with a brilliant white light that left us nowhere to hide.

All we could do was run.

The Beach Road steepens as it approaches the main part of town – where it merges into Main Street – and as we pounded up the hill we couldnt actually see what lay ahead of us on the other side, but when we reached the top and our view became clear, it was obvious we were in serious trouble. A group of about 10 or 12 Fighters were striding along Main Street towards us, and behind them we could see dozens of other townspeople following in their wake. They were all carrying weapons of some kind – firearms, knives, clubs, machetes – and theyd all become crazed by the hunt. Even the ones I knew to be relatively reasonable had madness in their eyes. It was as if the cloud of confusion and fear theyd been living under for the past few days had suddenly burst open and rained down upon them in a poisonous torrent of mindless rage.

Over to our left, another group of Youngers had spotted us and were charging up from the beach, and as the first shots were fired – I couldnt tell where from – I heard the sound of guttural shouts and clattering boots coming up the road behind us. When I glanced over my shoulder, I saw the Fighters and Youngers wede just left behind making their way up the hill.

As more and more gunfire began raining down on us, we darted to our right and dived for cover behind the wall at the side of the road. We returned fire, doing our best to keep the Fighters and townspeople at bay, but although we managed to slow their progress – forcing most of them to scatter and take cover – we knew we couldnt stay where we were. We were surrounded on 3 sides – Youngers to the east, Fighters and Youngers on the road behind us, and even more Fighters and townspeople directly ahead of us on Main Street. The only place left for us to run was a broad stretch of wasteground to the right of the road, but it was so flat and wide open that we didnt stand a chance of getting across it without being shot.

We need to get out of here, Jeet! Chola Se yelled, letting off a shot towards Main Street.

I was running low on ammunition now, and as I took aim and fired at the nearest Fighter, I knew I only had a couple of rounds left.

Chola Se swung round and blasted away at the Youngers coming up from the beach, then immediately reloaded, swivelled round, and fired off both barrels at the mob on the road behind us.

Theres too many of them! she called out, turning back and reloading again. If we dont get out of here soon—

East Walk, I said suddenly.

She snapped the shotgun shut and looked up quickly, following my gaze and staring ahead at Main Street.

East Walk is a covered passage leading off Main Street that cuts through to an area called Southwall, a winding maze of narrow backstreets and closely packed rows of terraced houses. The passage was about 30 yards ahead of us, on the right of Main Street, midway between us and the main group of Fighters and townspeople. Wede have to run straight towards them to reach it. The roadside wall would give us some cover for the first 15 yards or so, but after that the stonework had collapsed, leaving us no cover at all for the final stretch. Wede be right out in the open, running into a hail of gunfire.

Do you think we can make it? I said to Chola Se.

We have to. Its the only way out, isnt it?

We glanced at each other, both of us knowing that it wasnt really a way out, because even if we reached the passage – which was far from certain – wede only be delaying the inevitable.

But right now that was all we had.

And it was better than being dead.

Ready? Chola Se said.

I held her gaze for a moment, then nodded.

We ran hard and fast, keeping low and shooting over the wall as we went, and when we broke out from behind the wall onto the open road we just kept going, running even faster, swerving and jinking from side to side as we raced towards the turning into East Walk. Gunfire was crashing all around us – bullets screaming through the air, shots ploughing into the ground at our feet – and up ahead of us I could see that some of the Fighters had realised what we were doing and were moving towards the passage in an attempt to head us off. But we were nearly there now, just a few yards away from the ancient stone archway that leads into the walk.

Go, Jeet! Chola Se yelled, firing off both barrels.

Bullets smashed into the archway above my head as I lunged into the gloom of the passageway, and a moment later Chola Se came hurtling in after me. She was already reloading the shotgun as we moved off down the tunnel-like corridor – me facing the front, with the Beretta in one hand and my knife in the other, and Chola Se with her back to me, covering our rear with the shotgun.

The stonewalled passage was too narrow for the Fighters – or anyone else – to come after us all together, and anyone foolish enough to try it alone would be blown to pieces the moment they showed their faces. So for the moment we were relatively safe. But I could already hear barked commands coming from outside – THAT WAY! ROUND THE BACK! SEAL OFF THE EXITS! – and the bootsteps of Fighters running back along Main Street. It wasnt hard to guess where they were going – there was another way through to Southwall just along the street – and the danger now was that if they got there before us and blocked our way out, they could trap us inside the passage.

We need to get moving, Chola, I said, picking up speed.

How much further is it?

It was hard to see in the gloom. My eyes were still adjusting after the glare of the sun, and as I peered down the passageway it was hard to make anything out. I knew there were 2 exits – one on the left of the passage, about halfway along, which led out into a little square in the middle of Southwall, and another one at the far end – and I knew that the one at the far end had 2 separate ways out – left into Southwall, or right into a street that led back towards Eastside.

I could see the exit halfway along now – a narrow archway in the wall just a few yards ahead of us – and as I stared straight ahead, I could just make out the exit at the far end, about 20 yards further along.

I was just about to ask Chola Se which one she thought we should go for when a figure appeared from the leftside exit at the far end of the passage. I knew who it was straightaway – his corpulent frame was unmistakable – and as our eyes met and we both stopped in our tracks and raised our pistols, I could tell this was the last place he wanted to be.

It was Van Hesse, the Grocer.

There was no rage or madness in his eyes, just fear and uncertainty, and from the way hede walked into the passage – with a reluctant and heavy-footed trudge – it was obvious he was just doing what hede been told.

The order had been given – find the dogchilds, kill them if you have to.

And somehow, much to his dismay, hede found us.

And now here he was – his great bloated body dripping with sweat, his battered old 6-shot revolver visibly shaking in his hand

– and I could see the panic and desperation in his eyes as he tried to work out what to do. He didnt want to kill me – he hadnt even wanted to find me – but he didnt want to be shot dead either, and he knew Ide pull the trigger if I had to.

He knew me.

He knew what I was.

And I knew him.

I knew what he wanted to do. He wanted to lower his gun and walk away, but I knew hede never do it---he couldnt. He was Van Hesse, the Grocer – a man of some standing. Hede worked very hard to get where he was, and everyone knew it was only a matter of time before his service was rewarded with a place on the Council. If it ever got out that hede found the dogchilds whode attacked Deputy Pilgrim, but instead of apprehending them – or killing them – as ordered, hede lowered his gun and let them go---

No---he couldnt do it.

The consequences were unthinkable.

What are you waiting for, Jeet? Chola Se said.

Just then I saw the Grocers eyes dart to his right, and as he quickly looked back at me – at the same time taking half a step to his left – I knew we only had moments to spare.

This way, Chola! I snapped, running for the exit to our left. Come on!

I kept the Beretta raised as I ran the few yards to the narrow archway, and just as I got there I saw 2 Fighters rushing into the passage and bundling Van Hesse out of the way. Chola Se was right behind me now, and as I stepped aside – covering her as she lunged for the exit – I just had time to see the Fighters raising their rifles before she grabbed my arm and dragged me through the archway out into the square.

The sudden glare of the sun blinded us both for a second, but as we shielded our eyes from the dazzling light and gazed around the little square in search of the best way out, we saw straightaway that we only had one choice. There were 2 narrow streets leading off the square, both on the side furthest away from us, and just off to our right was the Stoop, a steep flight of stone steps with houses either side that led all the way down to the rear of the Quarterhouse. Half a dozen townspeople were gathered at the corner of one of the streets, and 3 Fighters had just emerged from the other one and were crossing the square towards us. And from inside the passage we could hear the 2 Fighters coming after us, the hollow stomp of their running boots rapidly approaching the archway.

Chola Se swung round and fired at the Fighters in the square, and as one of them tumbled to the ground and the other 2 began shooting back, we turned and ran for the steps.

There was a cacophony of noise all around us now – gunshots, shouts, barking dogs, people yelling out from upstairs windows, THERE THEY ARE! OVER THERE! THEY WENT DOWN THE STOOP! – and as we raced down the steps, taking 2 or 3 at a time, the sounds seemed to follow us down, swirling and echoing around the walls of the houses like seabirds swooping around cliffs.

We were both on our last legs now – exhausted, weak, dehydrated – and I knew we couldnt keep going much longer. Our bodies had had enough. And when I saw Chola Se stumbling to a halt in front of me and wearily raising her shotgun again, and I looked down past her and saw Captain Luca and 2 young Fighters taking aim at us from behind a barricade of heavy oak barrels that were blocking the steps about halfway down, I very nearly gave up there and then. I didnt have to look round to know we couldnt turn back – I could hear the stampede of boots on the steps behind us – and as I gazed around at the houses either side of us, searching desperately for somewhere to run, all I could see was an endless stretch of solid walls and locked-up doors and shutters.

Wede run out of places to run.

LOWER YOUR WEAPONS! Captain Luca called out.

Remember what I said before, Jeet?

I turned to Chola Se, momentarily confused, but when I saw the way she was looking at me, I understood what she meant. Shede looked at me like that once before – when shede made me promise that I wouldnt let the Dau take her alive – only now it wasnt the ways of the Dau she was worried about but the way shede be treated by our own people if they took her alive.

But they arent our people, are they? I suddenly found myself thinking. They never were. Theyre people, theyre humans---we no more belong with them than we belong with the Dau. Weare Deathland dogs. We belong to no one. Weare the unwanted, the hunted, the trapped, the slaughtered---

DROP YOUR WEAPONS, NOW!

Jeet? Whats the matter? Open your eyes, Jeet.

I opened my eyes. I didnt know what was happening. I didnt know where I was or where Ide just been---

IF YOU DONT LOWER YOUR WEAPONS IMMEDIATELY YOU WILL BE SHOT!

When the highpitched whistle suddenly screeched through my head, I thought for a moment that it was coming from inside me – a dream, a memory, an illusion – or that maybe it was the sound of a bullet piercing my skull, but then – as the whistle abruptly stopped – I saw Chola Ses head turn sharply to the left, her eyes full of life as she stared hard at something. And I knew then that the whistle wasnt a dream or a memory or an imagined bullet, it was real. But at the same time it wasnt just an ordinary whistle. It was so highpitched that it was beyond the range of human hearing, a whistle that only dogs – and dogchilds with heightened senses – could hear, and as I turned my head and followed Chola Ses gaze, I could see the half-open door where it had come from. The wooden door was in the wall to our left, less than 10 feet away, and there was no doubt in my mind that it hadnt been open when Ide looked at it just a few moments ago.

The whistle sounded again – 2 short blasts – this time from slightly further away, and even before the second blast had finished we were already hurtling towards the door. It only took us a couple of seconds to get there, and by the time Captain Luca had given the order to shoot – FIRE! – and the Fighters had opened up with a volley of rifle fire, we were clattering through the wooden door into a narrow alleyway between 2 houses. There was another open door at the end of the alleyway, and beyond that another backstreet---but that wasnt where the whistle had come from.

The whistle had come from Cruke.

He was standing beside an open door about halfway along the alley on the righthand side, waving us towards him and urging us to hurry.

Can we can trust him? Chola Se said breathlessly.

What choice do we have?

I could shoot him.

I looked at her. Wede be dead by now if it wasnt for him.

She thought about that for a moment, then nodded, and we ran down the alley towards Cruke.

As we approached him, he stood aside and ushered us through the open doorway. It led directly into the hallway of the house, and as we stepped inside we saw Crukes wife – a plump old woman called Gilder – standing quietly at the foot of a staircase halfway along the hall.

Go with Gilder, Cruke said quickly, glancing anxiously along the alley. Youre safe now, okay?

As we began heading down the hallway Cruke put his hand on my shoulder and stopped me.

Hit me, Jeet, he said.

What?

Just here, he said, putting his hand to his forehead. Use your gun. Make it look real, but dont knock me out.

I dont understand—

Just do it, Jeet, he said firmly. Hurry up. Weare running out of time.

I suddenly realised what he was doing – I knew why he wanted me to hit him, and I knew why it had to look convincing – so I raised my gun, held it still for just a moment, then cracked the barrel into his head. I meant to hit him hard enough to draw blood but not too hard to seriously hurt him, and as he staggered backwards, almost losing his balance, I thought for a second Ide overdone it – the blood was already streaming down his face – but after a few faltering steps he steadied himself, leaning against the wall and shaking the dizziness from his head, then he looked at me and gave me a quick nod of approval, and I let out a sigh of relief.

Go now, he said, lowering himself to the ground. Quick, before they get here.

I moved off down the hallway. Gilder and Chola Se had begun climbing the stairs now, and Gilder was beckoning me to join them. I glanced back at the doorway and saw Cruke lying on the ground in the alley, holding his bloodied head and moaning, and I knew that when Luca and all the others arrived and Cruke told them that hede tried to stop us, but wede overpowered him and run off down the alley, theyd believe him. He was Cruke, the legendary exFighter Captain and respected Councillor, and he was flat out on the ground with his head split open. There was no reason not to believe him.

I turned back and began following Gilder and Chola Se up the stairs.

When we reached the third floor of the house, Gilder led us along a short corridor to a locked door at the far end. She reached into her pocket and pulled out a leather cord threaded with keys, and after fumbling her way through them for a while – squinting at each one in turn – she finally found the key she was looking for and stooped down to unlock the door. She waited a moment before opening it, standing up straight and cocking her head to one side at the faint sound of muffled shouts coming from outside. The short burst of shouting was followed almost immediately by the hurried clomping of running Fighters---dozens of them from the sound of it. Gilder carried on listening until it was clear they were moving away from the house, then she bent down to the door again, opened it up, and gestured for us to go in.

It was an odd little room – 2 chairs, a small table, a rickety old cupboard, patterned rugs hanging on bare stone walls – and the only source of light was a small window with iron bars across it high up on the far wall. There was nothing obviously out of place about the room, it was just that I couldnt work out what it was supposed to be. It clearly wasnt a bedroom, and it wasnt a store room or a workroom either. And if it was meant to be a place for just sitting and relaxing, what was it doing at the far end of a corridor on the third floor?

It didnt make sense.

And then there was the smell.

Ide seen Chola Ses nose twitch as soon as wede entered the room, and a few moments later Ide caught the scent too. It was only very faint – too faint for humans to sense – and it seemed to be coming from somewhere nearby rather than inside the room, but there were definitely traces of it in here – in the air, the walls, the furniture, the floor, the ceiling. It was a scent of the past, of another time and another world---the scent of another life. And it shouldnt have been here. It didnt belong here.

None of it made sense.

And when I glanced at Chola Se I could see that she felt the same. There was an uneasiness about her, a wariness, an instinctive sense of disquiet. Wede both secured our weapons as wede made our way up the stairs – Ide pocketed the Beretta and Chola Se had slung the shotgun round her back – but as we looked at each other now, silently sharing our concerns, Chola Se quietly reached round and pulled the shotgun forward so that it was hanging at her hip.

Ile get you some food and water in a minute, Gilder said, smiling kindly at us as she crossed over to the wall on our left. And Ile bring some bandages too. Your leg needs looking at, Jeet.

I looked down and realised that my knife wound had opened up again and my leg was soaked in blood.

We just need to make sure youre safe first, okay? Gilder said.

The faded red rug hanging on the wall in front of her was roughly the size and shape of a door. A wooden baton was attached to the top edge of the rug, and it looked as if the baton was securely fixed to the wall, but when Gilder reached up and pulled at one end of it, both the baton and the rug swung outwards, opening up like a shutter to reveal a small wooden door in the wall. It was no more than 5 feet high and 2 feet across – and set about 6 inches off the ground – and it was fastened with 2 heavy bolts. Gilder had to stand on tiptoe and stretch up as far as she could to reach the bolt at the top, but she managed it with practised ease, as if shede done it hundreds of times before. She unlocked the lower bolt, then opened the door and gestured us forward.

Its all right, she said, noticing our hesitation. Theres nothing to be afraid of, I promise. Youre safe here, I give you my word. No harm will come to you in this house.

She ushered us forward again, and this time – after a quick glance at each other – we cautiously made our way over to the hidden door. On the other side of it was a steep flight of uneven stone steps leading up to another door, which again was secured with bolts.

You go first, Gilder said. Ile be right behind you.

Ide put my hand in my pocket now and was gripping the butt of the Beretta, and as we stepped through the doorway and began climbing the steps, I saw that Chola Se had hold of her shotgun. Gilder followed us through the doorway, then stopped and turned round to pull both the rug and the door closed behind us. The light in the staircase dimmed, but there was still a faint stream of sunlight coming in from somewhere, and when I looked up I saw a narrow shuttered window in the wall at the top of the steps.

The faint scent wede sensed in the room was much stronger now, and it was getting stronger with every step. There was no doubt what it was anymore – not that there ever really had been – and it was equally clear that it was coming from somewhere behind the door at the top of the steps.

It still didnt make sense.

The stairway was so narrow that when we reached the top we had to squeeze in close to the wall to allow Gilder to get past us and get to the door. She unbolted it, reached for the handle, then stopped. She didnt move or say anything for a good 10 seconds – she just stood there, staring blindly at the door, deep in thought. Eventually, after seemingly making up her mind about something, she turned to us and spoke quietly.

You already know, dont you? she said.

We both nodded.

She smiled. I should have realised---Ime sorry. You must be wondering what on earths going on here. Come on, let me show you---

She started turning the door handle, then stopped again.

His names Juddah. I dont how hese going to react when he sees you, but dont be alarmed if hese very frightened at first. He hasnt had any contact with the outside world since he was 5 years old.

She opened the door and we went inside.

I was right behind Gilder when we entered the attic, and as I peered over her shoulder I caught a momentary glimpse of a creature so wretched and pitiful he was almost unrecognisable as a dogchild. If it hadnt been for his unmistakeable scent – which was so overwhelming now that I could feel it permeating my skin – Ime not sure I would have known what he was.

He was no more than 15 feet away from us, and when he saw me and Chola Se he reacted so suddenly – shooting across the attic in a blur of speed and disappearing into the dark interior of a large blanket-covered cage in the corner – that all I consciously saw of him before he fled was a brief flash of yellowed teeth as he bared his lips in a silent snarl of fear. But the image of him in that very first moment was so intense that it somehow went beyond conscious vision, burning into my minds eye with a clarity of detail that I can still see right now.

I can see his face – a patchwork of jagged scars, the ugly red slashes vividly clear against skin so unnaturally pale its almost translucent – and his wild staring eyes, unblinking and petrified. I can see his long black hair reaching down to his bare shoulders, and his naked torso, as scarred and disfigured as his face. I can see him half sitting, half lying on the floor – his legs splayed out to one side, his upper body leaning over at an angle, propped up by an elbow on the floor. And I can see his poor legs – the right foot missing, the left leg ending at the knee---the stumps of both limbs withered and rotted black---

And then he sees us and hese gone.

He ran on all 4s, his damaged legs causing him to move with a strange irregular hopping motion, but the awkwardness of his movement had no effect whatsoever on his speed, and in the fraction of a second it took for him to streak across to his cage, he barely seemed to touch the floor at all. I dont even remember seeing him get up. One moment he was there – half sitting, half lying on the floor – and an instant later he was a flash of hobbling limbs flying through the dusty air and disappearing into a black hole.

Its all right, Juddah, Gilder called out softly as she followed him over to the cage. Its okay---Ime here---everythings all right---

As she stooped down in front of the cage and spoke quietly into the darkness, I heard footsteps behind us, and when I turned round I saw Cruke coming through the attic door carrying a jug of water. His head was still bleeding from where Ide hit him, the wound already swollen into an eggsized lump.

You must be thirsty, he said, passing the water to Chola Se. He looked over at Gilder, concern showing in his one good eye. How is he?

Not too bad. Ime just telling him about Chola Se and Jeet.

Cruke nodded and turned back to us. Chola Se was taking a few careful sips from the jug.

Its all right, Cruke told her. You can drink as much as you like.

What about the rationing? she said.

371

Ime a Councillor, Cruke said with a cynical shake of his head. Rationing doesnt apply to us.

Why not?

Because we make the rules.

Thats not right.

Of course its not. He smiled. Drink up, both of you, then come and sit with me. I need to tell you about Juddah, and you need to tell me what the hells going on.

As we sat down with Cruke on some battered old chairs, Gilder stayed with Juddah for a while – sitting on the floor in front of his cage, whispering softly into the darkness, calming his fears – and then, after about 15 minutes, she quietly left the attic and went downstairs. A short time later she returned with a tray of food – soup, bread, dried meat – together with a bowl of hot water and a clean white sheet. While Chola Se and I helped ourselves to the food and listened to Crukes story, Gilder tended to my knife wound – removing the old bandage, carefully cleaning the cut, then rebandaging my leg using strips torn from the sheet.

Juddah came into our lives just over 10 years ago, Cruke told us. He was found during one of the last hunting trips into the Deathlands before they were outlawed. No one knew how long hede been living with the dogs, or where the dogs had taken him from, and because he wasnt claimed by any of our people – and no one seemed to know anything about him – it was assumed his birth parents were Dau.

Cruke paused for a moment – helping himself to a chunk of bread and washing it down with a big gulp of water from the jug – then he carried on with the story.

Because of his physical condition, it was difficult to tell how old Juddah was when he was brought into town, but we think he was probably around 3 or 4 years old. He was barely alive when the hunters found him. They discovered him with the remains of 5 or 6 dogs in a cave to the west of the mountains. Its impossible to know exactly what happened, but from what the hunters told me – and from the state he was in when they found him – it seems likely that Juddah was living with a small family of dogs, probably just an adult pair and some of their offspring, who for some reason were attacked by a much larger group, possibly a marauding pack of male dogs from the east. It was an astonishingly savage attack. Every dog in Juddahs group had been slaughtered – their bodies ripped to pieces, skulls crushed, limbs half-eaten---the hunters told me theyd never seen anything like it. But somehow Juddah had survived. They found him cowering under the butchered remains of a large female, probably his dogmother. His lower leg was torn open to the bone, he had terrible bite wounds all over his face and body, and his right foot was missing, bitten off at the ankle. Hede lost so much blood that the hunters were convinced hede never last the 10-mile journey back to town, and they very nearly put him out of his misery there and then. But eventually it was decided that since theyd have to take his body back to town to be identified anyway, they might as well give him a chance. So they did what they could for him – binding his legs to stem the blood, making him as comfortable as possible – and they set off back to town.

As Cruke was telling us all this – his voice very quiet now – I sensed a very slight movement from somewhere behind him. We were sitting on the righthand side of the attic, not too far from the door – Cruke facing the door, Chola Se next to him, with me sitting opposite them and Gilder on the floor between us – and I realised straightaway that the movement had come from Juddahs cage, which was across the other side of the attic. I didnt look over at it immediately, but instead just carried on focusing on Cruke for a while. When I did finally glance up – making sure not to look directly at the cage – I caught a brief glimpse of 2 dark eyes peering out warily from the darkness. They disappeared back into the gloom the moment I saw them, but a few moments later they edged into sight again. They were a bit further back in the cage than before, but this time they stayed where they were.

I smiled quietly to myself and turned my attention back to Cruke.

---but he was only just alive when they got back, he was saying, and by the time the hunters got him to Doctor Shiva, Juddahs heart had actually stopped beating. And even when the Doctor got it going again, it was still touch and go for a long time. Shiva couldnt save his left leg – he had to take it off below the knee – and when we offered to be his mentors, Shiva warned us that even if Juddah recovered physically, he might never fully recover from the trauma of the attack, and it was also possible that his brain may have been damaged when his heart stopped beating.

Cruke paused again then, and as he reached out for the water jug and took another long drink, I remembered the time when Ide met him at the Olders Home, when Ide thought he was just a battle-scarred old Fighter, and that all hede ever done, and all that had ever mattered to him, was fighting and killing the Dau.

It was strange to realise how wrong Ide been.

Shiva did as much as he could, Gilder said, taking up the story, but Juddahs legs never healed properly, so hese never been able to walk upright. And he never learned to talk either. She smiled sadly. We dont know why---whether its a problem up here – she tapped her head – some kind of physical damage, or if its something else---psychological, emotional---whatever you want to call it. She shrugged and smiled again. It doesnt matter to us. We understand him, and he understands us. Thats not to say he doesnt have his problems, and of course his life up here is far from ideal---but hese as happy as he can be most of the time, and thats all that matters really.

But whyse he up here? Chola Se said quietly. I dont understand it. Whyse he hidden away like this?

For the same reason you are, Cruke said. Deputy Pilgrim.

Pilgrim?

Cruke nodded, his eyes suddenly hard and hateful. You wont be aware of this, he said to us, but when you were being rehumanised, your progress was under continual monitoring and assessment by the Council and Deputy Pilgrim.

No, I said, shaking my head, I was never assessed.

Me neither, Chola Se added.

You were, Cruke said calmly. Trust me. It happens to every dogchild. Monitoring and assessment is a condition of rehumanisation, and unless a mentor agrees to it – and agrees to it being carried out without the dogchilds knowledge – the process will either be passed to an alternative mentor or abandoned altogether.

Neither of us said anything, we just sat there, staring at Cruke, trying to digest what he was telling us. I found it almost impossible to believe – Starry would never have hidden anything from me – but at the same time I didnt get the feeling that Cruke was lying,

375

and I couldnt think why he would be.

The assessment is based around a series of targets, he went on. Which basically means that if the dogchild doesnt meet certain standards and qualifications within set periods of time, Deputy Pilgrim has the authority to terminate the rehumanising process and remove the dogchild from its mentors care.

What sort of standards and qualifications? Chola Se asked, frowning.

Good question, Cruke said. I asked the same thing myself on countless occasions during Juddahs rehumanisation, but the only answers I ever got were the same meaningless platitudes about human values and social integration---He shook his head despairingly. They just wouldnt tell us what they wanted from him.

Why not? Chola Se said.

Because thats how they do it, he told her, his voice gripped with bitterness. Pilgrim told us once that it was up to Juddah to prove himself, and when I asked him what he actually meant by that, he just told me to hurry up and get the dog out of Juddah or else.

Or else what? Chola Se said.

Cruke sighed. About 6 months later, we were summoned to a Council meeting and informed – by Pilgrim himself – that Juddahs rehumanisation process was being terminated due to insufficient progress, and that we could either hand him over to the authorities for disposal or deal with it ourselves. We were given 48 hours to decide.

Disposal?

Cruke nodded. Its what happens, Ime afraid. Juddah wasnt the first, and he wont be the last. If a dogchild cant live a life of at least some value to our people, then its life isnt just deemed to be worthless, its deemed to be positively harmful — a burden, a liability, an unnecessary strain on our limited resources---

But—

I know, Cruke said, its wrong. Its not how we should be. He shrugged. But it is. And thats how it was. And there was nothing we could do to change it. So we just had to deal with it.

He gazed down at Gilder.

She smiled — her eyes wracked with tiredness and sorrow.

We told Pilgrim wede dispose of Juddah ourselves, she told us. And we worked out a plan---She shook her head. It doesnt matter how we did it. We just did. We faked Juddahs death, and ever since then hese been living up here.

It was clear that Cruke wasnt comfortable talking to us about Juddah, and once hede told us as much as he thought we needed to know, he was more than happy to change the subject and start talking about the current situation instead. And the first thing he told us was that wede been officially denounced as traitors.

The story Pilgrims putting out, he explained, is that hede suspected you of working with the Dau for quite some time, and that in the last few days hede finally discovered proof of your betrayal, and thats why you tried to kill him.

And does everyone believe him? I asked.

Cruke shrugged. His storys backed up by Kite and Glorian. They were both there when you attacked the Deputy. They say you broke into his house and tried to kill him with a shotgun.

Cruke looked at Chola Se.

Is that true?

Yes, she admitted. We did try to kill him. But weare not traitors. Hese the traitor.

Pilgrims a traitor?

She nodded. Hese also a rapist and a murderer.

It was Pilgrim who abducted Chola Se, I told Cruke. He took her and the babies, killed Aliaj and Berch, and planted evidence to frame Yael. And he killed Starry too.

Can you prove any of this?

I shook my head. Thats why we had to kill him.

But you didnt.

No, he knew we were coming for him. He was waiting for us---

I closed my eyes, trying to remember exactly what had happened in Pilgrims house – the room suddenly erupting in a burst of light and a roar of shouting voices---the deafening boom from Chola Ses shotgun---the billowing cloud of smoke and feathers and straw---

Pilgrim wasnt even in the room, Chola Se said. There was a figure in his bed, under the sheets, and we could see Pilgrims boots sticking out---but it wasnt him. It was just a straw dummy---

She looked at me.

Ime sorry, Jeet, she muttered. Its my fault. I should have waited---She shook her head. I was just so—

Its not your fault, I told her. Weare together, remember?

378

Live together, fight together, die together. Weare one.

She smiled. Weare useless.

Yeh, but weare useless together, okay?

Okay.

Cruke went on to ask us how much we knew about the battle.

How much do you know? I asked him in return.

Very little, he admitted. I probably know a bit more than most of the townspeople because of my position on the Council, but Gun Sur hasnt shared any details with us—

Why are you on the Council? Chola Se said, interrupting him.

What?

Youre not that kind of person, are you?

What kind of person?

You know what I mean. Youre not like the rest of them. Youre not greedy and corrupt and self-obsessed, youre just---I dont know. Youre a good person.

Ive done a lot of bad things in my time.

You were a Fighter – Fighters have to do bad things. That doesnt make you a bad person.

Cruke shrugged.

Youve got a heart, Chola Se told him, glancing at Gilder. You both have. You wouldnt have helped us otherwise. And all this – she waved her hand, indicating the attic – everything youve done for Juddah---I just dont understand how someone like you can be a Councillor.

Thats the whole point, he said.

What do you mean?

If Ime a greedy and self-obsessed Councillor, no ones going to

379

suspect me of having a heart, are they? He smiled at her. Does that answer your question?

Ime not sure———

Well, it will have to do. Because I need some answers from you and Jeet now. I need to know exactly what Gun Sur and Pilgrim are planning———

His voice trailed off and he stopped to listen as the clamorous toll of the assembly bell began ringing out from the Quarterhouse Square.

Damn it, he said under his breath. What now?

Maybe Gun Surs going to answer your questions, I said.

Cruke looked at me.

He promised hede explain everything in due course, didnt he? I said, remembering Gun Surs speech in the Square last week. He said that when the time comes, everyone will be told exactly whats happening and what their duties will be. I glanced at Chola Se, then turned back to Cruke. I think this is it, I told him. The time has come.

Cruke nodded slowly, then started getting to his feet.

I have to go, he said to Gilder. Ile be expected, and theres bound to be a Council meeting afterwards———He looked down at Chola Se and me. But Ile still need to talk to you when I get back, because Ime not going to get the full story from Gun Sur, am I?

I shook my head. He doesnt even know the full story.

Cruke nodded again, then leaned down and kissed Gilder on the top of her head.

Ile be back as soon as I can, he told her. Lock all the doors when Ime gone, and dont let anyone in. And I think its best if you stay up here until I get back. If you need to—

380

Its all right, she said. Dont worry, wele be fine. She smiled at him. Go on, off you go. And be careful.

Cruke held her gaze for a moment, then turned towards the cage.

Ile be back soon, Juddah, he called out softly. Look after your mother and our friends for me.

A low whine came from the depths of the cage – a sad and gentle sound.

Good boy, Cruke said.

Then he turned round and left.

After Cruke had gone, Gilder went downstairs to lock the front door and the shutters, then she came back up to the attic again, closing all the doors behind her. The smile had left her face the moment Cruke had walked out of the door, and when she came over and sat down with us – perching herself tensely on the edge of the chair, her hands clamped together in her lap – she didnt waste any time on small talk or niceties, she just got straight to the point.

Is this really it? she asked us. The final battle with the Dau?

Yes, Chola Se said.

Do you know whats going to happen?

Chola Se looked at me.

We know whats supposed to happen, I told Gilder. But its---well, its complicated. Things might not go as expected.

She nodded. I just need to know as much as possible---for Juddahs sake. I need to know how much danger hese in. I realise youre both very tired, and Ime sorry, but please---I need to know.

It felt very strange telling Gilder about the battle plan. It was so central to everything – so much a part of all that had happened and was about to happen – that up until then Ide just assumed that I knew it all off by heart. But when I began telling Gilder what I knew – or what I thought I knew – I was surprised to find that the details of the plan didnt just roll off my tongue as Ide expected, but instead I had to keep stopping to consciously think about them.

It was, as I said, a very strange feeling, and its only now – as Ime writing about it – that Ive realised it reminds me of a sensation Ive recently begun feeling about Starry. He was everything to me – my father, my teacher, my only friend---and in the past 6 years thered barely been a day when we hadnt seen each other – and yet sometimes, when I think about him now, I cant remember what he looks like.

The battle plan is based on deception, I told Gilder. And the key to the deception, complications aside, is that Deputy Pilgrim has fooled the Dau into thinking hese a traitor.

I hesitated, thinking hard, trying to unravel the tangle of truth and lies in my head.

The Dau are convinced that Pilgrims given them the full details of our battle plan, I continued. They think weare planning to fill an armoured truck with TNT, blow a hole in our wall to let it out, then drive the truck across Nomansland and blow their camp to pieces.

That was the truck we saw at the storehouse? Gilder said.

I nodded, closing my eyes for a moment as I tried to concentrate.

So thats what the Dau think weare planning to do, I went on, and what Pilgrims told them is that on the night of the attack hele disable our watchtower guards so that the Dau can bring all their people across Nomansland without being seen, and as soon as the hole has been blasted in the wall, hele detonate the TNT in the truck – killing dozens of our people – and then the Dau can simply stream in through the hole in the wall and finish off whoevers left---

I had to stop and think again then – partly to make sure Ide got it right so far, and partly to remind myself of what came next. And as I was thinking about it, searching my mind for the facts, I kept seeing something else in my head. It was formless, without shape or definition---not even a thing. Just a sense really. A sense of a great drifting darkness, a looming presence---

Jeet? I heard Chola Se say. Are you okay?

I looked at her.

Do you want to stop for a bit? she said. I can tell Gilder the rest—

No, I said. No---its okay. Ime fine. I was just---

I blinked.

The presence in my head crept back to wherever it had come from, and I turned back to Gilder and carried on.

Theres an old tunnel beneath the storehouse, I told her. It goes all the way across to the town wall, and at the end of it – positioned inbetween the Central and East Towers – theres a massive underground cavern.

I stopped again, this time picturing the cavern in my mind---the ancient vastness of it, the towering stone walls, the orange glow of the burning torches, the little caves and ledges cut into the rock walls, all of them crammed with tools and equipment---and the biggest cave, the one filled to the brim with wooden crates---and I remembered Gun Sur opening one of the

383

crates to reveal hundreds of bright orange rectangular bars, each one about 5 inches by 3 inches---

The roof of the cavern has been rigged with TNT, I told Gilder. When the explosives in the wall are set off, and the Dau come pouring in through the gap, theyre going to be crossing directly over the cavern. So when the TNT in the roof is detonated, most of them will either die in the blast or fall down into the cavern. If they survive the fall theyle be trapped, and weare going to have Fighters and armed civilians strategically positioned around the outskirts of town to pick off any stragglers who survive the blast and remain above ground---

I turned to Chola Se.

I think thats about it, isnt it?

She nodded. Thats how its supposed to happen.

But it might not? Gilder said warily.

Pilgrims not just pretending to be a traitor, Chola Se told her. He is a traitor.

Are you sure?

Chola Se glanced at me. Are we sure?

As sure as we can be, I said.

So whats he planning to do? Gilder asked.

We dont know.

And that was it really. We didnt know what Pilgrim was planning to do. That was the truth of it---and the truth of that was that there was nothing more we could say. We didnt know what was going to happen – to us, to the town, to Cruke or Gilder or Juddah---we didnt know what was going to happen to any of us.

We slept for a while then. There was a small bed at the back of the attic – which apparently Juddah sometimes slept in, but mostly he preferred his cage – and Gilder told us that we were welcome to use the bed if we wanted to, but we were both so exhausted that we just closed our eyes and fell asleep in the chairs.

I dont know how long we slept for, but it couldnt have been more than a few hours, maybe 3 at the most. At one point I was woken by something touching my face. I sleepily flicked at it, assuming it was just a fly or a mosquito, but instead of feeling nothing – as I expected I would – I felt my hand brushing against something solid. It felt big too, and strangely familiar, but at the same time unknown. It definitely wasnt a fly. I instinctively jerked away from it, and as I sat up suddenly and opened my eyes, I was just in time to see a blurry figure hopping away from me on all 4s, darting across the attic back into the cage.

Sorry, Jeet, I heard Gilder say quietly. He didnt mean any harm.

I looked over at her. She was slumped in the chair across from me, half asleep herself.

I didnt think hede wake you, she muttered. Sorry.

Its okay, I told her, glancing across at the cage.

I could see Juddah watching me. He was still hiding away, but not so far back in the cage as before. I could see more of him than just his eyes now. I could see his poor disfigured face, barely an inch of it unscarred. I could see his mouth, the lower lip torn and hanging down at one end. I could see enough of his right ear – partly showing through his long black hair – to see that half of it was missing. And in the darkness of the cage I could just make out the blackened flesh of his withered left stump, sticking out at an angle beneath him.

He was still frightened.

I could see that too.

But it wasnt a lonely fear. It was the comforted fear of a child being watched by their mother.

There were 2 small skylights in the attic roof, both of which were unshuttered, and there was another small window in the north-facing wall which was closed up behind padlocked metal shutters. I couldnt see the sun from either of the skylights, but I was fairly sure that it was gone midday when Cruke came back, and I guessed it was some time in the early afternoon. He wasnt the same as he had been when he left. He had the look of a Fighter about him now, a Fighter about to go into battle – grimfaced, controlled, his eyes cold and steady.

Its happening tonight, he said bluntly.

What is? I asked him.

The battle – its tonight. An hour after sundown.

No, I said, shaking my head. Thats not right---its tomorrow night, Sunday. Thats the plan.

The plan must have changed then, Cruke said. Because its definitely tonight. Ive just come from a Council meeting and thats all anyones talking about – why tonight? why such short notice? why didnt Gun Sur tell us earlier? Theyre not happy about it, I can tell you.

Did he tell the whole town whats happening? Chola Se asked.

Not exactly, no. He told them what they needed to know, and then afterwards he called all the Senior Fighters and Councillors to a private meeting with him and Pilgrim and the Captains, and he told us what he hadnt told everyone else. Cruke looked at

Gilder. Weare setting a trap for the Dau. Theres a tunnel—

I know, she said. Jeet and Chola Se told me. Ime worried about Juddah and I wanted to know—

Juddahs going to be fine, Cruke said, putting his hand on her shoulder. Weare all going to be fine.

Ide realised by now that Gun Sur had probably always intended to change the day of the battle at the very last minute in order to minimise the risk of the Dau finding out what the real plan was. On the face of it, it was a good move, designed to catch any possible traitors off guard, but the reality was that Gun Sur was guarding against something that had already happened. The Dau already knew what the real plan was – Pilgrim had told them – so changing the day of the battle wasnt going to make the slightest bit of difference.

All right, listen, Cruke said to me and Chola Se. Ive been put in charge of the civilian force thats backing up the Fighters, so Ime going to have to leave again in a couple of hours, and theres a lot to do here before I go. So I havent got long, okay?

We both nodded.

I want you to tell me everything you know about Pilgrim, he went on. I dont care if you can prove it or not. I need to know everything – what you know about him, what you think about him, what youve seen him do and heard him say---I need it all, do you understand? I need to get inside his stinking heart and find out what hese doing, and I need to do it in no time at all. So please, start talking. Tell me everything.

I was hoping that Crukes military experience might give him a different perspective on Pilgrims intentions, but after wede told him everything we could think of, and hede talked it all over with us – asking question after question about every little detail – he was just as perplexed as we were. He agreed that Pilgrim was definitely up to something, and that he was rotten to the core, and cruel and vicious and quite possibly insane, but he also agreed that in terms of what he was actually planning to do, a straightforward betrayal made no sense at all.

The Dau wont let him live if they destroy us, he said. Pilgrim knows that. And he knows hele die at our hands if his treachery fails. So it cant be that simple, can it? He has to be planning something else.

The only other option that Cruke could think of – and this was something that none of us had considered before – was the possibility that Pilgrim was doublecrossing (or triplecrossing) the Dau so that theyd lose the battle in a way that somehow benefitted him.

How do you mean? Chola Se asked.

Power, Cruke told her. He wants to become Marshal.

It seemed at first as if Cruke might have found the answer, but the more we thought about it, the more we realised that it made no more sense that a simple betrayal.

The ends dont justify the means, Cruke concluded. If all hese trying to do is take over from Gun Sur, theres just no need for such an elaborate and multifaceted plan. There are far easier – and much safer – ways of getting rid of Gun Sur than that---

And that was about as far as we got.

The 2 of us carried on thinking about it while Cruke went off to talk with Gilder, but we didnt make any progress. It seemed so impossible to work out what Pilgrim was doing that I even began wondering if we might simply be wrong about him, and that he wasnt actually planning anything treacherous at all but just doing exactly what he claimed to be doing – pretending to be a traitor in order to defeat the Dau.

Maybe he didnt kill Starry, I suggested. And maybe it really was Yael who abducted you—

Yael didnt rape me though, did he?

No.

And Yael didnt have the phial that Starry found either.

No, he didnt.

And if Pilgrims not a traitor, why has he told everyone that we are? And why—?

Yeh, okay, I said. I was only thinking out loud. I know weare not wrong about him. Sorry, it was a stupid thing to say.

She smiled at me. I forgive you.

Thanks.

Just dont do it again, all right?

An hour or so later, Cruke came back over and sat down with us again. He was dressed for war now – heavy boots, equipment belt, a sturdy old leather jerkin – and he was carrying a large and heavy-looking canvas bag. He had a Sten gun slung over his shoulder, 2 automatic pistols and a long knife in his belt, another knife in one of his boots, and when he dropped the bag on one of the chairs, I heard the dull clank and rattle of more weapons.

I want you to promise me something, he said, sitting down beside us. I dont want to leave Gilder and Juddah, but I dont have a choice. Ime a Fighter. I have to fight when Ime told. Its my duty. I realise that might be hard for you to understand, but its just---its how it is.

He went quiet, staring thoughtfully at the floor, then after a while he reached for the canvas bag and began opening it up.

I want you to look after Gilder and Juddah for me while Ime gone, he said, searching around inside the bag. Ile leave you some extra weapons and ammunition – he pulled out an automatic pistol and a 6-shot revolver – and Gilder will show you where we keep our emergency rations. Theres enough food and water to keep the 4 of you going for at least a week, but I doubt if youle need that much.

He put the pistols on a chair, then leaned forward and lowered his voice.

Whatever happens when the fighting starts, its not going to last very long. This is it – the big one. Its all or nothing. And the way its set up, weare either going to win quickly or lose quickly.

He glanced over his shoulder and smiled at Gilder – who was busy searching through a boxful of tools on the other side of the attic – then he turned back to us and reached into the bag again.

Ile watch out for Pilgrim as much as I can, he told us, pulling out several boxes of ammunition and a hand grenade from the bag and placing them on the chair with the 2 pistols, and if I get the chance to take him out Ile do it. I doubt if Ime going to have much time to spare though, so I cant guarantee anything. But you dont have to worry about him. He doesnt know where you are, and whatever hese up to – no matter what it is – its going to need his full attention, which means that as of now youre the last thing hese going to be thinking about.

We didnt look at each other, or say anything, as Cruke carried on talking, but we didnt have to. I could sense the uneasiness in Chola Se, and I knew she could sense it in me. We didnt like what Cruke was asking of us.

So all you need to do, he continued, zipping up the bag, is stay here with Gilder and Juddah until I get back. You dont go anywhere, okay? Just stay right here and wait for me—

What if you dont come back? Chola Se said.

I will.

Yeh, but—

The grenades got an 8-second fuse, he said, gazing down at the weapons on the chair. And both the pistols are fully loaded. He looked up at us. If anyone tries to get in while Ime gone, you shoot them. Understand? It doesnt matter who it is – the Dau, one of our people – if its not me, you shoot them, and you dont stop shooting until theyre dead. Is that clear?

He had the look of a killer about him now – his icy stare unbreakable, his voice a chilling whisper.

Is that clear? he repeated. Yes or no?

Yes, we told him.

Good.

He lowered his eyes again then, and this time he didnt say anything for about 30 seconds. He just sat there, thinking---or maybe not thinking. It was impossible to tell. He seemed to have gone somewhere else.

Eventually he just took a deep breath, let out a heavy sigh, and slowly got to his feet.

I have to go, he said calmly, picking up the bag. He raised his head and looked at us. Wele talk again when I get back.

And with that he slung the bag over his shoulder and walked off towards the door.

He didnt look back as he went, and when I glanced over at Gilder I was surprised to see that she wasnt looking at him either. She seemed to be just getting on with whatever it was she was doing. But as I watched her taking a screwdriver from the box, then slowly putting it back in, then just as slowly taking it back out again, I could see the terrified emptiness in her eyes, and I realised that she wasnt just casually ignoring Cruke, she was simply doing what she had to do to cope with the possibility that she might never see him again.

I looked across at the cage.

Juddah had edged back into the darkness, and all I could see was the watching gleam of troubled eyes.

I heard the attic door shut, and when I turned round Cruke was gone.

We didnt talk about the situation wede found ourselves in at first. I dont know what it was that held us back, but instead of discussing it we just sat there together, quietly checking our weapons. As well as our own – my knife and sling and the Beretta Ide taken from Sweet, plus Chola Ses shotgun and a handful of shells – we now had another 2 pistols, 3 boxes of ammunition, a box of shotgun shells, and a hand grenade. The automatic pistol was a 9mm Glock with 17 rounds, the revolver was a Smith & Wesson 629.

We worked slowly and steadily – inspecting each weapon to make sure it was clean and in good working order, making sure Crukes pistols were fully loaded, reloading the Beretta, filling our pockets and Cholas bandolier with ammunition – and once wede done all that, I spent another 20 minutes cleaning and sharpening my knife.

Juddah was nowhere to be seen now. Hede retreated into the furthest reaches of his cage a short while ago when Gilder had left the attic to fetch some supplies from downstairs, and although I kept looking over to see if he was watching us, there was no sign of him at all.

As I carefully honed the blade of my knife – using a small piece of quartz that Starry had given to me years ago – I found myself thinking back to the day Ide bumped into Chola Se on my way to the Olders Home. It seemed like a lifetime ago now – and I suppose, in a way, it was. The only things worrying me then had been the account – and whether or not I could actually write it – and what kinds of questions I should ask the Olders. In fact, I was so busy thinking about what I was going to ask them that I wasnt watching where I was going, which was why Ide turned the corner into Main Street and walked straight into Chola Se.

The moment came back to me then – I could feel it, hear it, see it. The impact of the collision knocking the writing book out of my hand---apologising as I stooped down to pick up the book – Sorry. I wasnt looking. Are you all right? – then freezing at the sound of her voice – Ime fine – and feeling a strange tingling sensation in my belly, a feeling Ide never experienced before---then straightening up and looking at her, and the sight of her taking my breath away---her sad-looking woodbrown eyes, her shaggy mop of soft black hair, her slightly crooked mouth---her black smock, her black moccasins, her necklace, the long thin-bladed knife tucked into her belt---

I stopped cleaning my blade and turned to her.

What happened to your knife? I said.

What?

Your knife---the stiletto you kept in your belt.

I lost it on the night I was taken. I dont know if Pilgrim took it or the Dau, or if I just dropped it somewhere---She shrugged. Its a shame. I really liked that knife.

Yeh, me too. Are you going to get another one?

I dont know, she said, smiling at me. I think Ile wait to see how the battle goes first---

Oh, yeh. Ide forgotten about that.

And besides, she added, patting the shotgun in her lap, Ive grown quite attached to this now.

Its not the same as your knife though, is it?

No, she agreed. But we wouldnt be here without it, would we?

Thats true.

I suddenly remembered something then, and I started searching through my pockets until eventually I found the pearlhandled switchblade Ide taken from Sweet.

Its nowhere near as nice as yours, I said, passing it over to Chola Se, but you might as well have it.

Thanks, she said, taking the knife.

She examined it for a while – running her finger along the smooth white handle, nodding contentedly at the feel of it, then trying out the switchblade itself, flicking the button, snapping the blade in and out – and then we both looked up as the attic door opened and Gilder came in carrying a box of supplies – bread, nuts, meat, milk, potatoes. She smiled at us and carried on over to a small kitchen area in the corner of the room. As she started emptying the box and putting things away, Chola Se turned to me and spoke quietly.

What are we going to do, Jeet? she said. Weare not staying here, are we?

I shook my head. I dont know---

Cruke shouldnt have asked us. He had no right.

He saved our lives.

I know, but that doesnt mean he can tell us what to do, does it? We shouldnt be in his debt just because he helped us. Thats not how it works.

It is for him.

Weare not him though, are we? Weare us. And we should do whats right for us, not for anyone else.

I nodded. So what do you want to do? What do you thinks right for us?

She looked at me for a moment, then sighed. I dont know. I just---I dont want to be here anymore. She gazed over towards the window. I want to be out there---

In town?

No, I mean the Deathlands. I want to be out in the Deathlands. She turned back to me. We cant be here anymore, Jeet. Whatever happens---we dont belong in this world.

What about Pilgrim?

What about him?

Last time we talked about running away to the Deathlands, you said you couldnt do it because Pilgrim was always in your head--- always hurting and humiliating you---you said you couldnt run away from that.

I know.

Thats why we had to kill him.

I know.

Do you think you can run away from it now?

She stared at me for a long time before answering, and when she did finally speak there was so much pain in her eyes that I wished Ide never asked the question in the first place.

I dont know, Jeet, she whispered. I just---I dont know what I want anymore.

We slept again for another hour or so, and when we woke up we found a pair of binoculars on the chair next to Chola Se. As she picked them up and looked around, wondering where theyd come from, we heard Gilder calling out to us from the kitchen.

Theyre Crukes, she said. I thought you might want to see whats going on outside. She glanced over at the little window in the north wall. Ive opened the shutters for you. Theres a fairly good view from there. You can see most of the town and all across to the wall. She smiled at us. You dont have to look out if you dont want to, of course. I just thought---well, you know---if you do---

Yeh, thanks, I told her.

Are you okay? Chola Se asked her. Is there anything we can do to help?

She smiled again, trying to show us that she was fine, that she could cope without Cruke, that she was used to him going off to fight and not knowing if hede come back in one piece, or come back at all---but her smile couldnt hide the truth. And the truth was that she knew this was different. Cruke had said it himself – this was the big one, all or nothing. And Cruke wasnt even a Fighter anymore, he was an old man. And if that wasnt enough, there was Juddah to think about too---

Of course she wasnt okay.

No, Ime fine, thank you, she said. Are you feeling better now that youve slept?

Yeh, a lot better, thanks.

Good---well, Ide better get on. Theres plenty of food and drink here if you want anything. Just help yourselves, all right?

We thanked her again, then Chola Se picked up the binoculars and we went over to the window.

The view was as good as Gilder had said. We were high enough up that even without the binoculars I could see most of the town spread out down below. I could see most of the wall too, and as I gazed out at the familiar crescent shape with its 5 towering turrets, it was hard to believe that in a few hours time that massive block of solid stone – which had guarded us from the Dau for so many years – would be deliberately blown apart to let our eternal enemy come streaming in. But the sun was already beginning to sink down towards the horizon now – the evening sky a haze of blue and orange-red – and nothing was going to stop it. The night was coming, and when it came the thunder would roar and the wall would come crashing down.

And then thered be blood.

It was coming.

The town was busy but surprisingly quiet. Everywhere I looked there were Fighters and civilians preparing for battle – scurrying around, moving into their positions, checking the explosives, building barricades – but although a few shouts were echoing around now and then – Fighters barking out orders – and I could hear the occasional short burst of running boots, there was a strangely muted feel to the air, an unnatural hush, as if the town itself knew what was coming and was waiting in silence for the onslaught.

Do you think theyle bring out the truck? Chola Se said, without taking her eyes from the binoculars.

Theres no point. The Dau wont be able to see it if theyre all behind the wall, so bringing it out would just be a waste of manpower. Have you seen Pilgrim yet?

No.

What about Kite and Glorian?

No sign of Kite, but I saw Glorian going into the Quarterhouse just now. Luca seems to be the one doing most of the work out there.

Have you seen Cruke?

She nodded. Hese with a group of civilians over on Eastside at the moment, handing out weapons and getting them into position.

She lowered the binoculars and looked over at the wall, peering thoughtfully at the towers.

What is it? I asked.

I cant see any guards, she said, putting the glasses back to her eyes.

Pilgrim told Hensch hede take care of them, I reminded her.

Yeh, I know. It still seems a bit odd though.

Why?

I dont know---it just doesnt feel right.

Weve never seen the towers without guards before, I said, studying the empty guard posts myself now. Its bound to feel strange, I suppose. Can I have a look with the binoculars?

She passed me the glasses and I put them to my eyes and scanned the towers, one by one. She was right, there was no sign at all of any guards, not even a hint of a hidden presence.

I dont think theres anything to worry about, I said. I know it

398

doesnt feel right, but the plan depends on the Dau believing that the guards have been taken out, and theyre going to be watching the towers as closely as us. If they see anyone hiding up there, or any sign at all that Pilgrim lied to them, theyle call off the attack.

Chola Se nodded, but I could tell she still felt unsettled. There was something about the towers that instinctively bothered her, and although my explanation made perfect sense, I didnt blame her for not being convinced. It hadnt convinced me either. There was a wrongness to the towers that defied explanation.

I spent the next 15 minutes scanning the town through the binoculars, searching for anything at all that might give us a clue as to what Pilgrim was planning – anything out of place, anything not quite right, anything that shouldnt have been there, or should have been there but wasnt---anything that just felt wrong.

I focused on the wall, picking out the rows of laboriously drilled holes where the TNT had been planted, and the dozens of fuse cables streaming down the wall and running along the open ground before disappearing into a low-roofed stone blockhouse on the edge of town, where I assumed the cables would be joined together and connected to one or more of the detonators. As I studied the blockhouse I noticed a Fighter standing beside the entrance, and as I focused on his face I saw him looking across to the east of town and raising his hand. When I lowered the binoculars and gazed in the direction he was waving, I saw another Fighter waving back at him from the roof of a building on the outskirts of Eastside. This Fighter then turned round and waved again, and as I looked further to the east I saw a third Fighter – a young woman called Ysabel – positioned outside the storehouse, signalling back. And when I put the binoculars back to my eyes, I was just in time to see her opening the storehouse doors and calling out to someone inside.

It didnt take long to realise that what Ide just seen was the signalling system that had been put in place to synchronise the 2 separate explosions. Once the first explosion had blasted a hole in the wall, and the Dau had begun streaming in, someone in the blockhouse would give the order to blow the cavern roof a few seconds before the Dau were in the optimum position – that is, when the majority of them were directly above the cavern. The signal would be passed from the blockhouse to the storehouse by the Fighters Ide just seen practising the process, and moments later the detonator would be triggered – presumably by someone inside the tunnel – bringing down the cavern roof and hopefully most of the Dau.

I focused the binoculars on the area in front of the wall between the Central and East Towers – the area which covered the underground cavern – and as I imagined the massive chamber below, picturing its dimensions, I scanned the open ground for any sign of the explosives that had been rigged to blow off the roof and open up the great black chasm that would send the Dau to their graves.

The ground showed no sign at all of what lay below. There was nothing amiss, nothing out of place, nothing wrong.

I couldnt find anything wrong anywhere else either.

I searched every inch of the town that was visible from the window – the Quarterhouse, the Square, Long Avenue, Main Street---the storehouse, the ruins, most of the Beach Road and the upper edge of the beach. I examined all the battle preparations – the barricades, the gun posts, the newly dug trenches, the hundreds of unlit torches positioned all around town – and I studied the faces of everyone I saw – every Fighter, every Worker, every Younger---Muqatil, Ovan, Tomas, Diedle, Van Hesse, Jemelata ---Ghauri, Luca, Doctor Shiva---I studied their expressions, their postures, the way they walked, the way they looked at each other, the way they breathed---but the only wrongness I saw in them was the natural wrongness of what they were, the wrongness of being human.

I dont hate them for it, not anymore. Hating humans for what they are is as pointless as hating dogs for what they are. Their wrongness, our wrongness, is beyond judgement.

It just is.

The sun was almost down now, its dying red light still burning low in the sky, and the town was beginning to fade into the bluegrey dimness of dusk. The torches were still unlit, and I guessed theyd stay that way until they were needed. When the wall came down and the Dau came storming in, the torches would be lit, the ground would roar, and the guns would open fire.

I lowered the binoculars and rubbed my eyes.

Anything? Chola Se said.

I shook my head.

Here, she said, holding out her hand, let me have another look.

I passed her the binoculars and moved away from the window so she could look out without being too crowded. As I sat down on the floor and leaned back against the wall, I was surprised to realise how dark the attic had become. There was very little light coming in through the skylights now, and Chola Se was blocking out most of the remaining daylight from the window.

We cant light any candles, Ime afraid, Gilder said to me from the kitchen across the attic, noticing my slight puzzlement. No one can know theres anyone up here.

Yeh, of course, I said.

Juddah sees very well in the dark.

I smiled. So do we.

I thought you might.

She went quiet for a few moments then, staring down at the bowl she had in her hands, toying nervously with it as she thought about something. Then, without looking up, she said, Ive often wondered why---

Why what?

Juddahs nightvision, and yours---why is it so well developed? I mean, its not a physical thing, is it? Your eyes are no different than mine. You werent born with better nightvision than me, were you?

I asked Starry the same thing once, I told her. His theory was that all humans are capable of seeing in the dark as well as dogchilds, its just that most of them dont make the most of their ability because they dont have to. Dogchilds have to learn to see at night because dogs dont have candles or torches.

Gilder nodded, smiling. That makes a lot of sense.

Starry usually knew what he was talking about.

Her smile faded. Ime so sorry about what happened to him, Jeet. It must be very hard for you. Starry was one of the good ones.

It was a simple but perfect compliment, and I knew Starry would have appreciated it. The saddening thing was that it made me realise that apart from Chola Se — and Pilgrims cynical words of condolence — no one else had even mentioned Starrys death, let

402

alone said anything nice about him or shown any genuine sorrow.

It wasnt right.

But it was what it was.

As darkness fell and the light in the attic lowered to a gloom, I just sat there quietly, idly watching Gilder as she prepared a meal for Juddah. I was watching without thought, neither concentrating on what she was doing nor thinking about anything else. I didnt want to think about anything else. But I was too wrapped up in myself to care too much about what Gilder was doing. I was just watching her for the sake of it---watching the duality of deadness and love in her eyes as she cut up strips of bird meat and placed them in the bowl---watching the care in her knotted old fingers as she picked out the needle bones and sprinkled a little cornpepper on the meat---watching the age-old stiffness in her bones as she broke bitesized chunks of bread from a loaf and dipped them in fat---and watching the fleeting smile on her face as a low grumble sounded from Juddahs cage---

All right, she muttered softly, just a minute. Its nearly ready.

Juddah whined.

I know, Gilder said, pouring water into another bowl. Ime coming.

I watched her take the 2 bowls over to Juddahs cage and place them on the floor. She didnt put them right next to the cage but a few yards away from it instead, so if Juddah wanted to eat hede have to come out and get it. She stood by the bowls for a few moments, talking so quietly to him that I couldnt hear what she was saying, then she turned away and went back to the kitchen. I kept my eyes on the cage, and after a short while I saw Juddah edging cautiously out of the darkness. He stopped at the entrance and gazed across at me and Chola Se, his eyes flicking anxiously between us, then he looked over at Gilder, glanced over at the bowls, and let out another quiet whine – asking her to move the bowls closer. She ignored him. He whined again, a little louder this time, but when she still didnt take any notice, he went quiet almost immediately, glanced over at us again, then tentatively moved out of the cage and began crossing over to the food and water. He moved on his hands and knees – his left leg swinging out awkwardly to one side – and at first he didnt take his eyes off us, but the closer he got to the food the less wary he became, and eventually he forgot about us and just scuttled over to the bowls and began eating. Instead of eating straight from the bowl, as I thought he might, he picked it up first, then settled into the same half-sitting, half-lying position as before, and ate from the bowl with his fingers. He ate with remarkable delicacy – carefully selecting one piece of food at a time, examining it, sniffing it, then unhurriedly putting it in his mouth and chewing it slowly, savouring it as much as possible before swallowing it and turning back to the bowl to pick out the next piece.

Hese always liked his food, I heard Gilder say gently.

I looked over and saw her watching Juddah with a quiet smile, and this time the smile wasnt hiding anything. She was, for the moment, perfectly happy.

Jeet, Chola Se said suddenly. You need to see this.

What is it? I said, going over to her.

She handed me the binoculars and pointed to 2 familiar figures heading along a backstreet away from the Quarterhouse. The sun had gone down now, but there was still a residual paleness to the sky, and even without the binoculars I could see the figures clearly enough to recognise them. I put the glasses to my eyes, adjusted the focus, and as the magnified faces of Pilgrim and Kite came into view, I knew wede finally found the wrongness wede been looking for. It was right there – in their faces, their eyes, the way they were walking---

It was there.

Everything about them was wrong.

Can you still see them? Chola Se asked me.

Yeh.

Where are they now?

They just crossed End Row into Back Lane.

Theyre heading for Eastside.

It looks like it, yeh.

Why are they going to Eastside when the walls about to be blown?

They must be heading for the storehouse. Maybe theyre going to the cavern---

They wont be able to get in though, will they? The tunnels been blocked off, remember? And why would they want to go there anyway? And why are they keeping to the backstreets?

I dont know.

It doesnt make sense—

Hold on---

What is it?

Ide lost sight of Pilgrim and Kite. Ide been watching their heads moving along behind the shoulder-high walls of Back Lane, then theyd disappeared behind a higher section of wall, which should have only blocked my view of them for a second or 2, but for some reason they hadnt reappeared again. I lowered the binoculars and leaned forward, squinting through the window.

Whats going on, Jeet? Chola Se said. What are they doing?

Just a second.

Ide spotted them again. Theyd turned left down a little pathway that was hidden by the height of the wall, and now theyd turned right again and had come back into view about 20 yards further along---and they hadnt just changed position either.

I quickly raised the binoculars.

Its Diedle, I said.

What?

Diedles with them.

Where did he come from?

I dont know. I lost them for a few seconds. He must have been waiting for them somewhere---

Are they still heading for the storehouse?

Yeh---

She went quiet for a while then, and as I watched the 3 figures moving ever closer to the storehouse, I knew what she was thinking – I could hear her thoughts in the silence – and I knew she was right.

Jeet? she said quietly.

Yeh, I know, I whispered, lowering the binoculars and glancing across at Gilder.

She looked away the moment I caught her eye, but it was clear shede been watching us, listening to us, trying to work out what was going on.

We have to go, Jeet, Chola Se said. Whatever Pilgrims doing, hese doing it now. We cant just stay here—

I know—

We have to stop him.

Shese right.

It was Gilder.

We both turned and looked at her.

Chola Ses right, Jeet, she said. You have to stop him. Her voice was calm but her eyes were burning with hatred. We should have killed Pilgrim years ago. If wede stopped him then---She shook her head. Go, now. Get it done. Finish him.

Which of Crukes pistols do you want? Chola Se asked me as we headed down the steps.

Ime fine with the Beretta, I told her, fixing Sweets automatic into my belt.

Okay, Ile take the Glock. What do you want to do with the revolver?

Ile take it in the knapsack.

The house seemed unnaturally quiet now, almost as if no one had ever lived here, and as we carried on down the steep stone steps – our footsteps echoing loudly – it was somehow hard to believe that the attic wede just left still existed. Cruke still felt real to me – presumably because hede left the attic too – but Gilder and Juddah had already faded to memories, and although I knew Ide never forget them, especially Juddah, I also knew Ide never see them again.

How much time do you think weve got before they blow the wall? Chola Se said.

Not much — half an hour---maybe a bit longer.

Wede reached the ground floor now and were approaching the front door.

Whats the quickest way to the storehouse from here? Chola Se said.

Through Southwall and along Main Street. But I think its probably best if we keep to the backstreets. I know everyones busy getting ready for the battle, but we still cant afford to be seen.

Chola Se nodded. If we cut across Main Street somewhere near East Walk, we can take the same route as Pilgrim and Kite — along End Row and Back Lane.

Yeh.

How longs that going to take? 10 minutes?

5 if we run.

Runnings going to draw more attention.

10 minutes is too long. We need to run.

All right. She looked at me. Now?

I nodded.

She opened the door and we stepped out into the cold black night.

It was good to be outside again, and as I took a deep breath, filling my lungs with the sharp night air, I could sense the apprehension hanging over the town---the fear, the tension, the waiting, the silence---

We were nearing the end, I realised, just as Gun Sur had predicted. And when it was all over, there would only be us or the Dau left standing---

I looked at Chola Se.

She smiled at me.

We started running.

About 5 minutes later we were crouched at the end of an alleyway just across the road from the storehouse. One of the double doors was half open, letting out a faint glow of torchlights from inside, and in the low orange flamelight I could see Ysabel – the Fighter Ide seen from the attic – standing in front of the doors. Ysabels about a year older than me – shese only been a Fighter for a few months – and as we watched her, she kept looking up at the roof of the building across the road where the other Fighter was positioned, the one who was waiting for the signal from the blockhouse. He was only partially visible from where we were – the top of his head just showing beyond the edge of the roof – but we could see enough of him to see that he was facing away from the storehouse, his attention fixed on the distant blockhouse.

She doesnt need to keep looking up at him, does she? Chola Se commented. Shese not going to get the signal until the explosion in the wall goes off.

Shese probably nervous, I said.

Chola Se shrugged, and we carried on watching the storehouse.

Thered been no sign of life inside the building since wede arrived – no movement, no shifting shadows – and we werent even sure that Pilgrim, Kite and Diedle were in there anyway. The trouble was, we didnt have time to wait and find out. We had to do something, and we had to do it right now.

We need to get inside, I said.

Chola Se nodded. We cant take out Ysabel.

409

Why not?

The Fighter on the roof will see shese gone and raise the alarm.

What about using the side door? I suggested, looking across at the exit in the side wall that Diedle had used when hede come after us during the truck display.

Its probably locked, Chola Se said. And if its bolted on the inside---She shook her head. We cant risk it. If we cant get in straightaway, wele be stuck out in the open.

Wele have to use the main doors then, wont we? I said, reaching for my sling. Its the only way.

But you cant take out Ysabel—

Ime not going to, I explained, looking around at the ground. Ime just going to get her away from the doors.

I spotted a suitable rock, picked it up, and fitted it into the cradle of the sling.

Check the Fighter on the roof, Chola. Make sure hese not looking this way.

She leaned round the corner and looked up at the building.

I cant see him---no, hold on, there he is. It looks like hese---yeh, hese still facing the other way.

I straightened up, testing the weight of the rock in the sling, and kept my eyes on Ysabel as she paced up and down in front of the doors. I watched as she stopped and looked up at the Fighter again---I watched as she nervously adjusted her rifle strap---I watched as she turned round and began pacing again, this time walking away from us---

Is he still looking the other way? I quickly asked Chola Se.

Yeh.

I stepped out of the alley and swung the sling in a smooth

looping motion. The rock sailed up high into the air, arcing across the road, then up and over the front of the storehouse, before dipping down and landing with a heavy thump on the other side of the building.

Ysabel instinctively flinched at the sound of the impact, but then almost immediately she was up and running – snatching her rifle off her shoulder as she went – heading towards the far corner of the storehouse.

We waited, watching as she stopped, raised her rifle, and cautiously peered round the corner, squinting into the darkness as she tried to work out where the sound had come from---we saw her glance round, looking up over her shoulder in the hope that the Fighter was watching, and as the hope left her face and she turned back again, it was clear that he wasnt---and then, at last, we saw her take a steadying breath, tighten her grip on her rifle, and move off round the corner of the storehouse to take a closer look.

The moment she moved out of sight, Chola Se glanced up at the roof of the building to make sure the Fighter was still looking away.

Okay! she hissed. Go!

We sprinted silently across the road, leaped over a low wall into the storehouse yard, then ran full pelt towards the half-open door. Just as we got there, no more than a fraction of a second before we slipped through the door – with Chola Se just ahead of me – I caught a momentary glimpse of Ysabel coming back round the corner. I was almost certain she hadnt seen us, but I wasnt taking any chances, and as soon as we were through the door I grabbed Chola Ses hand – gesturing for her to keep quiet – and quickly led her away from the doorway towards the nearest place to hide, an area by the wall to our left littered with piles of scrap metal and heavy machinery.

Did she see us? Chola Se whispered as we took cover behind some large metal drums.

I dont think so.

We crouched down and stared at the doorway – hearts beating hard, guns levelled at the doors, waiting for any sign that Ysabel had seen us---

Her figure appeared through the gap in the doors---

Then slowly passed by again.

No hurry, no urgency, no sense of alarm---

She hadnt seen us.

For the next few seconds we just stayed where we were – crouched down behind the drums – and gazed all around us, scanning every inch of the massive building. The torches around the walls were burning brightly, and we could see everything there was to see – the workbenches and tables lining the walls, the tools and equipment strewn around the floor, the massive truck in the middle of the room, now looking abandoned and forgotten--- but there was no sign of life. No movement, no sound---there was no one there.

I heard Chola Se breathing in deeply through her nose, and when I glanced at her I saw a puzzled look in her eyes.

What is it? I asked.

Ime not sure---I thought I smelled something.

She sniffed again, raising her head and turning to the left, her eyes searching out the source of the scent.

What is it? I asked her. What can you smell?

I think its—

She froze, her eyes fixed on something.

412

Over there, Jeet, she said quietly, pointing towards the far end of the building. By the tunnel.

I looked where she was indicating, focusing on the open hatchway that led into the tunnel, but at first I couldnt work out what she meant. All I could see was the hole in the ground and the heavy iron hatch beside it. But as I looked closer, studying the stone floor around the hole, I saw something on the ground just to the left of the tunnel entrance. A patch of something---something dark and moist. And as I raised my hand to shield my eyes from the glare of the torchlights, thats when I saw the flies.

Blood, I muttered.

Chola Se looked at me.

We glanced over at the doorway to check that Ysabel wasnt watching, then we straightened up and began making our way over to the tunnel.

Its Raoul, Chola Se said.

We were standing together at the edge of the hatchway peering down at the Youngers lifeless body. He was lying on his back on the ramp, his legs dangling off the edge, his dead eyes staring back up at us. His throat had been cut.

I looked at the pool of blood on the ground to our left.

He must have been standing over there when he was attacked, I said. They probably got him from behind. And then he either fell or was pushed into the tunnel.

I gazed down at his body again. A makeshift bandage had been wrapped round the gunshot wound on his arm – the wound Ide inflicted earlier that day – and the ends of the bandage had come loose. Dribbles of blood had dried on his skin. His handgun was still tucked in his belt.

He was waiting for Ysabels signal, I muttered.

Chola Se looked at me. Raoul?

Hese the only one in here, I told her. Its the only thing that makes sense. Ysabel gets the signal from the Fighter on the roof, she passes it on to Raoul, and Raoul passes it on to whoevers at the end of the tunnel with the detonator. He was probably only given the job because he couldnt fight well enough with his injured arm.

And now whoevers at the end of the tunnel wont get his message.

Theyre probably dead too.

This is all Pilgrims doing, isnt it?

It has to be. Pilgrim, Kite, Diedle---theyre all in it together.

If the signal isnt passed on, Chola Se said, the explosives in the cavern roof wont detonate. The Dau wont be caught in the trap. The walls going to be blown wide open and theyre just going to come pouring in---its going to be a massacre.

We need to stop them blowing the wall.

How?

Ysabel. If we can get her to listen to us she can send a message—

She wont listen to us. Weare traitors, remember? And theres not enough time to explain everything anyway. No ones going to listen to us, Jeet. Weare on our own.

All right, I said, thinking quickly. You stay here and Ile go and find the detonator at the end of the tunnel. When the wall blows and Ysabel gives the signal, you call out to me and Ile set off the TNT in the cavern.

Ysabel wont give the signal to me—

She doesnt have to. Once the explosives in the wall go off,

all you need to do is wait for her to come through the door. Thats your signal, okay?

Chola Se nodded.

I stepped down onto the ramp, edged round Raouls body, and started to run.

Do you know how to work the detonator? Chola Se called out after me.

I raised my hand to let her know that I did, then ran off into the underground silence.

I should have realised then that we never had a chance. Pilgrim had been planning this moment for months, maybe even years — imagining all the different scenarios, assessing all the options, foreseeing every possible pitfall — he was bound to have put all kinds of safeguards in place. I should have known that. But I wasnt thinking clearly. All I could think of was hordes of Dau flooding into town---hundreds of hate-crazed humans, all of them hellbent on slaughter and destruction---and all I kept seeing were pictures too sickening to describe---pictures of death, blood, butchered bodies---Juddah and Gilder, Cruke, Chola Se---and all I could do to make the pictures go away was run.

I ran---

Feet pounding, arms pumping---

I ran.

Past the flaming torches on the black stone walls, past the age-old graffiti and ancient black beams---

I was about halfway along the tunnel when the entrance to the cavern came into sight. It was still about 100 yards away, and at first all I could see was a solid wall of darkness where the entrance had been, but I was running so rapidly now that within a few seconds I was close enough to see not just the wall that had been built to block off the tunnel from the cavern, but what lay in front of it too---

And it was only then that I finally realised the futility of what we were trying to do.

The freshly built stone wall was at least a foot thick, and if it had been intact it would easily have been enough to prevent anyone inside from escaping into the tunnel. But it wasnt intact. A hole had been smashed in the bottom righthand corner – not big enough to collapse the wall, but big enough for someone to squeeze through. The rough-sided opening was about 3 feet high and between 2 and 3 feet wide, and as I slowed down and jogged to a halt a few yards from the wall, I guessed the hole had been made with the sledgehammer and pickaxe that Ide just noticed lying on the ground. And if the cloud of fine dust I could see floating in the air was anything to go by, the hole hadnt been hammered out all that long ago.

But whoever had done it – and I was reasonably sure I knew – that wasnt all theyd done.

Over to my right, lying up against the tunnel wall, was the body of Muqatil, the senior Fighter Ide worked with in the storehouse. His throat had been cut too – just like Raoul – only this time the knife wound was so deep that his head had almost been severed. There was a lot of blood – his clothes were soaked red – and even from a few yards away I could tell it was still fresh.

A few feet away from the body lay the battered remains of the detonator. The metal casing had been pummelled into the ground, the T-shaped handle bent out of shape, and the ruined workings were scattered all over the ground. The only pieces I recognised were the screws that connected the cables to the detonator. Both of them still had short lengths of cable attached, and both lengths of cable had been cleanly severed. The main parts of the cables – from which the shorter lengths had been cut – snaked along the ground before disappearing into a small hole that had been drilled through the stone at the base of the wall. On the other side of the wall, I imagined, these 2 main cables would be wired up to the dozens – if not hundreds – of connecting cables that ran up the cavern walls into the fuses embedded in the bars of TNT planted around the perimeter of the roof---all of which were now utterly useless.

No connection, no detonator, no one to activate the detonator.

Safeguards.

I stared down in despair at the pulverised detonator.

Wede never had a chance.

But even as I stood there, with the weight of reality bowing my head to the ground, I began to feel a faint glimmer of hope. The town wall was still standing, I realised. Thered been no explosion yet, no signal from Chola Se---the hordes of Dau still hadnt broken through. And whats more, I knew where Pilgrim and Kite and Diedle were. They were in the cavern. They had to be. There was nowhere else for them to go. And if they were in the cavern, they were trapped. Their only way out was the opening in the wall---

The glimmer of hope was beginning to grow now, flickering ever brighter like a flame in tinder, and as I raised my head and turned to the wall, I could feel myself coming alive again.

But then I saw Diedle.

And I knew I was dead.

I dont know if I was so lost in my thoughts – or just so lost – that I simply didnt hear him coming, or if – despite his enormous bulk – hede somehow managed to creep across the cavern and into the hole in the wall with the whispered silence of a ghost. But either way, Diedle was there – crouched down on his haunches, squeezing sideways through the opening---his arm outstretched and the 8-inch barrel of his Colt Python revolver levelled directly at my head.

Put your hands on your head and take a step back, he said, his voice cold and flat.

When I didnt move, he simply cocked the hammer of the massive revolver and purposefully straightened his arm. I knew he wasnt bluffing. He was going to kill me whatever happened – I could see that in his eyes – and although hede prefer not to do it right now, it wouldnt bother him much if he did.

I put my hands on my head and took a step back.

He didnt move a muscle for 3 or 4 seconds, and as he crouched there in the wall – like a giant beast frozen in stone – I thought he was going to go ahead and shoot me anyway, but eventually he blinked, breaking the stillness, and then he began to move. His eyes never left me as he carefully heaved himself out of the opening, and the gun in his hand never wavered.

There was nothing I could do. If I tried reaching for my knife or the Beretta in my belt, Ide be dead in an instant. So I just stood there, hands on head, watching the big man as he straightened himself up, hitched a knot from his shoulders, and stepped towards me. Ide guessed he was responsible for killing Muqatil and Raoul, and as I glanced at the foot-long curved dagger in his belt, the silver blade darkened with blood, I knew I was right.

He was standing about 10 feet away from me now – his arm still outstretched, the long-barrelled revolver still levelled at my head. The pistol was so close to my face – less than 3 feet away – that I briefly thought about reaching out and making a grab for it, but with the hammer already cocked and Diedles finger resting on the trigger, I knew Ide never make it.

You killed my brother, he said.

I shook my head. He was alive when—

Save your breath, boy, he said. Theres nothing more to say.

I saw his finger tightening on the trigger, and the next thing I knew a burst of thunder ripped through my skull and the world exploded. I felt my legs buckling, the ground moving, the air thickening---and as a muffled roar filled my head, and I felt myself staggering to one side, I couldnt understand why I was still feeling anything at all. I was dead, wasnt I? Why could I still hear and feel? Why anything?

Theres no why when youre dead.

Theres not even nothing.

I breathed in then, and as I sucked in a lungful of dust and violently coughed it out, everything suddenly became real again. My eyes were open, I could see the cloud of dust in the air--- and as the ringing in my ears began to fade, I could just about hear the distant sound of heavy rocks thumping to the ground high above me---

The wall---

Diedle hadnt shot me.

The town wall had been blown.

Diedle---

I spun round and saw that hede fallen, knocked to the ground by

419

the explosion, and was just starting to get to his knees. Hede dropped the revolver. I could see it on the ground a few feet away from him. He glanced up at me, rubbing dust from his eyes, then quickly began scanning the ground in search of the gun. He spotted it almost immediately and began reaching out, but Ide already drawn my knife now, and as his hand closed on the pistol – and he turned to face me – I raised my arm and threw the knife. I knew I had to kill him outright to stop him, so I went for his head. He jerked sideways at the very last moment in a desperate attempt to save himself, but he wasnt quite quick enough, and the knife caught him in the neck, just below his ear---the 9-inch blade slicing through his throat and instantly dropping him to the ground. For a few moments, his hand kept scrabbling weakly for the gun, but by the time Ide stepped over and kicked the heavy revolver away, he was already lifeless.

The tunnel was quiet now, and in the deathly silence I could just make out a very faint popping sound coming from above ground. It was muffled and dull, deadened by the rock, but when I cupped my hands to my ears and strained to listen, there was no doubt it was the sound of gunfire. And I could hear something else now too, just the faintest hum of a sound – a droning, a whirring, like the faraway massing of insects.

I raised my head and looked up. Hundreds of feet above me, the Dau were swarming in through the demolished wall---

The battle had begun.

A moment later – with uselessly perfect timing – Chola Se called out to me from the other end of the tunnel – NOW JEET! BLOW THE ROOF NOW! – and as the urgency of her voice echoed around the tunnel, I heard a scuffle of movement from somewhere inside the cavern. I pulled the Beretta from my belt, hurried over to the wall, and squatted down to look through the opening.

The vast underground chamber on the other side of the wall was still clouded with dust from the explosion, and as I peered through the shifting grey haze – the torchlights glinting through the dusted gloom – I saw the blurred figures of Pilgrim and Kite standing together on the far side of the cavern. The dust was too thick to see them clearly, and as far as I could tell they werent doing anything in particular, just standing there talking to each other, but unless I was mistaken – and I knew it was quite possible – there seemed to be something about them that was somehow unfamiliar. I couldnt work it out at first – there was nothing obviously different about either of them – and as I carried on gazing through the slowly drifting haze of dust, I began to think it was just me---my mind playing tricks, distorting my perception, distancing me from reality---

But then the dustcloud lifted for a moment, and as I saw the 2 of them relatively clearly, I knew it wasnt me – it was them, together---the 2 of them were together. There was no question about it. There was a closeness between them, an intimacy---it was evident in everything about them – the way they were standing together, so close they were almost touching---the way their eyes never left each other---the way they mirrored each others movements and gestures as they talked---

It was so blatantly obvious I couldnt understand why I hadnt noticed it before. Something caught the corner of my eye then, an unseen movement about 25 yards to the left of Pilgrim and Kite, but when I looked over to see what it was, there was nothing there, just a slight swirling in the dustcloud – the echo of a movement – and a momentary flash of darkness that disappeared as soon as I saw it---or thought I saw it.

When I looked back at Pilgrim and Kite they were embracing, and from the way they were holding each other – tightly, intensely, knowingly – it was clear they were used to it, and I realised then that this wasnt something new, or something I simply hadnt noticed before – it was their hidden truth.

For a few moments then I was rocked with a dizzying torrent of memories – words, voices, images---all mixed up and streaming through my head at the same time. I heard Kites voice – Starry was with me last night---we kept our relationship very much to ourselves – and I heard Starry telling me how hede found out about Pilgrims obsession with Cowboys – an old friend of mine knows a woman who stayed with him one night – and then the remembered image of Starry and Kite at the grocers came to me again, Starry making her smile with the talking fish---

And I didnt know if I was sad or angry or just losing my mind.

Another memory came to me then – a much closer remembrance – and I saw myself walking through the tunnel with Gun Sur and Pilgrim and Chola Se---a week ago, a thousand years ago---and I saw myself running my finger along the wall, then pausing, examining the residue on my fingertip, rubbing at it with my thumb---and I remembered thinking about it, wondering what it told me about the history of the tunnel, then suddenly realising that it meant nothing---it was nothing---it was human thinking ---a complete waste of time---and that I should have been thinking, or nonthinking, like a dog---Ime in a tunnel, where does it go?---and that any other thoughts were meaningless---

I shut down the memory and stared through the dust at Pilgrim and Kite.

Ide been wasting my time again, I realised. Ide been thinking about them like a human when I should have been thinking about them like a dog. I should have killed them the moment I saw them. I should have just shot them dead.

Everything else was meaningless.

Theyd let go of each other now and it looked as if they were getting ready to go their separate ways. I lowered myself to my knees, leaned in through the opening in the wall, and raised the Beretta, fixing the sight on Pilgrims chest. I breathed out, steadied myself, and began squeezing the trigger---

Then stopped.

A thick swirl of dust had momentarily blocked my view. I thought about shooting through it, but decided it was too much of a risk. I couldnt see Pilgrim at all. If I fired now, I wouldnt know if Ide hit him or not. So I held my breath, keeping the gun still, and waited for the cloud to disperse---

1 second, 2 seconds---

3---4---5---

And then at last the air in the cavern shifted again and the fog of dust spiralled around and cleared, and I could see again---but now there was nothing to see. Pilgrim was no longer there. I lowered the gun and scanned the immediate area, hoping hede either just moved a few feet away or that I hadnt kept a steady enough aim, but there was no sign of him anywhere. And I couldnt see Kite either. I rubbed my eyes and tried again, this time looking all around the cavern, and after a few seconds I thought I saw something, a glimpse of movement in the far left corner, but by the time Ide swung the gun round Ide lost it again. But then a moment later I saw the same flash of darkness Ide seen earlier. It was just to the left of where I was looking – a vague patch of darkness – and this time, instead of disappearing almost immediately as it had before, the air around it suddenly cleared – the dust blowing outwards and away from it – and I could see it for what it was. It was a door in the far wall, in the lefthand corner---a door that had just been opened. The darkness was the darkness beyond the door, visible for just a moment or 2, then disappearing again as the door was closed---

A door in the wall of the cavern.

And Pilgrim had just gone through it.

As the door closed behind him – and the dustcloud swirled back around it – I heard a dull thump from the opposite side of the cavern, and when I quickly looked over – swinging the pistol round – I was just in time to see another door being pulled shut. It was a mirror image of what Ide just seen – a door in the far wall of the cavern, but this one was in the far righthand corner, the cloud of dust swirling away from it then changing direction and swirling back again as the door slammed shut---

I didnt understand it.

I was sure there hadnt been any doors in the walls when Ide first seen the cavern – I would have remembered them, wouldnt I? – and as I knelt there thinking about it, trying to picture the cavern as Ide seen it before, I wondered again if I was losing my mind – seeing things that werent there, things that couldnt be there---and in that moment I saw my hand reaching out in front of me, my fingers closing as I tried to grab hold of the dust---trying to feel it, examine it---trying to see if it was real---

What are you doing, Jeet?

The voice came from behind me, and before I knew what I was doing Ide spun round, jumped to my feet, and raised the Beretta.

Its me, Jeet! Chola Se snapped, instinctively raising her hands. Its all right---its only me. You can put the gun down now. Jeet? Did you hear me? You can put the gun down---

I dont know why I didnt lower the pistol straightaway. I knew it was Chola Se – I knew it the moment I heard her speak – but for a few cracked seconds something seemed to have broken in me, and whatever it was – whatever Ide lost – it had taken part of me with it. Or maybe something else happened, something---

I dont know. I just---

I cant think about it anymore.

I came back to myself, thats all that matters.

I came back.

Are you sure youre all right now? Chola Se asked me.

Yeh---sorry—

You dont have to apologise anymore. I just want to make sure youre okay.

Yeh, Ime okay. Ime just---I smiled. Ime an idiot.

She didnt smile back. She was staring down at Diedle.

What happened here, Jeet? she asked quietly, glancing across at Muqatils body.

I quickly went through everything – finding Muqatil and the smashed detonator, the fight with Diedle, seeing Pilgrim and Kite in the cavern. When I started telling her about the doors in the far wall, picturing them in my mind as I told her, the mental image triggered a sudden realisation, and all at once I knew where Pilgrim and Kite had gone.

The watchtowers, I said, squatting down by the opening in the wall and peering into the cavern again.

What?

Although the dust in the cavern was beginning to settle now, the haze was still too thick to get a clear view of the far wall, but I could see just enough to work out where the doors were. I fixed their position in my mind, then leaned forward – still focusing on the far wall – and looked upwards.

The doors match up with the 2 towers, I said.

I dont understand, Chola Se said. What do you mean?

The cavern stretches between the Central and East Towers, I explained, backing out of the hole and getting to my feet again. The door on the left, the one Pilgrim went through, is directly below the Central Tower, and the door Kite went through is directly below the East Tower.

That doesnt necessarily mean theyre connected.

The doors have got to lead somewhere, Chola. It cant just be a coincidence that theyre right beneath the towers. There must be steps leading up through the cavern wall into the towers—

We would have seen them though, wouldnt we? I mean, weve been in those towers dozens of times. If there were steps

426

that led below ground, we would have seen them.

Not if we werent meant to see them.

She nodded slowly. But even if youre right, that doesnt mean Pilgrim and Kite have gone up into the towers. They could have just used the steps to get out of the cavern.

So why did they split up? Why didnt they go out together?

Why did they split up if theyre going into the towers?

I thought about that for a moment, then shook my head. The only way weare going to get any answers is by going after them.

Whats the point?

I looked at her, taken aback by her bluntness.

Its all over, Jeet, she went on. Pilgrims done what he set out to do. It doesnt matter what hese doing now, or why, or whats going to happen to him---his plan worked. He won. Listen---

She gazed upwards, and we listened together to the distant sounds of battle filtering down through the great mass of rock over our heads – gunfire, muffled explosions, screaming, howling---

The Dau are up there right now, Chola Se said emptily, killing everything that moves. Theres nothing we can do to stop them.

She looked at me, and I could see the hopelessness dulling her eyes. They were losing their light as she spoke to me.

Its over, Jeet, she said. Its finished.

So what are you saying? You think we should just give up?

Give up what? Theres nothing left to give up.

Theres us.

I know, but—

We can still get out of here, Chola. We can still get to the Deathlands.

How?

The same way as we planned before---up a watchtower and down the other side.

She stared at me, and as I gazed back at her I saw the flame of a torchlight fluttering in the shine of her eyes. A hint of life was beginning to come back to her.

But even if we can get up into one of the towers, she said cautiously, how are we going to get down to the other side? We havent got any rope. We cant get down without—

We can use the TNT cables. Theres dozens of them in the cavern.

Are they strong enough?

We can bind them together if theyre not strong enough on their own.

She looked down at the ground, thinking it over, but I could tell shede already made up her mind. Shede come alive again, I could feel it. Shede come back to herself.

Ide found something true in myself too. I wasnt quite sure how Ide managed it, or where it had come from, but I felt right again. It was as if Ide been travelling in the wrong direction for a while, and now – without knowing how – Ide stumbled across the road home.

Ime ready if you are, Chola Se said.

I looked at her. She wasnt smiling, but she wasnt dull-eyed anymore either.

Just a second, I said, going over to Diedles body.

I stooped down and pulled the knife from his throat, wiped it clean on his shirt and sheathed it, then reached over and picked up his revolver. It was so huge and heavy that I almost decided against taking it, but it was a powerful weapon, and I had a feeling we were going to need as much help as we could get. We might be on the road home, but there was a long way to go just yet.

I put the Colt in my knapsack, then went over and joined Chola Se at the hole in the wall.

Okay? I said.

She nodded.

After you, I said, indicating the opening.

She smiled.

We were one again.

As we crossed over to the far side of the cavern, I quickly told Chola Se about Pilgrim and Kite.

Theyre together, I said.

I thought you said they spilt up? Pilgrim went through one door and Kite—

No, I mean theyre together---you know, like us---

You mean theyre mates?

I nodded. I saw them embracing.

Are you sure? Pilgrim and Kite?

I saw them, Chola. Ime sure---

I hesitated for a moment as an image of a hand reaching out into a cloud of dust flashed into my mind---the fingers of the hand closing, trying to grab hold of the dust, trying to feel it, examine it, trying to see if its real---

It was real, I muttered.

What?

It was real. I saw them together. Pilgrim and Kite.

Okay, Jeet. I believe you.

The air above us was just about free of dust now, and as we stopped in front of the wall and looked up, the connecting cables were clearly visible – scores of black cords hanging down from the scores of holes that had been drilled into the rock just below the roof of the cavern.

Are they long enough? Chola Se said, gazing up at the cascade of cables.

The cables stretched from just below the roof of the cavern to the ground, and then along the base of the wall to a junction point in the far right corner where they were connected to a series of thicker cables which in turn were connected to the main detonator leads. That meant they were at least 100 feet long, and some of them – the ones furthest away from the junction point – were even longer. And the height of the watchtower, from the turret to the ground, was 90 feet.

Theyre easily long enough, I said to Chola Se. Its just a matter of whether theyre strong enough on their own to take our weight.

Theres no point in risking it, is there? she said. We dont want to be climbing down and find out we made a mistake. I think we should double them up, just to make sure.

I nodded, and we got to work.

It didnt take us long to tear down 4 cables and remove the bars of TNT, then we took 2 cables each, twined them together, and wound them up into carryable coils. We helped each other hang the coiled cables over our shoulders – wearing them like cumbersome bandoliers – then I turned round, took a moment to get my bearings, and began heading off towards the far corner.

Its this way, I said to Chola Se. The doors just over there—

Hold on, Jeet.

I stopped and looked back. Chola Se hadnt moved.

What is it? I asked her.

This isnt going to work.

What do you mean?

If youre right about Pilgrim, and hese up in the tower – for whatever reason – weare going to have to get rid of him before we climb down, arent we?

Yeh, but we can do that. Theres 2 of us—

What about Kite?

Shese in the East Tower.

Thats what I mean. Shele see us, wont she? So even if we manage to take out Pilgrim, all Kite has to do is wait for us to lower the cables and start climbing down, and shele have us at her mercy. We wont stand a chance, Jeet. Shele just shoot us down.

Not if we shoot her first.

Chola Se shook her head. Shele take cover in the lower section of the turret and fire at us from a gunport. Wele never be able to hit her once shese in there.

I didnt know what to say. I knew she was right, and I knew what that meant---and I didnt understand why it seemed to bother me so much.

One of us needs to go after Kite, Jeet. Its the only way to take her out. One of us goes after Pilgrim, the other one goes after Kite. If we dont get rid of both of them at once wele never get out of here alive.

But we dont even know if theyre up there, do we? I reminded her. You said so yourself – they could have just used the steps to get out of the cavern.

If we go after them both and theyre not there, it doesnt matter, does it? We just go ahead and climb down anyway. But if we dont go after them both and they are up there---

She didnt have to finish the sentence. I still knew she was right. And I still didnt want to accept it. And the reason I didnt want to accept it – I realised now – was that splitting up and going after both of them was exactly what Ide been planning before Ide convinced Chola Se – and myself – that we could still get out of here and make it to the Deathlands---and I hadnt been myself then. Ide been broken, travelling in the wrong direction---Ide been lost. And I thought Ide found myself again and was on the way home. But now --

I didnt know what I was thinking.

Chola Se was right.

And I couldnt work out what that meant for me.

Youre dog, a voice in my heart said. Stop thinking. Just be.

I thought at first it was the echo of my own voice – the echo of a recent memory – but I knew now that the voice Ide remembered then had never been mine in the first place. It had come to me as my own, but it was a voice without a voice, thinking without thinking---dog to dog---mother to son---

My mothers voice.

She was close enough now for me to feel her in my heart.

Ile take Pilgrim, I said to Chola Se. You go after Kite.

What? No, hold on. If weare going to—

You want Pilgrim dead, dont you?

Yeh, of course I do.

Does it matter who kills him?

Well, no---but—

So let me do it, okay?

I looked at her, focusing my force of thought into her heart, letting her see what she already knew but didnt want to admit — that her hatred for Pilgrim was so allconsuming that there was a chance it could affect her judgement — just as it had before in Pilgrims house — and no matter how small that chance might be, it wasnt worth taking the risk.

All right? I said to her.

She hesitated a moment, then nodded.

All that remained of the dustcloud now was a waist-high layer of fine grey mist, and as I waited by the door in the wall, watching Chola Se as she glided through the mist on her way over to the door on the other side of the cavern, I remembered that morning on the beach with Starry — just sitting beside him on the old sea wall in the early-morning silence, gazing out at the sea---the dark yellow haze hanging over the surface in vast crawling clouds---the silvery twinkle of sunlight on his fishing line as it disappeared into the yellowy-brown mist---and I remembered recalling the time when Ide thought Ide seen a tanking ship, way out in the distance, moving slowly across the horizon---

I made myself forget it.

Chola Se had reached the door now. I watched her as she stopped in front of it for a moment — and just for a second I wondered if she was having second thoughts — but then she turned to face me and raised her hand, letting me know she was ready. I waved back. She nodded once, then took hold of her shotgun and turned back to the door. I watched her open it and go inside, waited 5 seconds---then another 5---then I drew my knife, opened the door, and stepped through into the darkness.

The relative brightness of the torchlit cavern had made the darkness beyond the door seem blacker than it actually was, and once my eyes had adapted to the gloom — and the surroundings had gradually become clearer — there was no doubt at all that I was inside the Central Tower. It was all so familiar from my Fighter training — the steep stone steps spiralling upwards, the ancient black walls, the taste of the cold dusty air in the back of my throat---Ide seen and felt it all before. But at the same time, I hadnt. Ide never been in this part of the tower before. I didnt even know it existed. And as I raised my head and gazed upwards, I realised that this part of the tower, the underground part, had to be separated from the main part of the tower, and that there had to be a secret entrance to it from above, otherwise — as Chola Se had suggested — I would have known about it. I would have seen these steps every time Ide entered the tower.

I carried on peering upwards for a while, looking and listening hard. A pale light was burning somewhere up above — just a faint glow of flame in the darkness — but I couldnt see anything else. And the only noise I could hear was the continuing sound of the battle outside. It was clearer now — louder, less muffled, more real — and as I began climbing the steps, I could smell the heat of gunpowder in the air.

The sound of fighting grew louder and louder the higher I went, and by the time Ide reached ground level I could feel the crash of explosions resonating through the walls. In the flamelight of a torch on the wall — the pale light Ide seen from below — I could see the stone floor of the main part of the tower just a few yards above me, and as I stood on the steps gazing up at it, I saw the secret entrance that Ide realised had to be there. It was a cast-iron drain cover — at least, thats what Ide always thought it was. Ide seen it countless times before, from the other side. Ide seen it every time Ide entered the tower, and Ide never given it a second thought. It was just a drain cover – a square slab of cast iron, about 30 inches across, set in the stone floor near the righthand edge.

The steps led almost all the way up to it. I moved closer – climbing another 3 or 4 steps – until the cover was directly over my head, then I reached up, put both hands flat against the cold hard metal, and pushed. It was heavy – heavier than I expected – but it was hinged, and once Ide got it moving, it wasnt hard to open. I moved up another step, gave it a good hard shove, and the cover swung back on its hinges and slammed heavily into the stone floor with a dull metallic clang.

As I stepped up and pulled myself through the opening into the main part of the tower, the sound of the battle outside erupted all around me, the air itself shaking with the thunder of violence – gunfire, grenade blasts, screams of agony, the roar of flames, the massive rumble of burning buildings crashing to the ground. The air was thick and hot – a sour metallic heat – and every time I took a breath I could taste the stink of burning flesh and blood---

I know violence, Ive lived with it all my life. I know it for what it is and why it has to be.

But this was something else.

This, I think, was some kind of poison.

The watchtower door had been bolted shut from the inside, which meant that – unless there was another way out that I didnt know about – Pilgrim was definitely still in the tower. I still didnt understand what he was doing in here, but as I began heading up the steps again – and the rage of the battle began fading away – I wasnt dwelling on reasons. I just wanted to be free now. I didnt want any answers and I didnt want to think. All I wanted to do was go home. Even if that meant dying.

I kept going.

Climbing the steps.

Steadily, quietly---

When Ide climbed high enough above the sound of the battle to hear the silence of the tower again, I stopped for a minute to listen. At first there was nothing, just the hollow hush of the tower, but then I heard something. It was very faint, coming from high above me, and I could only just hear it. It stopped for a while, then started again, and as I raised my head and cupped my hands to my ears I could just about make it out. It was a soft spitting sound – phht---phht---phht – irregular, intermittent. It would start up, spit once or twice, then stop again and go quiet.

I didnt know what it was.

I listened for a while longer, then carried on climbing.

About 10 steps later, I stopped again. I hadnt heard anything this time – the spitting sound hadnt started up again – Ide stopped because something was bothering me. I didnt know what it was, it was just there – nagging away at the back of my mind---something Ide seen or heard---or maybe thought. I knew it was important, but it just wouldnt come to me. I closed my eyes and opened my mind, trying to let it out---but all that came to me was a sense of darkness.

I heard another spit then – phht – just once this time, but louder than before, and much clearer. I still couldnt tell what it was though.

I opened my eyes.

I was near the top of the tower now. I could tell by the change in the air. It was fresher, cooler, touched with a faint breeze. But even up here it was still tinged with smoke and a surprisingly strong smell of gunpowder. It smelled of humans too – the dead and the dying, the bloody, the killing---

The living.

I could smell sweat.

My sense of smell wasnt as acute as Chola Ses, and I didnt doubt that if she was here shede recognise the scent as Pilgrims. But I didnt have to recognise it to know it was him. It had to be him.

I leaned to one side and angled my head upwards, trying to see how much further it was to the turret, but it was impossible to tell. It was too dark up there. The only light Ide seen so far was a torch on the wall about halfway up, and since then the tower had gradually darkened again. All I could see was the spiral of steps disappearing upwards into the gloom.

I knew the turret was close though.

Another 20 feet or so, maybe less.

Just another 20 steps.

I started climbing again.

1---2---3---4---5---

Phht.

---6---7---

Phht-phht.

---8---9---10---

An image of Chola Se floated into my mind. I saw her climbing the steps in the East Tower – padding upwards, just like me---

---11---12---

---her eyes alert, her nose twitching, the shotgun in her hands---

---13---

---and then all of a sudden the picture changed and I saw her falling---dropping down through the cold dark air---

I stopped and shook my head hard – once, twice – emptying my mind.

I breathed in slowly, breathed out.

I waited for my heart to stop pounding, then carried on.

---14---15---16---

Phht.

I froze midstep. The spitting noise was very close now, just a few feet away. I inched up to the next step, leaning forward, staring ahead---

I saw the opening to the turret.

5 steps away, a square hole in a stone floor.

There was no hatch, no door. Just a 3-foot-wide hole. The steps led all the way up to it.

Pilgrim was in there. I couldnt see him. There was no sign of movement, no more spitting, no sounds at all. But I knew he was there.

I sheathed my knife, drew the Beretta from my belt, and took another step---

And another.

I heard something---a nothing sound---a scuff, a small movement---and as I stopped to listen, something began edging into my mind, the vaguest hint of something dark---something important?

No.

I blocked it out, killed it.

Took another slow silent step.

And stopped.

The hole was directly above me now, no more than a foot from my head. As I gazed up through it, I could see part of the upper section of the turret – the perimeter walkway, the battlements – and above the turret I could see a patch of burning black sky, but the angle was too tight to see into the lower section.

I had no way of knowing if Pilgrim was in the upper or lower section, and the only way to find out without going in was to wait. The problem was, if I stayed where I was and just waited, Pilgrim might see me before I saw him, and if that happened Ide be dead before I knew it. And even if we saw each other at the same time, I wouldnt stand much of a chance. He held the high ground, he could manoeuvre – I was just a head in a hole. But then if I didnt wait, if I just went for it – either lunging up through the hole or cautiously inching my head through – I might get my head blown off anyway.

I couldnt wait.

I couldnt move---

I waited---

I moved.

Raising my left leg, placing my foot on the final step---gripping the edge of the hole with my left hand---lifting my right arm, bent at the elbow, bringing my gunhand level with my head---I straightened my leg and slowly pushed myself up, edging my head through the hole---

I saw Pilgrim immediately, just to my right – standing with his back to me, his submachine gun slung over his shoulder, aiming a

439

rifle through the slit of a gunport. He didnt seem to be aware of me. Pulling with my left arm, I inched myself a little higher, at the same time twisting my body round to the right to give myself room to lift my right arm through the hole and level my pistol at Pilgrim. It was just as I was lifting the gun through the hole that I heard Pilgrims voice.

You should have listened to me, Jeet, he said, without turning his head. I told you youd be sorry if you didnt.

I heard something behind me then – a sudden quick movement – and the next thing I knew something slammed into the back of my skull and everything went black.

As I drifted back up into semiconsciousness, I kept seeing the dust-filled cavern again. I saw it as a vast dome of burning black sky with swirling clouds of dustgrey stars---I saw it as my own cavernous skull with black tendrils creeping down the bonewhite walls---and I saw it again as Ide seen it through the hole in the wall when Ide been watching Pilgrim and Kite and something had caught the corner of my eye---an unseen movement about 25 yards to the left of them---but when Ide looked over to see what it was thered been nothing there, just a slight swirling in the dustcloud – the echo of a movement – and a momentary flash of darkness that had disappeared as soon as Ide seen it, or thought Ide seen it---

Ide seen it.

I knew that now.

Thats what had been bothering me all the way up the steps – the nagging thought in the back of my mind – that momentary flash of darkness. It had been the door in the wall opening and closing. Someone had gone through the door before Pilgrim. Someone else had been in the cavern, someone else had gone through the door into the tower---and hede been waiting for me in the turret, waiting to slam his rifle butt into my head---

And now, as my eyes began fluttering open, I could see him.

Glorian.

At first I couldnt work out where he was. He was closeby – just a few yards away, directly in front of me – but his great hulking figure seemed to be hovering above me, floating in the night sky, and the night seemed to be on fire, the blackness behind him red with flames---

I closed my eyes, waited for my head to clear, then tried again.

Glorian wasnt floating. I was in the upper section of the turret – sitting on the stone ledge of the walkway with my back against the parapet, my legs stretched out in front of me – and Glorian was standing on the walkway directly opposite me, leaning against the parapet. I was on the north side of the turret, facing town. From where I was sitting, I could see the night sky behind Glorian glowing red from the flames of the burning buildings 90 feet below, but I was too low down to see anything of the town itself. There was no doubt the battle was still raging though. I could hear it in the heat of the rising air – gunshots, explosions, helpless sobbing – and as I went to stand up, then immediately sat down again as a sudden surge of pain ripped through my head, I heard a massive crash of stone from below, the sound of another building collapsing, and a moment later an unearthly scream rang out, piercing the night like a needle, before dying away and fading back into the background chaos. I saw Glorian turn his head and casually glance down over the battlements. He watched something for a moment, barely even curious, then he wiped his nose on the back of his hand, turned round again, and stared at me with mindless indifference.

As I stared back at him, I realised that he wasnt holding a gun on me. He was carrying a 5-shot revolver in a holster on his belt, and his bolt-action rifle was slung over his shoulder — fresh blood visible on the butt — but his hands were empty. I looked down at my belt. The Beretta was gone and my knife sheath was empty, just as Ide expected, but when I looked up again and gazed around, I was surprised to see both the gun and the knife just 3 or 4 yards from where I was sitting. They were lying on top of my knapsack — together with the coil of twined cable — halfway along the walkway to my right. I stared at them, wondering if I could get to them before Glorian had time to draw his pistol — or unsling his rifle — and shoot. I knew Ide never make it from a sitting position, but if I was on my feet to start with, and Glorian wasnt looking---

I glanced over at him.

He smiled at me.

It was the first time Ide ever seen him smile, and I hoped Ide never see it again. It turned my blood cold.

Phht.

The sound came from Pilgrims rifle. I looked down into the lower section of the turret and saw that he was still standing at the gunport, still aiming a rifle through the slit — the barrel angled downwards — and as I watched him now, I realised that he was trailing a target – moving the rifle slowly to the left, his eyes calm and steady, his finger poised on the trigger---

And then – phht – he fired.

The rifle he was using was no ordinary weapon. It was a Remington R11 – a semiautomatic sniper rifle fitted with a telescopic sight and a silencer – and from the sound of it, he wasnt using ordinary ammunition either. It was hard to be sure with the silencer muting the sound, but the shots didnt have the familiar low crack of handmade bullets, and I guessed Pilgrim must have been saving up a stock of authentic ammunition, which hede no doubt plundered from somewhere – or someone – many years ago.

Any sign of Hensch yet? he said to Glorian without taking his eye from the telescopic sight.

I think hese still hanging back on the other side of the wall.

Let me know as soon as you see him. What about Gun Sur?

Still in the Quarterhouse.

Who else is left?

Henschs Deputy.

Li Jun?

Yeh, him. And their last 2 Captains.

Ive just got them.

What are you doing? I heard myself say.

Pilgrim turned at the sound of my voice and looked up at me.

Jeet, he said, feigning surprise. I thought you were dead.

All I could do was sit there looking down at him. I didnt know why Ide asked him what he was doing – I hadnt consciously meant to say anything – it had just come out, the mindless words of a broken head.

You want to know what Ime doing? he said, grinning at me.

Why dont you see for yourself? Go on, get up and take a look. This is what youre supposed to be writing about, isnt it? The last war, the final battle---? Well, this is it, Jeet. This is history in the making---the dawning of a new age, the birth of a new race.

He stared at me, his eyes burning with a strange black light, and as I looked back at him – still gripped with silence – his features seemed to shimmer. It was as if I was watching a series of masks flickering across his face, each of them changing so rapidly that they all seemed to merge into a single multifaced vision.

What are you looking at me for? the vision said. Do you want to see the end of the world or not?

As I struggled to my feet, a wave of dizziness flooded through me and I had to grab hold of the parapet to steady myself. Now that I was standing, I could see some of the southern edge of town in the distance – the black emptiness of the beach, houses burning along the Beach Road – but my view was still restricted by the height of the parapet. Down to my left, I could see the massive hole in the town wall where it had been ripped apart by the explosion – a 20-yard stretch of 8-foot-thick stone reduced to piles of rubble – and further along, from the corner of my eye, I could see the East Tower rising up into the firelit sky. I was desperate to know if Chola Se was all right, and there was nothing I wanted more than to turn my head and look directly at the turret to see if she was there, but I knew that I couldnt. Glorian wasnt stupid. If he saw me looking across at the East Tower, hede know I was looking for something – or someone – and if Chola Se had made it to the top, and if she had managed to take out Kite, it was vital that Glorian and Pilgrim didnt know.

The dizziness was easing off now.

I let go of the parapet to see if I could stand without support.

I felt okay.

Steady enough.

I could probably walk---maybe even run.

Without thinking, I glanced across at my knapsack again.

Try it if you want, I heard Glorian say. But you might want to check on your bitch first.

As I looked across at him and saw that savage smile again, I felt a terrible darkness sinking in my heart.

Over there, he said, jerking his head to his right, in the direction of the East Tower.

My breath seemed stuck in my throat as I turned to my left and looked over at the tower, and when I saw Chola Se in the turret, the world seemed to lurch beneath my feet, and if I hadnt grabbed hold of the parapet again I would have fallen back to the ground. She was standing on the walkway, her back to the battlements, facing my way. Her hands were tied behind her back, blood was streaming from an open gash in her forehead, and Kite was standing beside her with a handgun pressed to her head. In the glowing red light of the sky, I could see that she was badly hurt – her face white with shock, her head hanging down to one side – and that she was struggling to stay on her feet. But when Kite leaned in close to her and spoke in her ear, and she slowly raised her head and looked up at me, I knew she was far from beaten. She had the same look in her eyes that Ide seen in the dungeon at the Dau camp – the same fire and ferocity, the same will to keep fighting as long as she was still alive, the same willingness to die before giving herself up---

The cables were still looped across her chest, and as Kite took hold of them with her free hand and gave them a sharp tug, hauling

445

Chola Se around to her left, I saw something else in her eyes too. I only saw it for a moment – she didnt have the strength to fight against Kite for more than a second or 2 – but just before Kite swung her around, I clearly saw her eyes dart twice to her right.

She was telling me to look out to the north, away from town---across Nomansland and out into the Deathlands.

Kite was dragging her along the walkway now, and all I could do was watch in futile rage as she stopped about halfway along, shoved Chola Se against the parapet, and secured her bound hands to a cast-iron bracket bolted to the wall. She then forced her down to her knees, put the gun to her head, and looked across at Glorian. She waited a moment – her grey eyes glinting like silver – then she nodded at him.

The bitches life is in your hands, he said to me. You do everything right, she lives. You do anything wrong, shese dead. Understand?

I turned slowly to him and nodded.

Pilgrims rifle spat.

Just the 2 big ones left now, he said.

Glorian glanced down over the parapet.

And I turned round and looked out across Nomansland into the Deathlands. I knew what Chola Se had been telling me now. I knew they were out there – Ide sensed their coming---Ide felt their running hearts in mine – and now I could see their invisible shapes in the darkness---streaming down from the mountains---loping across the glassrock plains---heading towards town in their hundreds---

The Deathland dogs were coming.

Come over here, Glorian said to me.

I held my ground for a moment or 2, just long enough to stare into Glorians eyes and let him know that I intended to kill him — but not long enough to antagonise him — and then I started heading towards him. As I crossed over the walkway, I glanced across at the East Tower again. Kite still had her gun to Chola Ses head, but her eyes were focused on me, and I didnt doubt that shede pull the trigger if I tried anything. On the walkway to her right, a sniper rifle with a silencer was propped up against the parapet wall, and I guessed that if it wasnt for Chola Se, Kite would be stationed at a gunport in the lower section of the turret picking off targets, just like Pilgrim.

I was fairly sure I knew what Pilgrim was up to now, and as I reached the walkway on the south side of the turret, I found myself wondering what Starry would have made of it. The sound of his voice came to me then — not just as a memory, but as a presence. He was with me, within me---talking to me inside my head — *Pilgrims a psychopath, Jeet, and a self-obsessed savage, but hese definitely not an idiot---he knows what happens to traitors when they no longer serve any purpose---*

The voice and the presence suddenly stopped dead as I stepped up to the parapet and looked down at the town below and saw for the first time the carnage that until then Ide only been able to imagine.

It was a sight Ile never forget.

In the blazing flamelight of torches and burning buildings I could see that the battle was still being fought — fierce gunfights and skirmishes raging all over town — but as I gazed around at the ravaged streets it was clear the town had fallen. The dead and the

dying lay everywhere – Fighters, Workers, Youngers, Olders---
people Ide known all my life – their bodies littering the ground
below in a nightmare vision of torn flesh and twisted limbs. There
were scores of Dau casualties too – Fighters, civilians---it didnt
matter, they were all the same in death – but I didnt know
them---I had no connection to them. They were nameless. And as
I looked around at the bodies I did know, I realised that they were
nameless too. Cruke, Van Hesse, Leven Rai and Lolo, Tomas,
Ghauri, Luca---their names didnt seem to belong to them
anymore. Whatever it was theyd belonged to was gone.

Cruke was gone – lying on his back in the middle of Main Street,
a single bullet hole in his head.

Van Hesse was gone – slumped to his knees in the grocery
doorway, machine-gunned in the back.

Leven Rai and Lolo were gone – their frail old bodies
smouldering on the ground outside the still-burning Olders Home.

Tomas was gone – lying in the dirt in front of the blockhouse,
his rifle still gripped in his hands, his belly sliced open.

Ghauri was gone – just one of the many dead bodies sprawled
on the Quarterhouse steps, the back of his head blown off.

Captain Luca was gone – lying beside Ghauri, shot in the face.

The Quarterhouse was surrounded by dozens of Dau Fighters,
their weapons trained on the doors and windows. The building was
badly damaged – the walls riddled with bullet holes, the roof
partially collapsed, smoke billowing from a grenade-damaged
window on the second floor – but it hadnt fallen yet. There was
no sign of anyone inside the building, but the Dau wouldnt be
holding back if it wasnt defended, so there had to be a force of
some kind in there.

When youre ready, I heard Glorian say.

I turned and looked at him.

Youre going to do something for me now, okay? he said. And youre going to do it right, arent you?

I nodded, staring at him.

Hensch is down there somewhere, he said, pointing at the ruined wall. Hese keeping out of sight at the moment, waiting til he thinks its safe to come in, which should be any time soon. All you have to do is keep your eyes open for him, and let me know as soon as you see him. All right?

What does he look like?

Youle know him when you see him. Glorian stared at me. What are you waiting for?

I held his gaze for a second, then turned away and looked down over the parapet at the shattered remains of the wall. I knew Pilgrim was going to kill Hensch as soon as the Dau Marshal showed himself, and I had no qualms about watching out for him and pointing him out when I saw him. My only concern was keeping Chola Se alive, and right now the only way I could do that was by doing exactly as I was told.

So thats what I did.

Or, at least, thats what part of me did.

Glorian watched me for a few moments, making sure that I wasnt just going through the motions, then – seemingly satisfied – he turned away, leaned against the battlements, and gazed out towards the Quarterhouse.

And the part of me that wasnt watching out for Hensch carried on thinking like Ide never thought before – thinking about Chola Se, thinking about the dogs, thinking about Pilgrim and Glorian

449

and Kite and my knife and the guns and the cables and the grenade in the knapsack---

After a few minutes, the other part of me – the watching part – saw something moving over by the base of the East Tower, but when I glanced over – without raising my head – I realised straightaway that it wasnt the Dau Marshal. It was a group of our people – about a dozen young women and children – being herded along towards the tower by 2 Dau Fighters. These were the ones the Dau were keeping for themselves, I realised – the females for breeding, the male children to be raised as Dau. Among the young women was Prendy, the other female dogchild, and I could see shede been badly beaten and was struggling to stay on her feet. When her legs suddenly buckled and she slumped to the ground, one of the Dau Fighters stooped down, grabbed her by the hair and yanked her back to her feet again, then viciously kicked her back into line.

I couldnt watch anymore.

I couldnt carry on doing nothing anymore.

Theyre going to kill you, you know, I said quietly to Glorian.

He didnt respond at first, just carried on watching the Quarterhouse, but after a few seconds, I heard him let out a weary sigh.

Ime beginning to think you want that bitch of yours dead, he said. Youre going the right way about it if you do.

I dont get it, thats all, I told him. I mean, youre not stupid, are you? Youre an experienced Fighter, a Captain---you know what the Dau are like. Theyre not weak, are they? Theyre not going to just lie down and—

You think you know everything, dont you? he said, his voice

suddenly cold and hard.

I know what the 3 of you are trying to do.

He turned to me. Yeh? And whats that then?

Youre taking out everyone on either side whose got any power – Hensch and his Deputy, the Dau Captains, Gun Sur, our Fighter Captains and Senior Fighters, our Councillors---anyone with any authority or influence over their people – youre getting rid of them all.

And why would we be doing that?

Because youre traitors, and you know the price of betrayal. You knew from the start that Hensch would have you killed as soon as hede got what he wanted from you, so youre getting rid of him and anyone else you think might be a threat – and youre making it look as if they all died during the battle – because you think that will leave the rest of the Dau so weak and disorganised that Pilgrim will be able to manipulate them into thinking that it was him who won the war for them, not Hensch---

A sudden memory of Pilgrims voice flashed through my mind as I was speaking – and when Hensch finally retires, or upon his death, I heard him saying, Ile be made Marshal. And since the Dau will have wiped us all out by then, that means, in effect, that Ile be the leader of the entire human race.

And thats the only reason you havent killed me yet, isnt it? I said to Glorian. Pilgrims going to use me to help him win over the Dau. Hese going to tell them that Ime the dogchild theyre looking for, the one who ripped out Skenders throat, the one who murdered their Marshals only child, and then hese going to give me up to them and let them take their revenge.

Glorian didnt say anything.

And neither did Pilgrim.

I was sure he could hear everything I was saying – he was only a few yards beneath us – and Ide been expecting him to show some kind of reaction, but for some reason he was keeping his silence.

You realise Pilgrims out of his mind, dont you? I said to Glorian. Thats why this is never going to work and the Dau are going to cut you all to pieces as soon as they find you. Its why Pilgrims still obsessed with killing Gun Sur. Theres no need to kill him anymore, is there? The only reason you needed to get rid of him – and Cruke and Luca and all the others – was to cover yourselves in case something went wrong and the Dau didnt win the battle. Because if that happened, Gun Sur and the others would know youd betrayed us, and the 3 of you would be hanged as traitors. But its not going to happen now, is it? The Dau have won, so you dont need to cover yourselves. You dont need to get rid of Gun Sur. And even if you did, the Dau are going to kill him anyway. But Pilgrim still wants to do it himself, doesnt he? He wants to kill the Marshal because he despises him, because hese always wanted to kill him, because he likes killing people, because hese a madman—

BOOM!

The sudden earthshaking blast came from the Quarterhouse – a massive explosion that lit up the sky with a blinding white flash – and when I looked over at the building I saw a gaping hole in the wall where the door had been and a massive crack in the stonework above that had almost split the building in 2. Great lumps of stone and twisted metal were scattered down the steps, and plumes of thick black smoke were beginning to billow out from all around the building – the shutters, the roof, the hole in the wall---

A Fighter suddenly appeared through the smoke, running out of the building with a rifle in his hands — bent over, choking, holding a cloth to his mouth---the Dau Fighters opened fire, cutting him to pieces, and he fell to the ground without firing a shot.

I heard more shots then, but these were much closer and quieter.

Phht-phht---phht.

A wail of pain came from somewhere below---

Phht.

The wailing stopped.

I looked down over the parapet and saw 3 dead bodies lying amid the rubble of the wall. 2 of them were Dau Fighters, and the other one had to be Hensch. He was lying on his back inbetween the other 2, his face staring up at me, and although he didnt look exactly like Skender, the resemblance was too close to be a coincidence.

Hensch was dead.

I dont know how much of what Ide told Glorian was true — I was only guessing about most of it — and I dont suppose Ile ever know for sure what Pilgrim was really planning to do, but it doesnt matter now, and it didnt matter then. Whatever the 3 of them were aiming to do, the only thing I wanted to know about it was how it affected me and Chola Se. And the only reasons Ide been talking to Glorian about it were firstly to see if I could get anything out of him — which I hadnt — secondly to see if I could rile him into a mistake — which also hadnt worked — and thirdly because I was playing for time.

I didnt know if I was right about why they hadnt killed me yet, but they obviously needed me alive for some reason, and as long as I was alive they needed to keep Chola Se alive too, because without her they had no control over me. But they werent going to need us forever.

The dogs were getting close now though, and I was with them. I was with my mother, running through the night with her, seeing what she could see, feeling what she could feel – the burning town up ahead, the smell of charred flesh in the air---the closeness of the pack all around us---the big grey male, the 3 adult females, the 2 juveniles, the 2 young sisters---

I was with them all.

And all around us, everywhere we could see, hundreds of other dogs were running in resolute silence – large packs, small packs, families, lone dogs---

The Deathland dogs were coming, drawn together by the scent of human blood, just as they had been all those years ago when theyd attacked the wagon in the Black Mountains, only this time there werent just 30 or 40 of them---

This time theyd risen as one.

I could hear Pilgrim moving now – stepping away from the gunport, leaning the sniper rifle against the wall – and as I turned away from the parapet and looked down over the walkway into the lower section of the turret, I saw him standing there staring up at me – composed, cold-eyed, confident.

He drew one of his Colts and calmly aimed it at my head.

Youre right about one thing, Jeet, he said. I do like killing people.

It looked as if my time had come.

JEET!

It was Chola Se, calling out to me from the East Tower. As I spun round and looked over, I saw Kite hurrying across the walkway towards her, her pistol raised, yelling at Chola Se to keep quiet, and I saw Chola Se standing against the parapet wall, her hands still tied behind her back, her body twisted round in a strangely awkward position. Her head was facing me – her eyes burning into mine – but her legs were side-on to the wall, one in front of the other, her feet about 18 inches apart.

She glanced at Kite, saw that she was closing fast, then quickly turned back to me and called out again at the top of her voice.

WELE STILL DIE TOGETHER, JEET! FIGHT FOR US---NOW!

And then, with a graceful bound, she launched herself up and over the parapet wall and was gone.

I knew she couldnt survive the fall. It was a sheer 90-foot drop to a solid mass of glassrock---no one could live through that. I knew it, and for a fraction of a second after shede jumped the pain screamed through me like a dagger plunging into my heart---but then, in an instant, she came back to me, and I saw her again just before she jumped – the life in her eyes, the telling sound of her voice – FIGHT FOR US---NOW! – and I knew---

I knew what shede done.

And I knew what she wanted me to do.

I waited a moment.

Ide moved across to the eastside walkway when Ide seen Chola Se leaping from the tower, and as I stood there now – still pressed up closely to the parapet wall, watching Kite as she leaned out over the battlements and gazed down at the ground, searching for Chola

Se – I knew Glorian would be coming for me. Without Chola Se they no longer had a hold over me, and Glorian had to put that right---and hede want to do it right now, while I was still in shock, still stunned by the sight of Chola Se jumping to her death---still frozen to the spot, blinded by grief, unable to see him coming---

I could hear him crossing the walkway now – rapidly, silently---

I still waited.

I could sense him right behind me – his presence, his breath, his sweat---

I heard Pilgrim shout, DONT KILL HIM!

And I moved, dropping to my left just as Glorian lunged at me from behind. He sailed past me, stumbling wildly, and his momentum sent him crashing heavily into the parapet wall, and as the ancient battlements cracked and gave way under his massive weight, and he lurched down over the crumbling wall, I spun round, threw my arms round his legs, and heaved him over the edge.

I didnt wait to see if Pilgrim had changed his mind about killing me now, I just leaped back across to the southside walkway, threw myself flat on the ground, and rolled til I hit the wall. As long as I kept down and away from the edge of the walkway, Pilgrim couldnt see me from below. And if he couldnt see me, he couldnt shoot me. But I was only safe for a moment. Pilgrim knew I was unarmed, so all he had to do was cross over to the steps and climb up here---

I heard him moving – his boots clacking quietly across the turret floor---

I jumped up and ran for my knapsack – keeping low, running on all 4s---streaking along the stone ledge, leaping across the corner – and as I landed on the westside walkway, just a few yards away from the knapsack, I saw Pilgrim coming up the steps at the opposite end of the ledge. He was moving slowly, cautiously, edging his head up over the ledge to see where I was. He saw me, then I saw his eyes flick down at the Beretta on the knapsack, and just for a moment he hesitated. I dived headlong for the pistol, grabbing it in my outstretched hand as I hit the ground, and as I rolled quickly to my left and opened fire – working the trigger as fast as I could – I saw Pilgrim ducking down out of sight. I stopped firing, and in the sudden silence I heard his bootsteps hurrying down the steps, and I knew then that he still wanted to keep me alive. He didnt have to run from me. He had an MP40 submachine gun and 2 Colts – he could have fought back. And whatever he was, he wasnt a coward. He wasnt running from me, he was retreating, saving himself so he could take me alive---saving my life as a gift to the Dau.

His footsteps had stopped now, but I could still hear some kind of movement – a faint shuffling, a grunt of breath, a single muffled step---

I crawled across to the rim of the walkway and very cautiously peered down into the lower section, and the first thing I saw was the top of Pilgrims head disappearing down into the hole in the floor. I jumped to my knees and fired off a couple of quick shots, but I knew I was wasting my time – I could already hear his bootsteps clomping rapidly down the spiral steps. They slowed after a while, then faded completely, and for a moment I wondered if hede stopped on the steps somewhere and was waiting for me to come after him, or if he was still going down but simply wasnt hurrying anymore. And if he wasnt hurrying---

Dont think about it, my heart said.

It was my mothers voice, loud and clear and true. She was very close now.

Just do what you have to do, she said.

I went back to my knapsack, picked up the coil of cable and my knife, then shouldered the bag and crossed over to the northside ledge. As I sheathed the knife and put the pistol in my belt, I began to feel something – a rising---a sense, a power, a force---

It was everywhere – in the air, the sky, the stars---in my flesh, in my mind, my memories, my blood---in the tower itself, in the walls, the stone---

It was everything.

The rising.

The dogs were here.

I looked down over the parapet and saw them – a ragged army of silent beasts waiting outside the wall, their vast gathering stretched out across an area of glassrock the length of the wall – and half as deep – with more dogs arriving all the time, streaming in out of the Deathlands to swell the ranks of the hundreds---

My mother was there. I could see her sitting with her pack, calm and serene---and I could see myself through her eyes.

I was with her---

I was with them all.

We were one.

The rising.

I didnt understand it, but I knew it.

Just as I knew that Chola Se was down there somewhere, waiting for me to join her.

I got to work.

First I tested each of the battlements to see if they were strong enough to take my weight. One of them was visibly cracked and loose, and another was slightly unsteady, but the rest felt sturdy enough. Next I unwound the loop of twined cable, checking it wasnt tangled, and tied one end to the strongest battlement, winding it round twice and knotting it tightly. And finally I took hold of the rest of the cable, leaned out over the parapet, and launched it into the air. As I watched the coil of cable tumbling down, unravelling as it went, the image of Chola Se came to me again – the moment before shede jumped – and although I knew now that shede somehow managed to fix her cable to the bracket in the wall before shede jumped, I still couldnt imagine how terrifying it must have been for her to have to just leap over the wall into the unknown – not knowing if the bracket would hold, or how the cable would unwind, or how she could possibly control the fall and somehow stop herself from either hurtling straight down to the ground or slamming into the wall or falling halfway before the cable suddenly caught hold and snapped her spine or her neck---

No.

Shede made it, she was safe.

She had to be.

I looked down. The cable hung in a straight line all the way down to the ground. I reached into the knapsack and took out the hand grenade that Cruke had given us. Ide never actually used one before – theyre too rare to practise with – but Ide been taught how to use them in Fighter training. Cruke had told us that this one had

459

an 8-second fuse, which meant that once Ide thrown it, Ide have 8 seconds before it exploded.

I didnt know if that gave me enough time or not, but I had no choice. Whatever it took, I had to kill Pilgrim.

Whatever it took.

I pulled the pin from the grenade – making sure I still held down the safety lever – then I moved to the edge of the walkway, focused on the hole in the floor for a few seconds, and lobbed the grenade towards it. I waited a moment, just long enough to watch it arc through the air and drop down into the hole, then I turned and crossed quickly to the parapet.

1 second---

I heard the dull clank of metal on stone as the grenade hit the steps, and as I climbed over the parapet and grabbed hold of the cable, I briefly heard it clattering downwards, picking up pace as it went.

2 seconds---

And then I was off, not listening to anything, just scrambling down the cable – hand over hand, slipping and sliding, the cable ripping the skin off my palms as I let myself drop as fast as I could without falling---

3 seconds---

4 seconds---

I was about a third of the way down when a heartsense came to me from my mothers eyes – a vision without sight or time – and as we looked up at the tower together we saw a bloodied dogchild in a giants coat scrabbling down the wall like a broken insect, and at the top of the tower, leaning out over the parapet and looking down, we saw a dead-eyed human in a black Cowboy hat.

The vision left me.

5 seconds---

I grasped the cable, twisting it round my bloodied hands to halt my fall, and as I hung there – spinning and swaying – I looked up and saw Pilgrim scrambling hastily over the parapet.

6 seconds---

I had no understanding then.

I realise now that Pilgrim must have been waiting on the steps somewhere near the top of the tower when I threw the grenade. He would have heard it coming – bouncing and clattering down the steps towards him – and then, as it sailed past him, and it suddenly dawned on him what it was, his instincts had kicked in, telling him to run, and hede run back up into the turret – not knowing how he was going to escape, but knowing that if he stayed where he was, or ran down the steps, hede be killed when the grenade exploded – and when hede reached the turret and seen that I wasnt there, he must have spotted the cable tied to the battlement---

And now he was clambering down over the parapet and grabbing hold of the cable, and any second now he was going to start climbing down---

The cable was never going to hold.

He was at least twice my size, probably more.

And even if the cable could take the extra weight, the battlement never would.

I looked down.

I was still at least 60 feet from the ground. If I let go and jumped now, the fall would kill me.

7 seconds---

I loosened my grasp and let myself slide, and as I hurtled down

– keeping hold of the cable with just enough grip to stop myself freefalling – I closed my eyes and saw in my heart the dead-eyed human plunging down the cable above me, plummeting even faster than me, dropping down on me like a great black bird swooping in for the kill---

8 seconds.

I dont know where the grenade was when it exploded.

My memory of the moment is unclear.

I vaguely remember hearing the blast – a low muffled boom from inside the tower – but I cant recall if it came from above or below me. There was an unearthly sense of silence for a moment – a strange hanging hush – and then something slammed into me, a massive jarring impact from above, and the silence erupted in a great rumbling roar of crashing stone---and all I remember after that is falling, tumbling down through the darkness in a thunderous torrent of rock and dust and howling black air---thoughtless, blind, breathless, gone---engulfed in an avalanche of pounding stone---

Then a sudden shattering crash.

A crack of bone---

Then nothing.

Pilgrim was standing over me with his gun in his hand when I opened my eyes---the dead-eyed human. Standing over me like a living corpse – a thing of dust and earth and tattered rags, a thing of the underground, a thing of the grave. His skull was caved in – shattered bone, torn flesh hanging down, raw red, blackened blood thick with dirt---

He could barely stand – his body swaying like a drunk man – and it was taking him every last ounce of his strength to keep the Colt in his hand levelled at my head – his arm tensed, quivering---his broken teeth gritted---a film of sweat oozing from his pores, glistening pink with blood---

There was nothing but death in his eyes.

Mine and his.

He was dying, he knew it. But he was going to kill me first.

I saw all this the moment I opened my eyes. I saw him looming over me, the burning black sky above his head, and I saw his finger tightening on the trigger, and in the next moment my eyes closed and my heartsense opened and I was with my mother – streaking across the rubblestrewn glassrock towards the dead-eyed human, and as we looked together through her killing eyes, I saw myself lying there at his feet---sprawled on my back in the dust, limp and motionless, ready to die---and I saw the humans finger tightening on the trigger---and then his eyes flickered, and he turned and saw us hurtling towards him, and then we were flying, leaping up through the air at him, launching our massive jaws at his throat---

My eyes opened.

I saw Pilgrim swivel round and raise his gun just as my mother leaped at him. I saw him sighting the pistol at her head as she flew through the air towards him, and in that moment I knew she wasnt going to make it. I saw his finger pull on the trigger---

463

Then something flashed, spinning through the air, and a pearlhandled switchblade thudded into his back.

He froze for an instant, his eyes widened---

And then a savage blur of crushing jaws engulfed his head and he crashed to the ground with my mother tearing at his throat.

I heard Kite screaming as Pilgrim died – howling from the depths of her heart – but by the time Ide managed to get to my feet, there was no longer any sign of her in the East Tower. Not that I cared. The only thing I cared about was finding Chola Se, and as I turned to my left – where the switchblade had come from – and I saw her hobbling through the rubble towards me, I felt the same strange tingling sensation in my belly that Ide experienced when I first met her. Shede clearly been hurt when shede jumped from the tower – she was limping badly, her left arm looked broken, and the side of her face was grazed raw – but she was alive.

Shede made it.

She barely glanced at Pilgrims body as she came over and stood beside me – he was nothing now, nonexistent – and as my mother trotted over to stand with us, licking Pilgrims blood from her lips, Chola Se didnt look at her either. She didnt have to – theyd killed Pilgrim together – she was in my mothers heart.

The 3 of us were together now, and as we stood there amid the wreckage of the fallen wall, looking on as the burning town lit up the night sky with a crimson glow, and the haze of gunsmoke drifted slowly in the dying heat of the battle, I could feel the presence of the Deathland dogs behind us. I could feel them all in their hundreds – every single one of them. I could feel their beating hearts in mine, their blood running in mine, their breath in my lungs, their hunger in my belly.

Theyd moved closer now – drawn in by the scent of carnage – and were massing together just outside the boundary of the fallen wall.

The Dau were aware of them.

Although the fighting wasnt over yet – sporadic gunfire was still erupting all across town – the fall of the watchtower and Pilgrims death had drawn the attention of dozens of Dau, and as theyd become aware of the dogs, and the news had quickly spread, the crowd had kept growing, and there were now at least 50 or 60 Dau facing us across the glassrock, no more than 20 yards away. They were all armed, and they were all watching us just as much as they were watching the dogs. Some of them were curious, others wary, and others just wanted blood.

It was one of these – a wild-eyed young Fighter – who suddenly stepped forward, pointing at me and shouting out in recognition, Thats him! Thats the cur who killed Skender!

He raised his gun and started towards me, and a moment later 5 or 6 others joined him, marching across the glassrock with murder in their eyes.

Take him alive! a voice from the crowd yelled out.

Skin the monger!

Watch the bitch!

Ide lost my pistol when the tower had fallen, but the knapsack was still slung over my shoulders, and the moment the Dau had begun to move, Chola Se had reached into the knapsack, pulled out the big Colt revolver, and levelled it at the approaching mob. My mother reacted instantly too, baring her teeth and letting out a bonechilling snarl, and at the same time – acting in perfect unison – the army of dogs behind us made their move---all of them advancing as one, stalking slowly through the ruined wall in a great mass of savage silence---their bodies low to the ground, their ears flat, their lips drawn back, their eyes fixed unerringly on the Dau---

My voice came to them as their own. I didnt tell them to stop – we told ourselves.

Stop.

Wait.

We stopped as one.

The group of approaching Dau had halted at the sight of the advancing dogs. They still had their guns raised though, and now theyd been joined by the rest of the crowd, all of them standing there with their weapons at the ready and their fingers poised on the triggers.

Listen to me! I called out to them, taking a step forward. This doesnt have to happen. If you let us leave, the dogs will come with us and wele go back to the Deathlands and leave you in peace. But if you try to take us---

I paused, gazing down at Pilgrims body.

The dogs might not get all of you, I said, looking back up at the Dau. But by the time its all over, most of you will be lying in the dirt with your throats ripped out---and all for what? For Skender? Skender was worthless. You all know that. You despised him, every one of you. He didnt deserve to live. So why waste your lives avenging his death?

I took another step forward, holding my hands out at my sides.

Its up to you, I told them. If you want to die for him, go ahead and shoot.

I stood there for perhaps 30 seconds, gazing around at them all, looking into their eyes – letting them see that my death meant nothing to me – and then, without another word, I turned round and began walking away.

We stayed together at first, hundreds of dogs running as one through the silent darkness of the glassrock plains, and as we headed ever deeper into the heart of the Deathlands, I felt the world coming back to me again – the closeness of the other dogs, the hypnotic rhythm of our movement, the cold night air freshening the skin of my aching body---this was where I was meant to be. With Chola Se and my mother, running together with the Deathland dogs---

Going home.

I let my voice come to the dogs again as we neared the foothills of the towering Black Mountains. Beyond the mountains, the alliance would begin to dissolve as the packs and families and solitary dogs split up and began heading back to their own territories, but for now we were still all together, and we needed to know that while our rising tonight was over for now, it would come again.

We knew it.

We could see it.

Wede heard the voice.

Our time will come.

When I first started writing this account, I didnt think I knew how to do it. 3 months have passed since then, and so much has changed that I can barely remember the way things used to be, but Ime still not sure if the words on these pages are anything more than dust in the wind. All I can say is that Ive done my best to follow the advice that Starry gave me when I sat with him that morning on the old sea wall.

Just take all the feelings from your heart and mind, he told me, and put them into words.

Its early evening now, and Ime sitting in the shade of the old blackwood tree at the far end of the plateau with my writing book open in my lap. The sun is still high and white in the sky, the air still thick with the Deathland heat, but the first faint breaths of a cooling breeze have just started fluttering in the tall dry grasses scattered sparsely around the hillside slopes, signalling the beginning of the end of the day.

Ile finish writing soon.

There isnt much more to say.

Everything is quiet for now – this world, our mountain home, is restful.

My mother is stretched out asleep on a patch of sandy ground in front of our cave, her feet twitching occasionally as she dreams – she spends most of her time sleeping now – and I can hear Chola Se playing with the pups in the vale beneath the plateau, splashing around with them in the shallows of the stream, keeping their minds off their empty bellies until the pack returns from hunting.

Chola Ses injuries are mostly healed now – her nightmares mostly a thing of the past.

I try not to think about that past if I can help it. It happened, its done. That world has gone. What good can come of reliving it? Thats not to say it isnt still with me – its in me, part of me--- it is me – and sometimes I cant think of anything else. I think of Starry, of course – he comes to me with every breath – and sometimes I find myself thinking of Juddah and Gilder, wondering what happened to them, wondering if theres any possibility they survived---

But the rest of it, the rest of that human world, I try to forget.

The pups arent the only ones with empty bellies. Weare all hurting with hunger. The hunting hasnt been good for some time now, and I know that if it doesnt improve very soon, the big grey male and some of the others will begin to feel themselves being drawn by the desires of their blood. The ghosts of their ancestors will start whispering to them of hungers past, bringing memories to them of times they wont remember – scavenging scraps from wagon camps,

469

the taste of horseflesh and human young---or running steadily through the Deathland night, their jaws laden with stolen meat, then gorging on the plundered feast and falling asleep with bursting bellies – and these whispered dreams of the past will become their hunger and turn their minds to the night of the rising. Theyle remember the smell of raw blood and burning flesh, the promise of human meat, and theyle begin to be drawn to the town again.

My mother will do her best to persuade them from going, just as she did all those years ago. Shele tell them of the dangers, and shele remind them that weare living flesh ourselves – meat in a world of starving dogs – and that we need to stay together to keep ourselves alive. And if they dont listen to her, Ile let the voice come to them and tell them they want to stay, and I think theyle accept it for now.

But the rising will come again.

I know it.

Ive already seen it beginning.

I saw it through the eyes of a neighbouring pack from the mountains as they scavenged the carcass pit dug by the Dau in the woodland to the west of the town wall---I saw them feasting on the rotting dead, and I saw the Dau Fighters opening fire from the watchtowers---I saw 6 dogs shot dead. And the following night I saw the rest of the pack – 15-strong – returning to wreak their brutal revenge on a family of Dau civilians---and I saw 5 humans torn to pieces---

The killing will continue – an eye for an eye, a tooth for a tooth, a claw for another bloodied claw – until eventually it will be war.

I know it.

Its coming.

Dog against human.
Human against dog.
The skies will burn again.

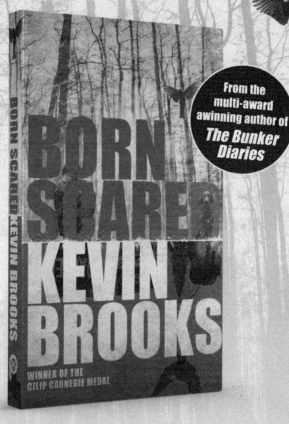